When the Jade Emp
common Cowherd a
uproar in the celestia
star-dragon to fetch
'There are many revo
for the star-dragon,
and chaos wherever F

As the lovers flee t̲h̲e̲ ̲s̲t̲a̲r̲-̲d̲r̲a̲g̲o̲n̲ ̲s̲a̲v̲a̲g̲e̲ ̲w̲a̲r̲s̲ ̲b̲r̲e̲a̲k̲
out all around them in ancient China. The star-dragon has
set in motion an inexorable chain of events which will
determine the destinies of all the gods, and all mortal men.

By the same author

Asgard
Krishna
Jormundgand

DRAGON

Nigel Frith

UNWIN PAPERBACKS
London   Sydney

First published in Great Britain by Unwin® Paperbacks, an
imprint of Unwin Hyman Ltd, in 1987

UNWIN HYMAN LTD
Denmark House, 37–39 Queen Elizabeth Street,
London SE1 2QB

and

40 Museum Street, London WC1A 1LU

Allen & Unwin Australia Pty Ltd
8 Napier Street, North Sydney, NSW 2060, Australia

Unwin Paperbacks with Port Nicholson Press
60 Cambridge Terrace, Wellington, New Zealand

British Library Cataloguing in Publication Data

Frith, N.
    Dragon
1. Title
823′ .914 (F) PR6056.R58
ISBN 0-04-823351 X

Set in 10 on 11 point Times by Computer
Typesetting Services, and printed in Great
Britain by Cox & Wyman Ltd, Reading

To Alexandra Cichon

Contents

Characters   *page* viii

Part One: Jian kang   1

Part Two: Shou chun   95

Part Three: Chang an   183

Part Four: Dun huang   235

Characters

All the characters, except those starred, are from Chinese myth, folklore or history, the historical events belonging to the year AD 383.

Gods

The Jade Emperor	Lord of the Gods
Confucius (Kun)	philosopher and scholar
Lao zi (Lun)	'founder' of Daoism
Guan yin	Buddhist goddess of mercy
Xi Wang Mu	Queen Mother of the West
*Wo Long Wang	Dragon of the Stars

Mortals

*Xie Nai	a poet
General Xie Shih	his uncle
Wei	his friend, a scholar
*Ling Xiang	his love, a sleeve-dancer,
Jen	a fox fairy
*Tawny	a serving-boy

Other Gods

*Solid Pear	Guan yin's old maid
*Dragonfly	Guan yin's maid
*Sugarplum	another
Yu lu	a door-god
Shen tu	another
King of Tai	God of the Eastern Peak
Mandarin Wu	a courtier
Guan ti	god of war
Xai shen	god of wealth
Zhou xing	god of longevity
Fu xing	god of cheer
Ly xing	god of salaries
Cheng o	goddess of the moon

Tou Mu	the Bushel Mother
Weng Chang	god of literature
Kuei xing	god of examinations
Redrobe	god of last minute passes
Ba xien	the Eight Immortals

Other Mortals

*True Pearl	Nai's maid
*Snowgoose	a girl at the tea-house
*Chrysanthemum	another
Gu Kai ji	an eccentric painter
Tao Qian	a retiring poet
Fu jian	monarch of the Northern Chin kingdom
Fu hung	his general
Mu jung Chui	another
Mu jung Chung	another
Dao an	his Buddhist adviser
Wang Zhia	his seer
Xie An	Chief Minister, Southern Jin
Fa xian	a Buddhist traveller
*The Abbot	a Buddhist of Dun huang

DRAGON

PART ONE

Jian kang

Chapter One

Of the flight of the lovers from the evening sky, and the dragon's pursuit of them through the turning seasons of earth, this is the story, and of the wars and turmoil that came to the great Middle Kingdom of China, when the sky-dragon undertook the mission of the gods and flung himself down from the river of the stars.

For long ago it was the Celestial Lovers, the Cowherd and the Weaver-Girl, ran away from the galaxy-meadows, and the Jade Emperor sent in terrible anger his emissaries to search for them in the world about Kun Lun Shan. And none of them returned with any news of them. The springs and the autumns of over thirty years went gliding by, while the stars stayed empty.

But the August Personage of Jade, before the last messenger had returned from the lovers' search, sent to seek for powerful aid: for beyond the dim horizon where the constellation of the Archer was lowering his bow, there writhed the dragon of sparkling scales. And here he sent a groom flying on a blue phoenix, tracing the Yellow River to where it falls from the Milky Way, and the groom came in winter to the snake of the horizon, the swingeing of whose tail causes disasters upon the earth.

And the groom looked on the dragon and said, 'All hail, huge Wo Long Wang! Hail, great pearl-bearer, wielder of the five imperial claws! Permit a trivial groom to disturb your regal peace, for the Jade Emperor has sent me to rouse you to earth again, for the Celestial Lovers whom your star-stream separated have not been found by any of the Emperor's emissaries, and needful it is to seek the help of a great power.'

3

But the dragon Wo Long Wang writhed his rainbow-coloured scales, and sparked up his bristling nostrils, and burned open his furnace eyes, and 'Wake not,' he said, 'the sleep of the constellations. Most foolish is he who takes a hammer to brain a gnat. Tell your Jade Emperor in his palace on Kun Lun Shan: better what is hid should ever remain hid than the world be turned upside down for the sake of a pin. The Celestial Lovers have fled from heaven. It was fated they would go. But gods cannot stop the progress of Fate.

'For this let me tell you from the depths of my sleepiness: once stirred from slumber I am vengeful. Many centuries it is since I came to earth. Then I set mankind a-boiling. If I should return this time, not anything would be safe, nor in the Middle Kingdom, or beyond. My fires would inevitably stir up the whole world, and shake the pantheons of the cosmic gods. So tell your little Emperor what a dragon has sleepily told you: you a little groom of low estate: leave well alone, leave the lovers to their destiny, and let sleeping dragons lie!' And the serpent ceased speaking then, and the tinkling bells were still, and the groom turned away from the stars.

Now the blue globe floated below, turning its mighty miles, as the groom came floating like a midge in the breezes of space. The limits of the whole world were stretched below his boots, the flat dust-lands, the crinkled white-capped mountains. There were deep seas, streaked with clouds, there were vacant vasts of grass, there were desert, steppe, and frozen tundra. But the little groom went winging now to the peaks of Kun Lun Shan to where was the heaven of the Jade Emperor. Herein the rich pagodas rose, fragrant above the mists, for the gods this night in heaven were holding a banquet.

Now the Jade Emperor was in his private apartments, laying on the brocaded robes for entry into the halls, and he gazed at himself in a mirror, practising various frowns. But when the groom arrived in the palace, he was brought in by clanking guards, and he was thrust down before the presence, where he kowtowed a thousand times. And the Emperor with his long moustaches drew his eyes from the looking-glass, and contemptuously he sneered at the groom, waiting to see what he would say.

And the groom said, 'Ten Thousand Years, forgive my loathsome presence, but what you have bade me, I have done, and visited Wo Long Wang, the dragon. And I have succeeded in waking him and reminding him of the Celestial Lovers' flight, and I have told him you wished him to go to earth, and seek out where they might be hiding. But the dragon refuses to come, my Emperor, and says what is hid should remain hid, and warns that the world might be all set fire, if he should once again come twirling upon it.'

And the Emperor raged and cried at this, 'Aiee! Does the slothful snake refuse to come? Does he dare to deny me, Emperor of the Gods, the king who leads the mighty deities of the Middle Kingdom? What is this vile serpent doing? I shall send others to him. The lovers must be found. I cannot any longer brook their flaunting of my laws! My own disobedient daughter to go careering about the world, the noble Weaver-Girl with that idiot Cowherd? How can I be expected to bear all this? Let the world of men all sink to ruin! But I must have my daughter back. Yet soft! I must be calm! I will send some generals. They will rouse the dragon. But as for me now, I must attend to other things, be calm, and cut a good figure. For the banquet abides me, and see where my Chamberlain comes into my presence with a look of anxiety.'

And the Chamberlain approached, that was an old, sooth man, and said, 'Salutations, Ten Thousand Years. I am come to tell you that all is ready for the banquet, and the historic feast is thoroughly prepared for. The Great White Queen of the West, the Buddhist Goddess, Guan yin, she and her train are all now gathered in their quarters, and they are eager and ready to attend the festival this evening, and cement by these celebrations the harmonising of the foreign religion. So let us hope all China now will

5

follow your enlightened lead, and accept the new faith with friendship and tolerance.

'Yet my Emperor, I must warn you: there are presences among us tonight, who might not want to let things go so easily. Indeed it is as we feared, for the leaders of the old religions do not share your broad and tolerant attitude. Indeed, great king, this very evening the two gods most likely to be offended have suddenly appeared unexpectedly at the banquet, and I have to inform you that Confucius and Lao zi, the great sages of the old faiths, are waiting for an audience. And I do not doubt, my lord, that they will object to the presence of a new deity, and what is more: a goddess.' And the Chamberlain bowed his head, and looked up again anxiously, to see how the Emperor would take it.

But the Jade High King did not rage, but merely looked peeved and sighed, 'What, are those two old duffers come to the party? Why does our land have to be in the thrall of old men and old sages? And why do its chief faiths have to be in the charge of two such eccentrics? What ever did Confucius do, but fail to be competent in any office, and what did Lao zi, except shun any form of responsibility? It is easy enough to be a philosopher. Anyone can have an idea of what is best. But how to achieve it? There is the point. Well, we shall just have to put up with them. I shall not be angered by them. I have a mild temper. And they will not dare to insult the goddess.' And the Emperor rose then, and with the Chamberlain still looking doubtful, processed from the antechamber.

Now when the Emperor had left one chamber, he glided into another, where the floors were glossy and great urns reflected in them. And once in the chamber, he moved again, and through other halls he went where gilded lions guarded the fretted doorways. Once in those state rooms, he shuffled in his brocade robes, reflecting the lamps in the yellow silk, and he came then to a reception room where numerous courtiers stood, who seeing him kowtowed with their topknots to the floor. The Emperor sat then, and

6

received the homage of these officials, and casting his eyes about them thus saw with disquiet the two great gods standing opposite him, staring with unforgiving eyes: Confucius in his purple scholar's robe and black silk hat, and Lao zi in the habit of a Daoist monk. And neither of them he noticed wore the omnipresent mask of diplomatic contentment.

And the Emperor said, 'There is snow on the roofs tonight. But there will be no frostiness in our welcome. The Buddhist goddess, Guan yin, compassionate one of the new faith, comes to us in tenderness and vulnerability, and so I warn: let no one here seek to tear this trust, for we must make welcome what our mortals have already made welcome. Therefore I have good hope, Confucius and Lao zi, who are most her rivals in religion, that neither of you old ones will betray any jealousy of this new school of thought in the Middle Kingdom.' And the Jade High King ceased, and stared about the court, and none there dared make any murmur.

But Lao zi stared at him and shouted, 'Sell your empire then, monarch! What do we care if you hand it to foreign devils? Yet you are hardly the ancient ruler of this ancient land. I am the one called Ancient of Days. And lecture yourself on courtesy. You are the one, I recall, who flies most easily into rages: witness this pet you are in over the Celestial Lovers. Rage away then, sell, burn, bring all down. The Dao presides over all. And this goddess you make much of here: tomorrow she will probably be your worst enemy. But there will be sense in that, for you should guard against evil, and not throw open the gates to barbarians!' And the Emperor blanched, and pulled out his moustaches at the assaults of Lao zi's eccentric tongue.

Then Confucius sighed and said, 'Your humble servant would not offend Ten Thousand Years with unpleasantness, and to my worthless eyes your highness tonight rivals Yao and Shun in your festivity. But talent is hard to come by, and even the founder of Zhou suffered from submitting

7

to the female. Your highness invites chill winds, if you open your doors too wide to visitors from afar.'

The Emperor glowered at them and said, 'If this is so, why have you pair of critics come to the banquet? We consider all our subjects, and we reconcile new things with the will of heaven. But our brothers should be harmonious to our care for the people, and not bicker or be jealous about petty matters. Let me hear no more talk of this, or there be some here who will regret stirring up disharmony.' And the Emperor continued frowning so that all became silent, and the chamber was full of uneasiness.

But now there came a scuttling noise and the sound of rattling armour, and there hurried into the presence mandarins who kowtowed begging the Emperor's mercy, and a flurry of figures behind them. And tottering into the pillared hall then, bedraggled and ragged as a beggar, there came a person who yet held in his hand the staff of an imperial messenger. And the Emperor stared long at the man's face, till the man in a hoarse voice addressed him.

'Is it so long since,' he said, 'and my face so changed by horrors that you, Son of Heaven, do not know me? Thirty years ago, my lord, you sent me from this chamber, in pursuit of these white hairs and wrinkles. Do you not remember then the emissary you empowered to seek the Great Wall for the lost lovers? Ay, I have returned at last, and more horrors have I seen than is in the power of any here to credit.'

The Emperor gasped and said, 'Then have you found my daughter? Quickly tell me what you have discovered, for I have already sent again to the dragon of the stars, and he may well be sliding to the earth. What did you find beyond the Great Wall?'

'Hell,' replied the man hoarsely, 'I found it beyond the wall, for that is where it lives: Hell, great king, and I went in it. Among the massing Mongols and their milling hordes of ponies, among the limitless dunes of the Gobi Desert, among the horrid tundra, where the wind blows ice in your beard, and the clouds hang for ever over the permafrost,

Hell was where I was taken, lord, by the fiends of the wastes, and hell was where your messenger has been sojourning.'

'But have you found my daughter?' screamed the Emperor, slamming down his mace, 'To Hell indeed with you and your traveller's tales! It is my daughter I wish to know about. Tell me what you discovered? I care not of the Cowherd. But is she in hell?'

'No,' said the man hoarsely. 'Neither your daughter, the Weaver-Girl, neither Zhi nu, nor the Cowherd, are in Hell. I was taken into Hell, and there I saw many stirring fiends, many a multitude of demons, longing to roam, but in those milling faces never saw I your daughter, nothing but the millions that long to spawn upon earth. I tell you, king, the steppes are seething. Soon they will break out. Be careful you stir not the hearts of barbarians or fiends.'

'You impudent wretch!' yelled the Emperor, leaping to his feet. 'Do you dare give your lord instructions? You have been away for thirty years, and is this the best you can do? Tell me you have seen nothing and warn me against fiends? I care not for the desert fiends! I care not for those beyond the wall! I care not for the milling hordes of the barbarians! It is my daughter I wish. And all Hell will stir for her. Ay, Hell and earth, for no longer will I brook her absence. You talk to me of threatening things, but I care not for threats. If the earth needs stirring. Well, come dragon. So be it!' And the Emperor ceased then, and ordered away the messenger. And they dragged him off from the hushed throne-room.

Now when there was this silence in the room with the Emperor staring maniacally, Confucius rose and bowed and said, 'Your imperial highness, this news is timely. For it raises another issue with which I and Lao zi would wish to deal. Your attempt to rouse the star-dragon; we have heard this very night you sent a groom on a phoenix, to try to stir up the dragon of the stars to seek for the Celestial Lovers.' And Confucius paused a while, raising his eyebrows, and the Emperor froze with fury.

9

'The rousing up of Wo Long Wang,' said Confucius, 'would bring dire results. Who knows not that the dragon is ferocious energy? The raw lust that is under the earth, the fierce fire in all human hearts, the rage of greed, of lechery, of conquest: these are the fire of which he is made. To bring down the dragon is to set upon the earth all forces of turbulence and confusion. At the best of times, his fury can hardly be withstood. At this time all chaos will engulf China. I need not remind you, your imperial highness, that China is fatally divided. The North is ruled by barbarians, descendants of the Tibetans, with Fu jian, a restless, arrogant monarch. The South is host to the legitimate imperial court, yet weak and dissipated it is. If you bring down the dragon, there will surely be civil war. These powers will rise up against each other. And who knows what will happen? Will there be China to survive? I beg you, great Emperor, do not bring down the serpent.'

And Lao zi said, 'Ay, the fool speaks true. We can do without wars in China. These lovers have their own life to live, and a right to be together. Let them alone wherever they may be, and let them seek out their own destiny.'

But the Emperor looked at them and said, 'It is too late. I gave orders before I came into this chamber. I have sent a troop of generals to speak with the dragon: they can talk to him in language which a dragon understands.' And the Emperor then spitefully kicked his foot-stool across the floor, and the mandarins knocked their heads together retrieving it.

But now there loomed a white shape at the door of the chamber, and there came a waft of fresh-scented perfume on the wind, and the company turning saw a goddess at the doorway, dressed in white robes and pure, with ivory-sleek features. And the Emperor composed himself and roused him from his throne, and all demure he went with soft eyes graciously to greet the goddess.

And Lao zi said, 'See how the hard throne is softened by the Great White Goddess of the West. All hail to you, pure lady, all hail goddess of mercy! The softest in the universe thus overcomes the hardest!' And he cackled with a little old voice like the winter's wind in the trees.

But the musicians struck up beyond the door, and the Emperor's wife came in shuffling, and she inclined her swaying body to the Great Goddess of the West. So the Emperor shot back his cuffs and gathered his robes about him, and sweeping across the hushed pale carpets, he led the courtiers forth to the hall. Confucius and Lao zi exchanged looks with each other, looks of anxiety and longsuffering. Then they left the hall together, though Confucius held back his warmth to distance himself from Lao zi's unmannerliness.

Bright now were the lanterns of the feasting-pavilion below the look of the honey-coloured moon. Shrill now was the music of the flutes that went echoing round the empty courtyards. The snow was on the curling eaves, dusting the wooden monsters, but the air was balmy in the environs of heaven. So came the company forth from the ante-chamber, led by the flowing-robed Emperor. So bustled the servants, pulling back the square stools from the huge, low tables. Spread over the glossy tops in regimented lines the porcelain tea-cups and flagons, the steamy rice-bowls, and dishes of celadon-ware, filled the eye with an endless banquet. The Emperor led his guests to their seats. The Great White Goddess sat. The mandarins nodded and simpered. Then they toasted each other in small dishes of hot rice wine, and the purple-perfumed company fell to feasting.

Now when all were happily eating, the musicians clanged their bells, for there was a host of ladies sitting with harps and lutes. And when they had played a while, the sleeve-dancers came on, and one led the rest in daring. In lilac-coloured robes, fluttering her sleeves like butterflies, in the lantern light with the bare fruit trees behind her, she seemed like the ghost of a lover lingering yet on earth, with faded cheek gazing forbidden on the banquet. And when the silks and ribbons were still, the feasters applauded her warmly, for she had caught for them the beauty of snow that melts more quickly than its cousin, the blossom. And

11

the Great White Goddess sighed as she watched the dancer, and lowered her eyes to stare on her faint green tea.

Then did the Emperor call for silence in the feast, and lifting his cup to the goddess he said, 'A week has passed by of your state visit to our heaven, O Great White Goddess, Guan yin of the Buddhist faith, and yet it seems you are already one of our family, so easy and compliant have you been to our importunate. Wherefore on this, our solemn feast, I welcome you yet again, and hope that relations between your heaven and ours may keep prospering, for assuredly your own heaven of Buddha in the West is, as we know now, refined and advanced like our own.

'The Middle Kingdom is the centre of the world, and long has been China's rule of the universe. Our emperors stretch back beyond the records of all other kings, our country has had its governing longer than all others. But though we are harmonious, and attuned to the will of the cosmos, this does not mean that more is never to be learned. From the South we found rice-grains, the buffalo entered our herds, the pig came frolicking from southern jungles. And in just such a way we are open to foreign faiths, and welcome them to our realm to contribute what they can. And so Great White Goddess of the West, welcome! We lift our cups to your compassionate eyes.' And the company murmured in agreement to this, and raised to the goddess their brocaded sleeves.

Now Guan yin heard all this with a tinge of rose to her cheek, and her head was bowed in humility at such praises. But when the speech was done, she darted her eyes to the company and panted nervously, bashful at seeing such lordly ones. None the less she rose, and bowing to the emperor said, 'Jade High King, master and son of heaven, your words have deeply impressed me with their wisdom and tact, and I am profoundly flattered to be so accepted. Indeed, so accepted, so greatly do I feel at home, and so much at one with your governance, that I venture to trade on my role as goddess of compassion, and plead with you, my king, to be compassionate.

'It is well known, mighty king, that long ago, due to pressure of wars, you put a daughter of yours away from you. This daughter was Zhi nu who, in her absence, learned the craft of weaving and making great tapestries. Nimble with her fingers she was, and wove into the brocade scenes of all gods and human history, and she was called the Weaver-Girl, and lived by the Silver Stream with her maidens in happiness. Yet during the time, my lord, that you left her to this noble art, she fell in love with a songful Cowherd and married him, and pretty is the tale of this, though we have no time for it here, yet angry and unforgiving was your reaction. For you put upon the married pair hard conditions to punish them for their love, and they were forced to dwell apart from each other.

'Great Emperor, this is your land, and I am but new here, and your people are only just getting to know my woman's ways. But women, you must know, O Jade-King, have a soft spot for marriages, and are often the mainsprings of compassion. Wherefore, in hearing this tale, I have often pitied the lovers, and often thought your penance for them was too harsh. And when I consider that the lovers have some years ago run away, I cannot find it in my heart to blame their flight. And so, O great Emperor, I hope you will allow this compassionate view, and accept this point along with your great tolerance to my new faith.

'What I am asking for, O Ten Thousand Years, is for you now to practise compassion yourself, and to seek no longer to persecute the lovers. If they have run away from the stars, then let them flee and be happy. If they are hiding, let them be well concealed and forgiven. Do not seek to find them, or harry them any more. Do not send any further posts or guards after them. Allow them to fade, my lord, into the oblivion of the world, and let their anguish slip also into the past. Humbly I make this plea that you will no more seek to rouse the dragon, whom I fear in rolling to earth would set all the world in hazard.' And the goddess of

13

compassion thus finished her heartfelt speech, and gazed at the Jade-King with bashful sweetness.

The August Personage did not know how to answer, and he sat, his eyes burning, his breathing heavy. He wished to give an answer, but he hesitated to be ungracious towards an honoured guest. So his Chamberlain made an answer.

'Ten Thousand Years,' he said, 'may I speak on your behalf to the Great Goddess? For I know your highness would wish above all things to comply with the goddess's request. Yet I have to inform you that, anticipating your commands, I have already ordered a troop of generals to hie to the dragon of the stars, and by now almost certainly, they will be stirring the dragon to descend to earth to seek the runaway lovers.' And the Chamberlain spread his hands, half smiling to the Emperor, as if to say, 'Unfortunately so!'

The Emperor arose then and said, 'We have dined our fill. Let us retire to the gallery and drink tea there, for I have many objects there of artistic and technical use which I would take delight in showing to the Great White Goddess.' And the Jade High King stood up, and the company bounded to their feet. So it was a little suddenly the important ones left the pavilion.

But Confucius and Lao zi stayed behind a little from the others, and they watched until the mandarins had gone from the heaped-up tables, and the shadows from the lanterns had left with all their echoes.

And Confucius said, 'The Emperor seethes. He has ignored the goddess. And Wo Long Wang will rage his way and unseat the earthly rulers. There has never been true stability since the time of the Duke of Zhou. What may we hope now if this turbulence occurs?'

But Lao zi said, 'Let them all come down, big dragons and little! If floods sweep away the market towns, more men will follow Dao in the hills. I care not if these lovers are never found. I care not if the dragon makes his home in a mountain. But this White Goddess, that steals the Dao's very analects, why, she should be run out of this realm like

14

a fox that steals our hens!' And Lao zi pulled his moustache taut, as they both stared at the scattered dishes.

As they dallied in the banqueting pavilion, and the murmur of voices came from the gallery where the Emperor and his guests had gone a-strolling, there sidled into the chamber a groom in travelling clothes, with thick boots still matted in damp-clinging snowflakes. And the groom saw the pair of old gods, and instantly he waved to them, and as they waited, he moved away the stools and came over towards them.

And Confucius looked at the man and said, 'Well, groom, what is it? I see from your boots you have been visiting the outer realms. If I remember your face, you are a scout on earth-duty, who has to visit the world of men to see how our affairs are proceeding. Is all well on earth? Is the North still troubled, and the South still dissolute yet faithful? Come, tell us your news. You came here to do it. And do not be afraid of speaking frankly before Lao zi.'

'Indeed not, my lord,' then replied the honest-faced groom soberly, 'and especially as my news pertains to him as much as you. For I have a report which touches both of you together, and a matter you were engaged upon some winters past, which is still unfinished. Very unfinished, as you'll see.'

And Confucius sighed and said, 'Well, groom, give us your record precisely.'

And the groom looked at them puzzled, and at last he said, 'Down below by the Yangt zi, the grand capital Jian Kang is humming as usual with the airy hordes of scholars and courtiers. On one of the main boulevards, not far from the imperial palace, spreads a great compound with high walls and impressive gateways. Here, as you may remember, lives the family of the Xie, where General Xie Shih, the military expert, rules over a large household. Now there are wives and concubines, servants and guards, aunts, uncles, relatives of various sizes. But you may both of you remember there lurks a certain scion of the Xie, a nephew who rejoices in the odd name of Nai.'

15

There was laughter from the gallery, as the groom reached this point, and the sound of a lute being plucked by unskilled fingers, but the two gods froze as they heard this and shot a dark glance at each other, and even more they stretched their ears to what the groom was saying.

'Now Xie Nai, as you know to your cost, is a somewhat feckless person. A scholar of sorts, who though he has passed a good half of the civil service examinations, yet has a dream of being a court-poet, and beguiling with odes an emperor. He once lived in the North, but losing his parents there, came to stay with his uncle, and ever since he has sponged off his relative in a shameless manner. Just recently, of course, he has shot to fame but that does not really matter, what is important for us is, as you know, he has tawny-coloured hair.'

There was the sound of a voice now echoing from the others, as a woman began to sing, and the twangling of the lute sprinkled the air around, as if of feminine fragrance. But the gods did not listen, they eyed each other angrily, and stared at the messenger with impatience. The groom held his finger up and nodded at the noise, and conspiratorially he continued with his story.

'Well,' he said, 'I don't need to remind you of your dealings with Xie Nai. Let us just say he is a person, who for reasons of pure chance, became of crucial importance to you both. It was a strange state of affairs. Nothing he did was of merit. And yet of vital interest to you was the state of his mind. If he was obedient to his uncle, you, Confucius, were delighted. If he ran off into the country, you, Lao zi, began to smile. He was indeed a man for whose mind you two battled with each other, each seeking to win him either to Confucianism or Daoism. I think my summary of your dealings with this poet meets with your agreement?' The man paused and looked at the sages.

Confucius and Lao zi nodded, unhappy about where this account was leading.

'Well,' continued the groom then, 'you may remember your battles, and you well remember that neither of you

16

won him. As is often the way in China, the man inclined to both faiths and used whichever at the time seemed relevant. When it became obvious that neither of you were winning because he had the habit of agreeing with both of you, eventually you left him, at least in the happy trust that he was faithful to two, if not to one of you. But did you know he had a girlfriend, a sleeve-dancer, Ling Xiang? I seem to remember that you met her when you were living down there. You were probably impressed with her dancing. But I have discovered something about her: would you believe she's a thorough-going Buddhist? Not only that but she's talking to Nai now, and he is becoming fascinated by it. You should not have ventured to fight for the soul of such a variable Everyman. True to his poet's whimsy, he is now ditching you both. And Buddhism has the triumph!'

The old men were stricken. They looked at each other, and dismay was on their faces. 'Nai is always Nai!' then said Confucius wearily, but Lao zi stamped his foot in anger.

And then coming from the further rooms, they heard a woman's voice again, and the voice of Guan yin praising the song, and suddenly Lao zi froze and grabbed his comrade's arm and stared at him maniacally. 'What if she has done this?' he said. 'What if she has broken her word? What if she has done this proselytising?' And the old men stared amazed at each other, even more horrified. Then busily they went towards the Emperor.

Meanwhile, through the Kun Lun Palace, the Jade-King happily moved, showing his wondrous collection to the goddess. Here hung the dusky-painted silks of mountains and streams, and here the gold-embroidered yellow banners. Here stood the great bronze cauldrons from the early days of his rule. Here the carvings on granite, with the relief processions. The Emperor pointed out everything to Guan yin, and himself summarised the history connected with each object.

When they had finished with these, they progressed then to the inventions which demonstrated the powers of Chinese genius. Here they saw the compass, a marvel to all the world, where a lodestone on a wooden fish floated in a bowl. Here they saw the harness and the stirrups which made Chinese horsemanship more advanced than all others. On shelves they saw paper, and models of inventions, such as rudders for ships, drills, wheelbarrows, and at the end of the corridor a great vase-like object, where dragons dropped balls into mouths of frogs, for this was a seismograph whose frog would catch the ball in whichever direction the world was touched by an earthquake.

But last of all the Jade High King took the goddess to an alcove, where artefacts stood that had not yet been discovered in the earthly kingdom, and sitting down he passed to her softly the bowls and dishes which were made of the unique china or porcelain. They smoothed in their fingers the vivid glossy yellows lipped like lotus-petals, and they held in their palms the white stem-cups painted with trees and figures, and they pinged with their finger-nails dishes as thin as eggs, whose glazes stained pale green their milky colours.

But into this alcove now came bustling the two great gods, and Confucius and Lao zi bowed to the smiling Emperor.

'Unworthy though I be, high king, to reprove any in your sight,' Confucius said, 'yet sometimes duty forces one to confront the prince with unpleasant facts, since to overlook them would surely be a greater neglect of duty, but I must beg to turn, prince, your mind to troublesome things, concerning this your honoured guest, the compassionate goddess, for I fear the lady has broken the assurances she gave to refrain from proselytising in the capital!'

'Indeed!' yelled Lao zi. 'She sits smiling in our heaven, but her attendants are busy seeking to undermine us on earth. For a thousand years Confucius and I have swayed the minds of men, but we do this not by hawking and selling our wares. We do not struggle for men. They are free to follow of their wish. Yet what does she do, this cunning woman? She picks the very man we did struggle for, and tries to make him a Buddhist merely to make us look

18

stupid! A typical woman's trick, and it goes completely against what we agreed. She is seeking to subvert Xie Nai!'

The Emperor waved scornfully. 'Not that fool again! Have you not yet done with Xie Nai? This is no place to drag him into the conversation. Have neither of you any sense of decorum? The Great Goddess, I am sure, could have no possible interest in that little tawny-haired idiot, and what business have you two disrupting our celebrations for the sake of your private quarrels? It is totally irrelevant, totally futile, totally insignificant!'

Confucius bowed his head, he folded his hands in his robes, and sighed into his beard. Then he said, 'If he who leads is fond of rites, the people will be easily led. If the Emperor observes justice, all will be harmonious under his sway. In the world of man, the Middle Kingdom is faced with a disturbing crisis. The old faiths which have served him a thousand years are being eaten away. It is no light matter, your imperial highness, if an alien faith comes to the country, wins the minds of men, turns them from their old paths, and directs them onto new and foreign ideas. If this thing progresses, then the people we know as Chinese may end up worshipping Indian gods! If you allow Buddhism to grow, then what we think of as our country will no longer be ours.'

'Too true!' then interjected Lao zi. 'What is Buddhism anyway but the Dao: gone in a circle? It wanders off like a corkscrew frogleaping the Himalayas merely to come back to its nest! Yet how does it come back? Reeking of the incense of those Indian temples, filled with all sorts of foolery, phoney metaphysics, and now her: Guan yin, like a holy cow breathing on us female compassion! The last thing we want is another mother-in-law haranguing the people about compassion! To Hell with compassion! Tell her to leave Nai alone. Tell her to close down all her temples. Tell her to get her lazy, good-for-nothing monks out of our nice clean landscape!'

Lao zi paused for breath. He was staring at the goddess, whose head was lowered in shame and horror. But the

19

Emperor's head was raised. His eyes were red with rage, and the bottom of his teeth were showing. Yet Lao zi carried on. 'Oh, you can scowl, your highness! You are quick enough to act when your daughter is involved. But once it is *our* protégé, what do you care? The whole country is falling in ruins, and you hand the people of Han on a plate to this foreign devil! Well, how much longer do we have to sit here obsequiously entertaining this harlot?' And Lao zi gesticulated, so that his robe flew open. And the Emperor stood up, blazing with anger.

But a bugle sounded far off, and there was a flurry of wings, and down beyond the gallery, a troop of generals all flying on cranes settled and dismounted from their saddles. Across the light snow that had dusted the courtyard there now came servants rushing to the flyers, and exchanged reports with them. Soon the yard was filled with grooms who led away the long-necked birds.

But the goddess of mercy sat still quivering with fear in her seat for she blushed and blanched, and did not dare to lift her eyes, and her maids crowded about her anxiously. And so there was a silence, as she arose with tears streaking her cheeks, and opened her mouth to refute the accusations. But then too overcome, she gestured feebly to her womenfolk, and fled with a flurry of silks from the feasting.

'You fatuous pair of ancient interferers!' then screamed the Emperor. 'With your idiotic games you have ruined the purpose of my carefully arranged state visit! I can hardly believe it! Lao zi, you decrepit madman, it is your usual round of chaotic mischief! But you, Confucius! What can possess the god of rites and piety to act with such brain-amazing crassness? Is this all a manic dream? Do I feast of nightmares? Be off, the pair of you, from my palace! Confound me if I ever invite either of you again to this sorely tried heaven.'

A bugle sounded through the hallways. The Emperor paused. Then a pair of generals clanked into the gallery, followed by the pattering feet of the court officials. The generals flung themselves on the floor, and kowtowed to their governor. The Emperor ceased, and stood a while staring down at them.

The first general spoke then, 'All hail, great son of heaven. With the greatest of speed have we returned from your mission to the dragon. We put to Wo Long Wang the substance of what you told us. We impressed on him the long-lasting sin of the Celestial Lovers. We told him of your rage: a wounded father, impiously scorned by a daughter who married beneath her. We told him of the hopelessness of our searches though the heavens. Then we begged him himself to seek out the Cowherd and punish him, and to bring the Weaver-Girl back to her father's arms.'

'Well?' whispered the Emperor. The court were all silent.

'The dragon refuses to come, your highness.'

'Aiee!' screamed the Emperor. 'As if I haven't enough to suffer! As if these idiots and that foreign woman were not enough to madden me for ever! Must I be taunted by a daughter running away from my embraces? Summon up my carriage! Hail me a troop of flyers! I will go to the dragon myself and demand his obedience!' And the Emperor shot up his cuffs, and with his long finger-nails flung his beard over his shoulder.

But now at the end of the gallery there hovered again the goddess, and Guan yin came white-faced once more to confront the Emperor. And the goddess said in a humble voice, 'Great King of Jade, I am come to say I am departing. My maidservants and I, my sister-attendants, my fairies and all will be this night leaving you. I thank you for your entertainment. Hospitable and gracious has been my stay this night in Kun Lun Shan. But now I see my hesitant ways have stirred up antagonism against me, and the faith which I fulfil has on your soil an implacable opposition. Wherefore I think it friendliest if I abstract my person and my train from your heaven, and thus I hope, your imperial highness, that my presence troubles you no more.' And the Great White Goddess bowed low, full of composure.

21

And the Jade-King answered, 'Not from me, Great Goddess, have you implacable opposition, nor is there antagonism on my part to prompt you to quit my person and heaven. Rather I have sorrow to hear your words, and shame at the nature of your departure. But there are those not of my court, over whom I have no sovereign power, that have behaved this night in a manner that brings odium and ignominy upon them. And it is through them, goddess, that you see fit to withdraw, while for myself I assure you there will always be a place for you in my empire.

'But your words none the less are just. And as you sense, compassionate one, the temper of our court is not now for feasting. For there are high things mooted, and a long-drawn sorrow is, as you know, gnawing at my inwards. Wherefore for this while, goddess, I bid you adieu, and for this moment seek no kind of dissuasion. But we shall meet again, White Queen, when all these things are done. Then shall we have cause for rejoicing.' And the Jade Emperor bowed then to the goddess of mercy, and she responded again bowing. And then did she withdraw, looking no more to left or right, but with her lovely maids floating slowly from the hallway.

But the Emperor stood and gazed on the two great sages, and he frowned, pointing his arm to the door. And glowering did he stare upon them, while Lao zi looked stubbornly back, and all the court frowned on them. Then they bowed and went, and the senexes shuffled moodily from the great galleries. And they went and gathered their cloaks and things from the antechambers, and the grooms saw them muffled up against the cold, and then did they plod sombrely from the steps of the palace, and make their way through the lantern-hung spaces of Kun Lun Heaven.

Meanwhile, the Jade Emperor in fury summoned his guards and swept with thwacking robes and steps from the galleries, and he clattered down the snow-dusted stairways, as the servants came running to his side, and the grooms got ready his chariot in the courtyard. For now were led the long-necked cranes squawking to the cart, and beating

22

their wings were they harnessed to it. And the Emperor came to it, and leapt into the seat, and he ordered his charioteer to crack the whip and set them fleeting. The mighty birds struck the air, and with great thundering claps, they climbed up over the curly-eaved palaces, and above the golden pagoda towers of the heaven they flew, and over the mists of the snow-hung passes. And they winged above the many heavens that lie in the Kun Lun Range, the heavens of Confucius and of Lao zi, and the paradise of the ancient Queen, the Queen Mother, Xi Wang Mu, where ripen the jewel-like peach trees of immortality. And the Jade-King then launched his chariot up above the airs of the earth, seeking the rare scent of the ethery spaces.

But Confucius and Lao zi walked on, and came to the last gate of heaven, where from they might have view of the turning world. And they stood a while together in that lofty spot, gazing down on the many headed snow-caps of the Western Mountains. And they saw beyond the snow-fields the dark hills and plains of China, still glittering under the snows in the Northern spheres, and the mighty rivers roamed there, reflecting the silver moonlight: the Yang zi, and the Yellow River, and the rivers moved Eastwards through the Middle Kingdom, bearing the fertile silt of the ancient mountains. And the gods looked at each other, and they saw wrinkled faces, just as below them there lay the wrinkled mountains. For the bald head of Lao zi gleamed in the faint moonlight, and the beard of Confucius was white as any frost. And they pulled then about them the wool-padded jackets, and prepared themselves to float on their clouds to their homes.

And Confucius looked at the ancient god and said, 'China was born old. Age gives her greatness, continuity unmatched on earth. It does not do to have new faiths swaying the common people. At such times it is one's duty to speak out, even if it risks impropriety. My friend, I am weary. I am flying to my heaven. There will I rest a time. It is not needful to go busying about earth to seek to counter

23

this woman's preaching. But when the weeks have gone by, then let us meet together, and consider what has occurred, for we must go again to the poet Nai, to see just how deep in Buddhism is our protégé.'

'You're right,' said Lao zi. 'We must take a look at our boy. But first, as you say, let us rest a while in our heavens. For why, my glorious patriarch, we are both now approaching a thousand, and neither of us can afford to scamper about as he used to. So farewell a while, old-faced friend. I think this whole affair has drawn us closer, you and I.'

And Confucius looked at him, judiciously he nodded, and then beneath the massive gate with gables branching upwards, in a landscape of snowy peaks and a solitary heaven, the two old men embraced and comforted their souls. But then they soared into the night sky, and travelled the cold air towards their own heavens on little puffs of cloud.

But the Emperor in his chariot approached now the Silver River, and they looked out for the Pole Star, and the great Bushel which swings its pan-handle to the North, and they passed beyond the pivot of jade, and the stars of Wen chang, the god of literature. And the million sparks that twinkle together and form the sky-dragon they beheld. From eternity did the river seem to wind, devouring in its jaws its own tail, and its scales were like speckles, red dwarfs and azure giants, and its oval eyes like galaxies lay sealed again in sleep.

But the Jade-King cried out, 'Awake, Wo Long Wang, awake! The Jade Emperor bids you, yellow king to yellow king! From Kun Lun Shan have I travelled, I, even Lord of the Gods, and now do I bid you attend to dire things that have need of your fieriness and strength. For some thirty winters hence, dragon, my precious daughter, the Weaver-Girl, and her husband, the base-born Cowherd, these two have run away to avoid the terms of my wrath, these two have left their destiny in heaven to live in lust together. And none of my spirits, in spite of countless searches, has ever been able to find them upon the globe.

'Now there are those who tell me, dragon, that your spirit is unendurably fierce. They warn me against rousing you. They say your descent brings death. And there have been many mandarins and councillors who have begged me to eschew you. They say you will spill war on the globe, plunge the Middle Kingdom into chaos, upset the perilous hold the South has on its own realms, and strengthen the barbarians of the North. They say you will aid the uncivilised ones, the Tartars and Huns and marauding tribes. They say you will set the rough ones upon the towns, and China's great heritage will die.

'Well, I tell you, dragon, I do not greatly care. Set all in turmoil, if you will. Bring the bad days again, as you did after the Shang fell, or when you visited earth in the time of the warring states. Bring chaos on the Middle Kingdom. It is divided in any case. Set armies marching, civil wars, ay, even Hunnic invasions. I care not what. But I must see my daughter! You must carry her again to heaven!'

'Wherefore, O serpent of night, sleep no longer in the stars, pitch yourself down and snuffle about the mountains. Seek in every corner, in town and hamlet, in the palaces of the dappled earth and brocaded paradise. Find these lovers in their wantonness, and pitch the Cowherd into Hell and her into my arms! For I tell you this also, serpent, when she left the heavens, she stole from me a golden cup most precious. The cup of stability she stole from her father, whence comes all this time of turbulence. And the cup of stability I must have again, for that is the essence of China!'

Now when the Emperor was done, and looked around him anxiously, to make sure he had not been overheard, the dragon Wo Long Wang slipped open his huge eyes and said, 'What is this whining of midges on a summer night? A strange, small tale you tell me, of jealousy and pique, of miserliness, and missing a little goblet. Well, I will do your bidding, king. I will descend to earth. I will sniff all China and find your lovers.

'But hark you a word, O Emperor, these lovers you persecute: it is long since you first set upon them since she strayed from her weaving, and the company of her girls, and went to the Cowherd's lodgings. It is long since you seized them and forced them to live apart, giving them nothing, but sundering man and wife. You caused my Silver River to swell and separate them, for them you saw as leading a rebellion against you.'

'Yet herein you are wrong, king. No such crime was theirs. Rather to greater service was their impulse. For the journey they planned secretly to the wilder strands of the stars: this was in service of her true purpose. Did you not make her the Weaver-Girl? Was she not to weave all into the web? Was her task not to record all deeds in the robe's texture? And the singing of the Cowherd: was this not his real task? Was this not also the purpose of his creation? What was this journey therefore but to seek to be themselves? They were not running away from heaven. Will you not think upon these things a little before you rouse me? The world would benefit from such discretion.

'For I tell you, Oh Chinese king, you have sharpened my lust for mischief. You have put me in mind of thrashing my tail so that gods and all shall mark it. You have irritated me, and an irritated dragon is not good to have at your door. Wherefore a final time I bid you: will you think again, for upon my track come war and ruin and famine? Upon my head sits lust and plunder, ravage and rapine in my belly, and at my tail universally wailed annihilation? If you rouse me, Oh Emperor, this time all earth shall shake. It will not just be China.'

'Do it!' said the Emperor, and he turned his chariot away, and flew back towards his cloud-hung mountains.

So the dragon began moving, and the prow of his vast snout, that hung in the heavens with scales of glittering stars, began to slide against the blackness, following the tiny king, who whined away mosquito-like into a dot. The broad blue face of the speckled globe still turned beneath the speck, cloud-swirling under the trail of the milky galaxies, but the Silver Stream commenced to slide and peel

26

itself from the sky, sloughing its shiny skin like a snake from space.

And Wo Long Wang slid downwards ever, blazingly at the earth, his camel's head and weird horns brushing the planets, and he poured towards the dusty continents, curtaining the Northern sky, and he left but a skin of himself, a wraith above. Meanwhile, the monstrous head now protruded through the stratosphere, breaking the rays of the ultra-violet. Through the noctilucent clouds he peered, sniffing the airs of the countries, stuck like a foot through the ceiling of the globe. There lay Eurasia. There lay the West, sparkling beside the Middle Sea. There lay the central mountains of Kun Lun Shan. The sparkling dragon roamed his horns, then with a thundery noise, he fell through the undulating dawn towards China.

Chapter Two

On the earth, meanwhile, in the capital of Jian Kang, the tawny-haired Xie Nai awoke and shivered in the cold. And seeing his breath steaming, he turned over and pulled the coverlet up to his ears. Hearing him stir so, his maidservant True Pearl came in and set down a charcoal brazier, about which she warmed his clothes. Then, rising from this task she fetched fragrant tea into the room and thus she brought it to him and pulled back the cover of his bed.

And True Pearl said, 'Come, master, it is no good moping all morning. The General has gone to court, and so you will not bump into him, and you can get up and attend to your writing without any thought of chastening words. Or go to court yourself even, since you are such a grand man now. But it is unmanly to lie grieving there over a letter.' And True Pearl pointed to where on a spindly table there lay a folded-up letter and a piece of orange ribbon.

But Nai sighed from his bed and said, 'True Pearl, do not pester me. You are just jealous that I have no heart to frolic with you as before. But I tell you my heart is leaden. This woman possesses me! Never have I met such a being, whose every word enthralls me. And yet she sends me this negative nonsense, drooling like a monk over leaving the world! Oh, I am going to ignore her! Put out my boots and quilted overjacket. I shall call on my friend Wei today, and we'll go drinking away our miseries.' And Nai got up from his bed, and caught hold of True Pearl amorously. But then he sighed and let her go about preparing his clothes.

When he had washed and dried himself, Nai pulled on his grey silk breeches, and fastened about him a dark red jerkin, embroidered with butterflies and flowers. Next he tied on his shoes, and set on his head his purple and gold-trimmed hat, and then did he sit down and eat the dish of noodles and sip the green-tinged tea. Yet when he stepped outside, he saw the sky was heavy, and not a good day to go jaunting in the city. But Nai went off at once, and walked the length of the compound, where stood the many houses of his uncle and his dependants.

Nai felt sad and grieving as he strode along, and he thought continually of the girl who had sent him the letter. And Nai sighed and considered, 'Alas, she will not have me! She is too shut up in her own, strange world. Such a beautiful girl! Yet that was not the fire for me, but – Oh, her words, her words! And is she to go from me? She whom I love so much, she who for me inevitably seemed destined? Oh, love, why does it wrack me so? Why do I always land myself in such suffering?' And Nai stumbled in among the frosts, and slid about on the twisting paths.

But when he had gone past the gardens outside his own apartments, and plodded beside the duck pond and the halls of his aunts and cousins, he came to the first courtyard where there lay libraries, public rooms and rest-rooms, in which the great Xie family gathered and radiated its influence. And as Nai sighed despondently, he saw the major-domo coming towards him, who gazed at him reprovingly, as he shuffled forth from the verandah.

And the major-domo said, 'The Prince General has gone to court, but he has asked me to inform his nephew Xie Nai that court will not detain him all day. The Prince General has important words which he wishes to communicate to his nephew, and he asks especially that in the afternoon the nephew may be ready for an interview. It seems the nephew has on his overjacket as if venturing forth into the city. Under the circumstances I'm sure he will agree that this is far from wise.'

The despondent Nai looked at the servant's pious face and hooded eyes, and irritation boiled up inside him over this restriction, and so he said. 'Oh, I'm going out a while, and the world will recover from the unwisdom. But if you

29

can tell me what the Prince General wants, I can know how earnestly and quickly I need to return. But I don't suppose you are at liberty to be so helpful?' And Nai looked at the major-domo, who slid his hands into his sleeves, and piously shook his head. So Nai left him.

And so Nai came at last to the gateway of the General's palace, and this went through a courtyard wall and an outer wall, and when he came to the lodge there were servants squatting about, all dressed in the livery of the Xie family. And the triple-arched gateway was flanked by marble lions, and the great red pillars went up into the curling eaves, and above the arch was a scarlet-painted sign whereon were five characters, which spelled out the words 'General Xie Palace, built at Imperial Command.' And Nai, nodding to the servants who desultorily got to their feet, left the rich pageantry of his uncle's quarters.

But when he came into the street, there was ice and mud and carts and pushing porters, and there was a bustle of peasants carrying planks and a tramp of halberdiered soldiers. The steam and smoke rose from the braziers of the trays of roasted nuts, charcoal-scented, and the flags on the ropes fluttered outside the shops and the banners against the grey clouds. And Nai made his way through the straight avenues of the city, threading his red-silk path through the hemp-clad crowds.

He reached the little bridges which crossed the canals, where the willows sprouted leafless at the water's edge, and here beneath umbrellas were the sellers of shoes and tools, and there were pies and knives and beads spread out on the floor and on tables. And Nai crossed the hump-backed bridges, where the barges were moored, and the children waddled across the planks to the shore. And here the women moved about the boats, hanging up the washing, and a flautist sat under a canopy serenading the ducks. And Nai went on through these tumults, till he came to a poor quarter of the city.

And when he came to Wei's house, it was up a back alley, and a stream ran down the middle clogged with peel and rubbish. But he knocked at Wei's lodgings, and an old man opened the door, coughing, and Nai went then past the broken table and through tattered curtains into the dingy digs. And when he came to Wei's room he found it stacked high with scholarly books, and a cake of ink and a brush on a plank by the window. And Wei sat at it writing, oblivious of any noise, crouching over the paper in the cold light of the window. But then Nai coughed, and the fresh-faced Wei looked up, and arose cheerfully to greet his old comrade.

And Wei said, 'Nai, my good friend, how pleasant this is to see/you! It has been a long time. You catch me here studying. There are examinations not too long away. Let's hope that I can do as well as my distinguished comrade. But you, great courtier, how is it with you? Do you preen yourself daily in the Emperor's presence? Or are you immersed in dallying with the delectable Ling Xiang? It is no wonder with all your good fortune I have not seen you!'

But Nai sighed and said, 'Alas, none of these things is mine. I am too perplexed and miserable to do anything. I have come here hoping that my old friend, Wei, would give me the pleasure of his company, and come with me today to the tea-houses. For there the wine and the girls are perfumed, and there we could drink and take our minds off our troubles. That is, if his studies are not too pressing on his time?'

'Of course not!' said Wei merrily. And he called then a servant-boy, and gave him some piece of cash, and sent him off to the stalls down the alley. Meanwhile, he himself pulled out and dusted a chair for Nai, and got him some rice-cakes out of a great pot, and when the serving-boy came back he poured them fragrant tea in chipped dishes, and offered this and the cakes to his brocaded comrade.

And when they had eaten for a while, Wei looked into Nai's eyes and said, 'Well, this news you bring is only partly surprising, for distinction at court is not necessarily a blessing, and Ling Xiang is not the easiest of ladies. But why can

31

it be you are so crestfallen? You are becoming distinguished, and I thought that with Ling Xiang you had found a woman with whom you might at last settle down and create a household, for she if anyone is as mad as you are!' And Wei laughed then to see his friend's mournful face, and sat back prepared for the story.

Nai did not answer him, but fumbled in his pocket, and brought out the folded letter and passed it to his friend, who undid the orange ribbon, and opened it to gaze on the characters. It was a poem, written in a feminine hand, and the characters were of the type of slender gold. As Wei read it through, Nai rehearsed in his head the succession of seven syllable lines and rhymes.

> Bustling the city awakes.
> It is time to run again.
> Grieving the heart creaks open.
> The white tiger leaves his den.
> What heart is there for laughter
> Now when the blooms are fallen?
> Who would sport in the red dust,
> A would-be catechumen?
> My friend, the perfumed blossom
> Glitters no more in the glen.
> The cries of the winter geese
> Accuse the misty heaven.
> Lichees you offer me,
> Who finds her hunger barren.
> And in russet only thirsts
> To flee from the world of men.

Now when Wei had read this over, he paused for a while, frowning, but then he stared at Nai again, seeking to read his thoughts. But then he sighed, 'Ling Xiang was once your pupil for instruction in the Five Classics. You undoubtedly instructed her in the Book of Odes, and in the techniques of composing poetry. She is merely showing you here the results of her studies, paying compliment to you as she does so, and she says nothing more fearful than that she is world-weary and has thoughts of the Buddha. The winter has come. Her days of laughter are over. She has little zest for life. But I can't see that this poem is a cause for great anguish. Have you discussed it with her? What is so deadly in it? And anyway: what is a catechumen?'

Nai smiled at this and said, 'That you may well ask. I also had never heard the word before. And I looked it up in the dictionary and in the encyclopedia, but it was not in either of them. But apparently it is a Buddhist word for one studying to take the vows, a neophyte, training to take the Buddhist catechism, and being of a new foreign faith we have not got it yet in our official language. But as for discussing it with her: well, that is the point: I cannot discuss it with her. She has gone away for several days, leaving about a week ago, and this was the little present she kindly left for me. I was enraged at its defeatist attitude. Why can she not tell me to my face that she wants to throw me over?'

But Wei frowned again at his friend and said, 'Yet surely you run ahead. There is nothing in this poem to suggest she means to leave you. It is a lament at the state of affairs, but she does not repudiate you: she bewails, if anything, her own heart for being sluggish. And yet you must remember she does live at a Buddhist convent, and she is almost upon the road of a religious life. It is too much to expect her to come bounding over to your arms, when she is obviously thinking of dedicating herself to a higher cause.'

'Oh, higher cause be damned!' cried Nai. 'What is all this Buddhist rubbish? The desire to snuff yourself out: the whole thing is morbid and effete! I can't stand all this wailing alone in the darkness. You ought to be happy to be alive and have all your faculties. But what a thing to send me, just as she leaves for the country! She is bent on giving me heartache and trouble and frustration! Get your cap and coat on, Wei. We're going to the red lanterns! At least those women don't sit and wail all day about Buddhism!' And Nai got up impatiently and stood already to go. So Wei shrugged and found his coat to follow him.

Now when the scholarly pair had come to the tea-houses, the streets were gay with banners and flags. At the entrances to the inn-yards the porters called out to them, extolling the virtues of the particular houses. Crossing the street on pattens, their silk robes lifted up, the courtesans tottered and the singing-girls. There was a jingling of cymbals and a screaming of flutes from the balconies. And when they came to the Tea-house of the Red Dust, Nai was greeted by the concierge and nodding cheerily at him, he took Wei in, and brought him to the pleasant courtyard.

Laughter and drum-beats greeted the pair, as they entered the lascivious tea-house. Fat merchants sat drinking in fumey alcoves, where singing-girls like butterflies waited on them. Above on the second storey the lanterns were lit, since the grey day was dark and gloomy. The painted faces of courtesans peeped over the balconies, and between the festive poles with their decorations of paper flowers, and above them piercing the clouds the pagoda tower of the restaurant waved its coloured tassles and tinsel serpents. The spirits of the two men cheered at the merry sights, and they bounced together into an upper chamber.

Now when they had sat down, wine and food were brought them with due ceremony by the tea-house servants, and when they had nibbled on the sauce-dipped crispies and pancakes, there entered at the door two beautiful courtesans, who bowed to the gentlemen with much glittering and simpering. And the tallest one, called Snowgoose, said, 'Well, here is Xie Nai again! What a wretch he is: he has deserted us for months!' And they came and sat with the pair of scholars and pretended to look angry.

And the other one, called Chrysanthemum, said, 'And this is Master Wei, isn't it? I seem to remember he has not been to us for months either. What a pair of rogues we have here! You can't trust men a bit, can you?'

But Wei smiled and at once said, 'Ladies, you can trust a poor fellow like me. The only thing I have been doing is studying for my examinations, so my absence from you is not from any sort of perfidy.'

34

'Which means,' said Snowgoose again, 'that this one has been unfaithful, because we all know that of the pair, Nai's the one with the money, and this poor scholar can't even afford to come unless his friend brings him. So what is it has kept the great Xie Nai away from us? Who or what can it be that has detained this midwife-poet?'

'Midwife-poet!' laughed Wei, smiling broadly. 'Why, he has earned that nickname!'

But Nai looked at them seriously and said, 'You may joke as you will. But what has kept me from this place has been beyond any form of joking. There are such things that touch the heart with ecstasy and pain, and at that time the pleasures of the tea-house seem shallow!'

Snowgoose screamed with laughter at this, and held her long sleeve over her eyes. 'Oh, what a philosopher we have here suddenly!' she cried. 'He'll be going off to India soon as a Buddhist! We are shallow creatures beside whatever it is that brings him ecstasy and pain! What can it be this new interest of Nai's? Kite-flying? Fishing? Fireworks?' And Snowgoose held on to her colleague, and for a while shook with tearful laughter.

'I don't think we should tease him,' said Chrysanthemum sadly. 'We all know what Xie has been up to. And when you really fall in love, there is, of course, nothing else which holds its savour beside it. Love is a measure against which all other things are brought and at last discarded. We should be glad that he has fallen in love in this, the true fashion.'

'I have heard that the Xie family are thinking of staying in the capital this summer,' said Snowgoose suddenly. 'Usually the whole entourage moves West and goes into the hills of Ta Pieh Shan. But this summer for some reason, the General is not leading the emigration, and we in the Southern capital are to be honoured by them staying with us and sweating it out.'

Wei looked at Nai.

'Yes,' Nai nodded. 'That is probably the case. But my uncle wants me to go none the less near Ta Pieh Shan, and smooth things over. The patriarch lives there as a hermit by the lake of Shou chun.'

'But let us get back to love,' sighed Chrysanthemum. 'I want to hear about Nai's feelings. I want to know if he's ever been in love before in this the true way?'

Nai smiled at Chrysanthemum. 'It is strange to call it true love, but I think you are correct. I love this girl because I enjoy being with her. We have the same interests. It's weird, after falling in love in so many different fashions, to be in love at last in the most common way.'

'It sounds positively repellent,' said Snowgoose. 'Why rejoice in being bourgeois?'

'Let's hear about these different ways of falling in love,' said Wei. 'We are all hanging on the master's lips!'

Nai smiled at Snowgoose. 'I was in love with Snowgoose here once. And this was because she was a master of her trade. But this was just sex-love, where the feeling arises from the feast of pleasure. But is this true love? Forgive me, Snowgoose: it faded. Then I was in love once with a proud beauty, whom I barely laid a finger on. Yet I worshipped her. My spirit was unbearably aflame even just to look at her. And this was worship-love, where the woman is an object you adore from a distance. But is this true love? Well, it is a kind that could not survive in marriage. And then one of my other times was when I was in love with an unpleasant woman. She would love to torment me. She would go off with other men. Yet she would upbraid me viciously if I looked elsewhere. Yet I couldn't forget her. This was hate-love. It possessed me. But was this true love? No, I think there's very little true about that.' Nai sipped on his drink.

'What a wonderful sermon!' said Snowgoose. 'I'm sure we are all much enlightened. Let us now sing a hymn in praise of the ordinary love of the ordinary, boring little homebody!'

Wei let out a laugh. 'I'm afraid not, Snowgoose,' he said. 'No one could call Ling Xiang ordinary. Have you ever seen her? She is very beautiful, very vivacious, very intelligent. And surely, ladies, such artistes as yourselves must have heard of her reputation? She was the highest paid sleeve-dancer in Hang Chou, and had even the Dukes squabbling for her services. I think this is maybe worship-love just as much as it is true love.'

Nai nodded his head. 'You are probably correct. But why are we talking about *my* love? I came here to forget it. Why don't we put him on the slab? Let's cluster round and examine his entrails!'

Wei shook his head. 'No,' he sighed. 'With me there is nothing to hear about. I know I have a love destined in the stars, with whom I shared a former existence. But I have never met her, and so I have nothing to say.'

The others turned quietly towards him.

'Do you really think that?'

Wei nodded his head.

'You were lovers in a former existence?'

'That's very Buddhist.'

Wei nodded again.

'But don't you think you will ever meet her?'

'When the time is ripe,' Wei paused and drank. 'When the winter's night has fallen softly.'

They were quiet for a while. It was growing darker outside. But then there was a noise of footsteps on the stairs.

There was a knock on the partition. Suddenly into the room came a servant-girl of Snowgoose's, looking flustered. 'There's a sedan-chair,' she said, 'outside, arrived from the Xie Palace. Prince General Xie believes his nephew is here, and has sent for him. But also there has arrived a horse all saddled from the Xie Palace, and this the General or someone has also sent for Xie Nai. What shall I tell them? There's a crowd outside. Everyone is fascinated!'

Snowgoose laughed. 'Oh, honourable nephew, you are much in demand!'

But Nai sighed and said, 'Oh, that moralising old post!

Why can't he leave me alone? I've got my own money now. I'm not dependent on him any more. Why does he have to dog me around like an old woman? Wei, I'd better go and see him. I'll take the carriage home. Which leaves a horse standing around idle. Why don't you borrow it for a while, and ride home yourself in state? A man like you should always ride everywhere.' And Nai smiled at Wei, as he went from the room, and Wei accompanied him down the stairs.

'What do you think he wants you for?' said Wei as they arrived outside, and looked idly on both the horse and the carriage.

'Who knows?' sighed Nai. 'I should think someone's been having a word with him. My stake at court is not as good as it was. He's had to keep quiet for a while, ever since I became rich and famous. He's lost his usual basis for lecturing me. But I should think he now senses things turning against me, and wants to crow a little. I'll give him crow! O gods, I want to leave this place. I want Xiang to come with me and begin the great voyage into the world!' And Nai smiled again at Wei, who looked back somewhat blankly, and the poet then rode off in his carriage.

But when he arrived at his uncle's palace, hardly had he entered the gate, before he was whisked off by officious servants, and taken through the grand courtyards to the massive halls of his uncle, where he strode through the conference chambers and banqueting rooms. And he found his uncle sitting frowning and tapping his fingers on a chair, staring at the door waiting for his entrance. So Nai went forward and impatiently kowtowed to the General, and then waited for him to speak.

And the General said, 'Nephew, I left word that I would see you, and you saw fit to go instead to the tea-houses. I am afraid this is all too typical of your otiose attitude, and is the behaviour of one who refuses to grow up. Why do you ever seek to lead a life of pleasure, fooling away your years in trivial pastimes? Is there no sense of duty in you, which might spur you to more estimable deeds?' And his uncle glowered fearfully from his wide chair, the shadows gathering on his brow.

'Why do you say all this to me?' said Nai. 'I have explained it to you a thousand times. Do you never remember anything I tell you? I have heard you say this for ten years at least, and for ten years I have given you the same answer, yet still you keep repeating it as though all my replies were just written on water! What's the point of saying it again? I'm not leading a life of pleasure. I am training myself in a great task. Do you think it is trivial? Do you think the Classics trivial? Do you consider trivial the Spring and Autumn Annals?'

His uncle look black. 'You will moderate your tone, sir!' he said. 'Ever since your success with the Emperor you have become impertinent. How dare you accuse me of forgetting the substance of our interviews! I am afraid they are all too gravely engraved on my brain! Of course I do not consider trivial the Spring and Autumn Annals: they are a precious record of the origins of our glorious empire! But do you think your fairy stories are on a par with that? Is that the gist of what you are implying?'

'Yes it is, and yes I do!' shouted Nai. 'Otherwise why should I devote such time to it? And grander things than the Annals also, if I could but learn the tasks. What are the Annals but court-records? There are grander things in the world, vaster and more powerful than these! And they are all in the shape of these stories. But the craft must be discovered. That is what I work on: the Great Tale, and the craft to tell it. And that is why inevitably I must soon embark on the vast journey to the West.'

'Oh, you and your journey!' cried the uncle. 'For ten years too I have been hearing of this journey! Ever since those musicians came to the court. How can you pay heed to such foolery? Well, I wish you would go on this journey. I wish you would go to the West. Ay, and I wish you'd never come back. For as long as you are in my house, the opprobrium of your presence tarnishes the glitter of my name. Ay, I would you were gone, or become a man. That is what I would wish of you, nephew. But I did not summon you to bandy words with you, or descend to your ridiculous fantasies. I have things to say to you. Wherefore give good ear. The hearing may not be pleasant.' And the uncle sighed then, and reached over to a table, and took a sip of some hot rice-wine.

'Now you may think,' said the General, 'that you are now firmly established, and that with the Emperor's approval your position is sacrosanct. You have received great gifts from him, which have made you to some degree rich, and you think that many more are to be forthcoming. I have heard that you imagine soon you are to be granted a sinecure. Was not the post of mythic historiographer mentioned? I may tell you that such a post is by no means established, and that there is considerable opposition to it in court. To put it bluntly, nephew Nai, what treasure you have you can keep. But there will not be any more forthcoming. It will behove you shortly, therefore, to seek about the world for some means of gainful employment. A tutor perhaps you will once more have to become. That at least is a post of some dignity.

'Yet I have a suggestion for you which if you take, will do much to expunge your shame. You must know, nephew, that we live in dangerous times, and that our state is far from unthreatened. Indeed, I have to tell you that very great danger approaches, and our empire may well be forced to defend itself. Wherefore a time of war approaches, when men such as myself will be needed, and even fools like you will have some usefulness. You must know then that today I have seen the Emperor, and my memorial to the throne has been read with more than usual interest. It is probable that soon I shall have command of a battalion, empowered with the right of conscription and requisition. I could force it upon you. But I would have you choose. Is it not time for you to think of the defence of your country? You may give me your reply when you have meditated my words. I might be able to get you a troop of cavalry.' And the uncle ceased his speech there, and stared into Nai's eyes, as though expecting him to be impressed.

But Nai was not impressed, but instead bowed his head dutifully, and left the room, eager to be out of his uncle's presence. And when he was outside again in the frosty gardens, walking to his apartments, he sighed and said, 'Heigh-ho! This is clearly the time for Nai's punishment sessions! With Xiang leaving me with that letter, clearly wanting me little, with my new fame at court already being chipped away by jealous officials, and with old groaner going on again, as I have heard him for years, I am clearly not in luck, and must keep my head down.' And Nai walked moodily, stamping on the puddles and cracking the ice that glared at him.

'Why,' he mumbled to himself, 'does everything have to be difficult? Here I am struggling away to do things my people have never done, while all about me I have to fight off these continual demands and troubles! Here I sit, cracking my brain, trying to discover things unknown, and no one even sees what I am doing, let alone understands it! I have got to learn metres no man of Han has mastered, I have got to learn arts none have in China. I have got to unearth the whereabouts of the great story of the world, so that all men can have one tale to unite them! And all they do is nag and harry me, call me this way and that, demand I grow up, settle down, get a job, join the army! Oh, why can't all these phantom nothings blow away to the moon, and leave me to get on with the endless battle?' And Nai thus went stomping irritably up the steps of his house, and slid open the doors to his charcoal-scented chamber.

But Wei, meanwhile, before he went back into the tea-house, took charge of the horse that Nai had left him, and he took it to the stables and bade the groom there see to its housing. But the man said to Wei, 'You must pay me in advance, if you wish me to stable your steed, for by the time you have finished I shall have gone home, and there's no one else to take the money.' And when the man had said this, he held out his hand, intent on not moving without it.

But Wei stared back at him, and he thought to himself, 'Alas, I have no money to pay this man. Nor have I any money to pay for the feast in the tea-house, or anything that the girls offer there. Nai has gone now, and with him all hope I might have had of affording such entertainment. How then can I go back in there, when it will be impossible for me to fulfil my obligations?' And the man still stared at him, as Wei continued his thoughts, plunged in suspended dismay.

Then he said to the groom, 'You have reminded me by your words, and indeed it is not practical for me to stay this night in the tea-house. Wherefore I will take my horse and trouble you no more, for it is time I went home.' And he turned the steed about then, and leaving the man staring, wended his way homewards, and as he moved away from the tea-house, he stared about him, thinking on all that had passed.

As Wei came to the wide boulevards, and rode on his horse below the fire-towers looming in the dark, the ways seemed all ghostly, and the tree-shadows menaced him, blackly scampering over the ground in the silver moonlight. And Wei felt chilled by the spookiness of the place, compared with the rich and perfumed place he had been in. He thought of the glittering life which Nai naturally led, and he contrasted it with his own doggedly toiling existence.

Approaching the avenues of his own district, Wei thought for once he would take a new path back to his old home, and so he spurred the horse towards a district where canals and ditches gleamed and clumped across a hump-backed bridge into a weird space. And when he was there the wind went whistling through the bare willow trees, and all was gloomy, reminding him how he went alone. And Wei sighed to think how Nai had all the girls he wanted, and he none.

Then as he went riding high through this strange district, he saw a cheery procession going with lanterns along before him. Three girls there were in lovely brocades, strolling with their servants, holding their silks against the wind, as the lanterns were blown this way and that. And as Wei rode

42

towards them quietly, they saw him and cast him a glance, and gayly did the girls talk about him. And Wei looked down upon the rouge-cheeked girls, and sighed to himself.

But one of the girls looked up at him, and laughingly she cried, 'Hi there, you bold rider! You look so fine on your horse! You're clearly such a cavalier, won't you give us girls a lift, and escort us to our mansion hereby?' And the other girls fell laughing at the merry talk of this one, and Wei at first was startled by her frankness.

Wei looked seriously down at the girl, and weighed her joking request, and with seriousness he gave his answer, and said, 'A lift is difficult. For there are many of you, and but me and one horse. Yet certainly I will be glad to escort you to your mansion. And make sure in this burly night that no one should attack you.' And Wei nodded, as the girls fell laughing again at his serious style.

Yet they let him come with them, and so the party continued, strolling with their paper lamps beside the canal. And reflected in the slimy green water the capering procession went, and threaded through the blowy streets, and the ghostly rearing willow trees. Meanwhile, the dogs and hounds of the district fell to barking and howling now, disturbed by the procession and wailing to get at the girls, and Wei rode soberly, guarding the girls, which they seemed to think a great joke.

But then as he rode seriously, his eye roamed among them, and he noticed then what seemed to be the third sister, for there was a shy girl who tiptoed along with the others, and whose face was beautiful, round and silver like the moon. And just as Wei was gazing at her, she shyly looked up at him, and the beauty of her eyes made him sigh with love. But now they had come to the gate of a great house, where the girls were stopping, and Wei saw this was their home. And a red-bearded porter came, and opened the gate between the ceramicked tigers on the walls.

And when the girls had started to go in, the one who had spoken turned and said, 'Thank you, bold rider, for your brave escort. There might not have been many attackers, but at least your presence kept the howling dogs from attacking us.' And with a smile she nodded then, and delicately picked up her hems, and tiptoed over the threshold of the gate.

And when this girl had gone, Wei found another one smiling at him, and the second girl said, 'A fine horse you have got there too. Bold rider, you must be rich and lucky!' And when she had said that, like the former sister, she picked up her hem and stepped into the gate.

But when the others had gone in, Wei stood stricken and nervous, for the final sister, the moon-faced beauty, now came to the door. And as she passed by Wei so softly, tenderly she looked up at him. And shyly she said, 'Yet sir, won't you come in for some wine?' And then she looked at the ground again, trembling to wait his answer. And there was shock and tension in the air.

But Wei tied his horse to a post, and without speaking he let the rustling girl lead him over the step of the threshold, and he followed her quietly then into the gloomy house, and through the dark walls with their circular gates. And she led him into the creaking house, and her shuffling steps led Wei to a door, and holding up her lantern she took him in.

And when they had entered the room, she looked at Wei shyly and the look she gave him seemed to dart into his very soul. She stood there, holding the lamp which trembled, her eyes shining in its glare, and she seemed to stare gently into all his thoughts, and read there everything he desired. But then she moved away from him, and bustling she poured him some wine, and shuffling with tiny steps brought him some fruit and sweetmeats on a dish of silver. And she fetched a little table up, and gestured for him to sit in a lacquer chair. And she faced him again over the bamboo table, urging him with her eyes to drink and eat. And the time passed softly then, as they sat together, and they ate and drank in the vibrant silence.

And as Wei looked round the chamber, he saw that it was rich, with a perfume that melted his very bones. And screens were there, painted full of woodland scenes, with

44

pheasants and rabbits feeding among ferns. And Wei saw a great bronze mirror, which reflected the melon-shaped lantern, and a couch, jewel-studded and hung with pearls. And the maid sat on a red dais, with a fan of feathers, made from mandarin ducks and ornamental cockerels.

And the girl sighed to look at him and said, 'You have come at last, and here in this room all is at rest. But now we are together again from a former life, and being so, there is no impropriety. I saw it in your eyes at once. I recognised my friend. You will not leave me now we are reunited?' And she set her eyes on the floor again, bashful at having spoken. And Wei's wine steamed before him.

But Wei said, 'Distinguished maiden, your words are strange to me, and yet how many echoes they call up in my heart! Your face indeed I recognised, so familiarly fair, and indeed I felt drawn as if we were long acquainted. But is all this a slumber? Allow me to know your name, and of what family you come. For long I have had a vision of such a meeting with such a girl, and yet my fate in poverty has made me mistrustful.'

The girl smiled at him relievedly and said, 'My name is Jen. I have lived here a good time. My sisters you have just met, and I must also tell you I have two brothers. Indeed of them I must warn you, for at the Emperor's court tonight they play their lutes and flutes to entertain him. And they return at dawn. Before light then you must steal away. But as for the rest, it is both dream and real.' And she looked up at him bashfully, and got up from her chair, and kneeling by him laid her head on his thigh.

Now Wei when he felt this did not know what to do, for the fires of love and lust stirred in him, and he said, 'Fair maid, you have done me much honour tonight, and both kind and generous is your entertainment. But my sweet girl, you lay your head on a man who lives alone, a poor scholar, not one for high living, and the nearness of your lovely face, and the warmth of your sweet body trouble me with much fever. Wherefore I beseech you, do not make my welcome too sweet, lest I am tempted to take it further.'

But the girl looked up at him and said, 'You may take what you will. Is this our night of meeting a time for timidity? You do not seem to credit my words. I meant what I said. To me we are already united. And indeed I have seen in your face the craving of a man troubled, and my whole fate is to release such fever. It is not foolishness or dangerous innocence in this. The time is vital between us.' And the maid looked up at him, her long neck twisted upwards, and she seemed like a beast for the sacrifice.

But Wei could talk no further, but he bent down towards the maiden, and he set his lips upon her lips, and he twined his arm about her lifting her up towards him, so that she slithered in her robes over the floor. Then did the passion rise in him, and he bent her against his knees, and strongly and lustily did he kiss her, and the maiden gasped when she broke from his embrace, so that he was once more a little dashed. But then she sunk upon him, and he lifted her up in his arms, and to the bed of love he took her.

Now the time was silent when the midnight hour came, and the pair lay silent late in the bedroom. The mansion was steeped in the cold stillness of winter, and the moon intermittently shone on the frost of the roofs. But as the night went on, the winds began to blow, and the eaves were set a-creaking and the flags fluttered from the poles. And in the perfumed chamber, as the tempest passed, the draught set the lanterns flickering shadows on the walls.

And so the time was quiet again after the midnight hour, as these two lay still talking from their hearts. The gongs of the night-watchman sounded afar off, and the hooting of the owl that hunted among the willows. But the strong winds came again, and blew the leaves through the streets, and the bare branches of shrubs tapped the wooden walls. And the pair of lovers came thus to swear eternal love in the house that stood firm in the storm. Then the watchman in the streets with wooden clappers announced the hour before the dawn.

And Wei said, 'Jen, the dawn approaches, and with it I must go. The cockerels in their roosts have scented the

46

morning. But fear you not that I will return, for my sweet, now am I a wooer, and tomorrow I will return to win you honourably from your father. For I will work for you henceforth and achieve what I have dreamed. For I will make a home and a worthy life for you. So farewell a while, a little while, my love that was destined in the stars. A little while farewell, for we are together.' And so Wei left his sweetheart, and in the darkness crept away, to be shown by the maid from the mansion.

But as he untied his horse, and rode off into the gloom, he had a sudden thought which made him hesitate, for he still had not learnt the name of the house or Jen's family name, and he feared that this might lead to confusion. Yet the day was growing grey now, and he could not return to the house, so he stayed on his horse and looked about in the twilight. And he saw far off a marketman moving in the mist, by a stall with lamps hanging over it. So Wei rode over and said 'Good dawning, marketman, there is down that street there a gloomy mansion: that street there on the left, as far down as you may go: what is the name of the folk who own it?'

And the marketman looked up at him and said, 'Woe for you! Woe for you, stranger that comes with the dawning! For at the end of that street there, at the furthest you may go: there is nothing, bare land, which the wind howls on. It is a vacant plot there, empty ground which no one will buy, because it is haunted by the fox-fairies. And if you have seen ought there but a ruined plot of land, then you have been bewitched by spirits!'

Wei pulled his horse about, and jerked his spurs into his sides, and rode back down the street to seek for the mansion. But all the street was different now, for the morning had come on, and normal were the huts and the willows. But at the very street-end, as far as he might go, there was nothing: the land was drear with weeds upon it. And where had been the mansion, the perfumed chamber, the lacquer chairs, all this – just as smoke does – had vanished. And there was nothing left at all but the frozen grass, and the post he had tied his horse to.

47

Chapter Three

Now while dawn dallied in the East, silvering the canals of Jian kang, in the West it was not heard of. For darkness hung where barbarians prowl, and the camels look up lugubriously, and the ghastly deserts of Takla Mahan howl for ever in their agony. And the stars look down impenetrable and immense.

But high above the dreary dunes, and above the forest ranges of the wolf-haunted Nan Shan, where the ways of men are lost, there in the icy night with teeth bared to the thin air, the mountains of Tu Fan glitter in loneliness, their frozen slopes forbidding all life to come to them, save for the snowman of solitariness abominable, upon whom the stars look down impenetrable and immense.

But high above these rigid peaks, and the frozen air and clouds, there is a waterfall descends, falling from the night sky. Nor of water, nor ice it is, but of stars eternally tumbling, descending from the heavens and the figured constellations, the very end of the great Milky Way of the sky. As in the Emperor's parks in winter, when the alchemists from salt-petre make the fires and rains of flame, and the courtier-enrapturing cascades, reflected in the palace lakes, rivers of milk-white fire, so did there the pathway of the stars descend on the barren ranges.

To this sight came Wo Long Wang, the dragon, and he said, 'Hail, O sparks of my tail! Hail, O end of me that showers the inhospitable peaks of Qinghai! I have descended to the earth, you see, and circled China's hills, I have roamed one revolution of the courts of Zhongguo, and here have I come thus to circle upon myself, and gaze with admiration on the might of my extremities.

'Ah, see how they receive my glitter, the mightiest mountain of earth! See, the vaunting Himalayas, how they turn me into the creeping rivers! In splashes the stars fall from the Milky Way upon the snow sublime of earth's bosom. And look thus how the Huang he, first flood of the Central Realm, the Yellow River, teems from my fallen frosts! Rash Emperor indeed that called me down, such a mighty power. Why, with one shake, I could burst its banks and send the empire into deluge! Incautious man to put me in world, when so many things can break from my sporting!

'But for this end the Lord has called me, and I have a taste for the trip. For I have been viewing the state of this little world, teeming with hairy angels. I have looked upon China, and all is confusion there, with no settled government. One Emperor in the South thinks he is heir of Han. Another in the North thinks he is the true Emperor. There's sport enough in setting these two biting the ears of each other.

'I have looked upon the coasts, and there I see slackness brewing from lax administration. What point in trade when what's wanted may be taken with impunity and total profit? I have looked upon the frontiers, beyond the Great Wall, and I have looked West into Central Asia: what prize barbarians of the Huns, the Turks, the Xien pi, loiter and grumble looking for employment! A long time it is since I came into the world, and how the pot needs stirring!

'Wherefore, having looked for a day since he summoned me, I see it is time to be sporting, and say in thunder to the cowering earth below: have a care, the dragon is coming: the king of the dragons whose battling in the clouds brings down the rain and lightning, whose coiling about each other for a pearl in wrathful play sends the floodgates clanging back upon their hinges. Have a care, puppets of earth, have a care, men of clay, for dragons have long washed away your houses! Now comes the giant of them, a million million long, and there will be howling and snapping!'

And the massive almighty dragon of the stars then reared

49

up above his own head, and he shook his scales and his belly was in the zenith, and the whole sky bent to his cosmic circling. The planets were gathered up, stretched taut like the skin of a beast, and the meteors and comets down-cascaded, and then came a slithering throughout the whole spangled universe, as Wo Long Wang plungéd downwards towards the mountains.

But in his heaven amidst Kun Lun Shan, Confucius was gazing down, watching with concern the roaming of the lithe star-dragon. And he watched him now as from the mountains, and the blue lake the Tibetans call Koko Nor, the dragon followed the Yellow River from its source among the snow-forests of dragon-spruce. And he watched the dragon foaming in the torrents of the river, where the yaks breathe steaming among the sun-gilded ice. And the dragon writhed along the river, until he came to the Great Wall, and then did he stare across the Great Wall of China.

And Confucius sighed to himself and said, 'Ay, see how the dragon glares! He looks over the Great Wall and sees the barbarians, wondering if he might stir them to attack! He looks upon the Juan Juan there, that Westward are called Avars. He looks upon the Toba tribe, known in the West as the Turks. He licks his chops at the Xien pi, and the Xiung nu, the Huns. Why, there are millions there he might deluge upon the tottering cities!' And Confucius nearly started up, to see what he could do to prevent this, when he saw the dragon moving again in his search on earth.

For the dragon slid on from the Great Wall and came thus to the Eastern Ocean, and he descended South along the shores and came to the mouth of another river. Here does the Yang zi debouch and spew its tumultuous silt into the sea, and the dragon roamed over the Yang zi's banks and came to the city of Jian kang. And Confucius watched as the dragon fed his eyes now on the town with its canals and hump-backed bridges. And he watched as he gazed on the potteries and steel-foundries, and its rattling factories of veined brocade. And he saw the dragon stare upon the imperial way to the palace, and here again Confucius grew concerned, wondering what mischief he might wreak among the true descendants of the ancient empire.

And Confucius said, 'Why now, the dragon looks with longing on the one place the imperial court is sustained. Is he looking for the star-lovers, or is he looking for mischief? Surely I think the serpent will not be diligent in his task. There are pirates on the shores to stir up, and plotters in the capital. May be I should descend and warn the mandarins.' And Confucius again was on the point of rising from his seat on his balcony.

But the star-dragon did not linger overlong on the Southern capital with its peaceful ways, but sniffing the air again, to find out turmoil, he slunk again towards the Yellow River. And where the river meets the Wei, a kingdom from Jian kang, he came thus to the old Northern capital, and on Chang an he now looked down, studying its decayed streets, peering at its mighty but fallen splendour. And the old capital of the Han, extended its great square, its huge ruined walls twelve miles roaming. And the dragon stared close in it, and Confucius stared too, and the two divine beings peered at the mortals.

And in the courts of Chang an, they saw the potentate, for there was Fu jian, monarch of the Northern Kingdom of the Jin. And Fu jian sat in the midst of his palace, Tibetan guards all about, and he studied with his counsellors the ancient maps. There came to them messengers, with news of recent campaigns. There came to them reports of military successes. And the monarch and his generals stared longingly at the South wondering how its riches might fall into their clutches. And the dragon pricked his ears at this, and breathed steam and lust into the men, and he settled himself there to work his mischief.

When Confucius saw this, he was horrified, and said, 'It is just as we feared! Rather than executing his orders, as a diligent official should, rather than seeking a small pair of hiding lovers, he is planning to stir up turmoil on earth, to set wars roaring about the globe, to whip up lust and spill the teeming plunderers, bringing down the walls of civilisation. And thus has he gone to where the men meet his own mind, and he sits in Fu jian's court, rousing them to battle. Alas, alas, has not China suffered enough? Must there be always barbarians sinking their teeth on it?'

Confucius gazed upon the two capitals, Chang an and Jian kang, and he sighed and said, 'Behold the state of China, that lies divided between the ancient and the modern. The capital of the ancient sons of heaven, there it lies: in the grip of nomads who usurp the old traditions, while a town of not much moment, till it was called a Golden Mound: there lies Jian kang, become the seat of the true sons of heaven. How many revolutions are in the Chinese dragon's tail?

'It is a thousand years now, since I left Shan dong, and walked among the courts of nobles, seeking to teach what it was to be a gentleman. The time was dark and turbulent, the feudal lords were feuding, and few indeed I found to hear my advice of ruling by righteousness. It seems now the turbulent time has returned, and the ancestors are forgot. When the thunder-clouds come, it is needful for the gods again to walk the earth.' And Confucius got up now, and left the verandah where he leaned surveying the earth, and he walked with sad steps among his halls, silent in the winter light.

But when he came across a servant he said, 'Summon my carriage, and yoke the cranes ready for flight, for I am descending to the earth once more to walk in the streets of Jian kang.' And Confucius then continued strolling along the wide-tiled chambers.

But when he saw another servant, he stopped him and said, 'Bring me now my travelling hat and staff, for I am going down again to the world of men, to march among them in disguise so that no man may know me.' And Confucius now paced busily among the echoing halls.

And he came across his Chamberlain, leaving his office in the courtyard, and setting his feet along the pavements where there was a light dusting of snow, and Confucius said, 'Lord Chamberlain, great arbiter and ruler of the court, lend me your ear a little while, for I have great things to put forward.' And the Chamberlain leaned eagerly with his hands folded, ready to hear Confucius's proposition.

And Confucius continued, 'You remember once, not two years hence, I had reason to go into the world of mortals? A foolishness it was, unworthy of my time, and rivalry of Lao zi made me do it. But I went to Jian kang, and in a certain household, set myself up as a tutor, wearing a scholar's robes, seeming ancient and infirm, and calling myself the scholar Kun. Lao zi and I were engaged in a battle there, competing for the favours of a mortal, but nothing we gained of it, except humiliation, and learning our lesson, we retired.

'It has occurred to me now that the time I spent there was not, however, thrown away. It was foolish to deal with Tawny-hair, for he has a mind that sails like a phoenix above sense. But the family he lives with, and part of whose clan he is, this is far from contemptible. His cousin is Xie An, the chief minister of the Emperor and one that can dictate the state policy. His uncle is Xie Shih, a general in the cavalry, and a vigorous promoter of careful defence. To have an entry to his household might prove useful for the salvation of China.

'My lord, you have doubtless heard that the dragon of the stars, Wo Long Wang, is in the world rampaging. I have watched his progress, and far from attending the mission which the Jade Emperor gave him, he has gone a-sniffing what mischief he can create in the world of men. He has settled on Fu jian, the Chang an usurper, intent on driving him to conquer. It will not be long now before the Northern state wages war on the South. Bring me my scholar's gown then again, my disguise as a mere mortal, for not as Confucius but the scholar Kun will I go into the household of the Xie.' And the Lord Chamberlain bowed at this, and went to the warder of the robes, and he fetched the gown of the scholar Kun, and Confucius put on its mortality.

Now in the capital of Jian kang, the chief minister Xie An

was progressing in his bannered chariot to see his cousin the General. The outriders went before him, but on either side another cart and a sedan chair bustled along, as two of his friends, officials at the court, accompanied him in their brocaded robes to join the drinking-party. The outriders blew their trumpets and shouted, and the people dodged out of the way, until the whole procession with their clinking bells drew up before the General Xie palace.

And the General was there to greet them, and he bowed from his own front gate and said, 'Now welcome, great cousin minister adviser of the Emperor. And who also has come with you? Do I see Gu Kai ji there? And Tao Qian? Are we having a literary party? My humble abode is honoured to have the great painter here, and the poet whose verses speak of the solitude of nature. Come in, come in.' And he turned to take them in through the door. But then he stopped, and they all gazed at a strange figure.

For there now in the doorway, appearing from the very air, stood Confucius in his disguise as the scholar Kun, and he bowed low to the company, assuming a humble air, and he folded his hands discreetly over the lengths of his grey beard. And the General cried, 'Now look also who has appeared! It is the old scholar Kun that taught my nephew. Princes, let me present you him, and let him join our party, for his advice we can also attend as we debate the difficulties of the empire.' And with this introduction, and with much bowing and smiling, effusively humbling themselves, the courtiers, ministers and scholars entered the compound, and were led to an antechamber.

So when they sat in the antechamber, taking their tea together, with a view outside of the weird rock-garden, they seemed a joyous lot of ancient gentlemen, though not all of advanced years. For the General was big and had a scowling brow, while his cousin the chief minister had a face as smooth as egg-shells. And Tao Qian, the nature-poet, had flowing loose-clinging robes, and Gu Kai ji was an odd-looking character, with tufts of hair sticking from his skull, and he fidgeted and stared, and scrutinised each

54

object, while the poet beside him smiled with lips sweet and womanly.

And when they were settled then the General said, 'It is long since I have presumed to trouble your footsteps to come here. Your stupid younger brother is well, and all his insignificant bugs, and the trifling acceptance of his unworthy report has given him a mean measure of glory. And this is why I called to see you, not to celebrate such paltry success, but to discuss what leads from my new powers of augmenting the imperial defences. So before we go into dinner together, may I hear your views on my memorial?' And the General turned then to the company, seeing who would speak first.

Gu kai ji looked at him, and said, 'It was a good paper. Your powers should be doubled, and at once you should be off to strike at the Chin before it is too late. And when you cut their heads off, stick them on poles, and it will do to frighten the Turks and Huns.'

But Tao Qian sighed at this, and said, 'How many million will this paper slice through? I am insignificantly young. I would hope to live to old age and tend chrysanthemums in my garden. But at this rate none of us will retire to the blue hills. Why can we not live in peace with ourselves and peace with our neighbours?'

Then Kun, the scholar, said, 'In all these things it is necessary to take the Golden Mean. Neither by over aggression nor over timidity should the government proceed. A gentleman is not swayed in his plans by fear, and never gives way to anger. In calm content and with rational mind he contemplates what policy is best.'

'But what policy is best?' said the General abruptly. 'To my mind, there is only one. And the latest reports from the North and the Chin court make any other decision seem absurd and inadequate. I would mobilise the armies now and send them to be ready for him East beyond Da Pie Shan. But what says my cousin? He is the chief minister who has the ear of the Emperor.'

And Xie An looked at him, and thought for a while,

Then soberly he said, 'I agree with you. If we do not resist Fu jian's attacks now, we may never have another opportunity.'

Now when the General heard this he was pleased and said, 'Come then, let us go into dinner.'

So the courtiers arose, and at a sign from the General the banquet-room doors were opened, and the company moved forward in due order of precedence towards the loaded tables and glimmering lights. But as Confucius went, humbling himself at the back, and smiling on all with dispassion, his eye suddenly caught another visitor at the feast, sitting waiting for them to come in. It was a ragged monk, a Daoist in dishevelled robes, with bald head, grinning at them. Confucius froze. His face went black. His breath came thunderously in anger. Turning on his heel he stalked out of the banqueting-hall and off through the anteroom. The ragged monk laughed, but the others looked at each other in pained astonishment.

General Xie none the less went ahead and settled his guests into their feast, for he sat them at their tables, and called forth the servants, and the maids brought the dishes of steaming food: of horseflesh was there, most delectable, and wild boar and golden hams, and in little bowls was the excellent roast dog served, juicily cut up into tasty titbits. On bamboo shoots and ginger and pumpkins and brinjal, the Chief Minister and the poet and the painter feasted, and the monk came and joined them laughing, and was received into their company, for they knew him also of old. But when all was jolly under the painted rafters, General Xie went out in pursuit of his lost guest. And soon did he come back, dragging Kun along, who wore on his face a sombre expression.

And General Xie said, 'See, I have prevailed on him to rejoin us. Bring to our guest the hot wine and steaming towels. There's no disrespect intended here, nor nothing at which to take offence, and so let us all practise calm content and rational thinking, as we were bidden.' And the company applauded as Kun came back, though he avoided looking at the monk.

Kun, the scholar, said, 'It was not so much disrespect or the giving of offence that drove me from the company of the monk, Lun, but as to what it was, though he knows it well, it would not be fit to divulge it here. Monk Lun and myself, as is well known, had many battles of wits in this house, when we were instructing that unique nephew of the General's, Nai, who so strangely distinguished himself in the Empress's service. Perhaps it was the memories of those battles of ours that drove me hence in anger, or perhaps it was the indignities brought on our names by the Poet Nai in his tending of the Empress. Whatever it was, however, that grinning monk knows well, and we need talk of it no longer.' And Confucius sat down, keeping a still face, and seeming to have no interest, fell on the food.

Lun, the monk, sat for some time his head bowed, though it was shaking with laughter, but then he said, 'Oh, po-face! A beautiful sermon! Full of lofty sentiments as ever! But I know this scholar: he's just jealous to see me here with these lords! But I'm not a Confucian. They mean nothing to a Daoist. It was Confucius who spent his whole time on earth toadying up to the aristocracy! But as for me: they're all robbers and bandits, and I don't need any of them. I sit here and eat their food because I amuse them and their food is worth eating.' And the monk drained off a cup of hot wine, and the scholar feigned to ignore him.

'But what I would like to know,' said the General chuckling, 'now that you two old combatants have got together again, is where have you been this past year? Our palace has been empty without you two skirmishing in it. One moment you both lived here, hobnobbing with my nephew, being unofficial tutors to him, the next – when he achieved eminence – you had disappeared, like some gods vanishing on clouds. Did he say something to annoy you? Did my servants mistreat you? I have never been able to make out the story.'

'My lord,' then said the poet Tao Qian, 'I should think they both vanished on the hot air they spend so much time producing. For vain is this duel between Confucians and

Daoists, which has been going for as long as the faith's founders. The forces of order are pitted against the forces of nature and profusion, and so goes on this battle, coming and going, just as do our pair of philosophers. History shows us this, revolving the past great dynasties with our own times of chaos. But for myself, a Daoist, I prefer to forget it all, and look forward only to opting out of it.'

But Gu Kai ji, the painter, said, 'Be that as it may, there are also times when the fabric of life itself changes. For may be, courtiers and officials, generals and poets, a fearful new age is dawning. I hear that Fu jian is very much under the influence of a sage called Dao an. If he seizes our empire we'll all have our heads shaved, and both Kun and Lun will be Buddhists.' And so did the company argue long as the food before them was diminishing.

Meanwhile, through the streets of Jian kang, as the sky darkened above the city, and seemed to be filled with the menace of sudden snow, the young scholar Wei walked up and down the boulevards, seeking among the faces of all that passed him. For he looked among the wood-bearers, stooped under their heavy loads, and he looked among the water-bearers, with their huge pails balanced on shoulder-poles, and he looked among the peasant women and bourgeois women and ladies. But never in any of the sea of faces did he see the face of Jen.

And Wei lamented to himself and said, 'No, I'll never find her. I have the bewitchment, without the joy of living in her presence. I have searched all day now. The place where I met her has no vestige of her laughter, and the empty ground of the plot mocks me cruelly with her absence. Oh Jen, Jen, why did you come to me, if you knew you could not live with me? If we were destined to meet, from another life incarnated, why could it not have been as equals?' And Wei sighed again, as he tottered among the crowds, wincing at the vigour that was rife in all about him.

But as he came now to the gardens by the lake, and the air was dim and heavy, he saw walking towards him a form he knew and which he found cheering, for Nai was approaching in his embroidered hat, and his red silk jacket flapping, and Wei raised his hand and said, 'Nai, well met! This is good comfort to see you. For when I delivered your horse this morning, they said you were still in bed, and so I did not disturb you. But now here you are, your usual colourful self. But what do you out in these garden suburbs?'

'Need you ask?' said Nai. 'Have you forgot this is hallowed ground here in the North part of the city? Overlooking the park with its lake and five islands, do you not find the Cock's Crow Temple? And is not this a convent, where the Buddhist nuns live, and where these of that persuasion live with them?'

'So you are going to see Ling Xiang?' interrupted Wei. 'She has returned then to the city? Ah, lucky is he who can march towards his sweetheart in the trust of an earthly reception!'

'I don't know what you mean by an earthly reception,' said Nai, 'but it is in fact *another* reception, for I had the first last night shortly after I'd left you. For she had sent word to the compound she had returned and would be glad to visit me. And so while you dissipated your time in the whore-house, I was being pure and righteous with a Buddhist.'

'So already you have seen her?' Wei sighed gazing at him. 'It must have been sweet! But what of the poem? Tell me how it went, my friend, and I will walk along with you, for nothing have I much to do today but gaze on the faces of the living.' And he walked with Nai then, as the hills of the lake came into sight, and the sky grew heavier and darker beyond the bare trees.

Nai looked frustratedly for a while, and then said, 'It's not going well, my friend. She's driving me crazy as a matter of fact, because every time I see her I get depressed. She is always going on about our love not being grounded. I don't know what the hell she means by it. And I get these great lectures on my not being serious, and her not being in love with me. You would think she was doing everything to put me off her.'

'Well,' sighed Wei, 'perhaps she is.'

'But I don't think she is!' replied Nai. 'Take the poem, for instance. It wasn't as bad as I thought it was. I thought it was a definite "you are not for me", but in fact she denies this. She seems to want to be with me. But she gives me all these stories about her past, which – if you took them seriously – are pretty horrifying.'

'How is that?' said Wei.

'Well,' said Nai, 'let's just say she has difficulties. She lives a solitary life. A nunnery is her home. She has forsworn any part of the life of the red dust. And now when she returns to it, and is friends at least with a man, there are such dangerous places lurking in her soul, that it is like dealing with a tiger. When you ply her too hotly, she freezes you into snow. When you show no tenderness, she rages as if she would rip you to pieces. It is like that clever substance of which fireworks are made, you never know when it might catch fire and turn into comets. Last night, for instance, opened a way dark and perilous.'

'Tell me more.'

Nai sighed, as they paced along. 'Well, Wei, we are old friends, and there have been mistresses we have shared, so there is not much secret between us. But certain things about Xiang I must not speak, or at least while the bond between us lies so deep. Oh, she is strange, my friend; a lady of the dance, who never has been a lady of liaisons, a peacock of the theatre who yet in her soul is shy of all display. But why do I prevaricate? I was angry with her last night, and in my rage I discovered . . . a capacity for rapine. Is that how I should put it? Ay, I could rape Xiang easily. And surely this would be one way ahead for us.'

Wei looked at him embarrassed. He did not know how to reply. But he was forestalled by their arrival.

'Look, here's the nunnery,' he said with anxious relief. 'I'll leave you. I must be going.'

Nai watched Wei disappear beneath the leafless trees,

surprised at his sudden embarrassment. But then he drew in his breath, and walked towards the nunnery, and climbed up the steps to its screened gateway.

But when the afternoon was waning, and the day was dark with winter, and they lit their lamps early in the stalls along the backstreets, the young scholar Wei grew weary with his searching, examining every face, still peering in each inn and each tea-house, longing to see his fox-maiden. And he shivered with the cold, and sighed to see no sign of her, and ever the sky got heavier with menace.

Wei groaned, as he stopped at last, and said, 'Why, this, this then is bewitchment! I did not believe them when they told me that he who loves a fox-fairy is lost. I did not believe the marketman when he said that by Jen's love I was put under a curse. But I believe it now, for the curse is love and never can I forget her. Nay, how can I forget the meeting with the soul with whom I am linked for eternity? O Jen, Jen, I do not blame you for bewitching me, but why did you have so cruelly to desert me?' And Wei went languishing through the busy streets, and sighed to see such endless streams of the world's people.

Then as he stood beneath an awning, where an inn-house rattled its plates, and the smoke came billowing from a stove that roasted chestnuts, he saw among the milling throng a sudden flash of scarlet. And Xie Nai he saw again, pushing his way morosely forward. And Wei ran across to him and seized him by the arm, and pulled him back with him under the awning, and said, 'Nai, go you home? It was not long you stayed. How did your meeting go with your lady? Tell me, was she angry then with your former treatment? It is cold and miserable in the city!'

And Nai looked at him sadly and said, 'Ay, I fear all's done. Over and over I hear from her the same messages. I'm going to send her a letter. I shall spell out to her the case. I must wipe away these delusions. And as for the consequences, I care not if all's finished. It is pointless going on when all's depression.' And Nai moved away from him, weary and glum-faced, and was gone in the gloom without waiting an answer.

And Wei sighed, as he stood there alone, 'Alas, for this weary world! If my friend Nai is lovelorn that loves so many, what may I have hope for, a poor scholar? The times are troubled. Crumbling, the old faiths. The darkness of war glowers over us. It is good that I went and entered my name for the troops of cavalry. In a war, perhaps, these forlorn and grim things can be forgotten.' And Wei left the awning, and went wandering towards his home, seeking the back-alleys of the city.

But just as he walked by a slimy canal, his mind full of thoughts of death, he saw coming in front of him a girl in a flowery robe, who walked with a modest step and sprightly. And Wei's heart bounded in him because the familiar walk was so like the walk of his beloved. And when he came much nearer to her, he saw that it was her indeed, and she saw him too, and gasped with amazement. And Wei called, 'Jen!' But she darted and ran away. And Wei at once ran as hard as he could after.

Now the little fox-fairy set her feet pattering along the bank, and Wei thumped hurriedly, panting and calling. And the fox-fairy dived into an alley and out again into some shops, and Wei bounded after, knocking over some boxes. But when the fox-fairy came into the great crowds, she lost herself swiftly among the pushing people. Yet Wei still hailed after, shoving the folk this way and that, until at last, he caught her. And he seized her and held her just outside the inn which he had left, and the smoke from the brazier again engulfed him.

And Wei said, 'Jen, my sweetheart, why do you run away? Why do you wish to avoid me, when you have loved me? Is it true you have put a spell on me, for surely I am enchanted by your love, surely after last night I cannot forget you. O Jen, why do you spurn me? I love you purely, my love. I want nothing else than to be with you and cherish you. O Jen, come answer me. Tell me you wish me no harm. Tell me you do not truly wish to flee me.'

And the fox-fairy looked at him, and said, 'If you have any money, we could go into this inn and discuss it.' And Wei sighed to hear her, and took her arm, and he entered with her the crowded inn-yard.

'You know I am a fox-fairy then,' she said to him as they drank, 'and you can see I was trying to avoid you. But this was not for my sake. The world becomes hard for the man who loves a spirit. But as for putting a spell on you, you can dismiss that from your mind. I am not of that vindictive sort of fairy. But as an embodied spirit, neither out of the world nor in it, I respect my place and live but in the dread and loneliness. Yet the night when I met you, I was with skittish girls, and there came to me this chance of a little happiness. Forgive me then, my mortal friend, forgive me my deception. I will see that you are never touched by bewitchment further.' And she looked at the table, and sighed a little, but then drank off her wine.

'My sweet one,' then said Wei, 'what is there to forgive? How can I forgive what has brought me such happiness? When I missed you last night, when I saw that barren plot, then my heart sank within me. I suffered as never before. Your kind words to me, your recognition, the fact that in another life we have known each other: all this made me realise you were my eternal love, and that our meeting was eternally destined. How can I forgive you bringing me all this? O Jen, you are with me now. All is happiness.'

Jen looked at him, and sadly shook her head, and she replied, 'My dear, you know little of this world of ours. There is no future for us. A mortal cannot take a fox for a wife or a concubine! Those words I said to you: I made them up. I wanted your love, so I said them. You must not think they are true. I am a fox. You should see me run. Out in the country I have a bushy tail. It cannot be, my little scholar. There has been joy. Keep that, and don't ask beyond it.' And Jen leaned over to him and put her hand on his, and Wei looked back at her dismayed.

Then he shook his head, and said, 'No, that is not the way. What passed between us was of more moment. What you said to me might have been feigned, your words might have been meant to catch me. But I recognised them, and knew them for a truth, and if you cannot see it, surely I can. We were destined, Jen, and we shall fulfil that destiny. And I am not one to speak from fleeting rashness. We met each other that blowy night. Our eyes conveyed the past. And now our ill-matched bodies must face the future. You are strange to me, fox-fairy. But I am not afraid. We must live together.' And Wei took his other hand, and placed it over hers, so that her palm was trapped between them.

But Jen snatched it away, and she ran to the inn door, and Wei leapt up from the table and hurried after. At the door she stopped, for outside it was snowing now, and the flakes were teeming down in the fading evening. And as Wei came up beside her, she seemed to rock and melt, and in a moment she gazed up into his eyes again. Then back she looked at the merry streets, where traders hurried in the snow, and the lamplights burned a smoky orange among the coolness.

And Jen was looking over the road, where a vacant shop stood with a board over the door, and a notice of sale. And she looked up at Wei again and said, 'You are kind to me. There has been no trace of fear or repulsion. I am not worthy of you, but what virtue I have, I will serve you with to the best I can manage. If you have the loans to cover it, you can buy that house there for us to live, and I will work as an embroiderer and seamstress. I will stay faithful to you, but you must remember one thing: I am a fox. The country for me is dangerous. All will be well if you never ask me to travel with you out of the city, for there in the wastes, where the woods are wild, my hold on mortality is fragile.' And Wei looked back on her, and tears were in his eyes, and he wound his arms round her and kissed her.

Chapter Four

Now in the palace of the General, by a door in the first courtyard, on either side guarding the guests' apartments, there were two door-gods painted, Shen tu and Yu lu, who stood there in their ceremonial armour. And it happened that these door-gods had been only freshly painted, so that the two warriors depicted were as yet new to the household. Shen tu stood there bearded, with goggle eyes popping, a sheaf of arrows bristling from his shoulders. Yu lu stood there grandly, his hand on a bejewelled lance, and a thin moustache from his smooth face quaintly trailing. And the two gods together were watching the scholar and the monk arguing, the untiring Kun and Lun.

And Kun was saying, 'This, then, makes it all the more serious that you cannot keep faith with me. We arranged clearly that neither of us would come to earth to investigate the Buddhist onslaught on Nai, but what do I find sitting eating in the General's hall before any of us had entered but this terrible filthy Daoist, whom you purport to be, and indeed who rather typically you personify? It is reprehensible behaviour! How true the *Analects*, when I said "Put loyalty first!"'

But Lun, the monk, yelled, 'Ha! What hypocrisy! Great grandfather of pots calling the kettle black! You did all the very same things you accuse me of doing. But it's all right for you. Why? Because you're Confucius, and you're good, and I'm Lao zi, and I'm naughty! I've never heard such fantasies! You self-righteous, one-eyed, pompous, bombastic old wind-bag! Remember my words in the *Dao de ching*: that those who would conquer must yield. And remember my next words, and beware of them too: that those who yield will conquer.'

Now the two door-gods had listened to this amazed and stood open-mouthed for a long time, when eventually the monk and scholar flung back the doors, and flattened the painted gods against the wall. Meanwhile, the pair, Kun and Lun, went into their quarters, and continued with the argument.

For Kun was saying, 'I did not come here for Xie Nai. That is why your remarks are out of order. I came down to the capital, because I had seen the dragon stirring up war in the North. I came down here to alert them, although I am glad to see that preparations are going forward. But my descent had nothing whatever to do with our battle over Nai, and so it is no accusation against me!'

'Oh, leave me your lawyer's logic,' then sneered Lun, twitching his robe. 'Why don't you find out my reasons before you condemn me? It happened that I also was watching Chang an, and it happened that I also saw Fu jian. But I saw him conspiring with this Buddhist the painter mentioned, this absurdly named Dao an – Dao be damned! And I saw at once that if Fu jian takes the South and East, then he will be forcibly spreading Buddhism. And that was why I descended. I couldn't care a damn if Nai becomes a Buddhist or a witch-doctor. So may we stop arguing now, and discuss the matter in hand: what are we going to do about these creeping baldies?' And Lun looked at Kun with piercing, ferocious eyes, and Kun was brought to consider.

But at that moment, unable to hold back any longer, the two door-gods came floating into the apartment. And they looked at the monk and scholar with popping and squinnied eyes, as they floated for a while over the Turkestan carpets, between the great bronze cauldrons where incense coiled up into the fretted ceiling. And the two would-be men paused a moment to see this vision, and they did not know quite how to react to it.

And the door-god Yu lu said, 'Excuse us for interrupting, but long have we been listening to your fascinating conversation. For you both seem to be mortals from an outward point of view, and yet you persist in addressing each other as Lao zi and Confucius. Moreover, we have observed in your account of human affairs a quite masterly sweep of detail. I say you are, but my friend says you are not. Are you Lao zi and Confucius? And if you are: what is the story of your entertaining Xie Nai, and why do you bother with such a waster, for from what we have observed, he sponges off his uncle, and idles his time writing silly stories?' But the door-god was silent now.

And Confucius stared and said, 'Indeed this is extraordinary! It did not occur to me that we might be overheard. Had we known we were, we would have moderated our language, for you must remember Lao zi and I are old comrades, and our intimacy lends us certain freedoms. But you are indeed right, Yu lu, I think? And is it not also Shen tu? We are whom you opine. And you have come at a good time, for I for one am tired of arguing, and I would relish the opportunity to relax in good company, and over wine tell you a beguiling tale. Lao zi, settle the gods down. I'll see to the drinks. This will be a pleasant way to spend an evening.' And Confucius went to a cupboard, and got out the rice-wine and set it in a bronze wine-heater.

But Lao zi, laughing, bade the gods come in, and showed them to the couch by a table, and the couch was a heated couch such as is used in winter, with a little stove burning inside it. So the gods bowed and sat, while in purple scholar's robes, Confucius busied about like a mother, and while the wine was heating, he went to the double-doors and shut them on the snowy scene outside. Then the wine was brought to the table, and poured and drank, draining the cups at one draught and toasting each other.

'Well,' said Confucius at last, 'you have asked for the story of Nai, and what makes us gods so interested in him? And the quick answer to this is that we have no idea: it was pure fate or chance the way it happened. For we happened to get into contact with him because of a squabble, the eternal squabble, such as yourselves have been witnessing, and we picked Nai to settle the squabble, as a sort of experiment, relying on his reactions as Mr Average. I hardly need say it did not work. We picked quite the wrong person, and the squabble has only grown worse because of it.

'For it happened one day, that Lao zi and I in heaven were sitting together peacefully, looking down on the world, when we saw the capital Jian kang, laid out before us with its waterways, and we came to consider which one of us had the most followers. Was the average man down there a Daoist and a would-be hermit, or was he a Confucian, honouring his parents and the state? And long we quarrelled about this difficult question until we decided, we must pick one at random and see.'

'Well, no sooner had we decided on this,' Lao zi took over the story now, 'than our eyes were glazed by seeing a sea of people. There were thousands of heads bobbing black-haired below us, and we were being spoiled for choice. Should we have that one, or that one? They all looked the same. Being the same you could not select one.'

'But then luck played up to us,' said Confucius excitedly. 'The subject of our experiment selected himself, for suddenly down there in the mass of black-haired people, we saw this tawny-haired person, bouncing along aimlessly, of no particular profession. This was the man for our test! Strange how these things happen! It did not take a minute. It was as if it was predestined. Yet where will it end? The whim of that little argument goes on expanding and expanding, and now it seems so serious, the very heavens themselves are all involved in this ridiculous creature.'

The door-gods gazed back at them.

'So this was Xie Nai?' said Shen tu.

The scholar and monk nodded their heads, and all paused while they drank the steaming wine.

'The cold is settling tonight,' said Lao zi, staring through the trellis-work. 'The pines on the Bell Mountain will creak with the loads of snow along their branches. The foxes that dart on the wooded hills will look forlornly to the Yang zi

River, and down they will come to scrounge round the capital for kittens and chickens. How still is the night when the gods come to earth! Yet, let us get on with the story.'

'Indeed,' said Confucius. 'I would not abandon the chronicle for the nature-poem. But strange it is how these things turn out, and we are here again in Jian kang. Undoubtedly there is some great fateful reason why we should come and sit as humans in the house of this dreamer and waster.'

'Are we going to have the story, or are we not?' said Lai zi, glaring at him.

Confucius smiled. 'Having selected our man, we were not slow in launching our enterprise. We summoned two clouds, and hurtled to earth, and flung ourselves immediately down in his path. The dreamer was startled. In a cloud of dust two ill-sorted old men had appeared to him, in their haste still clothed in the elaborate robes of the chief deities of the Chinese. Well may he have stared! "What are you?" he said at last. It should have been us asking him the question. But we managed to collect ourselves, and explain we were just travellers along the road.'

'Just idle travellers,' said Lao zi dreamily. 'And I was not short on invention. And as we had just come from Kun Lun Shan, I introduced us as: Kun, the scholar and Lun, the Daoist. And then I said to him at once, he could settle a bet between us, if he told us whether he was a Daoist or Confucian.'

'Well,' sighed Confucius, 'it transpired that we could not have picked a worse case. He was a Confucian surely, but he was also a Daoist, and also he was neither. He was also very stupid. Yet he was also very clever. Yet also he was neither. There could not be a man in China who was both so typical and yet was like a complete foreigner. He seemed at one point to be keener on hearing about India than he was of his own faiths. And then we discovered that we had picked a poet who had the most absurd and maniacal dreams, a waster and an idler, who in spite of his advanced

69

years had not yet even begun on his life, a glittering failure, who had mastered all sorts of abstruse arts, and yet had achieved success with not one of them, a kind of grown-up natural, who the more you pressed him on his beliefs, the wilder he got, until he was babbling like an idiot about Western fairylands. It became plain to us that Nai had been touched by some form of disabling lunacy. And yet we were stuck with him. He was the man we had picked to settle our argument. We thought of giving it up.'

'But then we went with him back to his house,' Lao zi now took over the narration. 'And though I myself still doubted, all thoughts of abandoning the idiot flew away when Confucius here saw the rank of his family. "General Xie Palace, Built by Imperial Command", we saw written over the gateway. Confucius was bobby-dazzled. It only takes a whiff of the aristocracy to get him going. It was decided to pursue our investigations, to insinuate and probe further. And so we formalised ourselves in the disguises we had adopted, and became unofficial tutors to this twerp. That was the beginning of our suffering. You two have lived here a while, you must know something of Nai's lunacy. We tried to talk to him of sense, of the ancient laws of his country, and all we got was fantasies of the cosmos. I really think he is more mad than all my monks put together. It was a strange fate that drew us to him.'

'Indeed,' said Yu lu, 'from our observation of Nai, this is what we deduced. He is so feckless and seems so unmoved by the ordinary considerations of life! We were puzzled by him for some time, and studied the way he lived. He is a very strange person. He spends hours, you know, fooling around with stories: studying old ballads, reworking the plots, turning out sketches of his own, telling fairy tales of the gods. It is all such foolery! What reputable scholar would bother himself with such vulgar claptrap? Yet we heard him talk once to his friend Wei: he revealed megalomaniac ambitions! He says there is a Great Tale, hidden among the earth, which once heard would unite humanity, and he honestly believes that in his ridiculous rhyming and story-telling, he is preparing to find it. But I am sorry to interrupt you. Do continue with your story. What did you decide concerning him?'

'Well,' said Confucius, 'it was not so much what we decided, as what Fate determined for us, for it was soon after we had come to the Xie household that the course of Nai's fortunes took him away from us. Till we met him, he was a failure. He had not completed the full course of the state examinations, and so could not undertake any proper offices in the service of the Emperor. While he fooled his time with stories then, he would earn a miserable pittance teaching the Five Classics, and indeed the girl Ling Xiang, who is reputed to have influenced him towards Buddhism: she started with him as one of his pupils. But as to what happened that finally drove us from him, the narrative is so undignified and ludicrous, I had better leave it for my colleague. Daoists, you know, seem to specialise in the ridiculous.'

'Oh yes,' said the monk Lun, 'I'll tell you this with pleasure, for the whole thing tickles my sense of the absurd. And Xie Nai in this, as with all his actions, revealed himself a master of absurdity. Indeed it was his finally involving us in his absurdity that irrevocably offended my comrade here. It all began when Nai went to stay for a year or so in Shou chun, to further his studies. In fact he did no such thing, for he loafed around the town all day, sponging off the patriarch's estates, and instead of studying proper subjects, gave his mind to the story-tellers who practise there, and their fairy tales. But he told his uncle he had been studying, and when he returned to Jian kang, he said he had just successfully completed a course in midwifery.

'Oh, this just shows you the madness,' laughed Lun, 'of this idiot's mind! Imagine him telling his uncle he had become a midwife! He did it because he knew that his uncle would insist on him practising whatever he said he had studied. But with midwifery – what woman in China is ever going to consent to having a man at her lying-in? He knew he was safe there, and he maintained it stoutly that this was

71

his proficiency, and said he would be glad to practise it in Jian kang, if his uncle could find the work for him. His uncle stayed quiet. He had no wish to get involved in this sort of indignity. And so it looked as though Nai's little plot had worked, and he beavered on compiling his myths and legends.

'The hilarious escapade which dented my friend's dignity,' said Lun, 'and thereby sent both of us back to heaven, arose because our protégé eventually had his bluff called in an elaborate manner. For soon after lying to his uncle that he had pursued studies on a subject upon which he knew he could never be questioned or tested, what should happen but the Empress, the first wife of Emperor Xiao wu, should fall into a protracted and difficult labour? The midwives of the court were running about, unable to bring things to rights, and the word went out to summon all the city's midwives, until at last whole crowds of them were locked up in the palace, all of them totally powerless in the face of the Empress's agony.

'The General sent for his nephew. "Have you heard the news?" he said. "No," said Nai. He had been mooching about as usual. "The Empress is in labour. All midwives have been summoned to the palace. I have ordered a sedan-chair to take you there immediately." He gazed at Nai with delight in his eyes. But we were surprised. "Thank you," said Nai airily. And to our shared amazement, he left in the sedan-chair and was gone, to be locked up in the palace.

'We heard about what happened later, first from reports going round the town and then from officials who told us the true story. But it seems that the two accounts were not so different from each other, so wildly were absurdity and reality mixed. It seems that Nai in his usual idle fashion had been fooling around with his nieces that morning, and he found as he bounced off to the Emperor's palace, he still had two of their dolls in his pocket, two glove-puppets with absurd grinning faces. These were to come in very handy.

72

'When he came to the palace, he joined the other mid-wives in an ante-room in the Palace of Earthly Tranquillity. It was in fact the ladies' apartments, where no men were usually allowed, but Poet Nai sat there in the midst of it all happily. When the officials rushed out to the midwives, crying, "She has been in labour thirty hours! Let the next volunteer be more sure of her mystery. The last was horse-whipped. The next midwife must deliver! Who's next then?" Xie Nai stood up and raised his finger.

'The official stared crazed at him. "What are you doing here?"

'"I'm the next midwife," said Nai modestly.

'"What are you talking about? You're a man, haven't you noticed? How can a man be a midwife and tend the Empress?"

'Nai shrugged his shoulders. He was about to sit down, when another official rushed out of the inner chamber.

'"Where's the next midwife?" he shrieked. "The Empress is dying!" and he seized Nai and dragged him off without noticing.

'So Nai arrived interestedly at the lying-in chamber of the Empress, and found both the palace and the labour fascinating.

'The Empress was at her last gasp. "Where is she? Bring her to me!" she groaned. Nai was thrust into the grasp of the feverish Empress. The Empress stared at him. "Madam," she breathed throatily, "my life, my life is in your hands. All your sisters have failed me. Time and again, I have tried to give birth. But there is no way. It is trapped. It cannot be delivered. Madam, you have a kindly face. My eyes are dazed with pain. My last hopes rest in your skill and cunning. Tell me what to do then. What can I do, O heaven, to drive this imperial baby from me?" And the Empress fell back then, gasping upon the pillows, as the spasms came again to transfix her entrails.

'The Poet Nai put his hand on the Empress's brow. "Have no fear, my Empress," he said tenderly. "You are so beautiful, you can understand the little baby not wanting

73

to leave you. But he'll come out. He is frightened of the world. Yet have no fear. We'll entice him." And Nai nodding affably, left the Empress, and walked about the room mysteriously.

'Then with all the eyes of an astonished court on him, he strolled down to the end of the bed thoughtfully, and stared businesslike before him, examining all with a frown, as he rolled up first one sleeve then the other. Then with an intake of breath, he dragged from his pocket his nieces' two dolls with their little hats on, and then flung himself down at the end of the Empress where things were most likely to happen. He held the dolls before him, and in a funny voice like a puppet, called, "Little Emperor, come out, come out!" and he waved the dolls again, nodding their heads and calling, "Come out and play, little Emperor!"

'There was horror in the court. Amazed officials and ladies stared at the lunatic, reeling with confusion. There was a slithering of silk, as some duchesses fainted away with shame at the sight of the world's most ill-placed puppet-show. In the frosty silence, the Empress herself ceased groaning, and raised her head, feebly to see what was happening. And her eye fell on the Poet Nai wagging his head and grinning, and waving two puppets at her nether regions.

'The Empress froze. The courtiers froze. The unspeakable at last was happening. But then the Empress started laughing, and she fell back on the pillows, and just gave herself up to this great laughing-fit. Everyone looked at each other, but somehow the horror was gone, and one or two others began chuckling. And then just like magic into the puppeted hands of Nai there popped out the next Emperor of China. Well, that's all there is to tell. From that moment on Nai became the court favourite. The Emperor himself became thoroughly interested in all Nai's literary experiments. He was given fees and sinecures, invited to all the parties. The story made him a little hero. But my friend here was not pleased when at length he discovered he had named the little puppets Kun and Lun. When the Empress sent for the two comical old men who Nai had named his dolls after, the scholar insisted we went. And I was not arguing. The story had reached its ending.'

Chapter Five

In the heaven of Guan yin, the goddess of compassion, the Pure Land, which is called Xi tian, the fields and the lakes were eternally green, though the snow from the cloudless air was trilling and twirling. In the High Western mountains, where China goes no further, by the great Jade Gate, beyond which are foreign devils, the blissful land lay in the sun, blooming and flourishing, and the pink cranes and phoenixes flew by with the streamers of their tails.

Now though there walked here arhats, and bodhisattvas serenely – those souls who delay nirvana to bring benefits to mankind – yet mainly about the hills and woodlands, beneath the blossoming trees, there skipped the goddess's fairy-maidens, laughing happily. For they wore pink and blue robes with ribbons and tassels flying, and their hair was bound up, sleek black, in combs of coral and tortoise-shell, and as they ran beneath the trees, plucking the apple blossom they giggled and tried to catch the snowflakes before they fell to earth.

And the paradise was ringing with laughter from the seven rows of terraces, where the trees hang forth their branches of jewels, tinkling in the breeze, and from the great pagodas and pavilions of the rose-roofed palace, where the gold-leafed chrysanthemums rustle in pots along the pearl-dusted paths, to the bird-haunted lakes, where the lotuses bloom and the sands of the strand are gold, so that all the Pure Land was musical under the touch of the early spring snow.

But hurrying back now through the sharp mountain air on clouds of speed and gloom, there came the Buddhist goddess, Guan yin, the mother of mercy, surrounded by hastening attendants, and she frowned as she flew, for all were still perplexed by the happenings at the court of the Jade Emperor. And she came upon her fairy-maidens, as they romped about her palace, throwing the whirling cones of diabolo. But when they saw the goddess, they stopped abruptly, and clustered around her, shocked to see her gravity.

And Guan yin said, 'Alas, fairies, what calamity is this, to be home so soon and so abruptly! Well may you look startled! Well may you gasp and blanch to see your goddess arriving back unannounced, prematurely! All has not gone well. The state visit to Kun Lun Heaven, long looked forward to, and much hoped for, has ended disastrously. Rows, recriminations! Oh, it has been the opposite of celestial! I am afraid the expected harmony has not been achieved, and we are not to go unopposed henceforward in China. For the great gods Confucius and Lao zi have taken against me, and I was forced to retire under their insults.'

Guan yin's old maidservant, Solid Pear, that accompanied her cried, 'It was despicable! You should have heard them! Call themselves gods! They are like a couple of misbehaving urchins, needing their heads knocking together. They think they can banish my mistress from the Middle Kingdom just because they are as old as mountains. Just because no one has ever said boo to them. Well, I'll give them boo! I could mix and mangle with both of them: the prim one with his manners and dignified voice, and the mad one like a scatty peasant! I'd stick a broom up their philosophies! Go and get your mistress some tea! Can't you see she's fainting for weariness?' And the beefy-faced Solid Pear startled the maids, so that at once they knew the bosses were home again.

But the fairies bustled round, and with whimpers and cries of horror, they swept Guan yin away to her inner apartments. And they hurried to take off her travelling shoes, and bring her a negligent robe, and hastened her to a couch with a view of the gem garden. And those bringing tea soon swept in with the steaming brew, and trickled it into the porcelain dishes, and at last the goddess of mercy was relaxing in her home, being comforted by her true companions. But still they clustered around, staring at her anxiously, and more of the fairies hung in the doorway.

But one of the fairies called Dragonfly said, 'We were wondering if something were amiss, for we were watching the world constantly, and horror of horrors, we saw only yesterday, the great star-dragon, Wo Long Wang, descending upon China. For he flowed down from the stars just where the Silver Way falls on earth, and deluges into the source of the Yellow River. And he went snuffling and sniffing, spying what mischief he could, and settled on the old capital, Chang an. Is this connected with your trouble? Is he after the Buddhists? Woe to whomever the dragon seeks!' But Guan yin merely turned white at this, and sat a long while in silence.

Another of the fairies, called Sugarplum said, 'And we have been watching the sleeve-dancer, Xiang, as you bade us. She had gone away from Jian kang, leaving Nai alone, but on her return he has been angry with her. It seems she is suffering. But there's a fairy now down there, watching on developments.' And Guan yin looked up at this, and sighed even more, and then frowned again thinking.

And a third fairy said, 'And also a strange thing happened to a friend of Nai's called Wei. He met up with a fox-fairy, and fell in love, and what do you think: the pair are setting up house together? Strange things are happening hidden on mother earth now that the dragon is coming.' And again Guan yin looked sombre, sighing and fretting inwardly. But then her face cleared and she stared at them purposefully.

'Fairies,' the goddess said, 'it is time I told you something. The flight of this dragon renders all most urgent. It is something that happened long ago, and has preyed on my mind for decades, but now is reaching unbearable proportions. A thing of great moment it is, a thing which if mishandled, might plunge all China into chaos. And I can see no way out of it, especially in these hard times. It is a thing which puts us all into grave danger.' And the goddess stared at the fairies, who looked back at her in horror, afraid almost to hear what was to follow.

She sat down in the midst of them and said, 'You have been speaking about the Dragon raging amidst China. As Solid Pear can tell you, he was summoned by the Jade Emperor specifically to hunt down two escaped lovers. The daughter of the Emperor himself, the Weaver-Girl, and her husband, have run away from their place in the heavens, and in order to be together are hiding unknown, contrary to the Jade-King's wishes. Well has Dragonfly said "Woe to those the Dragon seeks!" Well, it is the lovers. But woe also to the person, if there be a person, who arranged the escape of those lovers. I can tell you now, fairies, a secret of thirty years, which I have never told to another. I was the person who arranged the escape of the Celestial Lovers!'

There was silence in the palace, and the rooms were all hushed of the perfumed pagodas. The tinkling of the jewel trees could be heard outside the windows, and the fluting of the purple love-birds. But in the room all faces were drained white with fright, as the fairies stared at the goddess with horror.

'Ay,' the goddess repeated, 'thirty years ago I was moved by compassion of those lovers. So long they had been married, so long faithful to each other, and yet were condemned to meet only once every year. I was moved by pity of Zhi nu and her husband, the Herdsman, why should they spend eternity longing for each other? I thought at first to help them merely escape from the stars, to come and live here in happiness in the Pure Land. I thought to build a house for them, beside the Lake of Gold Lotuses, where they might live at peace among sapphire trees. But then I saw the Father would find them: they and I would be blamed. There was no place in heaven to hide them. If they must be hidden, it must be on earth. And thirty years ago in the Buddhist fashion, I decided to incarnate them as mortals in China, and to give them chances they had not in heaven. And so it was they went to earth, though separated by time and place, and in that vale of tears have dwelt ever since.'

A silence came in the afternoon of the Western heaven, as the fairies stared at the goddess with amazement. The sunlight froze as it came in through the window, dappling the pale pattern of the shaped carpet. They stared at her open-mouthed, coral lips fragrantly parted, their almond eyes ablaze with fear and admiration.

At length Dragonfly said, 'But who are the lovers then? Where are they? What mortals had their incarnation?'

Another said, 'Ay, goddess. Tell us that we may seek them, and watching them guard them from the dragon!'

And another said, 'Ay, does it bear on what we've been telling you? Is this the reason you take such interest in certain people?' And the fairies all gasped at this, and looked back at Guan yin, who sat trembling, with her eyes downcast.

Guan yin said, 'Fairies, I have kept this secret thirty years, and not without reason have I kept it secret. To steal the daughter of heaven, and with her herdsman husband: this is a crime fitting awesome punishment. To do this as a foreigner, recently come to these lands, in secret: this would rouse more against me. But to take away the Chinese lovers, and give them incarnations in the manner of the new faith of the interlopers: why, this would shock all Zhongguo deities, regardless of their tolerance. This would destroy our hopes as well as ourselves. Here are then good reasons for keeping this silent, and not revealing to you where are the lovers.'

She smiled at them then and said, 'But I will tell you none the less, for you are all of you my confidants. And I can trust you never, no matter who asks you, to divulge the secret of the lovers' incarnations. In any case, you would probably guess them. You mentioned Wei just now, and his new love, this new-found fox-fairy. Well, it is not these two lovers: it is Nai and Xiang: Nai, the poet, and Xiang, the sleeve-dancer. These are the mortals in whom the daughter of the Jade-King, and the songful Cowherd incarnated. But it is a strange story: a sad story for them, but for us it has a humorous piquancy.

'It happened a long time ago,' the goddess said, 'when I was new to China, when I looked on all the Middle Kingdom spontaneously and innocently, without regional understanding. The gods were in their heavens, and they seemed to be all men, ruling according to men's ways. And China seemed to be like a cowed and punctilious son, paternally dominated beneath them. How different it was from the lush and fertile confusion, in which I had grown up South of the Himalayas! And then amongst this stern masculine world, I caught sight of the Celestial Lovers.

'Now as you know, Zhi nu, the Spinning-Maid, and her Cowherd husband, lived in permanent absence from each other on either side the Silver Way. Two forlorn stars, separated by a river, set in different constellations, the Vega in the Lyre and yearning Aquila could never embrace or speak. When I learnt of this tale, and heard that, though married, they could meet only once every year, the time being specified to the seventh day of the seventh month and only moreover when it was a clear night, I was horrified at this and moved to pity by this prime example of China's rigid piety, and I saw the Jade Emperor as the worst of all fathers, and determined if I could to thwart him.

'So secretly I went to the Celestial Lovers, and had some words with them about it. Secretly I fixed with them that they might leave heaven, and have some place where they could be truly together. The star-lovers were fully in agreement, and only too keen to escape their fixed and cruel fate. And I outlined to them how I might transfer them to the shades below who wait for reincarnation upon earth, and infiltrate their souls stealthily into birth in the same place together. And then I bade them to take advantage of their mortal state and to seek nirvana while they were able. This was the plan. A time was fixed to steal them from the stars.

'But alas, Fate is impenetrable!' Guan yin sighed. 'Even

the plans of gods are often thwarted! And my scheme for their happiness instead became a scheme for even more suffering and frustration. For I took them from the stars. We crept away one night, first collecting the Cowherd from Aquila, then going illegally to Vega in the Lyre, where we met up with the Jade Emperor's daughter. She came out of her house to meet us. She brought nothing with her for the trip, save only a cup which her father had given her, a cup of gold stability, and so we fled away from the stars and down to the souls who were to be reincarnated.

'At first it was frightening for the divine pair to be lost in the scrum of humanity. The massed multitudes swirled about, babbling in unformed languages, yearning for earthly transformation. But I kept the two lovers strictly by my side, and first set about incarnating the Cowherd, and indeed this went well, giving him birth in the family of the Xie, as I have explained. But alas, then disaster struck us. The Weaver-Girl went frantic, seeing the Cowherd so weirdly taken away from her, and losing her head, she was swept away by the crowds from me, and lost in them. When I turned back from the Herdsman, I saw at once what had happened, and frantic now myself I searched for her. But I could not find her again. She was gone from me, tugged by the millions of the unborn.

'You may imagine, fairies, my feelings at this, and the horror which now swept over me. Rash I had been in snatching them from heaven, presumptuous in planning for them such a destiny. I risked the wrath of the heavens and the son of heaven in what I was executing. But now I had bungled it! I had compounded my sins into that fatal match: audacity and error! I did not find the Spinning-Girl. I searched for her in the underworld. But not till nine years later did I eventually discover her, when she herself obtained birth by due process, and incarnated herself as a mortal.

'But what further woes opened up from this! It seemed to be Destiny. The lovers were meant to suffer! For the Weaver-Girl was incarnated in a family miles from the

Cowherd, with never any likelihood of them meeting. And so instead of launching on life of mortality, in which they could share their love freely, they were lost in the pack of people, yearning for each other, and yet not even aware of each other's existence!

'So it was the pair set off: celestial spirits, banged about in the world of men. So it was they grew up, not knowing of each other: he in Jian kang, she in Hang chou. He was of a rich household, she of refugees to the South, each filled with a hunger for stars. And as the Cowherd grew up – and he was named Nai, as I told you, of the family of Xie – and as the Weaver-Girl grew up – Ling Xiang she was called, now nine years younger than her husband – the pair of them were like fairies, having appetites born in the heavens, the cravings of which could not be satisfied.

'They started much the same, launching out on sprees of celestial fantasy. Their minds still happy in the fumes of the constellations, they went shooting forth, grasping at the heavens, capering like eager kittens into the world, but soon the gruff bumps of human life came to them. He found no one to share his celestial lusts. She found men too eager to share hers. He was pushed from the banquet. She was set upon by the feasters. He was booted out. She was torn apart. It was pitiful and yet funny to see how these glittering creatures fared in the world of matter. And it was strange to see how their separation brought them inevitable distress and failure.

'Well, Destiny is ineffable. Just as by amazing fortune they had been lost to each other, so by convolutions they were brought together again, by remotest orbits stumbling upon each other. As you know, Xiang came to Nai as an unusual pupil to study the Five Classics. Listening to her words, he caught the unknown memories, the unconscious traces of starry paths. He wooed her at the last. And now they are on the path which will take them forward together.

'And yet why do I talk this way?' she stared at the fairies aghast. 'Why do I speak as though all had been resolved? It has not been resolved: a greater danger overhangs them now than did any other in any part of their story! For the Dragon of the Universe is after them to catch them: her he is bent on taking back to her father, him he is determined to plunge into Hell and to set ever in eternal suffering! What can I have been talking of? And yet what can I do? The Dragon's might extends all over the Middle Kingdom! I have only one course of action; I must tell the lovers, and get them both out of China!'

The goddess was silent. Her fairies did not speak. They had heard enough amazements for a week of silence. Instead they stared at the goddess, whose face now was set and firm, as though thinking on difficult matters. Meanwhile, the tinkling jewel trees jangled as roosting birds came bouncing to perch and sing on their ruby-decked branches, and the gem-pollen came in the window bringing with it exciting scents. Yet all were too stunned to notice it.

But then there came rushing in a fairy on a cloud, with pink ribbons streaming and flowers fluttering about her, and she landed on the verandah outside, and calling on her mistress, dashed into the room where they sat and knelt before the goddess. And the travelling fairy said, 'Guan yin, come quickly down to Xiang, your protégé, for the poor girl is in a terrible state, since her lover has sent her a letter, and the letter is the most horrible, wounding thing to read that anyone has ever clapped eyes on! She has sent for Nai to the nunnery, and he goes there all sardonic! Come and save your devotee from this horrible creature who thinks only of lust and literature!' And Guan yin shook her head at this, and wearily she arose, and went like a tired mother to a noisy baby.

Now while it was afternoon in the courts of the Western heaven, in Jian kang the morning still dawdled towards midday, and as the sun came slanting through the circular window, where the waxed parchment tinged the light with an intimate warmth, Nai, who was still in bed, stirred and stretched beneath the coverlet, and thus did he wake from a hazy but cheering erotic dream. But then he remembered. Soon was to come retribution, for he had now sent a stern letter to Xiang, and he wondered what would happen when she had digested its ill-tempered contents.

Then he remembered he had kept a copy of the letter, and indeed had left it by his bed, and so he turned over anxiously, and brought the copy from its place, and frowning his brow he read it. And he repeated to himself the words about making her face reality. And he studied the phrases about her stopping continually trying to deflate him, lecturing him on and on, as if wanting to devour him, like a lizard he saw with glittering scales mechanically munching a butterfly. And he said her lectures bored him, as did her incessantly going over the troubled times of her life, and he had had enough of it, and took back his proposals which he had made at that strange place, the Eight Formations.

Now when he had read the letter through, Nai sighed and stared in front of him. It was too late to take it back. But anyway he felt that he had only spoken truth in the letter, for truly she seemed bent on merely attacking him. Nai did not know what would happen. They had one or two commitments, but surely it seemed this would be the end of their friendship. It had to be. For it was no love-match, and it could go no further with the frustrating conditions under which it existed. And at least the balance had been struck. Nai sighed and lay with the letter in his hands.

But now there arose a shuffling at the door, and Nai's maid, True Pearl came in, and at once rushed over to her master's bedraggled form. 'Master Poet Nai, awake,' she said, 'there has been a servant to the gate, calling for you urgently to go out into the city. The maid of Ling Xiang has arrived, breathless from her mistress, who rages and tears things in her abode in the nunnery. And she demands to see you at once in the nunnery. O master, get up, get up at once! Your love is very angry. The maid says she has never before seen her like this.' And Nai looked up, and he grinned maliciously, and nodded that he would come at once to them. And he leapt up naked from bed, and put on his dragon-robe, and went and washed himself, and had the maid dress him.

As he walked through the winding paths of the wintry garden, in the channels which the servants had cleared from the snow, and went beyond the garden plaque of poetic inscriptions, wearing its hat of snowflakes, he crept past his uncle's quarters, with their grand red-painted rafters, hoping to avoid any meeting. But he was seen by his uncle, and a booming voice called to him, echoing round the cold, clear hallways. And Nai went over in his fur-boots and his tasselled and glossy fur-hat, and he saw the General sitting with his officers, and he came before his uncle, and kowtowed with his brow to the floor, and his uncle idly warmed his hand at a brazier.

And General Xie said, 'And are you going into town again, walking in your boots like some kind of peasant? You were seen down by the lake this last day, neither in a sedan-chair nor upon horseback. You may choose to demean yourself, but you will not demean the family name in Jian kang in the slush. But here's not why I sent for you. I asked you some days ago if you were ready to take a position in the cavalry? Or to assume some office, fitting to our family rank, or to command the troops assembling for the defence of the kingdom? But skulking you avoid me, and seek to avoid your duty. Answer me then: what are your deliberations?'

Idle Nai gazed back at him, not knowing what to reply, having given no thought at all to this sort of business. And he said, 'Good uncle, I have not yet decided. I have had many other things on my mind. But so kind is your offer to my unworthy, despicable self, I obviously owe you a dutiful answer. Yet have you forgot, uncle: I am due at the court soon, and the Emperor looks for my attendance at a banquet? And then I am to go on the mission to visit the patriarch at Shou chun, and explain how with the present state of affairs, it will be impossible for the family to spend the summer in the hills as usual. And this solemn embassy I could not neglect without seeming desperately unfilial.'

'You fool with me, you wretched insect!' the General replied. 'Since when have you shown filial piety? Neither of these social commitments debars you from honourable service to the Emperor in defence of the land of the ancestors. Will you answer me directly? You do not want to join the army because it will take you away from your precious girls! And from your ridiculous, vulgar songs and childish fairy tales, which may take the Emperor's fancy, but do not take mine! But you must understand, and all wasters like you: that war and death is threatening our total extinction. Cowardly and vile indeed would be the nephew that would seek to dodge out of these sorts of duties.'

But Nai looked at the General and said, 'Well, I will be plain. I will not undertake such services voluntarily. If you command me to head your platoons, well then, I must do it. And I must take what fate awaits me. But as for my own will in this, I have other things to do, and I need all the time I have to get on with them. Moreover, the Emperor sits yet on his throne, and while the dynasty stands we must pay heed to it. And he seems to favour what I am about. Why should we not respect it?' And Nai looked at the General. The General stared back. Then with a wave of disgust, he dismissed him.

And so Nai came again, the third time in those days, to the nunnery in the crunching snow. The sun was shining in the park, outlining the tall pines, and the air had a smell of freedom. He felt a sense of fatefulness: all the turmoils of the heart, which had dogged him for months, these were reaching a culmination, and he half expected that by the evening he would be free; lonely, sad, but untroubled. So he tottered upon the slimy ice, beneath the heavy hedges, and moved through the bluish shadows to the nunnery. Then did he climb the steps and clang on the bell by the gate-screen, that echoed in those holily-tidy courts.

Xiang came to the gate herself, sighing and tense to see him, in a plain robe of royal blue. Her hair was held back with a comb sleek on her head, so that her face shone smooth and frozen. She walked stiff-shouldered away from him, took him to the library, where was a chair with another set by it, and on the bamboo table Nai saw the letter with the creases in it, lying guiltily.

And Xiang said, 'I thought for once we could reverse our rôles. You could be pupil and I the teacher. I have your work there, as you see, and I have read it closely. I thought I could give you my comments upon it. Please sit down.' She gestured to the chair, and sat down herself, ready for hard lessons. Nai watched her softly, feeling somewhat sad to see her so pressed and tense.

'Well,' she said, 'it seems at last in this strange friendship of ours, you have decided to speak your mind. I'm sad at what you said, of course. I thought you were my friend. But I see you were sneering at me. I'm sadder that you chose to say all this in a letter, instead of having the courage to say it to my face. But then you are a poet, I suppose. Your defence is the brush. But where have we come to, you and I? Not a year we have known each other. I have talked to you like a friend, but what are we to each other, you and I? I swear I have never had such a strange relationship with a man. It is almost as if we were two children.

'You say I am always attacking you,' Xiang continued, 'like some malevolent lizard. Well, you can insult me so, if you wish. I am more reserved than you are, and you appal me the way you bound at me. You are so uninhibited and childish in your attitude! I feel just at times like cutting through it with a knife of acid, and making you face reality. You live in the house of your uncle. You have no experience of life. You avoid all contact with responsibility, and yet you make suggestions as you did at the Eight Formations! It is sheer childish irresponsibility!

'I see also,' she continued, dipping into the letter, 'that I have been boring you to distraction. I am sorry you find my life boring. I have already indicated to you how it has been for me something of a battlefield. You sneer at my self-analysis, but you must realise I am at least trying to do something about myself. I live in this Buddhist house, because I am trying to disentangle my soul, and it demands all my labour and concentration. I confided my secrets to you. You have flung them back in my face. Perhaps it is you should begin the great pilgrimage.'

She was losing something of her anger now. 'And then this sentence here,' she went on. 'You take back all your proposals. Here is a wondrous faith! And our social obligations! Do you think I care about them, if it means facing them like this? It seems you are bound to me on trivial conditions, but not by any deeper considerations. Is this then your great love? It seems to me cruel. How you have spun me along, while I revealed all to you! You don't like me, do you?'

Nai shook his head. 'No, I don't!'

Xiang gave a sigh, and the tears started trickling.

Nai felt his heart melt. 'But I love you,' he said, kneeling beside her, and for a while he embraced her.

But she drew back again. His impulsive heart once more made her shrink.

But then she dried her eyes. Nai sat back in his chair. It was hard and formal in the library. She poured out some tea she had made for him. He smiled and sipped it. She was trembling with dismay and wretchedness. Outside beyond the verandah the garden was all white, and there was snow on a statue of Guan yin.

'It is difficult,' said Xiang, 'when you have gone through so much pain, suffered with the inevitable abrasions, to have the heart to begin again, especially from the place where you have come for refuge from such entanglements. I did not want to love you. Nor am I truly in love with you. There is no sweep or urgency of any passion. How then can you expect me to rejoice at the road, which takes me out of this sanctity? And now you have done this! I cannot even look at you! I couldn't even touch you! How ever shall I get through the Emperor's banquet? How ever shall I get through all this?'

Nai sighed wearily. He opened his mouth. He was about to say: well then, let us end it. But suddenly there was a slithering of snow from the roof, which that very moment stopped him. The statue of Guan yin stood smiling over the garden, serenely scarved in snowflakes. There was a knocking at the door. Xiang went out to see to it. Nai sat in the still room sadly. Then Xiang returned. She had a puzzled look on her face. 'It was a message for you,' she said amazedly.

'There was an old woman at the door, whose face was covered with a shawl, and asked me if I was Ling Xiang the sleeve-dancer? When I replied yes, she said she had a message for Xie Nai, who she believed was with me. She said it was from your old nurse, who looked after you as a child, and lives in Shou chun in the country estates. She said she trusted all was well, and that you were being kind. And with that she was gone!'

Nai stared back amazed. 'It's Fate,' he said. 'In that case we must get on with it. I was about to say let us end this affair. But Fate prevented it.'

Xiang looked at him seriously. There was surprise in her gaze. 'I'll get some tea,' she said, and went out.

Nai sat still. There were tears in his eyes. How often had this happened! So many times with he and Xiang Fate had intervened and somehow thrown them together! The first time he saw her: it was so weird and fated: mirroring the story he was writing! Time and time again they found they shared so many hopes, inhabited the same country. When ever he had tried to break it off, as on the night of his birthday, the moment just glided by and was saved by some trifle. And now just on the very crisis. Who was this messenger? He should have jumped up and made after! Fate seemed to mean him to stay with Xiang. Why then, he thought, did Fate make her so impossible?

Xiang returned to the room with a tray. On it were delicate tea-things. She sat and poured him the jasmine brew in silence. As Nai smelt the water blossoms, he thought of summer and the country.

'In a few weeks,' he said, 'I have to go to Shou chun, as you know, and we did talk a while of you coming. There is nothing much I have to do there. I think you should come.

We could spend a long time together. It is no good this seeing each other in dribs and drabs. No sooner do I warm you, but you're away again. And every time we meet, you have some other problem, and I have on my hands another woman of snow.'

There was silence once more. The sun now streamed through the window, and the snow glared with its brightness. From the eaves with their curling corners the drips were already falling, making holes in the piled snow beneath. Xiang offered the plate of rice-cakes. Nai sighed and took one. He ate without hunger.

She looked at him with painful brow. 'You are harsh with me,' she said. 'You brutalise me with your feelings. Those poems you used to write me when you first loved me: they were very powerful. But I did not want to hear them. I was not ready to love you. The force in them made me shy from them. And this letter you have sent me. It might not be much to you, but to me it came like a sort of betrayal. All the time I was talking to you, I thought it was to a friend, but I see inside you were laughing at me. I feel betrayed by this. I know I have been hard on you. But you assault me. Therefore I must quell you. I cannot take such violence. And now you have undone so much. I just need to hide from you.'

'Well,' sighed Nai wearily, 'you can hide for some weeks, but then I think we should go to Shou chun. I have to visit the patriarch and explain to him about the family not coming to stay in the hills this summer. The way things are going, the patriarch may well have to come here, for Shou chun is near the Northern barbarians. If they should invade, then the Fei River will be an objective, and our estates are all in its path. But there in a little farm is a pavilion by the lake. We could have that to be at peace in. It's beautiful in springtime, for the whole place is full of orchards, and the lake comes right up to the verandah.'

'I'll think,' said Xiang. 'I'll think about it. We must at least try to be alone together. If you remember I wished for that some time ago, but it was you who said you were too

91

busy. I know I have been difficult, but this is a hard time in my life, and after all I have come here for refuge. And the last thing I wanted was another difficult entanglement. These are what I have been fleeing. I came to the Buddha because all other avenues had been shut off for me. I could not live in the world as I was. Here at least was fulfilment. And yet I have run into my troubles all over again! How can I expect to surmount them? This is what makes me so difficult. But perhaps we should try, for after all, so many aspirations have brought us together!'

'Indeed!' said Nai. 'That was why at the Eight Formations I proposed what I proposed. I feel this kinship with you. It is as though you were born my sister. And we both have this urge to make the great journey. I know there are the things in the West for which we are searching. I was sure we were meant to seek them together. I sensed in my soul that we had work to do, right from our first talks together. This was why I said what I said. I said it even though we were not lovers. I say it still, because it seems destined. So we should go forward. And perhaps in Shou chun Fate will work out a way for us to follow.'

But Xiang was frozen again now. She held herself stiff and looked down. Then she looked at him. 'You must not expect too much of me. I will live with you in Shou chun. I will even share your bed. But I cannot promise to be your lover. You have had enough experience now to know that that is not possible. And I know myself well enough to discount it. I cannot give myself to men. Something has always stopped me. And with you . . . well, my dear, I don't even have the impulse.'

Nai smiled as she said this. 'Well,' he said, 'this could be what you have been waiting for.'

As Nai made his way home in his snow-boots along the ice, the evening descended and wrapped around him. It was deep and secret, the dusk, and across the purple snow-patches, the lamps in the houses glowed both amber and acid. The city seemed to fold around him and take him into its sleep. And indeed he felt he could sleep now.

But on the snow-roof of the nunnery, hovering mysteriously, the gentle goddess, Guan yin, stood serenely surveying. And she watched the bouncing figure of the poet striding away, and smiled sadly at him among the snows. But then she spread her hands to the parklands, and brought the thaw on faster, and set the eaves shuffling and icicles dripping. And the air was filled with rivulets splashing into the canals, and the song of birds piercing the cedar trees. And the ripe sky was brave again above the snowy hills, and the trees held branches soft with sticky buds.

PART TWO

Shou chun

Chapter Six

In the halls of the Northern capital, in the council chamber of Chang an, the monarch Fu jian sat with his generals, conferring, and he gazed at them from his low throne, and scowled with many thoughts. And he said, 'Great warriors, generals of unification, you have now heard the reports of our dispositions and estimates of our strength, and you have seen how our mighty armies are on the offensive, how the Western regions have been stabilised in the face of the Huns, and the ship-borne army assembled already in the province of Shu. Yet now is the time to return to the debate of the greatest matter of our age. For the hour is upon us finally to decide whether this invasion is to take place. For spring is coming on, the season for campaigning, and we wish to strike while there is good time, and the year is before us to take the road to Jian kang and to bond by force the Southern capital to the new will of China. Fu hung, it was your turn to speak. What have you to say now?' And Fu jian turned then suddenly to the General, and bided him, glowering and fixed.

But Fu hung bowed sternly to the monarch, and spoke his mind fearlessly. And he said, 'I do not believe, mighty Fu jian, that an invasion should be mounted. For the Emperor of the South, of the house of Jin, has no crime, and men will serve him. Also his lieutenants, Xie An and his clan, are both competent and intelligent. The sovereign and vassals will unite their strength and rely upon the fastnesses of the Yang zi River, and those that are North of it will move South, and the long river will be used as a barrier. These tactics will exhaust us without even a fight, and lead us and your reputation into great danger.' And Fu

97

hung then sat down on his stool again, and Fu jian gazed at him contemptuously.

Then spoke next the Commander of the Left Guard of the Grand Heir-designate, and he said, 'I also hold with Fu hung that the invasion should not be mounted. We seized Xiang-yang now some time since, and it might seem a good time to take more cities. But the portents are not good. Need I remind you all of the visitation of locusts in the Yu province? And the Grand Tortoise with the trigram pattern on its back has only recently died in the Ancestral Temple. Now, moreover, the Year and the Garrison Stars guard the Dipper and the Ox, and the dynasty of Jin have the stars' blessing, for the suspended shapes have no irregularities. I would remind you of the master, Confucius's words "When distant people do not submit, cultivate civilising virtue in order to attract them."' And the Commander of the Left Guard resumed his seat, leaving Fu jian even more displeased.

But then arose Mu jung Chui, the General Cresting the Armies, and he said in a loud and booming voice, 'If we are quoting the Classics, then I refer to the Book of Odes; which is more apt to our condition: "If the counsellors are many, nothing is achieved." And here we all sit counsellors! But should we not be Generals? Why are we debating like elders, quoting the out-of-date Confucius? Are we not Buddhists now? Do we not hold to the people's faith? Is there not more vigour in our entrails? Our monarch's internal resolve and divine plan are sufficient to win this war for us. But let us not forget also the strength of our armies, myriads and millions strong! To sit here like old uncles, while those thieving phantoms in the South counterfeit the imperial title, this is despicable! Let me quote to you a people's proverb: "Trust in heaven and await the time!" Well, the time, I say, has come. Let us fall on those rebel caitiffs! And let us with all the strength that is ours unite and stabilise the world!' And Mu jung Chui sat down again, to a cry of approval from his monarch.

But a strange monk then arose, in Buddhist robes, at the

far end of the hall, and with bald head bowed, he shuffled towards the monarch, and stood in peace and calm before the throne. And the Buddhist monk said, 'Great monarch Fu jian, known also as Yung ku and Wen yü, leader of the Northern state from the capital Chang an, descended of the great Ti of the Tibetans, I am no general, and little can I speak here of military manoeuvres, but may not Dao an, a poor sage of the Buddhist Wheel of Law, speak to his monarch on behalf of his people? I think, honourable monarch, you bear me in good repute, you have often spoken of my wisdom. You have said it is your dream to see all the Middle Kingdom united under the one faith of the great Lord Buddha. Assuredly that would be well. But some have urged me to speak, relying on my influence with my monarch, and these folk bid me say: have a care for your royal person, do not weary it over the insignificant South!

'And also, my lord monarch, though I respect your unbounded faith, though my heart is proud of your devotion to the Great Doctrine, this would I say to you: that though your ideals are just, the manner of implementation has in it a danger. For the faith of the Great Ascetic is not one of conquest, though he himself conquered the realm of Maya. And the people cannot be truly won to the way of the law by force and military campaigns and conquest. Therefore would I also add my voice to those here who bid you desist from desires of conquest. Better rule your kingdom, and practise devotion now than risk all on a hesitant future.' And the monk turned away again, and slowly his bald head faded back into the shadows of the council-hall.

Fu jian arose and said, 'Well, you have given your views, and as is a monarch's duty, I have attended. And each of you has spoken well, and the points you made are not without consideration. Assuredly we must catch these caitiffs before they all flee South of the river. But our news is that they send forth to meet us. For we have heard some forces assemble ready to march West, and that others are ready to cross the river and strike North for us. Xie An may be intelligent, but his Emperor is a ninny, and he fills his court with poets and painters and eccentrics. And as we all know his women bully him far more than his generals, and his wife and her sister play with him like a ball.

'Now these so-called prognostications. Do not worry about them. They spell trouble on the enemy. For the cycle of the stars is explained to us anew by our Buddhist wise men, who show the three cycles in the history of dharma portend cataclysm on the South. And did not I also see, while practising asceticism in my apartment, a shooting star, big as a moon, fall on my palace? I know I am the chosen one to obliterate the old ways of China, and bring in the new rule with the perfect new faith! Those layabouts in the South are decadent Confucians and Daoists. It may be Dao an turns his back on violence. But he is a monk, and I am a king.

'So I am issuing orders forthwith, and sending the rescripts immediately: let the invasion be prepared, let the troops be gathered, let the armies begin marching! We will march on the South. We will drive them before us! We will capture those decadents and perverts. Three villas have I already built, gentlemen, to house our captives in their new appointments. The Chief Minister Xie An will be secretary for personnel, the General Huang chung a palace attendant, and the Emperor himself be my Left-hand Archer in Waiting. To it then! Bring in these humiliations! For soon will Fu jian set his foot on their necks, and reduce their paltry, lying kingdom. And the clamour of our arms will bring the faith of peace, and compassion will be rammed down their throats!' And so did Fu jian leave the hall, and stalk out waving his hands with triumph.

And when Fu jian had shouted this, there was a mighty roar of wind, and the tapers dimmed and trembled in the council-hall. And there reared up into the heavens a column of smoke and cloud, instinct with fire, brimming with sparkling brimstone, and as it twirled above the capital, then the dragon's limbs it put on, and scales appeared in the dust, and teeth jutted out of it, and Wo Long Wang, the

100

star-dragon, howled and laughed over the ruined streets, and crackling flames went trilling his limbs deliciously. And he sped away gloatingly, bearing the monarch's message, and village and town and hamlet he set thrumming.

Then, Fu jian himself sent forth and issued rescripts commanding mobilisation, and from the imperial bureau he flung his orders forth into his kingdom. For there was to be conscription thus for horses and for men, both public and private, over all provinces: from every ten able-bodied men one conscript for the war: from the Blazing Brightly families the officers and gallants; from the wealthy houses the cavalry, squires of the winged hosts; from the Tibetan aristocracy generals and commanders. And thus all families high and low were struck with female laments and war-fever.

Meanwhile, the dragon hurried on, drumming on the wayside, drumming among the inns and farmhouses. Behind haystacks he drummed, along channels of crackling ice, over field and frost-bitten plough-land. Among gorges he drummed on, along flats of the Yellow River, drumming at each step of the dusty loess terraces. Like the Great Wall he went snaking over hill and over dune, and the men came plodding, leaving copse and hamlet, plodding along every little road, while over the stubble plain the dying winter sunset hung drearily. And they streamed along the highways, until they came to Chang an, and there they massed in their clattering millions.

Now there was in the great Yellow River a huge channel near Chang an, where it coils to the left as the Wei River joins into it. There do the two hill-fed streams mingle their turbid currents, and the silt is mixed in warring stripes and colours. Below the murky surface of this in cloudy beds and groins, there live all manner of water-serpents, for here it is the dragons breed, which bring water and rain to men, growing through the various sizes to the monsters: the long which after five hundred years grow horns and become kioh, which after a thousand wing themselves into ying, and also the little water-snakes, which grow scales and become giao: these teemed like eels in the river's gravel. To them in fury came Wo Long Wang, and thus he abruptly addressed them.

'Giao, kioh long, ying long, waters all, idle lollers and coilers in the Huang he! Why have you not arisen now that the tumultuous times have come on earth? Why are you not out there inciting the millions into battle-fury? Do you instead lie all in one great bed here like sprats on a fish-monger's slab? Do you rather slop about in weedy lethargy? Arise I say! Arise! Take to the air, and follow my coils, for we are now to madden all men into conquest!'

But the wisest of the ying long there said, 'Wo Long Wang, why do you pester us? Return to your stars, O sleepiest of the earth's monsters! For we are proper drag-ons that look after the rivers and the clouds, that bring water to man in the channels and downpours, and ours is no business to stir up wars among men. Rather we deluge them with fertility. Wherefore I say go from us, and reflect instead on yourself, for you are the most sluggish and forgetful of creatures. Did not the Jade Emperor send you from heaven to look for lovers? Yet all you do is snuffle and slobber around soldiers!' And the ying and kioh all laughed at him, to hear how their leader struck home, scorning the neglectful serpent. And Wo Long Wang turned aside, and went hasting off again, seeking once more his hordes and banners.

But yet some lesser giao that could writhe and climb the air were wooed by the powerful voice of the monster dragon, and they left the slimy depths of the Huang he, and instead in mists and clouds mounted up into the air. Wher-ever Wo Long Wang went winging, they followed him in their droves, like eager tadpoles, or minnows that climb upon the current, and soon as the star-serpent flew about the world, the clouds and thunder began following. Great cumuli curled their heads over the dragon's troops and the lightning flashed over the armies. Then hissing down the unseasonal rains tipped flying from the sky, and lashed against the shields and flanks of the cavalry, till soon all over the Middle Kingdom downed the tumultuous rain, and even the Southern capital, Jian kang, was smitten.

And when the dragon Wo Long Wang saw these attendants, he said, 'Good boys. Now we'll have some sport. For if you are joining me, I have some deeds for you to execute on someone I am searching. For as your proud master said I am bound to earth to search for lovers, and one of them will I gladly hand to you for plaguing. Yet first let us fly a little, bringing the rain on the world, and see how the wars are progressing. For who knows as we fly, we may chance across our quarry, and there may be spite for you to dig into.' And thus did the star-dragon lead the eager little giao, and fly towards the South on adventures.

But in Jian kang, the capital, the drumming rain descended, as Nai drove in a chariot with curtains flapping. And he clattered down the Imperial Avenue, turning right through a gate of the city, in the drenching downpour swerving out along the canal. And he drove through the You Yuan Gardens, and here by Xuan Wu Lake, he came to the nunnery, with the clouded trees spattering rain around it, and he stayed his chariot outside and pelted to the steps and the gate-screen which gleamed wet in the courtyard. But Nai did not find the lovely Ling Xiang there at once, though he saw in the lodge her chests and luggage waiting. But then she came running from the town under an umbrella, with bundles of little boxes tied in yellow ribbon.

And after she had kissed him, and run away, and he waited, and loaded the luggage, and she had come back and run away again, and he waited and talked to his horses, she eventually returned with news that she had lost her purse with five strings of silver cash in it, and they made a search for it, and failed to find it, and dispiritedly went late to the carriage. But on the way they drove, they stopped at a market where Xiang had just purchased her bundles, and she ran around the stalls, and Nai waited in the rain, and checked the luggage and talked to the horses. And the purse was found, for Xiang came bounding back again, and

103

leapt with it into the carriage beside him, and heartened by the omen, the whip was cracked over the haunches, and the flight was made from the city.

So, soon were the lovers clattering down the road by the lake through the chestnut-dripping avenue, and they passed in the smoky rain the gardens of Sui, nestling poetically in the wooded hills, and they passed through the pedlar's gate into the ferry station, where the Lion Hill glowered over them in the mists, and here they took the ferry and crossed that mighty torrent which bore them from warm South to the North of China. And so they pressed on again, splashing through the fields, where the startled cranes launched up and wheeled against the grey clouds.

And Nai sighed and said, 'Well, at last we're off, and here we are together in spite of everything. No uncles and aunts impinge on us, no court obligations strain us, our differences have been buried. The heavens have opened, the dragons fight in the clouds: it rains down pearls and promise. Oh, won't it be sweet to loiter in the rain-drenched pavilion with nothing but the geese to disturb us?'

But Xiang looked at him sidelong and said, 'As ever, my friend, you incline to the chirpy view of the world. You seem to forget that half Jian kang is enrolled in the army, and daily they expect invasion from the North. We shall probably arrive in Shou chun just in time to be fallen upon by the marauding Tibetans. And I'm glad you assume our differences are buried. It is a tribute to my powers of sociability. When will you realise that I feel as bad as I say I do, and that I am still wounded by your letter?'

'Oh, you'll get over it,' Nai said cheerily, as he whipped the horses. 'You make out you're a fury, but really you're a good sport. I've seen this underneath all along. It's just a question of having a man who can handle you, one who is gifted with superhuman forbearance, and till me you've been unlucky. I'm the man you've been looking for, courageous, serene, inspired, gifted with the vision of the supreme artefact which will unite all humanity. It's impossible to resist. You're a lucky girl. Ah, look at the landscape!' And thus did Nai gesture to the passing farms, as Xiang gazed on him with narrowed eyes.

Now when they had been travelling for some little time, they stopped a while at a pretty village. The sun came out and lit the muddy streets, where the sheep were driven down to a ford in the river. A temple there was, where a little pagoda looked up with its stacked roofs, and the tombs about it ran tumbling together, while yellow jonquils hid amongst them. The lovers strolled a while, then Xiang undid the bundles which she had bought in the rain, and together they feasted, and laughing drank miao tai, as the elders of the village looked on disapprovingly.

But when they clattered on again, Xiang took Nai's arm, and said, 'Sweetheart, I don't want you to be offended. But what are your plans about these wars? It seems the battles are coming, and many are joining the ranks to fight. Your friend, Wei, for instance, has a post in the cavalry. He may win honour from it. But what will you? Are you really avoiding service, even when the enemy threatens?'

Nai shook his head and said, 'No. I've signed to fight. My uncle has been many times pressing me, and though I've not told him, I have put my name down also for the cavalry. I have enough money of my own for the garb and the horse and equipment. But I'm in no hurry to get on with it. First we have our holiday. Then if there's time, I shall save the empire. But as for Wei . . . ' Nai stared at the road thoughtfully. 'I'm not sure what has happened to him. We are good friends, but somehow I haven't seen him since a fortnight ago when we had our big row. I know he's joined the army. My uncle was singing his praises to make me feel awkward. But he seems to stay away from me. I went to his house, but it was all locked up.'

'Hm,' said Xiang. 'Then what has happened to him? Such good friends should not be put apart.'

The first night of their travel they spent at an inn, where the life of the small town went on busily, for the farmers had come in and were doing their deals, a money-changer sitting with scales at a table. The room in which they set their bedding was directly above the booming parlour where the labourers plied their 'nimble lads', and there below did the lovers dine on clear eel soup, and sitting round the copper cauldron, mix their own sauces and fetch from the teeming pot cabbage, mutton and noodles. They went to bed then, the candle lighting the stairs, the incense fuming the secret chamber.

But when they lay in bed together, and Nai took her in his arms, Xiang froze and looked with ice in her eyes, and though they had been smiling then, at once she was a fury, and her body rocked and leapt away from him. But Nai embraced her tenderly, and gazing with sadness he said, 'My sweet love, what's the matter?'

And Xiang answered, 'Fear. Fear! I want to escape!'

And Nai smiled and said, 'Well, so you may.' And he made no more advances on her, but only held her friend-lily, and reassured, she melted a little, till tired with the journey, and serenaded by the owls, the pair of them fell asleep.

But the next dawn they rattled on again, flying in their curtained chariot by the chicken yards and the melon farms, and they overtook along the road lumbering great carts, and buffaloes with their sway-backed horns. The fields were stirring. And in the distance hills were gathering persistently around them, gloomy mountains espied to the West, which moved along with them as a monster moves.

And Nai said, 'To the West all hills. Beyond those crags will be Shou chun, and there we'll find our farm-house and lake pavilion. And surely in those peaceful fields, there will be simple comfort, and time to breathe and dream of the mountains Westward. For do they not call to you, Xiang? The Westward hills of the gods? Ay, they call us both with a strange music!' And Nai stared to the hills with tears in his eyes, as the road spun on before them.

But as they rattled along, Xiang looked at Nai softly and said, 'Sweetheart, be patient with me. You were kind to me last night. You never take offence. It is as though you understand me. For you know well, my dear, that you have come to me so late, when I was about to give up the world of men, and from the world behind me I see in you all that has hurt me before. Bide for me then, for I wish to be true. Yet there are so many ghosts.'

And Nai said, 'Surely. Your little freaks and frights, my love, they do not sting my self-esteem, for you have beaten me down with your grim talks to the love that lies underneath the others. I have loved women hotly, plagued by jealous rages, devastated by adorations. With you, I am only allowed a comradely love. Yet amazement! What limitless play it fosters! All others at heart have bored me, yet little one, with you I could play for eternity. And indeed when I hold you, I feel l could fall into a pit which has infinity in it!' And Nai looked across at Xiang who smiled and laid her head softly on his arm.

Springlike was now the day, and the air smelt fresh after the long rains. The earth was trilling with rivulets and the birds looked up at warmer skies. In the bough-sheltered woods the snowdrops shyly trembled, with green-trimmed petals feeling the sun, and the snail came creeping over the wet stone, and the pussy-willow shook forth its pollen. Among the stirring countryside the lovers came to the track which led to the little farm-house and pavilion, and the horses nudged their way through the rank-smelling, rain-dashed elder, and brought them then to the curly-roofed farmhouse, where a watch-tower, like a pagoda, stretched up to the spring sky, and where a large farm-lady came running out to greet them.

And when they had been greeted by this prudent woman, they were given the keys of the pavilion, and provision was made for the lady to supply them with their food, and to see to the heating of the love-nest, and thus they sped away again along the road to the copse, between whose trunks the lake could now be seen glistening. The scene then swung before them: the lake with its catch of clouds, the climbing hills beyond, their heads in the mists fading, the pine trees clinging to the foggy pinnacles, the little bridges and tender goat-tracks, the clusters of spring trees drinking the green air, and about the farm and hill-sides the perfumed boughs of apple blossom, pear blossom, peach blossom, pink and white hawthorn and thick-crammed cherry.

'Oh, sweetheart,' then sighed Ling Xiang. 'What a para-dise this is! It's so lovely, as if Pure Brightness was upon us, not the Waking of Insects! Well, we must cleave to the former's appearance and not hold too much to the reality. I promise, my sweet, there'll be no more waking of insects. Truly I have not been well or in my best health lately. But now come and kiss me, for I am deep and slow, and now is the spring coming through me.'

And so fed the lovers on the softness of each other's kisses, for kiss they would, falling into the depths which the lips hold open. And hand in hand they moved towards the house, the little pavilion with lattices and red-painted pil-lars, where the curling-eaved roofs and creeper-hung bal-ustrades were set among chrysanthemum beds and wattle fences. The lovers went in then, and through the windows of the pavilion saw the lake waters that skimmed into the misty distance, where Shou chun raised its walls at the foot of the Eight Duke Mountain, by the windings of the Fei River, and the long lagoons that lead to the Yellow Ocean.

But when they came to sleep that night, and as before got into bed, once more Xiang froze, and looked all frost and ferocity.

And once more he said to her, 'What's the matter, my love?'

And she shook her head, and stared at him with loathing, her whole body tensed against him, jumping as each time he tried to soothe her and caress her.

So once again he said, 'Well then. Time is it we were asleep.' And he held her in his arms gently and tenderly, until they both breathed deep and slow with slumber and oblivion.

Chapter Seven

But Wo Long Wang careered now triumphantly about the world, and he exulted as he led the flocks of giao wriggling at his tail. He led them through the banks of cloud and he led them through the parchy air. With sizzling speed he flew above the woods and the crags of China, and from Chang an he flew and the North, across the peaks of Qinling, and the eager-sniffing dragonettes sped over the hills and plains.

The dragon laughed and said to them, 'Now my merry crew of disciples, you see what joy we have, bringing rain and turmoil among men? The dragon, he is a powerful beast, that loves to frolic and play. Great energy has he, a masculine force, that knocks down walls and cities with his exuberance. You see how the armies come racing at our heels? You see how they stream towards the South? Thus from our pranks breed the great new ventures. Yet snake-lettes, now we have other sport. I will take you to other great realms. For not alone men are troubled by dragons. Prepare then to see wondrous sights, and prim and proper heavens, and all the foolish dignity of immortals.' And the dragon then swooped upwards into the rarer sky, and like a comet he led his train a-clanging.

Now first did the star-dragon go skimming the Kun Lun Mountains and come to the heaven of Confucius. And he led his wriggling giao down to the spacious courts, and the ceremonial terraces and the regular-shaped hallways, and they came to the parade-grounds where the priests were offering incense, and the ancient rites of music were sounding through the courtyards. And the dragon at once settled down, and changed himself into a man, and bidding his little dragonettes to stay where they were, he went in his dignified man-manifestation up the steps and into the reception rooms of the god. And calling for an audience with the great Confucius, he sat on the benches in the ante-room, and waited menacingly.

But Confucius was not at home, and so his deputy Mencius appeared, and staring at the dragon-king said, 'Welcome, Wo Long Wang. We have not had the honour of seeing your terrible appearance in these halls for many long year, nor can we help you now, for in your quest of the star-lovers, surely we have nothing to tell you, for of them no god has knowledge. Yet in your request for an audience with Master Kong, we must also disappoint you, for he is in Jian kang, where he stays amazingly long, visiting his pro-tégé Xie Nai. But though we cannot help you, at least let us offer tea to your gruesome presence, and that of your tribe of serpentlings.' And Mencius stared at the dragon-king with an impudent smile.

The dragon said, 'A plague on your tea, and your imper-tinent manners. I have no wish to drink at the court of a complacent subversive. No doubt you are planning to over-throw your master, while he is away. He may be an old bore, but he's worth two of you jocular revolutionaries. Why don't you make your own heaven? And so farewell. Get back to your dialogues.' And the star-dragon resumed his own form, and coiling his scales into the sky, led off his serpents once more through the high, cold air of Tibet.

And he brought them next to the Tushita Palace, in the heaven where Lao zi makes his home, and they flew in among the mountains speckled with veins of minerals and gold, and they came to the palace, where the great furnaces burn so that all was glowing with orange light, and they landed on the steps, before which the clouds of smoke billowed forth, making even the snakelings splutter. But Wo Long Wang once again took on his human face, and stomped into the palace, calling loud for an audience with Lao zi.

But Lao zi was not to be found in the palace, and so his

deputy Zhuang zi darted forward, and slapping on the back the startled Wo Long Wang, he laughed and said, 'You robber, you'll not find him here! Lao zi has gone gambolling off for a life on earth with General Xie, for his nephew Nai you may remember is a favourite of the Ancient One, just as he is with Confucius. And it's all completely irrational! Isn't that good? That is Dao! I should go back to heaven. You'll never find those star-lovers. They are not in any of our furnaces!' And Zhuang zi ran laughing off from the dragon then, and dived back into his chemical experiments.

But the dragon was not impressed and mumbled, 'Go then, go! Make gunpowder of your bones, you mad-brained old Daoist, that spends all eternity fixing fireworks and golden pills! I care not for your crazed alchemy any more than those toadies' protocol. Yet strange that both Confucius and Lao zi should be visiting this Nai! Who is this charmer? What great gift has this being got? Perhaps we should make a trip to the earth to see of what nature is this paragon? But no. Giaos, come. We have another heaven to visit, where our reception may be more merciful.' And the dragon thus sped off again, winging across the snows, and flew further West now with his wormlettes.

And they came thus to the tinkling heaven of the merciful Guan yin, with its diamond-forests and jewel-orchards, sprouting from the gold rocks. And the dragon led the giao down to settle among the coral-groves, and to wriggle where the sapphire trees dangled their cool branches. And the giao when they saw all this, were bereft of their maliciousness, and ceased to spit fire, so that Wo Long Wang, who was a man again now, frowned and growled upon them, and urged them to spite, while he went and called loud for Guan yin.

But the goddess was not to be found at home on this sunny afternoon, and instead through the dusty snow-petals came Dragonfly the fairy, and when she saw the dragon, she blushed like a piece of rose-jade, and said, 'Forgive us, great Lord, for our mistress is not with us. Nor had we known you were coming, for we would have laid a banquet, and called up soft sleeve-dancers to entertain you. Yet our goddess has gone visiting down to the earth a while on some unknown business of compassion.'

The dragon looked hard at her and said, 'Is she gone to see Nai? Xie Nai, the one the gods are hiding? Is this the little secret which you would keep from me, and hide among your smiles and beauty and politeness?'

And the fairy-maiden gasped with horror at the suddenness of this, and before she could think said, 'Oh no, my lord, spare them! Let the star-lovers have peace! Let them live on earth! Be compassionate! What harm are they to anyone?'

And the dragon smiled grimly at this, and stared at the quivering nymph, then turned aside, and whistled up his snake-boys. And suddenly like a silent breeze they were gone from the garden, and the fairy stood forlorn on the steps behind them.

But the lovers on earth, Xiang and Nai, were at ease meanwhile and happy together, and the rest of that spring day they ambled by the shore, and fetched pebbles from the gravel of the lakeside. Laughing, they acted out characters on the banks, embracing each other and bouncing up and down. For Nai acted the sleeve-dancer and flew around like a bird, mimicking Xiang's looping swoops and attitudes, and she made fun of him, screwing her face up like a poet, and scribbling absurd characters in the sand. They laughed together, as though they were pair of hired clowns, fooling as the cold evening came around them, and afar off over the lake smoke darkened the sky, and there came a muffled noise of thunder.

Then when it was evening, they went inside and clumped into the cedar-fretted pavilion, and by the glow of the lantern they set ready to eat the lake crayfish and noodles brought them from the farmhouse. But when Nai went to make tea, Xiang threw away the tea-cups with a shriek, claiming she could not drink tea from bluish porcelain, for it made the tea seem pink, just as white made the tea seem red, and yellowish made it purple. The correct type of porcelain for the drinking of tea, she declaimed, was Yueh chou which made the tea seem greeenish. So up and down they searched through old boxes and chests and cupboards, wailing and keening like crazed mourners, and found at last the cups hidden in a chest, with a lute wrapped in a pair of strange Buddhist robes. And Xiang looked at the robes, and said they were fateful, and Nai said he wanted his tea.

And after tea, Xiang talked and said, 'Sweetheart, you are so stupid, it is just like having a little brother. How you make me laugh with your sweet little huge face, and your eager little big eyes and silly grin! Oh, I am so serious! I totter about shrieking. I suppose it's being for so long a prima donna. It's entered my blood. I shall be a little clown forthwith and have a holiday from my soul.'

She smiled. 'Yet we're alike. You're protected from life, just as I am in the nunnery. You live in your books, always thinking of plots and characters, living safe in a fantasy world. Mind you: you've always been there. I've been out in the cold. I've got the scars to prove it. If I have learned the normal prudences of life, it is from trying out all possible extravagance. And yet to what pain I was led by my hopeful heart. How was I to know it could not happen?

'I could not take a man. I did not know this at first. How is it one can know one is not like others? I fell in love easily. My emotions would sweep me away. Yet they led but to a torture-chamber. How can you love a man, submit yourself to his will, and yet not get your body to undertake it? What horrors did I slide into, what inextricable torment, to be in love and unable to give yourself. What place could I go but to a refuge? I need a refuge from life!

'When I was with the Count, and it finally struck me that there was never any hope for me, when I was locked with that man in such appalling struggles, all the time not wanting myself to be in them. I loved him greatly. Yet I was but a goad to him. Yet I couldn't stop myself being so. I knew then there was no way forward, I knew I should give up the world. I vowed then to go into a nunnery. The faith of Buddha, how sweet it was to one enmeshed in life, so wracked with pain!

'To Jian kang I came, my gold-tongued poet, resigned to give up dealings with men. Who should I see over a silver river? What should I hear but a poem? I had a dream about you soon after we met. It was just as we met over water. I heard a voice singing, and found you, standing there, and you were looking up at the stars. And when I looked up also, suddenly you were there behind me, holding me, your body pressed against me. But I was not afraid at this. Indeed I felt supported, and we looked up at the stars together. How vast they were, hanging about us like lanterns in an orchard, before a journey, in a house we shared! It gave me such a strange feeling. I felt so close to you, as if we had already been together.'

Nai smiled at hearing this. 'Then you are also mythofacted,' he said, 'held in a story which writes itself in reality! It was the same with me, sweetheart. For when I first met with you, I found myself acting out the very myth you are here in touch with. Is it not plain to you? Your dream is reminiscent of the Cowherd and the Weaver-Girl?'

Xiang looked at him ironically. 'The fairy tale?' she said. 'Yet have a care! Do you cast yourself as a god? I am afraid when you talk like this. I know you have much self-mania, but do you not fear the gods will strike you down?'

Nai shook his head. 'In everyone,' he said, 'there are gods. We are but amalgams of the immortal moulds. Nor is there very great pride in being two of the squashed, for that is all the gods are in our tale. But now is a night for poems, my love, rather than stories. Let me woo you like the Cowherd with my verses. What, I am your little brother. You need not fear me. Let me warble innocent seductions.'

'My little brother, yes,' she sighed. 'I think of you like that. You are not one of these masculine monsters.'

But then he took the lute, and as she lay in his lap, he twangled the strings and vibrated them, so that they

114

sounded forlorn, falling away into echoing chasms. The
five-note scale he played of the harmony of the sages,
listening in the hills for the pitch which would set the state
on sure foundations. And then he declaimed a shih of
seven-syllable lines, improvising the rhymes and parallel
constructions. And he sang:

> Since you, my love, came to live,
> The winter has departed.
> The lake laps at the pebbles,
> Cuckoos call through the green haze.
> Lighting the lantern at dusk
> I let fall my dazzled look:
> Warring with the gold sunset
> Your silver face's spring phase.
> How softly the hills hold us
> In their damp-scented embrace!
> How deep the watered crimson
> Of your jasmine-blossom silk!
> The petals fall in the lake
> And to the night-sky are raised.
> Our souls mingled together,
> In the stars finding their place.

Now when Nai had finished, he put his lute aside, and
taking Xiang in his arms he kissed her. As ever did they
sink in tenderness down to the quiet depths. In sighing
comfort he lay beside her. They stroked each other's faces.
Long, long did they lie with mouth on mouth, and the
breathing was calm between them. Nai set his soft hand to
press her breast, and he felt rise in his loins his hard,
unmaskable manhood. It stood on guard below, as all was
in peace above. Thus was the loving between them.

'My sweetheart,' then said Xiang, 'you are such a comfort to me, for in your love I find such understanding. You
never laugh at my laments, nor rage at my jerky fears, nor
ever take offence, or resent rejection. And yet so lusty are

115

you that I have only to kiss or touch, and there are you bounding with passion. How may you be so patient?'

Nai sighed and said, 'Supreme forbearance! Yet it is not so entirely. My sweet, in merely kissing you I fall into such luxury, this alone is satisfying. And moving to further pleasures, what are they but delights which one may take along the road? Sex has not merely one pleasure, and that in the act itself, and all else but preliminaries. Each step forward loses the delicacy of the step before, and the grosser frenzy succeeds the finer. I am as happy to be upon your lips as set here.' And he thrust himself hard into her soft lap.

She frowned at him comically, and said, 'Well, so you say. Why then can we not just be friends, or kissing cousins? You have always said to me that we must be wholly lovers. But will you really desert me, if I may not come there? O no, let me not ask that. This evening is too sweet to spoil it with such pronouncements. O kiss me again, my dear. I am for your arms. There can be enough of discussion.' And she held up her lips to him, and he kissed her warmly and strongly, and his hands pulled open her tunic and thrust inside.

With sighing did Nai take her silky breast then, naked and fallen into his palm. Soft was its skin, and tender his touch, so that it ripened to feel his kindly hand. He held it fast below and his tongue pressed in her mouth, and busily he fetched her tongue in his, and long he sucked on it, drawing its fresh juices, squeezing her breast beneath the silks. But delicately then he fell to browsing at her lips, while his fingers plucked and tenderly tugged at her nipple.

Xiang sighed and flowed under him. Suddenly now she stretched out flat, he lying on top of her. Groaning with the comfort of it, Nai bucked up his hips, and jammed his hard loins in her shut lap. He put his mouth on hers again. Restless his hands roamed. He pulled her towards him, holding her waist and her buttocks. He thrust up with his loins, as though he was fast inside her, tossing her about the

116

bed, disarrayed. She struggled against him fearfully. Tenderly he let her go, and rolled off beside her, stroking her soothingly. He brought her to smile once more, and fed again at her lips, and she closing her eyes, put her arms about him.

'O Nai, Nai,' she whispered, 'I would what I would, and yet if I could: Oh, I know not, I know not! O sweetheart, you are tender with me, and all my sudden frights, they slip away when you stroke me. Do you think I am a kitten? Yet if you would wish me a woman: well, by force you could have me. Who am I to fight you? Though I will, I will. Yet that would succeed, if you would truly have me. You see, I can conspire against me. Take it as a token of my love. The other night, remember, you might have done it?'

And Nai sighed and frowned, and said, 'Yes, I could have done so much. The anger you gave me, the sourness turned into lust. I did indeed force you. Why, I had you there on the point. It would be sweet again so to see you. Yet that is not the way for me, nor is it for you, my love. That is but to embark on long resentment. No, if I cannot have you of your own giving, then it is done, I will not have you.' And quietly he kissed her, and suddenly she wept, and he held her in his arms, as she lay sobbing.

But then he whispered softly, 'Come now, let us get into bed, and lie together naked as before, but to prevent anything happening, let us try a little plan. It is a device which will insure you against copulation.' And Nai looked at her with a rakish face, as Xiang dried her tears. But she was suspicious and slow and fearful.

But as she undressed slowly, Nai came to her aid, for he himself had already thrown tunic and shirt, and bare-chested he helped her, undoing her tunic's silken buttons, and taking it back tenderly from her breasts. And her blouse he slipped off also, and reverently kissed the fat of each breast, and the swell of her hips and dimpled navel. And hesitatingly shuddering Xiang let him do all this, as he unwound and slid from her her brocaded skirts.

Now when this was done, Nai fell to touching her soft

body, and sweetly and fluffily kissed each thigh and calf. And also did he browse about the sprouting of her pubic hair, until he felt her freeze again and hold his head. But then he got up himself and kicked off his shoes, and he undid the belt of his silk breeches, and without forcing her to touch, he slid them off from himself, and stood there quiet, with his manhood rearing in front of him. And it was fatter than Xiang had ever seen in all her past scrapes and adventures, wherefore the lady did not cheer much at a greater ordeal.

'And now,' said Nai cunningly, 'the court-poet's grand plan for the prevention of unwitting fornication! Come here then, my sweet, and lie you in this fragrant bed, for is not the meaning of Xiang fragrance? And let me lie beside you, and my love, only remember: you have here no need for shame or modesty, for the man you are with tonight beyond all men but the Emperor, has seen even the secret parts of the Empress.' And he gestured for Xiang thus to lie down at his side, and she did, but in anger and fright at his joking. And when she had lain upon the bed, he suddenly swerved upside down, and she found herself staring at his hairy monster.

But Xiang did not have time now to flee or protest, but she found, as had the dancing-girls alone together, that there was a nuzzling and kissing at her nest, and a stroking and cupping of her buttocks. And just as the girls do to each other when without men, there was a delicate touching of her loins, and she could not stop the flowing of the lust in that place, or cease from allowing her thighs to swim and open. Wherefore the poet Nai fell to kissing and licking her sweetly, sending the shivers and her hands roving. And she loved him with his head in that place, as he also was groaning with bliss at his feeding.

And Xiang sobbed aloud to see and feel so much, for he was like a baby to her, and he lay so still, his body stretched at her side, upended, yet tender beside her. And she found with all her feelings swelling she kissed him in his lap, and went herself to feed on his love-weapon, and they rocked there together, with much sighing and gasping and thresh-ing, for all the world as if they were perpetual lovers. But Nai with one swing now came round, and set himself to her lap, and twined her legs swiftly and easily about him, and his manhood was suddenly there against her sex, and all to do was to relax to him.

But she could not relax. A fierce anger and loathing seized her. Her whole body shocked, as though woken from a nightmare. And rigid did she freeze, as if to bound away, and steadily did Nai pause at the threshold. For his tip was set amidst it, and but one shove to have him in, and her eyes glared ice down on him.

'What's the matter, my love?' he said.

But she could not reply. She lay there panting and hard with fury. And he did not push into her, but softly lay still, and long did they stay thus together. And he gazed into her face, waiting to see a willingness, at which he would forge further.

But she could not yield, and so he merely held her sighing and sad, and advanced no further. And then she turned aside from him, and giving him her back, lay there frozen and quiet.

Chapter Eight

The dragon meanwhile, as the next day drew on, dived down upon the capital Jian kang, and he floated over the city, coiling about it, with his many-spitting giao in attendance. And when he had studied the avenues, he saw, in the grid pattern, the street which led to the palace of General Xie, and seeing it he smiled, gloating on its many courts, rock gardens and decorous residences. Then did he lead his dragonettes in a dive, and came down to the soil of the city.

But when he came to the streets, he turned himself again into his man-manifestation, and as a proud mandarin, with a grim face, all knobbly, he strode amongst the avenues. His giao, moreover, no longer hanging back, also turned themselves into mortals, and like a crowd of bullyboys they dogged the mandarin's heels, staring out aggressively at all who passed them. And the dragonettes had snakelike faces and hissed in their marching ranks, and wore a livery of coiling serpents. And thus they came to the gateway, and they sent in for Xie Nai, and they waited while servants came to and fro unproductively.

At the last from the gate there came hurrying Gu Kai zhi, the mad painter, and he glanced at the dragon and said, 'Sir, is it you have been sending inquiries within? Do you not know there is a war on? General Xie is not at home. He is flying North towards the invaders. And there I am to join him, hopefully to reach the infidels before they can do mischief on Shou chun. Good day to you, sir.' And the painter raced off, and leapt into a hired chair.

Then from the gate came another anxious-faced one, and his servants brought his sedan-chair out with him, and this was Tao Qian, and he looked at the dragon and said, 'Ah, sir, you have been inquiring for Xie Nai. A sensitive youth and distinguished in the literary arts, though inclining too much to crude popularism. Yet surely he is not here. Very wisely he has gone posting to the waste plot of the North moor, and there among elms and willows among ranks of peach and plum trees, he has leisure to spare. Would we all might flee the turmoil as he has done. Yet we must not forget he may very well be amongst it.' And the poet then set himself in his curtained-chair and was hoisted up and off by his team of footmen.

Wo Long Wang stared grimly dissatisfied at this news, and his twisted human face looked black with its bluff sneer. Yet just as he was staring, there came forth from the gate a scholar and a monk, who were talking in an animated manner of what had been heard within. And the dragon when he saw this pair stared at them puzzled, for there was something both mysterious and familiar in them. And when the pair of ancient mortals saw the human form of the dragon, they two stared amazedly at his proud, belligerent looks, for there was something in his face that they found reminiscent also. The two groups stood for a while, on the brink of challenging, as the life of the city went past. But then not wishing to tear the tender curtain of reality, having stared their fill, they both went their separate ways.

But Kun and Lun, the scholar and the monk, walked off together down the street, and keeping still their human forms which cloaked their divinity, they set their heads together gossiping hard, as they mingled among men. And Confucius said, 'A very strange apparition, and not entirely human. For that mandarin had a dragonish face, and those his roughnecks had a serpentlike look about them. How is it now upon the earth that you can't walk a street without bumping into gods? Can they not stay in their heavens, but must be dodging out from behind every cart and ash-can?'

And Lao zi said, 'Surely, and what mischief attends him! He is out to obliterate us! The Northerners have invaded. They are pouring across the country. They are hardly a hundred miles from the Yang zi River! What are we going

121

to do then? We have sat here for months! Isn't it time we did something about all this? Let us fly back to our heavens, and start making our thunderbolts. Nothing else will stop this mad Buddhist!' And Lao zi at once went to fly, except that Confucius caught him by the gown, and rocked him back on his heels to stay him.

'Impetuous monk Lun,' he said, 'will you go shaming us in the streets, and cowing men with displays of celestial flying-tricks? If we are to fly off at last, let us at least do it discreetly, from behind some back-door or in some unseen corner. For we have kept our mortal's frames now for months, and in that guise have we been working, and I think we may flatter ourselves we have assisted the war-effort. For it was as Kun and Lun, not gods, that we gave counsels to the great, and much of our advice was taken. But as for flying home now: no. That must wait a while. We must first fly and view the state of the armies. Only when we have seen the dispositions of both North and South, can we make a judgement upon it.'

So Kun and Lun went then, and dodging among the crowds, looking right and left to make sure they were not spied on, they came to a sort of privy place, round the back of an inn, and here they furtively tiptoed and crouched behind a wall. Meanwhile, a grinning passer-by gazed eagerly at them as they went, and closed in ready to surprise them. But when there issued from the gods the uplifting divine smoke, upon whose clouds the deities climbed graciously, the passer-by stopped grinning and watched hallowed by amazement, as the divinities swept off into the sky. And so they went winging North over the Yang zi River, and on towards the attackers and defenders.

And when they had flown down towards the Fei River, and the hills began appearing on their left, they saw now below them marching the many troops in the columns sent out from Jian kang. And they gazed upon the mule-trains and the catapults and the chariots, and the lines of footmen with their spears and shields clanking onward. And they saw the General Huan I leading the hosts, and spurring his horse to devour the miles that stood between him and the mountains. And the cloud-borne gods flew on again, till they came to the district of Shou chun.

And here approaching the Shuo Lake, they saw the General Xie commanding his forces, and sending out scouts to spy the land before him. And beyond his forces they saw the town Xia shih overlooking the waters, and here the Southern General Hu Pin manned the defences. But as the gods looked they saw to their horror that Hu Pin was surrounded by the enemy, and that the Northern forces had cut him off by circling down against the hills. And the gods were appalled at this, and looked at each other in dismay. But then looked back at the battlefield.

And as horrified as they had been seeing Xia shih besieged, they had even greater horror looking at Shou chun, for with smoke issuing from it, and soldiers marching about, they had not at first realised the true import. For Shou chun had fallen. It was in the hands of the North. The General Fu jung had taken it with his battalion. And there flew the Buddhist flag of the invading usurper on the temple of the Daoists, and the jubilant soldiers careered around the town, smashing up the shops and looting the houses, and the cowed citizens ran away in the fields, and hid in the reedbanks of the gloomy marshes.

Wherefore Lao zi said, 'Ai! We have been struck this day! How have these Northmen like tigers descended upon us! And see where the enemy flag, the Buddhist wheel of law, flutters in mockery from my temple! And look now: back in Xia shih, our General Hu Pin has sent a scout, and he hurries on his horse to greet our generals of the Southern armies. But see: the Northerners seize him, and they take him to the besiegers, and Mu jung Chui will learn now from the scout the weakness of our defenders! How long can we resist all this? We must act with speed, or China and its gods will be gone for ever!'

And Confucius said, 'Indeed. It is time to cease from talking, for a gentleman is prodigal in deeds. For we see here a picture of the threat that has come upon us all, the very outcome of the dragon's awakening. The streets of old China lie in enemy hands, an enemy faith triumphs over them. We must restore the power of the ancestors. We must invoke the rites of the land against these invaders. Wherefore, my comrade, good ancient one, do you stay here and watch the armies, and I will fly South to Jian kang again, and urge the priests there to rites of the ancient mountains. When I return, let us hope, the battle will not quite have broken, and the spirits I awake there may spread their powers to save yet these desperate reversals. Farewell a while, then Lao zi. Night hastens and I must also.' And thus did Confucius swirl away on cloud, and leave Lao zi to follow again the armies' manoeuvres.

Now when morning came to the Lake of Shuo, Nai woke stretching and writhing, and he felt the bed empty, and no Xiang there. So he looked up to see where she had gone. She was not in the room. He could not see her anywhere. His mind became full of misgiving. So he called out, 'Xiang! Xiang? Are you there?' And he heard his voice echo through the pavilion.

But then he heard a rustling, and to his relief, Xiang came into the chamber, wearing her scarlet dressing-robe, her face made up, looking sweet and radiant. She carried with her a golden cup, which Nai had not seen before, and which he could not help but stare at. But she did not make anything of it, but 'Good morning, my love,' she said, as she softly walked towards him.

Then did he notice that she had tea sitting ready, the little pot nestling on the charcoal stove. With one hand holding the golden cup, she reached over and delicately poured him some tea into a decorated dish. She gave it to him sweetly, and sitting up in bed, he thanked her and sipped it gratefully. And all the time Xiang held the golden goblet close to her breast, though still not drawing attention to it.

She sat down on the bed beside him. 'I could not sleep so well,' she said. 'I've had strange dreams, so I got up to think about them. I've been examining my soul, my dear, after what happened last night. I've had to do some hard thinking.' She stared ahead thoughtfully. Nai felt chilled by her seriousness. But he settled, waiting to see what would come from her.

'I know you understand the trouble I have,' she said. 'I know you do not think it is directed to you personally. You are very good at letting these things go by, without making a terrible issue of them. Oh, darling, I have such a fight in myself. It has happened so much. It overpowers me. I just want to escape, and yet I want to make myself stay, and this creates such a battle inside me. I have to follow the feelings that sweep me. It is only worse if I try to ignore them. But you are very kind to me. I wanted to say that.'

'Meanwhile, you have decided to break with me?' Nai looked at at her dispassionately.

'I'm not saying that,' she sighed. 'I am just trying to explain things. But as you have realised I am a very strange woman. I wish I understood my feelings myself. Why can't I be like other women? What has been stopping me? It is just that with all the men I have met there suddenly comes this curtain. Down it comes! Down, down at the moment it should be uplifting. And yet with you. I don't even feel the desire I felt with the others. What does this mean then? Is it that I don't love you? Yet you are very dear to me. And you are a friend.'

'And so you have decided after great consideration to award me a gold cup.' Nai looked at her seriously.

She gazed at him puzzled. But then looked at the cup and began chuckling. Nai nodded sagely.

'Well, I do deserve it, I have to admit,' continued Nai.

They both started laughing.

'My wooing of you,' he said, 'can only be described as truly heroic. Under constant assaults, I bore all silently, and yet never withdrew my advancing ardour. In spite of hideous wounds, I battled on, and yet never gave any quarter. From a howling horde of barbarians I reduced the enemy to a polite but deadly town of lecturers, and then undercut those with a resounding assault through secret mines laid under the city. By constant pressure of kindness the enemy was finally disarmed and at last negotiated into friendliness. And meeting at last as equals and allies in peculiarness, the great gold cup was handed over.'

'Oh, the gods,' signed Xiang smiling, 'I could never have got that far, if you hadn't made me laugh!'

She looked at him, chuckling. For a while they smiled and laughed. Then she leaned over and kissed him.

And Xiang said, 'When I was born, and they saw I was a girl, they were naturally not enthusiastic. We were not a rich family, and another girl was not a welcome addition. They put me in a corner, to be free to attend my mother, who had had a difficult birth. And there I might have perished, except that some malign Fate wanted me to go on and suffer.

'When they cast a look over to me again, they saw me clasping a gold cup, this very cup, in my blood stained hand. Some said it was a miracle: that I must have been born with it, bringing it from the womb with me. Some said it was neglected on the chair, and I grasped it, as babies will grasp anything when they are born. The cup was solid gold, far beyond the means of our family. It was wonderfully finished and refined. It also had a beautiful scent to it, as though just rinsed of some lovely perfume. I was given the name Xiang because of this, and some said I retained that fragrance.

'Though our family were poor, they let me keep the cup. Such was the kindness with which I was treated. I led a happy life then, was pampered and indulged, for through some strange quirk I developed beauty. Everybody loved me, and most of all my father: I was for him his princess. And then at some disgrace, he suddenly killed himself. My mother: she had to fend for all of us. That was the black day from which I have never recovered. Somehow I have never been able to forgive him. And always I have kept this cup, as if it was a piece of him, which I have never relinquished. Here, my dear, drink now. I have filled it with wine. Then I

126

have something else to tell you.' And she held it to Nai's lips, and tipped it for him to drink, and Nai sighed at its sweet fragrance.

'I had a dream,' she continued, 'a strange dream it was! It must have been through telling my other dream yesterday. For again it was as if I was the girl in the old myth, the Weaver-Girl: yet I'm not sure of the story! You must tell me how it really goes. But I was there dressed in fairy robes, and the Jade-King had come raging in upon me. And he had caught us together, you and I, as we were last night, and he was rounding on me furiously for my wantonness. All the time he scolded me, threatening me with punishment, I knew that we had not done the deed. And you he was accusing too, banishing you to Hell, and yet you would not tell him the deed was not accomplished. I was so hurt and angered by this, the dream woke me up. I have been lying here wild ever since. He had the face of my real father, my father who died and left me, and there he was: berating me for what had not happened! I went and got my cup. I felt somehow I had stolen it from him. That gave me satisfaction.'

She turned about to Nai now, and looked into his face. Then in cold anger, she kissed him. And she threw her arms about him, and pressed her naked body to his, and she opened her legs and threw her thigh across him, and holding him tight to her, she panted and was still, and his thing was reared up against her. But she felt down towards it now, and took it in her hand, and Nai sighed to feel her soft touches. And she stroked it with tenderness, making him writhe in the bed, until he lay back and stared at her with passion. And she yearned towards him, and her frame shook with sobs, and her eyes stared at him, hurt and shameful. Wherefore Nai took the cup from her, and set it beside the bed, and he smoothed her thigh and guided it up above him, and he slid in amongst her, and his manhood was aslant at her gate, and his knuckles felt her damp and swimming.

So once more did he perch himself in the lips of her sex,

127

knocking at the entrance to their fleshment. Once more did he gaze on her, reading in her eyes the extent of fright, or anger, or loathing. But he saw there now a different Xiang from the one he had seen before. Where there had been a girl, now was there a woman. And he saw the woman was strong for him, and the strength was in surrender, for the female overcame him in negation. And he pushed himself in now, pressing hard in that tight place, forcing with pain his flesh through the painful gateway. And he set himself inside her, spread raw against his fat tail, and the mad itch of their lust was amongst the searing. Wherefore she cried aloud, but met him at every point, and so to the fierce game they fell of pleasure.

Now never had Nai felt such heights as he scrabbled upon that mountain, skewering her with shouts of pain and smarting. Like a man cringing in agony as if with each thrust to shake her off, he daggered himself into her flaming cavern. Nor never had Xiang in all her scrapes given way to such flashy acts, as rich and ravishing as her own dancing. Like a creature that flees, leaping up corners, as if with each bound to escape, she rammed herself upon him, seeking the gulf of abasement, and flung herself with passion into the degradation.

As dogs, as salmon, bounding birds, as caterpillars coiling and creeping, as worms in the moonlight, as ants on the hot pavement, as elephants uprearing with trunks and tusks, as sloths that hang sucking the fruit from the branches, as octopuses enlocked in the bottom of seapools, while warm waters lap the many-tendrilled anemone, so did the lovers love, seeking all-figured wildness, in mimic of natures finned, fleshed or feathered, and send the day upon its way, through the drunken noon with animals, until the smoky evening came upon them.

But when the sunset streaked the sky, they lay exhausted on the bed, and Nai said, 'Well, my little one-time virgin, for one who has dallied for so long on the bank, you have rapidly learnt the arts of swimming. Can such things be thought on? From a duckling at the water's edge suddenly to become a whole shoal of porpoise! It would not be flattery to say I have never swum fiercer, sunk lower or splashed more rapturous. What do you think to do with me? Reduce me to a skeleton? I think it is I who feel like the virgin.'

But Xiang sighed and said, 'Desperation makes us learn fast. And I had a debt to settle. I see it well now: I have belonged long to a dead man, and against my nature I struggled for freedom. The hurt of his parting and leaving me in the world alone: this has long been my love-affair. But now it is gone. It is not that you have taken his place, it is just that I have taken another road. O heavens, how the air is sweet on this little path! And look the spring is about us!'

The dusk had grown deeper, and in their crimson dressing-robes, shifting the bed out onto the terrace, they took their wine and sweetmeats out onto the verandah, to lie and watch the night fall before them. The cloudless sky hung deep above, and the first stars looked on the lake. The ducks were winging home to the reed-beds. There were strange sounds coming from afar off over the waters: rumbling and rattling with ominous thunder. The lantern on the scrubbed boards made their rustling silks glow fiery cinnabar in the sunset. Nai stroked Xiang's head tenderly, and then in a soft voice, he spoke like a father at nightfall.

'Once upon a time there was a Cowherd who sang songs and lived right up among the stars. He had the gift of verses, and could warble words that were sweet, and send them flowing like nightingales and fountains. He sang about the summertime, when the meadows hop with butterflies, and the winter nights he sang when the quiet snow falls. And he sang about the stars, for all about him he saw them burning, and he longed to voyage amongst them and discover their secrets.

'But it happened one day, that as he walked beside the Silver Stream driving his magic ox before him – for the ox that the herdsman had was talented and could speak, and give good advice in the herdsman's language – he saw across the waters, strolling on the flowery side, the most beautiful maiden in imperial robes. And he stopped as he looked on her, for the sight of her face went through him, stabbing him to the heart with its loveliness, and all he could do was cease from driving his magic ox, and stand there stupidly lost and lovesick.

'Now the ox was not impressed, and he told his master that he should forget this vision of the walking fair, for the maiden he explained was the daughter of the Jade Emperor, daughter of the highest god of heaven. And there could be no thought of a common herdsman loving her, particularly one who neglected his labours to make poetry. The Cowherd should forget her and attend to his star-cattle. But he could not forget, and he lolled by the stream, and sang songs of love and loneliness.

'And the ox was not impressed. Yet the Cowherd kept languishing, and stronger and stronger the fever. And he could not do his work, but lied idle on the flowery banks, and sighed forth his songs to the star-flowers. And he lost the flesh upon him, and grew lighter and lighter, till the ox could see he was truly sickening. And so the ox told him how he might win the maiden by catching her when she came next with her girlfriends.

'Now it happened that the maiden went down to bathe with the star-girls from the Lyre constellation, and it happened that in bathing they left their clothes on the bank, for there are few thieves in the heavens. But the next time they did this, the herdsman was ready for them, and did as his ox had told him. He swam across the flood. He seized the dazzling clothes of the daughter of the Jade Emperor, and took them to his fields and hid them down a well so that nobody but he would know their whereabouts.

'But when the girls came out again from the Silver Stream, they saw footsteps troubling the star-banks. And when the maid came glittering with sleek flesh from the galaxy river, she found her own crimson brocade was missing. The girls were horrified. They ran up and down. The maiden hid in the water. But they could not find them, and at last they ran off, fearful, to seek for assistance. It was then that the ox went down to the river, and told the maiden to follow him, and the naked star-maiden went fearful forth behind him, and over the buzzing star-meadows.

'Now the Jade Emperor's daughter had always in her heart a soft spot for the art of verses. And it turned out that often while on the other side of the stream, she had heard the fragrance of the herdsman's songs. When she came up to the well, she could hear the Cowherd singing and her heart was glad at the sound of heavenly poetry, and she remembered listening to the love-songs of the evening that had wooed her in her strolls along the river. So as she stood there naked, and the Cowherd came towards her, his lips full of the honey of the songs she loved already, she felt herself strangely unafraid.

'Now the Cowherd did not leer at her, or jest about her nakedness, or seize upon her defenceless, but smiled and softly came, and wrapped about her gently a cloak to clothe her, and asked her in a soft voice if there was anything she wished. And when he took her to his hut, giving her wine to drink, he listened to her lovingly, and she asked to come again. And when she came again to him, she asked for honeyed verses, and he gave her the gold-combed poems, and laid them at her feet. And the Cowherd and the Weaver-Girl met and laughed together, and in the spring he married her, without any voices more.

'But the Jade High King now heard of this, and was exceeding angry, and he found his daughter had been wanton, and neglected her weaving histories, and he found that she had married a man unworthy of her rank. So he rose in wrath and came to her, and seized both her and her husband, and dragged them to his heavenly palace, ripping his clothes with rage. And a special curse he put upon them, that had transgressed his will.

'For the decree of the Jade Emperor was that the Cow-herd and the Weaver-Girl, on either side the Milky Way

131

should ever be asunder and to punish them for their hasti-
ness, they should go upon no journeys, but sit and slave at
unwelcome tasks each month of the turning year. And to
stop them disobeying him, he caused the Silver Way to flow
faster, and the stream be filled with galaxies, so that no god
might ever swim across. And thus did he punish them for
their lovely wickedness, and no more could they think of
voyage beyond the constellations.

'But the story did not end there, for the tender creatures
of earth, seeing the great grief of the Celestial Lovers, won
from the Jade Emperor a mitigation of his sentence, which
let the lovers have for their joy but one yearly meeting.
And to speed them to each other's arms over the Silver
River on the seventh day of the seventh month, there fly up
to the skies and planets, from the hedges and woods and
bowers, from the dusty roads and dried-up wheatfields,
stubble-harvested, the magpies of the whole of China,
fluttering black and white, who soar and form a quivering
bridge across the Silver River. And the lovers are united
thus that the Emperor put apart.'

Still was it now in the little pavilion, as Nai finished this
tale. The glow of the lamp fell on the scrubbed boards, and
caught the heads of reeds from the dark waters. The crimson of Xiang's silken robe burnt against her snowy flesh,
the brocaded petals lay frosty there like snowflakes. All
had come to stillness among the sheets and books and
incense-sticks, hanging so strange in the green twilight,
save that over the gloomy waters rumblings and clashings
came, far off, half heard, and yet smelling of menace. But
the lovers merely gazed at each other, oblivious of such
things, for the deeps of the heart have no room for terrors.

And Xiang said, 'My love, your story was so deep, it
seemed to me like a remembrance. The warbling of your
voice alongside these waters: almost as if they happened
within my soul. And see what strangeness there is here.
The whole night has sunk about us. Look there on the lake:
the stars are reflected, and the lights of the shore. And we
upon this bed together: does it not seem as though we were

already journeying through the deeps of space?' And she sighed as she spoke, and together they looked out now over the view from the shore.

For the lights of Shou chun now glimmered in the distance, and the stars were out in the heavens, and the reflection of both made it seem as though the galaxies were both above and below them. And softly did the waters lap against the verandah's planks and sweetly the pinpoint fires were washed towards them, the whole embroidered couch processing through the pageants of planets, with the rose and russet worlds abiding for them. But now in the blackness there came a strange figure, for a presence approached above the lake-waters.

It was a gentle goddess. Lilac robes she had on, which flowed and writhed in the perfumed breezes. Sweet was her ivory face, with smile soft and compassionate, and jade combs held up her sleek black tresses. As she came near to the bed, there wafted a fragrant smoke, sparkling within its grey with fizzling perfumes, and glittering about her was frosty fire, that shook through its limbs the glints of rainbows. And the goddess stopped and smiled at them, allaying their fears with her gaze, and then did she softly speak to them.

'Lovers,' she said, 'sweet lovers, canopied by the spring night, away, away! The high paths are calling. The greater ranges send their airs across the meadow-flowers. The snow hills call beyond the woodland. Away, away! I come to you from another world. For a while I tread my feet in the lake's pebbles. Guan yin I am, the Buddhist goddess, from the pure lotus land, hastening from the breath of the cosmic forest. For times there are, when the high world of gods breaks through to mere man. And it is now. Attend. Mark well. Be secret.

'For you must know in the dusty Chang an, far off in the ancient capital, in the temple of Tu fu, there sits a monk, Fa xian. Of far off things he dreams of seeking, in the Indian Buddha's land, of steamy fields and tanks beyond blue jungle. He waits for you. For you with his monks could go

133

on a pilgrimage, could seek the furthest things of the heart's desires. Why delay? Find that monk, and offer to join his travel. Be not afraid. Quest the vaster pleasures. For hear me well: the trembling goddess hangs on the crawling night. Indeed it is necessity sends me to you.

'You stare amazed. Yet surely my words ring in your very souls, for the quest has been long in your contemplating. You, Nai, have harboured long in your heart the lust to go West, and to discover the epic art of telling. You, Xiang, have also pondered and anguished on the road that leads to the extinction of the Buddha. Yet how could you go now? By what means pass through your foes to Chang an? How could you make this travel, when there is war? Did you not find yesterday in a chest a bundle of Buddhist robes? Are the armies of the capital not sympathetic to this faith? Disguise yourselves as Buddhist monks, and make through the Northern army. Indeed you must go. Necessity compels.

'For while we dally here, all about us, marching the depths of night, the forces of monarch Fu jian are defeating the Southerners. Shou chun is fallen. The town beyond is taken by Fu hung. Beyond Lo Creek, Mu jung Chui in darkness glowers. He has ordered his forces to advance by night suddenly upon Xia shih. He has bidden them bear torches and march by darkness. You must haste away, lovers, for they with their brands will burn through this very orchard, and surely will set aflame this little pavilion. Ay, you are surrounded. On all sides now, the Northerners are pitched. You cannot make your way to your friendly forces. Take note of my plan then. In Buddhist robes go as monks through the massing ranks. Pass through the war, and make your way to Chang an.

'A long, long journey, a dark, dark time, a turbulent turning world lies in your path before the riches of India. The high gods watch you. The stirred-up serpents slither on every side, and there is danger both by forest and mountain. Vast, craggy landscapes, huge sweeps of desert await your shuffling shoes. Can it be two specks can thread the whole world's mystery? Yet you must on, for know, lovers, there are dark things pursuing, and a story of stars lies beneath your travel. Wherefore –' But the goddess stopped her speech, for all over the lake now came turbulent sounds of war in waves advancing. And they looked to the shore line, and saw in the distance a mass of marching lights, as the army of Mu jung Chui carried torches towards Xia shih.

The goddess sighed sadly. 'Fear not,' she said. 'Their thousands are coming on, but I have thought of this danger in my tenderness. I have horses ready. We must take up the robes, and ride a distance in the night. Then you must disguise and seek the Buddhist path onward.' She paused again. They looked at the lights streaming by the lakeside. It seemed a massive army in close-packed ranks, roaming fierily over far hills, and skirting the rushes' edge, the glittering flames reflected in the waters.

But when the goddess stared at this, with a sigh, she looked at the lovers and said, 'Prepare yourselves now for other terrors. The cosmic forces are bearing upon you. This night all things meet fast. It may be other ways are opening before you. It may be that no pilgrimage is ever practical to man, when such an enemy roams in the world unruly.' And she looked again, and her soft face was wracked with dismay, as she stared at the scene before her.

Dread and aghast now at the sight of the goddess's fear, the lovers looked again along the lake. The army that was marching made a glittering line upon the shore, roaming and waving over the hillsides. The sparks of their myriad torches shone like so many scales, and the line like a serpent writhed towards them. They even saw a head to the beast, and it seemed with the marching fires that the snake-head of a monster sniffed the air. They watched the fiery eyes darting that appeared to be of a dragon, till the eyes fixed on them, and seemed to stare with glee. With fainting souls they watched the serpent glide out over the lake, and a thousand sparks went glittering on either side of it. It gazed on them, a vast dragon, hanging over the lake, surrounded by teeming fires.

135

And Wo Long Wang now grinned at the mortals, and shaking his head, he called, 'Why now, I behold at last the lurking lovers! See where they cower that have fled me from the silver river of stars to the muddy earth. See how they hide in mortality! And look who guards them! The lilac one! How might they all tickle my throat! How might my maw enjoy their triple spasms! What do you here, treacherous goddess? You challenge the pantheons. Yet your modest arts cannot protect these further. The Emperor this night bides on earth, on the mountain of Tai Shan. He sits and reviews the tortures of dead mortals. It would be good and apposite to take him his daughter here. And as for this other: giao, giao, set upon him!'

When the dragon had spoken, he rolled his eyes, causing the teeming sparks to fizzle and dive with shrieks down towards the pavilion. Meanwhile, the dragon lurched his head forward, and snatched up Xiang with fire, and twisting about flew up into the night sky. Whereat the dragonettes fell upon Nai, and sunk their teeth into his joints, and the wood of the house began to burn about him. And Guan yin ran from the smoky pavilion, and flew off after the serpent, and Nai tottered out, fleeing the roaring flames.

And when he was free, he looked about, and gazed forth over the lake, and into the darkness of the smouldering sky, and he cried, 'Ye gods, what is this hour? What are these visitations? Why have you made a mockery of my desires? If you did not mean me to come this way, O spirit of the world, why did you give me restless lust to do it? O gods, O dragons, sliding stars, why have you made this pain? To what have you snatched all in agony?' And he ran by the shore, and held up his hands, snake-hung, to the clouds, till calling on Xiang he fell senseless into the rushes.

Chapter Nine

Now the Emperor of Jade sat with the King of Tai Shan among the fluttering torches of a great parade-ground, for the Eastern Peak Deity had there his judgement of the dead, and assessed thereon the souls of the mortals who were brought before him. The Deity of the Mount of Tai sat in a silk-hung throne, while mandarins about him consulted their scrolls, and before him among rows of guards the souls were brought by torchlight, and the Jade High King looked on as his comrade worked through them.

Now there was a blue-skinned demon that tortured a woman tied to a post, and he stabbed her hands in the ground with bloody daggers. And another fiend there was green-hued, with horns upon his head, that rolled up his sleeves and buffeted an upside-down merchant. Great stakes of iron were ringing them about, wherethrough none could run to escape, and the smoke of the torture-fires billowed about the ground, streaming away into the night sky.

But as the punishment went forward, there came a messenger running, and he flung himself down before the Jade Emperor, and he gasped out, 'Ten Thousand Years, I come from the Lake of Shuo, and I am to tell you the forces of the North are triumphing. Shou chun has fallen. It lies in the Northerners' hands, and word has been sent to the Northern monarch. Wherefore we have good reason to think that Fu jian will be there by dawn, and he himself will share in the glory of its capture. The Southerners are marching towards the lake, but they have not half the forces. It seems, great Emperor, that the North will have the victory. Perhaps they will march on Jian kang!' And the messenger finished, as the monarch stared at him idly. But then was he waved aside.

But the Jade-King turned again towards his comrade, who was still surveying the damned brought to his court. And the mandarins read the crimes now of a woman who was brought in a kang, a collar of wood shamefully set about her neck. And a demon full of gnobbly muscles twisted the collar about her, and buffeted her face and her hands that were set through it, while all the time behind her a child wept and followed, tugging at the sash that held her skirts. Yet when the Jade-King heard that the woman was an adulteress, he smiled at the punishment she was given.

But there came rushing towards them now a further messenger, who cried, 'Jade High King, hear the news from Shuo. For the Northerners have sprung a great trick on the Southern towns and by a ruse they have captured also Xia shih. This town is set by the lake near Shou chun, and was commanded by Southern forces, but the Northerners attacked it at night with a small force, and fooled the town into terror and confusion and flight. For as they went towards it, the Northerners held boughs, and on these boughs they set torches, so that each man held aloft from him a branch bearing lamps all over it, seeming that where one went there were ten or twelve. And the holders of the town were afraid, and put up no fight against them. And so did the Southerners suffer a great defeat.' And the messenger was silent. But the Jade-King looked at him idly, and then did he wave him to go away.

And a further sinner was brought in now, a great fat man and replete, whom skeleton-fiends had loaded down with shackles, and they whipped him to the throne and whipped him onto his knees, and handed his scroll to the mandarin. And once more the mandarin read the name of the sinner and his crimes, while the guards stood ready to hail him to damnation. And the Jade-King stood watching, his eyes restlessly eyeing the guards, and he bided to see what this sinner would be given.

But then there came a roaring and a thundering in the

138

sky, and another messenger rushed into the parade-ground, and he flung himself before the Emperor, and was about to speak when the Emperor leapt up and forestalled him. And the Jade-King cried, 'Will you give over these reports? Can you not see I am attending to these sinners?' And the Emperor looked up and glowered, but instead his eye strayed from the man, and looked instead to where in the distant night sky a flickering of fire and writhing, a glittering of waving shapes, showed him that a vast dragon was approaching. And all in the parade-ground became stupidly still, as sizzling with fire the star-dragon lunged upon them.

And Wo Long Wang then settled his vast form on the smoking ground, and he cried, 'Hail, glorious Emperor of the dungeons! The star-dragon you summoned now in a winter's night, the sleeping serpent that wound in peace through the cosmos, now is he arrived before you, having executed your task, and brought you the prize you have whined and cringed for. See now, within my jaws, wrapt in a swoon of shock, enticing, ensilked, your long-lost daughter. I caught her in the very bed of the man who is the Cowherd, and neither of them were thinking of the Jade Emperor.' And the dragon put his tongue forth, and in the flickering fire, there in her rest they saw Xiang.

The Emperor dropped his mace, and looked, and sat stunned in his chair, and he could not speak, but tottered up from his throne, and he walked across the smoking parade-ground, dwarfed by the mighty snake, until he stood beneath the huge cliff of its lips. And the dragon set its burden low, and the Emperor stared at Xiang. And he clasped his heart as he saw her wrapped in the firelight. And he shouted, 'Put her down! Put her here upon the ground! You will burn her, you serpent, with your fires!' And Wo Long Wang thus set her, rolling forth onto the gritty ground, and Xiang lay still, senseless before the Emperor.

'And is the Cowherd dealt with too?' said the Emperor.

'Is he sent into Hell?' But the dragon did not answer his question.

'And is she living truly, as a mortal woman?' said the Jade-King. But still the serpent made no answer.

'How will she awake then? Is she in her right mind? Will she know me?' The Emperor knelt down beside her.

'Oh, Zhi nu!' he cried. 'So many centuries! Zhi nu! How long, how long! So long since you betrayed me! Have you not suffered enough? Well, now you are back. Now you will not wander. I will guide your steps henceforth, nor ever send you forth again. Always by my side for ever you will attend on me. But what of the Cowherd?' The Emperor looked up. 'Is he in Hell? Or is he here? We could have him here and judge him, and load him down with punishments. Why, even now I could see him judged and doomed. What have you done with the Cowherd, snake? Did I not tell you to bring him? Why have you not executed my wishes?'

But Wo Long Wang stared down at him, and said, 'The Cowherd, Jade-King: he is pitched on his head by the reeds of Lake Shuo. And as to what has become of him, he may be stunned or dead. I did not greatly care for his destination. What, I have brought your daughter! Is not that enough for you? Will you be abusing two now where you have one? Be satisfied with good fortune, king, for he who seeks for more may lose all in the hazard.' And the dragon squinnied his eyes at the king, who stared at him angrily back. And about them all was still on the parade-ground.

'Take her to my apartments,' then said the Jade Emperor. 'If she wakes here, she will think for sure she is in Hell. And if she is a mortal, these things would prove too much for her soul. Wherefore we must wake her in softer chambers. Well, dragon, you have done your deed. Fetch but the Cowherd along, and then you are free to return to your patch.' And the Emperor scowled at the dragon, behind whom now the pale dawn came, glimmering in the East below the great mountain.

And the Emperor now beckoned his attendants, and the

140

liveried servants came, and stooping down softly they lifted Xiang from the ground, and bearing her carefully on a canopy from the throne, they carried her amongst the grieving damned. As the yellow banners of the dawn streaked the sky beyond the roofs, the torturers and their victims suspended their agony, and the dragon watched the little procession bear the Weaver-Girl away, and take her up the wide steps of the palace.

But when the dawn came bleakly to the lake of Shuo, all about the waters were signs of chaos. The orchards were smashed and torn, the farm-houses burnt down. Smoke spewed from the embers of the passed army. There was blood among the paddy-fields. The buffaloes blundered lowing. Corpses were sunk in the reeds and the mud. And the vapours hung thick and black above the sacked town of Xia shih, where the Northerners now looted and ran rejoicing.

Wherefore when to these sights there rode General Xie of the Southern armies, his heart in his breast faltered to see such depredations. There rode beside him Gu Kai ji, the jester – now serious-faced – and the aides gazed appalled at their leader. About the clustering farms and fields of the peaceful lake, the path of the burning army could be followed. The town of Xia shih lay captured on its track, and the banners of the North fluttered from its walls.

Now when the Southern armies looked rightwards to the far side of the lake, they saw Shou chun itself, the garrison town, was captured. And the flags of the Northerners flew from its walls and heights, greeting the dawn with a change of sovereignty. Wherefore the Southerners grieved again, and doubted the task before them, and General Xie Shih, and Wei also there as a cavalry commander. Meanwhile among the reeds not far off the poet Nai lay senseless, his face in the mud, and his hands clasping the rushes.

Yet high above, among the clouds, tinged with the rising sun, the Ancient of Days, Lao zi, sat worriedly watching, for below him he saw the two great towns in the hands of

141

the enemy, and the pitiful Southern forces clustering at the lakeside. The smoke swirled below him. The towns were crawling with men. Further off the monarch's own columns came creeping. The landscape was all littered with signs of woe. And Lao zi was struck with anger, and cried, 'Alas, alas, see how Xia shih is taken! Where is that dignified oaf now he is wanted? For Confucius is elsewhere, while these cunning Northern devils have by a trick gained Xia shih for their regiments. They armed themselves with branches, and stuck on each bough several lamps, so that each man had a good dozen lights, and so they marched beside the lake, striking fear in the town, making them think their numbers were tenfold! Alas, alas, the Southerners are losing! What can save China now? Oh, let me think of a ruse to pay back these traitors!' And the old sage thus buried his head under his thoughtful arm, and a hum came busily from his brain.

Then suddenly Confucius was there, delivering his comrade a kick, and saying, 'Is this a time to sit like an ostrich? Lao zi, I have been busy, for to Jian kang have I flown, and sent forth the priests to the Bell Mountain. There they have said their prayers and beseeched the gods of the mountains to protect the true heirs of the Middle Kingdom, and therefore let us hope the god of the Eight Duke Mountain will do something to scare these Northerners hence.'

'You distrustful idiot!' Lao zi shouted. 'How dare you accuse me of sloth? I was about to think of the very plan which would have saved us! But you come up and kick me, and boast like a great general, of how you have stirred a few priests to their duties! O wonderful old campaigner! That's the way to win battles! Off and pray! You ritualistic old windbag! But you have given me anyway my grand idea. I'll tell you how to save this battle. If we have the Eight Duke Mountain on our side, this will prove very useful, for with it I shall cause deception. For I shall make the mountain deceive the eyes of Fu jian, just as he deceived the town of Xia shih.' And Lao zi bustled off then, leaving Confucius

142

standing on the cloud, grieving at the sight of the victorious Northerners.

But Nai in his rush-reed bed now woke from his long swoon, and at once he shook his hands and limbs in agony. And he stared down upon them, thinking to see snakes, yet upon his hands he saw nothing biting. But then he sat up fearful, and struggled to his feet, and every joint was seized up with stiffness. Yet he twisted about to the summer-house and stared to see the pavilion. But there was nothing there now but ashes. And Nai rushed towards it, and searched all about, and he stood mud-faced among the ruins.

And then did he fall to thinking, staring this way and that, for doubtfully he had to check his memory. But when he had convinced himself, again he looked all about, and he searched in the reeds, and about where he had been lying. To the shallows of the lake he waded, gazing back over the land. Then 'Xiang! Xiang!' he called forlornly, and he thrashed again to the shore, and went along the road to the farm-house. But that he also saw in ruins. And 'Xiang! Xiang!' he called, as his heart fainted within him, and the blackness of despair began to fall.

But then harkening closely, he heard far in the distance to the right the sounds of shouts and rattling. He stared about the horizon then, peering over the lake, seeking not for friends but enemies. Hearing the thronging sounds again, he stared once more about, then picked up a stick, and set his dressing-robe about him, and he ran towards the noise of the soldiers, splashing along the side of the lake, hurrying to catch the advancing armies.

Meanwhile, there came flying again Lao zi in the clouds, and he hurried up to where Confucius was standing, and Lao zi said, 'He, he! My little plot is laid for these devious-clever Northerners. They are not the only ones who can practise deceit, and make a few men look a hundred. See now: the Southern generals I have inspired to lay out their forces upon the Eight Duke Mountain. Look, there, where

143

the little trees dot the huge hillside, so that a man and a tree look but two dots indistinguishable. Also I have cast a mist to cover Fu jian's eyes, so as he looks now from the walls of Shou chun, he will see the trees confusedly mingled with the men, and think there is a millionfold army!'

And the pair of gods looked down now where, as the ancient one had said, Fu jian was striding up to the town walls, and below him were his troops massing at the hither side of the river, ready to take on the Northerners crossing the ford. And they bided for the Northerners until enough had come across, then were they ready, as ordered, to fall on them.

But as Fu jian looked out towards the hills behind the ranks, he saw now on the Eight Duke Mountain, befuddled with the mist of confusion spawned by Lao zi, and the influence of the spirit of the mountain, he saw the myriad troops and trees, standing like a nation ready, and his mouth dropped open amazedly at what he saw.

And he turned to his general and said, 'Why did you tell me they were few? This is a powerful foe before us. Call back the order to allow the troops to cross. Let others retire to the gates. Keep the teeming Northerners by all means from us.' And the messengers were sent hurrying down with this countermand, and confusion was sewn from the commander.

But from the rushes of his swoon, Xie Nai came hurrying now, and he searched always to seek the face of Xiang. Among the marching troops he looked, scanning the faces of the North, seeking among the prisoners, or the fleeing peasants. But no trace of her he found, but only the soldiers jeering, and they scoffed at him, as he hared about in his dressing-robe.

When he came to the River Fei, and looked across to Shou chun, he saw now the Northerners pouring over. And beyond upon the other side, he saw the Southerners withdrawing, and tokens of panic and flight in their racing ranks. Wherefore Nai caught on a riderless horse, and leapt up on its back, and through the bodies of the blood-clouded river, he thrashed across to the clashing banks, joining the spears beyond, and he seemed like a madman with his red silk robe fluttering.

But on the heights of Tai Shan, where the wailing sinners were endlessly having despatch to their punishments, while the Deity of the Eastern Peak still consulted with his mandarins and heard the crimes of each soul hauled before him, the dragon Wo Long Wang lay, breathing troubled smoke, still staring blankly in front of him, for the Emperor of Jade had gone now into the palace, and there had been no bidding for him to follow. And he stared at all the torments of humankind, and he saw how the creatures howled and pleaded, and slow was his great breathing in the morning light as he sent forth new clouds about the parade-ground.

Then at last came winging the goddess of compassion, and she descended in the great yard beside the dragon, and she said, 'So I have caught you again, disturber of the night, cruel snatcher and disrupter of fair lovers. And do you lie here gloating among all these wretched sights, you who have brought such torments on innocent young ones? Oh see, how vile is this punishment, and of what evil the guards! Oh, how may you bring tender Xiang to such a Hell?' And the goddess wept to look about her, wincing at man's pain, as the smell of blood and burnt flesh filled the mountain.

But the dragon replied, 'I am sleepy, O goddess. My mission is done, and now I should return to the stars. And yet your words dig into me with their feathered darts, and the cold face stings me of the Jade-King. I have not Xiang with me now. The Emperor has taken her within. He works to have her woken in soft apartments. Yet he has planned to keep her, ever an attendant at his throne, and me he has bidden fetch Nai to these tortures. Oh yet, O goddess, the sight of these things brings me in mind of sleep, for I have done enough with my cavortings.'

'Indeed you have, indeed you have!' said the goddess now with fury. 'For not just the lovers but all China you

145

have brought to torment. The land below us smokes with war. The dead lie piled in the streets. Your Northern barbarians, who think they espouse my religion: they have disobeyed the Buddha's great laws for man. They have done well in serving ahimsa! The blood they spilt this night-time cries ever upon their heads, and yours, O dragon, that spurred them into massacres. But you will not return now and slumber among the stars. No, you will stay, till some of these things you have sweetened. Come, turn yourself, serpent, into your man-form, and in yonder halls show me where Xiang has been taken. Trouble stands before me sure. For I must admit now the thirty-year truth. I must tell the Jade-King that it was I who stole the lovers from him. Yet first I will break it gently to him, tell him it piece by piece. There will be anger, when he discovers. Yet angry am I! And you, come! You may as well hear the tale, for just as much have you been cruel to the innocent.'

And the trembling goddess then walked determinedly to the crest of a ramp, while the dragon stayed lazily watching. But when she turned and scowled at him, with a yawn he turned into a man, and dressed in his dragon-robes, he walked behind her.

Hushed, meanwhile, was the silk-hung chamber, and incense-drenched, in the palace of the Eastern Peak, where the mandarins in rustling silks clustered about a bed, and the russet glinted decorated in gold pheasants. The physician with his hand on the pulse stood by the pale-faced form, as Xiang lay on saffron sheets amidst embroidered curtains. The Emperor knelt close beside her, staring into her face, then worriedly looking up at the physicians.

'Why can you not with your arts rouse the girl?' he muttered. 'Is this a death-trance? Is she mortal or spirit? By the stars, you have felt her, pounded her flesh, burnt things under her nose. But she sleeps still. By heaven, if the dragon has harmed her . . .' But as the Jade-King said this, the dragon-man came now into the room, and with him Guan yin, the lilac goddess, and as they came they argued still, so that their urgent voices, echoed in the hushed sick-chamber.

Now when the Emperor heard these voices, he swung about, and he stared amazed at the pair who had entered. And first to Guan yin he looked and stuttered, 'Goddess of mercy, what do you here? Here is no fit place nor state to give you due courtesy.' And then he looked at the dragon and said, 'And you, Celestial Beast, what is this you have wrought here? For you have brought my daughter, but look, she is in a swoon, and none of them here can rouse her. By the stars it were well for you if she can be roused, for you will feel my wrath if not!' And the Emperor turned again to Xiang, and took her hand and fretted it. But still the woman did not stir.

And the goddess said, 'Most noble Emperor, I have come to this place, since I myself was approaching Xiang already. I must inform you I was with the lovers when the dragon attacked, and had he not been so swift, he would not have had them. For I was with the Cowherd and Weaver-Girl, seeking to get them West, working to bring them free from the realm of China. And this I did for pity of them, forced by your senseless rage to live ever apart though they were married. This then is the reason, sir, why I have come here. Theirs is a cause in which I have interests.'

And the Emperor stared at her, grim-faced at hearing this, and at first did not know how to answer. But then he saw the deity of the Eastern Peak, the great King Tai, enter the room with perturbation.

'Ah, noble Tai, welcome,' said the Jade-King dismayed. 'You find us here distressed as to my poor daughter. Look how she lies senseless. So many years since I saw her. But what is this, goddess? What are you telling me? If you were there before the dragon, what led you to discover her? Why did you not first report this to me? Why did you not say you had found her? You knew well I was searching the length of Zhongguo for any sign of the runaway lovers. And what is this you claim? You were seeking to take them West? You

147

were striving to get them out of the kingdom? I know not what my friend here thinks, but this seems treasonous to me. Make ready with a good answer, goddess.'

'Sir,' said the goddess of mercy, 'in our Eightfold Faith, it is a behest never to tell lies. I cannot hide from you that I told you not of the lovers, because I did not wish you to know. I knew well you were seeking them, I knew the dragon was hounding them, yet I myself wished them to avoid both of you. Therefore I strove, though, alas, it was too late, to set them free from your pursuit of them. These are the reasons, king, I did what I did, and I renew again my plea to you to set them free. What right had you to persecute them, what right have you now? The justice of things demands that you relinquish them.'

'Hold, hold!' the Emperor cried. 'There is treason enough here. I have heard enough to condemn you outright. You are renewing the treacherous words which I heard in my own court so many months ago, though I chose then to ignore them. But what is all this interest you have, and how does it come you have it? How, indeed, did you know of the Celestial Lovers? I am not asking why you kept silent. This you have explained. No! How did you know where to find them? My mind misgives me! I see hideous sights! I see deeper treachery yet hidden! Be frank with me, goddess, or truly the tortures we have here, they will soon fetch the truth out of you.'

'You need no threats to get the truth from a follower of the Buddha,' said Guan yin. 'What dreams need deception? I will tell you everything, and gladly will I do it, for you have much need, king, of facing the truth. I knew well where these lovers lived. I had followed their lives. I will tell you what you have not asked. Prepare to know everything. She was from Hang chao, and he Jian kang, the Southern capital. She was born to a poor family. She was Xiang a sleeve-dancer. He was born to the Xie, and was called Nai. He was the poet whom Confucius and Lao zi befriended, drawn no doubt unconsciously by his flight.

148

And these two were incarnated some thirty years ago, and I was the god who stole them from heaven.'

Now the Emperor stood a long time, hearing these words, and his face was frozen anguish. And the court when they heard these things also were amazed, and no one there could speak for very astonishment. But as they were suspended there, there was a whispering at the door, and a disturbance of some one forcing entrance. So that the King of Tai turned, as the mandarins were murmuring, and a messenger came in before them. And the King of Tai said, 'Cease, will you, these disturbances? Here we have all heard dire wonders. Not ever will the court of gods recover from these things. What is the reason for this outbreak?' And the King of Tai stared glowering, as the messenger looked about, uncertain whether to speak.

But the timid messenger said, 'Your Highnesses, forgive me, but there has come great news from the earth. It seems the Northern barbarians, who looked to have triumphed, have instead been repelled. The taking of Shou chun and Xia shih has not resulted in the enemy success. Fu jian has tasted defeat. It seems the Southerners have forded the River Fei, and driven the Northerners in rout before them.' And the messenger looked about, as many of the courtiers there gasped and murmured with joy amongst themselves.

But then there came the dragon-man's voice. 'What? How is this? Fu jian, the North, the great armies I drummed up defeated? Are all my merry rioters thrown into disarray? Is the flaccid South still clinging to its antique glory? And all my little tribe of giao, has their cavortings been in vain? Why, this will call for ruin, this calls for turbulence!'

'Have you not done enough here?' shouted the Jade-King. 'See, still my daughter lies so deathly! O Zhi nu, Zhi nu, how have they all defiled you! How have they all wrought treachery on your person! Stolen by this vicious witch! She shall be tortured for it! And Confucius and Lao zi! Hale them here and set them in irons. They were in this

149

whore's plot. They will be tortured! Greatest of all treacheries against my throne! We have here a mutiny among the gods. Bring forth the torturers' implements!'

'Hold your noise, you braggart!' then roared the dragon, red-faced at the Emperor. 'Have you not done nauseating me with these wild outbursts all because of this woman, your daughter? By fires I could tear you apart with my claws, eat you now, eat all! What is this crew of minnows? And why, let us have battle then. Come, fight! I am for any of you, all of you! I could eat this mountain.'

'Stay, stay!' said the King of Tai. 'Let us have calmness here. This is my heaven, and I say be you all silent. Dragon, do you quench your fires, and leave your brawling be. And Jade-King, be calm, moderate your instructions. You cannot send for the great philosophers, you cannot have them seized and bound. They are equal to your throne. Why, the pantheon would be cracked. China would rock. Let us approach this with reason.'

'Ay,' said Guan yin, 'for see how Xiang fades away, see how her breath is failing momently. If I do not attend to her, you will lose all you fight over, and you boys will have broken your sport's prize. Let all be still now in this chamber. Fetch close the musicians in their costumes. Let incense be burnt and perfume sprinkled. We have now our work cut out to make this palace charmed, for its holiness is all fled in this braving and brawling. Come, fetch them forward thus. Place the masquers by the couch. Eyes now. Sleep, hearts. Come, reverence.' And Guan yin beckoned then, and ordered things in her quietness, her lilac robes swishing in the silence.

There came then to the front of the chamber with hesitant steps, a band of players dressed in strange costumes. One dressed like a tiger there was, with a great skin over his back, one in rustling silks like a blue phoenix. Another musician lumbered forward caped in an armour-like cloak, for he was set with designs like a great tortoise. And each player bore instruments, which when they shuffled, they took forth, a pipa, a lute, a pipe, and cymbals. And the priests lit the fumy incense, and the soft-footed servants drew up a screen, as the musicians began their magic. And a gently twangling music then sprinkled from their hands, with gongs beating tremblingly like a heart beat. Meanwhile, the room filled now with the scent of ashes of rose leaves, and it hung in layers in the stillness idly.

But Guan yin came forward now, and stooping to the girl, she drew forth the golden cup of stability, and she passed it over Xiang's eyes and said, 'Wake now, awake, sweet Xiang. Softly into this vision pass in your slumber. With this cup I conjure, the cup of stability, stolen from heaven to breed upon earth among men, that thus your spirit, stricken and stung, your soul's waves vexed and terrified, may sink and rest, drawing again together. The integration of this vessel, let it clear your mind, and with its focus draw your understanding. Yet all about you in this vision think it is but a dream. But in your dream, speak, speak for freedom.' And the goddess moving gently the cup before Xiang's face, caused at last the woman's eyes to flutter.

'She wakes! She wakes at last!' then cried the Jade-King, throwing himself on his knees before her.

'Ay, woo her well, you histrionic sham!' grumbled the dragon. 'Make hay while you have her.'

Meanwhile, Xiang sighed, and let her eyes open. She looked about the chamber with puzzlement. She cast her head aside to see where came the music. Then seeing herself in a strange place, she sat up with a start. And then she frowned. She found herself staring into the eyes of the Jade Emperor.

'What, father?' she gasped, and then with terror drew herself back in the bed, while the Emperor stared at her with anguish.

'It is! It is!' he sighed. 'Oh, my poor lost child! It is! You are back at last with your father! Such aeons of years, such infinity of being apart, so many lost millennia in the hands of the Cowherd. You are back, my treasure. Back with the cup and all. The cup of golden stability. Nor ever will you leave again, or take it from this place, for all now will stay frozen in perfection. Ay, all things, all things: all will be as it was, before you passed so vilely from me.'

'What is this place you bring me to?' said Xiang. 'And what are these robes you wear? And how are you alive? Father, what do you play with me? You must not be discovered, wearing these emperor's robes. Such blasphemy will bring death upon you. Take them back to the theatre. They are but from a play. I will speak to the girls of it. But never wear them in the streets. Yet how is it you are here? And father, what are all these people?'

'Do not fret, Xiang,' then said the goddess of mercy. 'All this is but as a dream to you. You need not know of anything, but truly here is your father, and Fate has contrived that you at last may speak to him. What is it you would say to him? Have the length of years not hidden any messages in your bosom?'

'Ay,' said Xiang bitterly. 'Why did he leave me in the world? Wherefore did he quit and bequeath me suffering?' And Xiang stared at the Emperor with a hard gaze, at which he himself grew anxious.

'It was not desertion, girl,' he said. 'My disgrace over the Shang, this forced me from my house temporarily. You had to be put from me. It was not safe to stay. The sweet days in the household were by Fate disrupted. You do not hold that bitterly. What, I am bitter to you? You it was deserted me for that fool poet! Is that the way to treat your father, that loved you so? What is he? A clown? An idler?'

Xiang stared back at him. 'There you speak like a fool. The ignorant have no understanding.'

'Ignorant?' said the Emperor. 'Have a care what you speak! I have had enough impudence here from these renegades! Do not you join in the rabble's jeers. Ignorant do you call me? Then what is that fatuous Cowherd with his cows? Practically a natural, that is what he is! Do you desert me for that sort of foolery? What does he do? He sings? Is that a task for a man? Do not you be so simple!'

'Nor you be so homely,' said Xiang. 'There are other

152

empires than here. There are other deeds and kings beyond China. And fools are they who live in their courts, busied but in their sphere, while all about them the thunderstorm is howling. Do you think this world is but all the dirt that lies in your hand, fixed by your rules, bowing to your favours? No, there are things beyond the Middle Kingdom, king, and to these vasts turn he and I. No task is it for a fool, father, to seek the ancient crafts, to spy in the depths to find the trace of pantheons, to find what underlies the changes of the transcendent world, to find the words for the song which earth sings in her slumber. Oh, this is not the task for a fool. Fools indeed are you, that none of you can comprehend the venture. And I and the poet will cleave together before any threat that is here. Nor do not you seek to sway me!'

But the Emperor looked aghast and said, 'Why, now I have the truth! Now I see of what heart is my daughter! She cleaves to that man before me or any here. Why, now I have it from her own lips! I see how in her very eyes she means what she says. I see how she has turned against me. It is thus for ever now. Take her from me then. I will think well what to do with her, whether to send her with the Cowherd into Hell, whether to take again her service, whether to imprison her with all these conspirators, all, all those who have betrayed me. Oh, how may be such treachery in the heavens themselves? How may the sky flush with evil?'

'Ay, how, how, Emperor? You were best think of that,' said the dragon now rousing himself to his man-height. 'Is it you turned traitor, or these that you accuse? Is it you or these are hollow? You have spoken well there, girl. Your words were firm. You are not the sport of postures like this father. And you have set smouldering the fires again in my bowels. No longer does sleep hang upon me. Ay, you have made me live again. Wherefore, petty Emperor, have a care for your whole realm and ruling. For I have a mind now to race about the world, and set the whole pitch of it ablaze and reeling. I have a mind now to romp again on my spree, and this time call forth greater agents. What, such a pampered actor to be in charge of Zhongguo? Is this the destiny of China? No, rather pull it down, set it all about his ears, set the Huns racing, barbarians of destruction! You have enraged me, king. You have stirred up my wrath. Not you, nor they, nor any can call off my sporting! All this I shall have upturned quite! Look out for your lives! All this I shall have swung upon its axis!' And the dragon looked with blazing eyes about the small chamber then, and all the clustered deities were fearful.

For as the dragon-man glared at them, all his skin was glittering scales, and round his angry eyes yellow flakes were forming. His shoulders furiously bunched behind him, swelling above his head, his leggings burst, and his boots were split open by talons. His spine on the fretted ceiling now made the rafters creak. Plaster descended on the staring gods. His horns dragged scrapingly across the painted beams, and splinters of wood fell as he shook his camel-head. Now Wo Long Wang burst back the doors. His tail thrashed forth into the court. His hind legs flung out the walls to the parade-ground. And his mighty snout lunged forward again, and he seized Xiang in his jaws, and he reared up his front above the building.

Then did the gasping deities run for their lives. The troops in the yard fled back from the furious one. The shattered palace gaped open at its roof, as the Emperor and his courtiers came running out, and the corridors and ante-rooms crashed about the tail. In the morning air then with smoke and fire, with scattering beams and tiles, the serpent lolled his front above the towers. Then did he fling himself madly on the sagging air, and spilling forth he dwarfed the torturers and the tortured. The wracks and impaling pikes of the guards suspended their grim work. The bullies flinched and the bludgeoned looked up in wonder. Then did the convoluting serpent float free with Xiang in his mouth, and twitching his fins glide forth into the morning.

Chapter Ten

Now in the heaven of Xi Wang Mu, the great Queen Mother Goddess, who presides over the celestial peach-orchards, the courts of the ancient mother were flowering and swooning with the fumes of early summer. A fragrant breeze settled and played among the golden roofs, bearing on its wing pollen from blossoming trees. In artificial grottoes, the jasmine hung in shade, spreading its creamy sweetness secretly. All was peaceful by the goldfish pond, and the spirit-gardeners, carrying their wicker baskets, moved among the lilies tending the waxy blooms, whose white trumpets showered them with orange dust. Along the speckled garden path stood the wheelbarrow and rake, and the bullfinch in the lilac sang.

In the cool, tranquil chambers of the ancient Xi Wang Mu, matters were similarly sunny. The mandarins moved graciously. The ministers in their scholars' caps debated matters of little urgency. On the sun-shafted verandah, the servants were sweeping the carpets. Little puffs went forth to disturb the butterflies. The pet dog of a fragile court lady stirred from its couch to scratch, and the parrot in the cage stared out over the garden. Plopping through all this bustle the only sound to be heard was that of the water-clock, the clepsydra.

But activity came, for one of the mandarins, Mandarin Wu, who had been talking with his fellows, at length with suitable bows and apologies, detached himself from his comrades, and went off shuffling through the hallways. Through shady rooms he made his way, among great porcelain bowls, past lovely tapestries, full of pheasants and dragons, and through numerous doors he went where

155

bronze statues of dogs were on guard, and at last he came to apartments still and quiet. As quiet as had been the summer courts of laziness and ease, so even quieter were these shade-filled secrets.

The mandarin now came to a room where time seemed to stand waiting. No breeze disturbed the hangings of silk on the walls. The very flowers seemed frozen, dense colours in cloisonné vases, and the dusty carpets hushed all footsteps. The secluded hall was empty. There were chairs for an audience. A throne there was before a yellow screen. But no one sat in any chair, nor throne, nor stood awaiting. Yet the mandarin came in and kowtowed with devotion. And he looked up then, as he knelt on the carpet, beyond the throne to the yellow screen, and at length he coughed slightly and addressed it.

And Mandarin Wu said, 'All honour to the great Dowager-Empress, may Xi Wang Mu live for eternity! Your contemptible, low servant, Mandarin Wu is before you, and has come with the fruits of his consultations with the chief ministers. We are happy to advise you, your imperial highness, that everything for the peach-festival is going forward. The gardeners have been examining the blooms this morning, and are quite certain the peaches will be ready in a few months. Word has been sent to the Jade Emperor that all is ready. He has but to send out the invitations.'

Then the mandarin, when he had finished this speech, kowtowed again before the empty throne, and softly sat back on his heels to await an answer. At length it came, as an ancient female voice responded, 'The Dowager-Empress is grateful for this information. The proposal is accepted, and news can be sent to my son, confirming what has already been relayed to him. But Mandarin Wu, there are things happening on the unhappy earth, of which I have heard most strange reports. I shall turn to them at once, for as ever our own affairs have the stamp of tradition and efficiency upon them.' And the Empress's voice paused a while, as the mandarin looked gratified, but then continued.

'I have heard that my unstable son's pursuit of the wretched Weaver-Girl has resulted in something like disaster. The dragon's sudden release upon the earth stirred up a civil war. Yet I hear that the legitimate Southerners repelled attacks. More credit to them! More disgrace upon my son! Foolish it is to seek to meddle with Fate. And I hear now that the dragon who at last tracked the poor girl down has in fact relented his chase and borne her off again. My thirsting son, the Emperor, is crazed and driven to grief by this double-blow to his self-esteem. And now I hear he plans to start the search for his daughter again, while hurling the unfortunate Cowherd into Hell. Are these things as I said them?'

'Indeed they are, great Queen Mother,' said the mandarin. 'Your mind is as sharp as ever.'

'Would that my son's wits were!' came the acid reply. 'But let me proceed to the urgent matters. It seems that the idle Cowherd, who on earth is the Southern poet Nai, is destined to be suddenly swallowed up by the earth. Yet as we have been thinking, this would be most ominous, considering the fact that he is a star in the constellation of Aquila. To toss before their time mortals into the mouth of Hell is hardly an action in line with the flow of things. But certain of us have been thinking the Cowherd is a crucial case, for our long memories remember some prophecies about him. We feel that these were omened words spoken about his case, way in the past by some important deity. But there we stick, for none of us can quite recall what or who or when it was. And I take it your inquiries have not reached any conclusion about this distant and misty matter?'

And the mandarin sighed at this and said, 'Alas, great queen, no. We have not discovered anything about it. But we carry on with our research, and there is also in the Jade-King's hall a certain scholar who eagerly pursues this problem.'

'In that case we must relinquish this matter,' continued the aged voice, 'and hope that while it is looked into, my wayward son takes no doomed action, or is persuaded to refrain by those his scholars who could have influence over him. Which leaves us with our final problem. I hear from the daily reports that nothing has been seen of Wo Long Wang in the kingdom. The whereabouts of the Weaver-Girl: these cannot be known, and we must trust merely to the dragon's mercy. Yet through all these dire things I am worried about my son, the effects on him of these troubles. I suspect him of further wayward acts, perhaps even greater in folly, and I fear for his mind turning in distracted mazes. Will you not go yourself, Mandarin Wu? Take the news of our peach-feast to the heaven. But spy on the Jade Emperor and study him. Then bring me report of your impressions of the state of his mind, for truly I fear with the dragon loose things might threaten.'

'I will, great queen,' said the mandarin bowing low, and backwards he withdrew from the tranquil presence.

But to the heaven of Kun Lun Shan, whither the mandarin went, had already come the great sage-gods, for Confucius and Lao zi swaggered, beaming and nodding about, basking in the glory of the recent victory. And they had come to heaven dressed in their best robes, with beards combed and perfumed most regally, and about the courtiers of the Jade-King they triumphantly went, smiling at those who did not seem to share their confidence. And thus they entered the galleries and gardens of the palace, and at last found the Chamberlain bustling.

And Confucius smiled upon the Chamberlain and said, 'Good day, my lord. All in the imperial palace is bustle I see, as usual. This is as it should be. Assign proper rôles with the rites. Provide unity with music. Indeed it is fitting that all should be busy in the palace, when we by following the system have yielded the victory.'

And Lao zi laughed at this and said, 'Ay, thus it flows! Though ritual is indeed but the husk of faith. But we have been busy and our work has been granted a harvest, and truly I think our determination has been well paid. For when a disciplinarian acts and no one responds, then he rolls up his sleeves and gets on with it. Will the Emperor be in court this morning? We wish to pay our respects. And no doubt also he will be wanting to thank us.'

But the Lord Chamberlain looked at them and said, 'Dear sages, you are merry. But I tell you all is not merry here. For this Emperor you talk of glibly, thinking to have his thanks, he seems in no mood for thanks or anything. Have you not heard what occurred upon earth, have you not heard of the dragon bringing Zhi nu to Tai Shan? The Jade-King had his daughter returned, but the dragon flew off with her again, and the horrible occurrence, it seems, has unhinged him! Ay, the Emperor sits strangely, all wrapped in a great white shawl, murmuring of all kinds of madness. He will indeed come to court today, but if it is anything like before, all of us are likely to have a baffling time.'

Now as they were speaking on the verandah by the garden, where the spirit-butterflies were fluttering happily, there glided into the peony courts among the bees and chrysanthemums, Mandarin Wu, looking discreet and unruffled. And when he saw the great gods talking, he smiled at them from afar, and seemingly floating, brushed towards them through the garden. And a cat came stalking from among the tiger-lilies, and rolled on its back in the gravel of the path, and the Mandarin Wu stopped to stroke it, and came on again cultivating an air of casualness. And when he was with the sages, he nodded at them and greeted them, and all of them looked again to the Chamberlain.

'It is good to see you, Mandarin Wu,' said the Chamberlain then, hurrying on, 'for as I was telling these great deities all is not well here. The Emperor as you know is stricken by this latest blow, and he grieves hourly for his restored and again-lost daughter. You must have passed the halls he is using to send forth messengers to seek. He goes in there every hour and asks for news of her. He has a thousand scouts searching all about the Central Realm,

attempting madly to discover the new whereabouts of the
Weaver-Girl. But all the suspense and anxiety are playing
upon his mind, and we fear now, he is turning to other
measures. Indeed he murmurs on about the Shang, and
talks of fighting the dragon. And he wears this strange
white shawl, and looks like a ghost. But you must come and
attend his court, and see what you think, for soon he will be
in audience.' And the Chamberlain worriedly darted away
on his business, and the three gods looked at each other
puzzled.

But the idle morning warmed on in the courts of heaven,
and the court ladies yawned and stretched on the terraces.
The little dogs were woofing happily at the girls who played
with a ball, and the studious lass read her scrolls beneath
the magnolia. The gods went strolling. They doubted the
Chamberlain's concern, and they passed beside the rows of
lavender smiling. And thus they mounted the gallery steps
and came to the ante-rooms, and joined the courtiers waiting in the Emperor's throne-room. And the Emperor
approached at last, wearing his strange shawl, and his face
had a strange look upon it.

Now when the Jade Emperor had swept into his throne-
room, and sat on the wide throne of the empire of Kun Lun
Shan, he did not begin by greeting the sages directly, but
instead bowed formally to them from his seat. And Confucius and Lao zi kowtowed to the mighty Emperor, and
raised their faces again in beaming and glossy confidence,
and at last the scholar Confucius, tall and dignified in his
twyform hat, looked about the court with satisfaction, and
began to speak.

'Ten Thousand Years,' he said, 'great one of our phrase
"beneath the foot-stool", with gratification and great relief
do we come to your court this day to make report. For the
things upon earth have suffered a brightness, the revolution of destiny has lightened, and joy is our tidings, the joy
of a great victory for the Southerners and for all of us that
love the Middle Kingdom. In Shou chun by the Fei the
forces of the rebels, the rabble sharked up by the Tibetan

160

braggart and usurper: these have been put to flight, the regiments decimated, the monarch himself driven to flee alone and starving. And thus do we answer the challenge made by barbarians to the true descent and legitimate rule of the Jin!' And Confucius stared about him, proud and stable, breathing forth the air of a gentleman of the *Analects*.

And then spoke Lao zi. 'High Emperor,' he said, 'lord of the heavenly mountains, what my learned friend here has said, this is all true, and far be it from me to contradict it. But the greater significance of this victory of the South is that it is not just that of civilisation against barbarity. But the followers of the Buddhist faith, the piglike Tibetans with their wizardry, these religious impostors have finally been given the lie. So let us no more have do with them. Banish the faith forthwith. And let us return to our own streams and mountains.' And Lao zi broke off abruptly, and sat on the floor, and the mandarins inclined and smirked to each other at the eccentricity.

'My noble gods,' said the Jade Emperor, 'your speeches would have moved me to tears, if I did not know that every word in them rings hollow. You boundless hypocrites! Have you not fooled me all the time, ay, here in my court, persuading me against Guan yin? Do I not know now the truth of it? Ay, you may well stare amazed! I know what you are, a couple of traitors! You plotted with Guan yin against my power. You knew of her stealing the lovers! Ay, you knew she was the one who sent them to earth! And to fool me you both pretended to oppose the march of Buddhism! A very clever ploy, I assure you! Masters both, I have summoned the gods. I have decreed a great council at the peach-gathering. There I will accuse you before all the pantheon of your plotting against my throne.' And the Emperor scowled at them, and they stood amazed, trying to understand what he had said.

But in the baffled silence that greeted the Emperor's speech there could be heard steps coming along a corridor. And the Emperor looked up, eager to hear if it was some

161

news of the Weaver-Girl. But instead there came in a scholar with a bundle of ancient bamboo books, and the scholar did not notice the strained atmosphere of the throne-room, but instead kowtowed to the emperor, and dropping open the clattering bamboo, was about to speak.

'If you have news of Xiang,' said the Emperor, 'say on. Where is she hidden? Where has the dragon flown with her? I am surrounded by these traitors, but I shall accuse them at the council, ay, when the time of peach-gathering comes I shall accuse them. They know of Guan yin's plot. Why were they so interested in this poet Nai? They said they were keen on him because of his fair hair! How could anyone believe such nonsense! Oh, deep are these dragons. But I shall be a dragon too. Ay, you may think I am mad, my deities. But I have put it in train. I have a sorcerer coming soon. From Lao zi's own heaven. I will become a raging dragon just like Wo Long Wang, and I myself shall snuff out Zhi nu's whereabouts. I shall not let her hide away, to slip out when it is calm again, and resume her lusts with that rabid poet Cowherd.'

'It is about that that I wished to speak,' suddenly said the scholar, who was still standing impervious to the Emperor's sternness. 'As I said I would, great Jade-King, I have consulted the books, and have found confirmation of my opinion. The Duke of Zhou did speak a prophecy related to the Cowherd. What the prophecy was I have yet to discover. But under the circumstances, I would advise you, Ten Thousand Years, to exercise caution in your treatment of Nai, the poet. For if he is an incarnation of this man of the prophecy, we should all be careful what we do with him.' And the scholar finished his speech smiling, and rolled up his bamboo book, which made a clattering back under his fingers.

But the Emperor rolled his eyes about, and looked madly around, so that many in the court gazed askance at him. And he murmured, 'When I am a dragon, I may do what I will do. A dragon does not heed prophecies. I will snuffle about the world doggedly, and smell her out. I will seize on her and bear her off to my heaven. Ay, that's the way to act in this. Too long I have sat idly on a throne. When one is surrounded by plotters, it is best to strike quickly.' And the Emperor was about to get up and stalk off from the room, when he started, noticing once more the two philosophers.

And the Emperor cried out, 'What, are you two still here? Have you not been led off into the dungeons? Why no, we are to wait for the peach-feast, when all the gods will be together, and there we may debate these serious matters. They tell me that the gods are all summoned and there is to be debate about the future of Buddhism in our kingdom. Well, we will have you all thrust out: Buddhists and Confucians and Daoists! Make a clean sweep. Then I will be a true Emperor. And yet I may be a dragon then. How will I preside as a dragon? Well, the King of Tai can do it for me. And do not all you stare at me! You will stare well enough, when I am come as a serpent to sting you!' And the Jade-King then turned his back, and wrapping round him his great silver robe, he slithered off from the throne and away down the corridor. And dismay and amazement held all who watched him go. And Confucius and Lao zi gazed ash-faced at the Chamberlain.

Chapter Eleven

But Nai, while his case was being debated in heaven, was sunk in the oblivion of sleep. And when the morning advanced, and his dreams began fading, he had yet the joy of sleeping still. But when he came to wakefulness, after a short pause, the sickening blow of reality fell on him, and he lay in giddy nausea, drained of all strength, wishing to fall into a pit of oblivion.

He lay there in weakness and bitterness. Weak was he in mind, for sickness and loss were at him. Since the day of the battle, all his joints had been wracked with pains, and a sickness had crept into his stomach. Never was there a time now when he did not feel a numbness in his nerves and a sense of nausea. His fortunes were at their lowest. Everything had been lost, and the very world was made of weakness.

Yet bitterest in the midst of him was the thought of Xiang. What terrible fate had overtaken her? He had searched the site for bones, but of bones were there none. He had searched the lakeside for her body. Body was there none. He had sought among the soldiers. He had dogged that day and the next and the next with searching. All prisoners he had watched over, all witnesses of the foe, each soul that he could he had questioned for trace of her. Nothing had he found. Yet what cruel fate had taken her? A greater nausea came to even think of it.

Nai got out of bed. Stiffly he rose. He hobbled across to wash himself. His fingers and his toes were cramped, his joints were aching. He wrapped his hair up in his scholar's top-knot. He put on his grubby robe. He let the light in through the screen, and went in the shafted sunlight to his low table. He sat on the mat, rubbed his ink-stone with water, prepared his pointed brushes, then returned to the lines he had written the night before, read them, and looked up unsatisfied. He hobbled to the shelves where his own works were piled high: heap on heap of unread manuscripts. He shuffled through the papers with numb, shaking fingers and got out a work of strange lettering: some slokas from an Indian text, which Nai believed were a fragment of a Hindu epic. He returned to his desk and frowned at the text, seeking to imitate more accurately its strange metre. For seven years Nai had worked on this new scheme. He did not want it to be a secret.

Nai put down his pen. 'Ah, the serpents are strong now!' he sighed. 'How can I deal with this terrible weakness? Sometimes I think that with their poison inside me, I will go mad with frustration! Outlawed by these pedants! Yet the pedants are the serpents. They seized me and pulled me under. When the Emperor favoured me, they could no longer ignore me, but now I am again out of favour: barred from the court because of my indignities in the battle, racing around, the General's nephew, in a dressing-gown! With my books thrown out of the palace again, I will never be able to hunt and catch the Great Tale! I should go on that pilgrimage. In India they would understand, and I could learn the true mastery. Yet how can I go anywhere? I am too weak to work even. I fret myself into decrepitude!' And Nai broke off, and put his head in his hands, and wept, 'O Xiang, Xiang, where are you?'

True Pearl came in now, and brought her master some tea and some fresh charcoal for his stove. As she busied about, she stared at him anxiously, for he sat still with his head in his hands. She put the things ready and then went over to him and said, 'Master, don't grieve for ever. Xiang may be gone and you may be cast out from the court, but it's not the end of the world. You sit here at your books all day, struggling with these stupid verses, trying to write things no one understands. Why don't you go out to the courtesans again, like you used in the old days?'

165

But Nai shook his head and said, 'Oh, True Pearl, don't nag me. What heart have I for that life any more? It was so shallow anyway, just as was the life in the court. The Emperor didn't really understand my stories. I was for them a kind of fool. They thought my ideas were fantasy, and anyway now I have not the strength to play that game any more. I have hardly strength to live. And yet still there is so much to do, so many questions, a whole world of asking and making. Yet what can I do here? There is no one to tell me these things. There is no one to talk to. They are all in India.'

'Oh, India, India!' said True Pearl. 'Always India! Why don't you go to the wretched country? What do you think you'd find there if you went? The people there would be just the same as here! You have got a mad idea that the Indians write these epics you talk of, and that Indians alone will teach you about them. But it's a whole life away and – what? Oh dear! O master, why can't you just be normal? When things fall apart for you, all your friends hold their breath: it looks as if at last you'll settle and become human. But what do we discover? Behind all these idiocies there is an even greater idiocy lurking! Can't you have any normal thoughts? Don't you want to be normal? Listen, I've got a piece of news for you. Guess who has come to the compound to see your uncle? Your old friend Wei! Isn't that amazing?'

'Wei!' said Nai eagerly. 'So he has come here! Oh, then at last he'll visit me! What does he want with my uncle? Well, perhaps it is some military task. Wei distinguished himself so well in the battle. No doubt my uncle is going to give him a higher command. He might even be made a General. Just think how Wei has risen, while I have sunk! It's a terrible warning to all poets. Join the army straight-away, whenever there's a war, and don't be caught in your dressing-gown! But it would be good to see him. It has been so strange, not being able to contact him. What has happened to him, True Pearl?' Nai stared at her sadly, but True Pearl stopped herself from replying.

She went to Nai's bed then, and began to tidy it up, while he sat still dreaming among his manuscripts. She smoothed his embroidered counterpane, and set his head-rest straight, and she slid back the screens to let in the sultry air of summer. She took out a little mat, and shook it in the yard. Nai felt so comforted by her movements. It was strengthening to feel her vigour helping him, while he felt so weak. There was a knock on the door, and True Pearl dashed up to answer it, and thus did she usher in Wei.

Nai jumped up to see his old friend, and ran and took his hand, and led him into his chamber. True Pearl was despatched to fetch more tea and rice-cakes, as Nai hurriedly tidied and prepared himself. The friends decided to take their refreshment on the terrace, so they went outside into the sun. And in the courtyard the victory banners still hung proclaiming 'Salute the Emperor! The Jin vanquished the Illegitimate!' The lanterns still hung among the thick, healthy leaves, as the comrades smiled and gazed at each other.

'I am come,' said Wei at last, 'first to ask your forgiveness for so long an absence, and secondly to tell you my good news, which will, alas, mean an even greater absence, for I fear, my old friend, who I have hardly seen for months, we are soon to be parted much more lengthily. Wherefore, my dear Nai, I hope we can part on good terms, in spite of my not visiting you for so long.'

Nai looked at Wei in friendly fashion. He was to assure him this would be so, but somehow he could not think of anything to say. But then returned True Pearl and brought them a little meal of sweetmeats with some fresh tea on a low lacquer table.

'My news,' said Wei eagerly, when they had begun sipping, 'is that I have been given an ambassadorial mission. While I undertake it, I am to hold the rank and to have the full trappings of ambassador. A ceremonial carriage, and guards and servants, all these will be mine for the journey, and I am to go to Chang an, the old capital, and beyond that Westward along the Silk Road. My mission, you see, now that the wars are done, is to seek to normalise relations between us and the usurpers, and yet to claim back with some of the command achieved by victory some of the traditions they have usurped. It is almost forgotten that when the imperial court fled South, there was left behind much ceremonial accoutrement. I am to demand the return to the Emperor in the South the oracle-bearing Grand Tortoise!' Wei looked at Nai brightly, and Nai nodded his head, as if deeply impressed by this image.

'My mission beyond that,' then continued Wei, 'is to travel West far into the state of Liang, and there with the governor, who is still in the Northerners' command, negotiate for the opening of the Silk Routes. With the turmoil of these times the old trade-routes which brought so many things of luxury much valued by the Emperor, these have been closed, and after this splendid victory, it is time to claim some of these great things back. That will be my embassy then. First to Chang an, and then to the furthest edge of Western China.' And Wei sighed satisfied, and sipped more tea, gazing on the spoils of victory.

'Well,' said Nai at last, 'these things are well deserved, for no one has worked harder or more faithfully than yourself. And though I'm sad to hear you are going to so distant a place, yet I am overjoyed that Wei has received his deserts. Your conduct in the battle shows that you can be fearless and punctilious at fulfilling orders, and in this great mission to bring South the Grand Tortoise, I'm sure these qualities will achieve success for you. Why, when you return to Jian kang, you will be a grandee. Perhaps a governorship will not be so far away. Wei, I am delighted, and indeed all this explains why you must have been so busy in these last few months. But listen to me, old friend. Seeing you again has quite buoyed up my flagging spirits. What do you say we go to the tea-houses of the town, and enjoy ourselves there with the girls of the Red Dust Mansion? If you remember, last time I left without paying for you. This time at least you won't be caught short!'

But Wei looked embarrassed and said, 'No, I must be

168

getting home. There are many preparations for this mission. And I have many things to see to of a gravity which would not put me in the right mind for a tea-house. I know I have been no friend of late. I have been caught in many concerns, and for a while, Nai, it was not good to be seen in your company. But I will hope to call again before I leave, and then perhaps we can dine properly together.'

But Nai hurried on. 'Yet let me come and visit you,' he said. 'That would be less pressing. Just tell me now where your new house is. I have been unable to visit you, since you moved from your old dwelling. I went gaily round to it, but found it all deserted. Let's do that, my friend. Then you don't have to trouble.'

But Wei still looked anxious. 'Perhaps that might not be wise at the moment,' he said sadly, but then brightened up. 'Oh, I know what I wanted to ask you. On my mission to Chang an, I am supposed to seek out Wang Zhia, the court astrologer. Someone suggested that I should take him a celebratory ode, written in the grandest manner. I thought of you immediately: you know about these things: you could recommend someone. I want someone really first class, who understands poetry. Is there any one in the Begonia Club who could help me?'

Nai stared at him, pained. At first he thought he was joking, but then he saw Wei meant it. He did not know what to say. 'I'll let you know if I think of someone,' he muttered at last, showing Wei out. Then plunged in gloom, Nai watched Wei walk off across the gardens of the compound.

Nai stood there and thought, 'They don't understand me, do they? They all think I am joking! Even my friends think I do all this idly, out of a whimsical interest. What does one have to do in this world to be taken seriously? Show is everything! Pompous looks and words, and everyone thinks you are a genius!' Nai returned to his books.

But True Pearl came into him, and stood for a while staring at him. 'I was listening to your talk,' she said at last. 'And I couldn't help noticing you weren't issued with an

169

invitation to his lodgings. Wei lives in Azalea Avenue, in a shop directly opposite the Inn of the Wild Pony. He's got a woman there. That's why he's never asked you round. A really beautiful girl, who takes in embroidery. I never told you this before, because I thought he was trying to hide her from you.'

In the heaven of Xi tian, the home of the goddess of mercy, the Taking-Away-Fear Buddha, the summer came on with its milky-blossomed lilies, and its swans that flowed proudly with their bosoms in the lake. The delirious bees went hovering over the waters, fell swooning into the lotuses, and the dragonflies darted and hovered over king-cups that were made of great pearls and solid gold. The mountain-fresh breezes wafted freely over the Pure Land, bearing the fairies with their joyful peals of laughter. But Guan yin amongst all this found she could not settle, as she sat on the silken carpet, spread under the coral tree.

'Alas,' she said sighing, 'how might I drink this nectar, when there on earth all is suffering? War and pillage, butchery and carnage, these have engulfed the people of Han. And all because of a dragon, a serpent called down from the heavens because of my own little scheme of help. Alas, alas, fairies, what misery we spread when we seek to right wrongs long forgotten! Yet I do not repent that. I do not repent the earthly creation of Nai and Xiang. Yet now she is gone again, stolen as I stole her, but by the very dragon who was sent to find her! What irony it is, my girls, that the Emperor's own beadle should be the very creature that turns against him. Have there been any new reports of the sighting of the dragon? Has any of my fairies reported seeing him?' And Guan yin looked round about, but none of them there had news, and they shook their heads.

But then winging across from the East a hot-faced fairy came, speeding immediately towards the jewel palace. But when she arrived there, the servants directed her on again, and the idle fairies about Guan yin watched her approach. By the time she came beside them, she was out of breath, and for a while could only look distracted and stutter, but then throwing herself down in front of Guan yin, she clutched her hand to her throat, and eventually could come out with her message.

'Great goddess of compassion,' she cried, 'flee, flee for your life! A terrible fate and ire and danger hangs over you. The Emperor of Jade is now angry beyond measure, and Confucius and Lao zi stir him up further against you. They want to outlaw you from China, plan to hold a council, debate to cast you out on the day of some sort of peach-ceremony. I didn't know what that was, but I hasted here none the less. Leave, sweet goddess. Leave this land before they come to you!' And the messenger went white-faced, and looked about her in fear, and the fairies about her whimpered in earnest.

But the goddess smiled sadly, and looked steadily on the fairy and said, 'Alas, my fairies, what trouble I have led you to, I, who poor mortals call on in their danger: "Great mercy, great pity, save from sorrow, save from suffering!" Surely now I could call on myself myself! Well, let happen whatever will happen. We can but follow our sense of righteousness. And if the Jade Emperor wishes to banish me, well, we will cross that bridge when we come to it. But now, my poor fairy-messenger, you are in need of compassion. Sit and drink this heart-returning nectar.' And she smiled on the emissary, and helped her to drink, and smoothed her hair softly with a gesture of loving-kindness.

But winging across from the West, bright in the summery light, a strange fairy, not of Guan yin's following, but with long pheasant feathers as a head-dress, came hovering towards the palace, delicately looking about, inclining her head courteously to see where she should go. And when she saw the goddess and her spirits under the scarlet boughs, she flew over to the coral tree, and bowed before the goddess, and at last raised her white-powdered face to smile at her.

And the strange fairy said then, 'All hail to Guan yin, goddess of mercy, hail from an unknown comrade. From an ancient and peach-laden court I bring you respectful greetings, and a long-delayed welcome to an ancient land, for I come from the orchard heavens, where the great Xi Wang Mu, the Mother goddess, the Queen Mother, heavy in years, lives in her quiet palaces, watching the springs go by, seeing all things, missing little.

'And Xi Wang Mu bids me tell you she welcomes you as a goddess. She is glad to see such female youth in Zhongguo. She treasures your brave advent here, and wishes you long stay, and intends to use her might to give you continuance. Wherefore she also wishes to greet you to talk more of these matters, and to discuss what needs to be done to win you favour, for she hears that soon at the peach-gathering festival, which is held in her own heaven, the gods of China are to debate the future of Buddhism. Whether Guan yin will be allowed to continue in their land, this will be the topic of their arguments. Thus she bids you come to her, and have good hope, for she is not without influence.

'But of a more urgent matter the Queen Mother wishes to consult you, for she has heard now of Xiang's recapture. She wishes to hear from you how it came about, and how it was the dragon once more seized her. For she has watched the dragon's progress from his seizing again of Xiang to his long romps and twisting about the Middle Kingdom, and yet she cannot spy in the gloom what he has done with the girl, where Xiang is now, what fate has taken the Weaver-Girl. And she wishes you to go to her, since she feels you also would want to try to settle this matter with her. In all then, goddess, Xi Wang Mu longs to meet you, and trusts that you and she can become allies. May I take her your answer?'

'More than that,' Guan yin replied. 'You may take me with you to meet this mighty Mother!'

But as the goddess wafted through the winds of heaven with the fairy towards the mysterious personage, Nai the poet stumbled madly through the streets of Jian kang, with ferment in his heart. The day was soft with summertime. The breezes rustled the willow trees that dangled over the green canals. But Nai seethed with fury, for from his anguished heart resentment and malice boiled in madness.

And Nai thought as he went along, 'Wei, my own friend, Wei! How he has sold out to these pedants! How he has sucked up all the smarminess of these courtiers, and plays the world and his friends so carefully! He didn't come and see me, because it was not prudent! I was not a man to be friends with. Did I think of that in his poor days? Oh, he is gone to the hoppers! He is all part of the mean, petty, bloodless, terrified, place-lusting hoppers! The big ones say jump: they jump that way. The big ones say jump the other. They jump that way too. They are grasshoppers, not men, and glossy, fat, complacent, dismissive slugs!'

Now Nai as he walked was buffeted by the crowds, yet did not seem to notice the people about him. He kept staring down at his hands, as if to shake away the snakes, but never did he see the serpents fully. He swayed as he walked along. Often in his movements, it would seem that his head was floating away from him. And the stiffness in his joints made him totter and go jerkily. But now he thought of Wei's other transgressions.

'And hiding in new lodgings, just because he found a girl! What does he take me for, a monster? Does he think I'll be after her? Gods, the girls I have put in his way! Why does he have to be so secret and deceitful? I will see what this paragon is like. Let me view this beauty! She will be some pious cast-off! But no, I hope she is good-looking. I do not wish him ill. Wei could do with a nice little mistress. But why be so unfriendly about it? Oh! well, people are mad. Why do I expect my friends to be otherwise? Should I turr back? Ah! Anyway, in my daze I have walked on too far.' And Nai stopped confusedly in the middle of his walk, and saw that he had missed the turning to Wei's.

As he doubled back now, quitting the road that would have led to the palace, he found himself walking by the canal again. He sadly thought of his first meeting with Xiang, when she greeted him, waving over the water. His heart burned with anguish and lamentation at the thought.

173

Surely this scar would never heal. He sighed. Why was he going then? He felt sad not angry. He had no quarrel with Wei. Yet as he stopped again confused, he still felt driven on, for he felt he wanted anyway to talk to someone, for his whole life of late had been filled with nightmares, so much so that he needed to test his sanity. He could talk with Wei of himself. Yes, he would do this. He could discuss with Wei his projected journey. All at once he stopped again. Wei's journey! His own journey! He had had a delicious idea. He could ask Wei if he could accompany him on his travel. In an ambassador's train, he could get to the West.

Nai walked on thoughtfully. He barged through the pedlars of a square. He came at last to the seedy Azalea Avenue. Children were guarding goats on the grass banks. He found the inn of the Wild Pony. There was a shop opposite. His heart leapt nervously. How would Wei receive him? Perhaps Wei would not be there. He paused at the door. A sense of fatefulness overcame him.

It was a pretty arbour. There was a chair by the door, and on the chair some sewing. A table stood against a wall with a pile of silks on it, all very artistically arranged by a bowl of peonies. It was soft and quiet. There was a faint smell of incense, and a tranquil, tender air after the hot bustle of the dusty streets. The street-noise sounded far off. A door stood before him to the rest of the house.

Nai knocked on this door. 'Wei?' he called. 'Wei? Are you there?'

There was no answer. But he thought he heard a rustling sound.

He opened the door. The room was screened by silky curtains, soft and cool as he put them aside. A small window gave a quiet light to a tidy bed, and over beyond, an alcove which was used as a kitchen. Again all was tidy. Flowers were set in makeshift vases. Bits of embroidery were pinned up as decorations. A screen in the corner had a scene of rocks and torrents on it, and spirits flying about on celestial pheasants.

174

'Anyone in?' called Nai again. 'Xie Nai has come on a visit. Is Wei there anywhere?'

There was still no answer. But Nai had the impression there were someone there. He suddenly angrily thought that Wei was hiding from him.

He walked into the room. He looked behind the curtains. There was nothing but darkness. He went over to the kitchen alcove. There was nothing there but sunlight falling on old plates and brass dishes. He strode over to the screen. He pulled a section of it round. A dress was moving in the corner. He pulled it further back. A frightened girl looked up at him. Nai was amazed at her beauty.

Nai sighed and stared at her. But then he said, 'I was looking for Wei. I've come to claim a favour. I was just checking he wasn't hiding from me. I didn't mean to sniff you out.'

She was standing up and straightening herself. 'It's I who should apologise,' she said. 'But I was not expecting a visit. I did not answer when I heard someone there, because I wished to avoid talking. When I heard you say your name, I was too ashamed to come out. We have nothing in this hovel of sufficient worthiness. Wei has just been in, but he has gone out again. I'm afraid he won't be back for several hours. Won't honoured Xie Nai revisit our contemptuous little home when we can make suitable preparations?'

Nai sighed and looked at her. 'Wei obviously doesn't want me here. But I came because I have something important to ask him. I want to presume on our friendship over this journey of his. I want him to let me come with him to the Silk Road. It's my only hope. I can't get there alone. So I have come to ask him.'

The girl started weeping. Nai looked at her puzzled. She sat down by the table and sobbed. Nai stood a while sighing, but then went across and leaned over the table towards her.

'What's the matter?' he said to her.

She looked up at him tear-stained. 'It's not because of your coming I am weeping,' she said. 'But as you have said,

Wei is going to Chang an and beyond. This is why I am weeping. I have lived with him so happily for several months now. It is sad to have to say goodbye.'

'Why say goodbye, though?' Nai said shrugging. 'Why don't you just go with him? He will travel as an ambassador. He will journey in all possible comfort, and I am sure you could stand it. Wei's days of poverty are over. He will have guards, and safe-conduct. Really, there will be no danger.'

'No,' she said. 'I cannot go with him. Now you know why I was crying. My name is Jen. I am sorry we haven't met before, but I would not let Wei bring you home. It is too humble here for people like you. But now alas, Wei will soon be rich also.'

Nai looked at her puzzled. 'Why do you say alas?' he said. 'So much seems to be hidden behind your words.'

She stared at him a while, but then gestured for him to sit, and sat with him in the quiet chamber. Then she sighed and said, 'Wei is a rich man. This is why I say alas. The story of Wei is much like a tale that has turned in a wrong direction. Wei was a poor man, and all his life he devoted himself to study for the examinations. Though not unduly brilliant, he made up for what he lacked in application and hard work. And the work he was engaged on became a life in itself: quiet, abstemious, unworldly. In fact this suited him, and it was more to his good that the posts he would gain by passing the examinations.

'When I came to stay with Wei, I saw him for what he was: quiet, pure, faithful. The world in fact did not attract him much, for in essence he was interested in the spirit. Just recently, while I was with him, he found great attraction in the faith of the Buddha. I was happy for him, for I saw this suited him, and was taking him inevitably towards becoming a monk. Do not be surprised at this. The circumstances of my life make this something I would not be jealous of. No, I was glad, glad that he was fulfilling himself, and moving towards the great extinction. It was indeed for me also something of a life's quest.

176

'When the wars came, because he was so dutiful, Wei enlisted and served in the cavalry. As bad luck would have it, he distinguished himself by being in the right charges at the right moment. The generals became interested in him. His talents became known. His ability at languages was bruited. In the fervour of new appointments which followed the great victory, Wei was given the grand commission. From the viewpoint of the now, Wei is a great success. He is on the path towards becoming a grandee. But from the point of eternity, Wei has, alas, embarked on a voyage towards waste and futility. And this is why I weep for him. Or at least in part, for I weep for myself also.' And the girl was silent, while Nai stared sadly at her, ruminating on what she had said.

'I can see what you say is just,' he remarked at last. 'Your sketch of Wei is correct. Though I would often take him about the lights of the city, yet I knew he was not really part of that world. We fool ourselves with such shows. It is not my world either. I also am myself when I sit among my books. Until about a year ago neither of us had had any worldly success. But then I received some, and lost it again, and now Wei has some also. And still you are right, for it is all but foolishness, and is achieved on the wrong terms. My success when I had it was based on my being taken as a kind of inspired and amusing fool. But that was a pretence on my part. I am not a fool. I am serious beyond comprehension. Which comes to the same thing. But a vain pursuit it is to seek your due of worldly glory. Yet when glory comes, it does not mean that suddenly its vanity possesses you. I cannot see therefore why you could not accompany Wei, and guide him still upon the path of the Buddha.' And Nai hunched his shoulders, and looked towards her brightly, thinking his solution was sound.

But she shook her head grieving. 'I can't,' she said. 'I can't. Don't question me, but I can't leave the cities. Here in the Southern capital, or there in Chang an, I can live safe among people. But out in the country, there is danger for me: there is death waiting if I step out. And so I cannot go

177

with Wei upon his grand embassy. And we must part, and he must fulfil his destiny.'

When Jen had finished this tale, she got up from the table, and turned aside, once more in tears. By the sunlit window, she wept into her handkerchief, her whole body shaking silent. Nai felt moved again, and going towards her, he put his arm around her to give her comfort. But she darted away from him, and stared at him disgustedly, her face showing amazement and horror.

'I'm sorry,' said Nai angrily. 'I only meant to comfort you. I didn't mean to be an ogre!'

'What's the matter with you?' she cried, staring at him.

Nai did not answer. He stood there, white-faced.

'No, I don't mean that,' she said. 'Your touch was so painful. It sent poison all over me.' She continued staring at him. 'It's as if,' she said, 'you were all hung over with serpents.'

Nai felt the hair on his neck rise. 'How do you know that?' he said, staring at her with horror.

'Yes,' she said. 'You see them. You know you are possessed. Come, sit down. Tell me what has been happening.' She gestured to the chair again, and Nai hesitating a while once more sat down opposite her by the window.

'You must tell me what has been happening,' she said. 'You are in a strange case. You are mortal, but demon fires attach to you. You have innumerable flames within you that drive you to seek for things, and the seeking and the driving sap your energies. Where did you come upon this madness? Where did you find these snakes? This is no ordinary possession. Do you know that you are haunted? Or do you think you are sane, and the rest of the world is mad?'

Nai looked at her and sighed. 'I have been seeing visions,' he said. 'I thought a goddess came to me, and a dragon. I have not mentioned them to anyone, because there is no one I can tell. And I can hardly truly say I saw them. I was caught in the wars by the Fei. The place where I stayed was burnt down. The girl I love was taken from me.

178

It seemed to me a dragon snatched her. It was a vision of vastness. The power of the stars seemed to sweep upon us. It seemed a goddess spoke to us also, and urged us forward. Alas, how we are led by celestial fancies! The fires of the enemy came. Ruin and grief disrupted. I have tried long to piece out what happened. I fainted in the rushes of the lake. My mind must have been crazed. My memory cannot retrace the reality. From that day turmoil and pain have seized me. She's gone from me that was my soul-mate. She's gone from me that came to me from the stars.' Nai shook his head.

Jen stared at him thinking. 'How old are you?' she said at last.

Nai looked at her, but then sighed. 'Thirty and some.'

She stared still at him. 'And how old this girlfriend? Is she the same age as you?'

'Not so old by six or seven years.'

Her eyes roamed his face. 'I have heard of your tales,' she said. 'Did Wei not say once you made a poem of the star-lovers?'

Nai nodded his head. 'I composed that poem just as I met Xiang. As it was in life, so was it in my poem. All the time I wrote, as things were happening in the made-up tale, so they would also find themselves in reality. It was a strange experience. It was almost as if we were both living in two different worlds.'

She stared at him for a long time. But then she sighed and said, 'Yet I am afraid I cannot help you. Go to the temple of Guan yin. There is a nunnery near the lake. Go there and pray to the goddess. You must not ask me any more. The goddess will guide you. And I will relay to Wei your message.' Jen looked at him impassively then. Nai was hurt and puzzled. But he saw that she had taken herself to silence.

When Nai came to the nunnery, he looked up at it gravely, so desolate was it now of Xiang. Through the slanted afternoon sunlight that dappled itself through the trees, he stared at the gateway with its carved screen. Once past its painted views, he stood in the quiet courtyard, and

179

all was silent and deserted. He went aside the mossy steps and moving through the garden came to the curving-roofed temple. The frescoes of the Pure Land, the paradise of Guan yin, glimmered through the smoke of the incense-sticks. Nai went in to the sanctum, and stood before the statue of the familiar lilac-robed goddess.

And Nai said, 'Great goddess of mercy, to your shrine I have come, sent by one who seemed to see into my destiny. From visions of you, pure spirit, and horrors attending them, and loss of Xiang, from these also I visit you. I stand before you, half-mad and hung with serpents, embarking soon upon a great journey. Is there some message you may give me, some word of my muddled state, before I leave this capital and country? For I am going Westward in search of the Great Tale. Can Xiang not return and come with me?' And Nai looked up sighing at the smiling face of the goddess. But there came no form of any answer.

It was a summer's evening. The sky hung deep above, the stars just being born. The jasmine in the corner, Nai passed in his home courtyard, sweetened the evening breezes, which floated up to the lanterns, and playing among the roofs of the capital, dallied on their quest of the horizon. Nai strolled among the flower-beds: delphiniums burnt so blue, it seemed as if something from the sky had fallen there. The stocks spilt their fragrance, and the heavy-lidded lilies hung spotted with pollen on their waxy tongues. As Nai passed the cedar tree, a sudden blackbird sung, echoing among the courts and red-painted terraces. The bats climbed in the golden sky, delicate and quiet. It seemed that the garden was full of messages. Nai went back to his room. The saffron light of evening filled it. He lay on his bed and fell asleep.

And as Nai lay sleeping, Xiang came into his mind, the image of her, white-faced and sober and chidden, and she whispered, 'Nai, Nai, look at me. See me even in your sleep, the wraith of that woman you once loved. I have stolen to tell you. Secrets there are beyond dreaming! Strange is here, but something bars me from speaking. Yet

180

this can I tell you. Take up the Fa xian pilgrimage. Go now to Chang an, and the Temple of Hung fu. Join the Buddhist pilgrimage, if you would see me again, to India. I can say nothing further. Beyond China. Hasten. Or else Hell lies waiting. There comes a time . . . but I must go now. Oh Nai, it is strange, beyond. Think of your old friend. Even in all this I miss you.' And thus did the image fade. And Nai awoke, and his heart roused at the limits that lay awaiting.

PART THREE

Chang an

Chapter Twelve

Now in the heaven of Kun Lun Shan and the Jade-King's palace among the mandarins there was consternation. For they ran this way and that discussing amongst themselves, and pondering the directions of each set of actions. And they clustered outside the Emperor's apartments, where the great gate was shut, and they gathered along the corridors to the throne-room. And busily they were talking, as Confucius appeared, puzzled from the direction of the audience-chamber.

And a mandarin went across to him and said, 'Great philosopher, it is true. The sorcerer is even now with him. Such an incident is unparalleled in the history of pantheons. Surely no good can come of it.'

'Indeed,' said Confucius. 'Yet we must consider the positive side. Still does the Emperor go forward with his duties. A strange scheme it is, I grant you. Yet it does not interrupt the usual progress of court business.'

But as they were talking, the gate opened wide, and a squat, mysterious figure came out of it. And the mandarins pointed, for this ill-kempt, long-haired man, whose fingernails were like claws was the Emperor's sorcerer. And as they watched the sorcerer go, Lao zi then arrived, and he laughed and greeted the magician, and together they talked a while, slapping each other on the back, to the horror of the whispering mandarins.

And Lao zi came up to them and said, 'He is an old friend of mine. His magic is impressive, but untrustworthy. I had him make a giant cat in Tushita once, and it left the mice and started eating my servants. But have you heard? It seems that Fu jian, the defeated monarch of the North, has at last made his way, starving, back home.' And Lao zi strolled about nodding, as though he at least were interested in what he said, for nobody else seemed to want to hear him.

But now there came forth litter-bearers of the Emperor's household, and they bore the palanquin of the Emperor, and the mandarins and all put their knees on the floor, when all of them stopped, seeing a monstrous sight before them. For the Emperor was brought forth now with an Emperor's head, and from his waist down a huge fat dragon body. Wherefore he looked like a great queen bee, and gasps of dismay greeted his appearance. But his face scowled at them, and he waved the way on, and proceeded still into the throne-room.

And when they had all come there, the Emperor did not ascend the throne, but stayed lying on his palanquin to address them, and he said, 'Now my people, you must not be alarmed at the sight of your king in such manifestations. The sorcerer has been with me, and assures me it will pass. Wherefore in a few hours I will have the true shape of a dragon. And I may moreover turn myself back into myself whenever I should wish merely upon thinking. And this way may I go seeking about the world, and returning each evening for the imperial audience. Continue with the business as usual. We hear the monarch Fu jian is returned, but now he is menaced by the Xien pi barbarians. It seems they are camped now not far from Chang an, and threaten the Northern capital with their presence. But do I see Confucius and Lao zi in our court? It is not yet time for you to answer the accusations.'

'Your imperial highness,' said Confucius, 'we have come here at request. It seems your attendants are concerned for your welfare. And as I look at my Emperor half turned into a serpent, I can, my Lord, identify with their fears. Yet also are we come, with news of the poet Nai, news which has disturbed us and may well others. My king, the threat of Buddhism grows. The barbarians stir on the frontiers. The danger of invasion is rampant. Is this time, my lord, to go disfigured about the world, putting your imperial majesty in danger?'

The Emperor smiled blandly at these remarks, and though the mandarins murmured in approval of Confucius's plea he said sweetly, 'When the sovereign's officers fail, he himself must take on the rôle of officer. What am I doing, but completing the dragon's task, finding my daughter, wherever she is hiding? And the Cowherd Xie Nai, I will seize him and bring him death, and pitch him into Hell, as I have bidden. I only delay from taking him, because while he is alive, he may lead us to Xiang's hide-out.' And the Emperor smiled easily, as he said these things, although all the court was chilled by such strangeness.

But once more into the court came, oblivious of the strained faces, the scholar who had come before, and he bore with him his bamboo books, and giving the Emperor a quick bow said, 'I have found, great king, the prophecy I spoke of earlier. The Duke of Zhou did make a prophecy concerning the Cowherd, and at last I have discovered its ancient record. It is in some obscure annals, and it says that the Duke of Zhou, soon after his translation to the heavens, was asked about the songful Cowherd and his idle ways, and thus did he make a gnomic pronouncement. "On the path the Cowherd treads will all China venture." He is said to have said thus to those who asked him. And so great Emperor, have a care where you should send the Cowherd, for the Duke of Zhou said thither will all China venture.' And the scholar was silent now, smiling on his bamboo, and he handed it up to the Emperor.

'Your majesty,' Confucius said now, coming forward in the court, 'this news comes as a mighty blow to us. For hear now what tidings I have brought concerning our friend the Cowherd, in his earthly manifestation as the poet Nai. For we have news today that Nai, after long dallying with the faith, and after long dismissing of my faith and my friend's, has decided to go the way of the Buddha, and leave the land of Zhongguo, and to travel with a Buddhist pilgrimage to India! What can this signify to us now with this prophecy?

187

What can this mean but the Westward march of China?'
And Confucius opened his arms at this, gesturing to the
Jade-King, while all the court murmured and gasped about
him.

And Confucius went on, 'Yet also, my king, before we
learnt of this prophecy, which prophecy also in fact makes
our task more urgent, my friend and I, in the interests of
Zhongguo, not liking to lose a soul, had decided to take this
poet's defection seriously. For we had determined – and
with this new news, how fortunate that we had, how good
for the nation and the Southern Empire! – for we had
determined, in spite of the grief, in spite of the trouble to
ourselves, in spite of our age and weary limbs and
exhausted spirits – new come from the wars, defeating the
rebels, holding up China's past, and rousing the traditional-
ists against the upstart Tibetan – we had decided to go again
to tread the paths of the world, merely to keep track on this
renegade spirit. Ay, lords, indeed, Lao zi and I are again to
visit earth, and will go along with Nai on his weary pilgrimage.' And Confucius looked round with stern, roused
face among those in the court, and watched as they nodded
their heads with approbation.

'All which I may say, O Emperor,' continued Confucius,
'might teach a lesson to yourself, of duty and martial vigour
and balance and discrimination.'

'Long live the great sage!' cried Lao zi sarcastically,
when Confucius had done his speech. But all now turned to
watch the Jade-King.

But the Emperor still read on the prophecy, studying it
with care, half-listening to the speech of Confucius below
him, and when he had come to the end of it, he put it down
in silence, and looked about the white-faced courtiers of his
throne-room. And he saw the two great sages bothered,
and the mandarins with worried frowns, and the scholar
with the bamboo also staring hard at him, and the Emperor
laughed and said, 'What is the Duke of Zhou? Here you
have a new dragon-emperor! Look, lords, how my scales
begin to quiver about my skin. See how my tail is growing

188

and advancing up my body! I am becoming a king of beasts, as well as a king of men. Power and magnificence are upon me. But why do you all stare at me? Get hence and call the King of Tai. Tell him to seize these all and take them to prison. Tell him to punish all the offenders who have conspired against my throne, and worked with the dragon to take my daughter. But let me get changing! Aiee! These claws fit me tightly, give pain! Aiee! How my hands are wracked with pinching!' And the Emperor shook his hands, and twirled about on his litter, and he began to roar and knot himself into weird postures.

But thus spoke the Lord Chamberlain, 'My lord, call the sorcerer back! He has put on you a ghastly spell and is shaming you. Cease from this beastliness. Return to yourself. Have a care of your empire and your servants. For how can we serve you thus, if you are transformed? Be patient and call but the sorcerer back again.' And the Chamberlain went up to his Emperor. But the Emperor hotly struck at him in the claw that held a mace, and fell back on his litter writhing and crying. And the Jade-King now gnashed his teeth, and a weird grinding noise came from them, so that all in the court were silent, listening to this rattling.

'Your majesty,' then said Confucius, 'your Chamberlain urges you well. Bide by his words and stay here and recover. For truly I and my sage friend, Lao zi, will once more to earth, and we will watch over Nai to see what follows. Great King, you cannot hound the poet and degrade yourself in this shape, for nothing will be achieved but your own shaming. We two will follow him as before, and seek to sway him from the path, and for the sake of the prophecy dissuade him from leaving China.'

'Go after him as you may,' said the Jade-king. 'But look now: I also go. See, I feel the scales now engulfing me. I feel the change of silver fires, dragonish flight sprouting at my back, and the snake's venom setting me lusty inside. It is a joy to feel this way. Take me quickly into the yard! Quickly up. I must seek the skies!' And the Emperor with a roar fell writing again on the litter, as the servants hurried once more to lift it.

But now running beneath the Emperor, as the courtiers groaned in horror, and Confucius stood hiding his eyes for shame, the servants took the twisting Jade-King into the wide-paced court, and they set him down fearfully in the air. Then did his body curl on itself, contorting like a snake, and hissing white mists came forth from his nostrils. And the Emperor's head grew, and snake-lips lined his mouth, and dragon's teeth chattered from his snout. And when the wings and feet had formed fully along his sides, then did he slide and creep upon the marble, till with a bound he humped himself up, and laughing in flight careered around the buildings. And the silver dragon with misty scales then cruised over the roofs, and soon was flown away into the sky.

But now Confucius looked at his friend and said, 'Alas, Ancient of Days, the things we have seen both on heaven and on earth! Does it not prompt you to think that this globe is but filled with lunacy, since always above it shed the beams of the moon? The Jade-King is gone from us. Down to earth he is gone to sniff again after his daughter, to seek where the dragon may be that has snatched her. Meanwhile, we go on a journey ourselves, to track the steps of a madman, seeking to persuade him to swerve from the path of the West. What times are these! The highest gods go bothering about the streets, and our own king seeks ultimate degradation. But come, let's on. A further study of shame lies before us, and we must down to the alleys of Jian kang.'

But Lao zi dallied, 'Wait a moment,' he said. 'This Jade-King's speech. Did he not say that Nai might lead him to Xiang? It seems to me therefore that as we go, we may not go alone, for the Emperor will also want to see where the poet wanders. Thus shall we go travelling: two old gods, in disguise at the side of a pilgrim, while back on the road comes sniffling and snuffling a silver dragon! We are mad indeed! But what, the world is made in such a fashion. All

190

the roads lead to the mighty Dao,' And the bald-headed
Lao zi cackled at this, and leaped up from the throne-room,
and hurled himself laughing into the deep-bosomed clouds.

And now soft-footed dawn came to the city of Jian kang,
stealing to the banks of the mist-hidden river. The birds
that filled the cassia trees spoke eagerly of her coming. The
cockerels hidden in the straw-filled yards broke up the
twilight's silence. In the palace of General Xie, the servants
rolled their beds up; they went with their weak lanterns
beneath the rose-flushing sky, and in the cool air of
daybreak they murmured to each other, as they shook forth
the sun-blinds and drew forth the carriage, ready for
another day of sluggish summer.

In the tender room of the poet Nai, the twilight stole
through the shutters, and in the haze the trunks and baggage appeared stacked ready and forlorn. The songs of the
birds pierced Nai's sleep. He awoke and remembered what
the day portended, and with a heavy heart in the bitterness
of dawn, he got from his bed and washed himself, and put
on his clothes, thinking that this was to be the last he would
see of his old home.

Now when all was ready, he called forth his servants, and
bade them steal forth with his luggage. Silently they moved
in the still-sleeping household, as the gold sunrise now lit
the curling roofs. The horse was brought forth, she was
harnessed to the cart, the baggage was loaded between the
high wheels. Nai looked with tears about the courtyards of
his home, and he rolled up his cloak for his journey into
autumn. The servants opened the side gate. Nai touched
the red-painted pillars. Then he mounted the cart and cast
a glance once more on the scene he was leaving.

'O sweet home of my idleness,' he said, 'home of my
protection, great stones and pillars of the mighty Xie, how
now shall I fare without you? What road do I now go on?
My loneliness and exile is now all about me. Hard and
bitter is the exile's path, when he journeys a winter landscape. Sweet courts, sweet gardens, kind servants, aunts

and uncles, now in secret Xie Nai bids you adieu, that have for so long to his pranks been indulgent. Alas, how suddenly this has fallen upon me! How wild and strange is my departure! Yet to seek the Great Tale do I go forth into the world, and perhaps a while the spirit of Xiang will guide me.' And such were his thoughts, as Nai went under the archway, and waved farewell to the weeping servants.

As Nai creaked down the street, the avenues were already stirring with shopkeepers setting up their stalls. In the haze of the morning light, the umbrellas were hoisted up, opening like flowers. Nai went towards the great crossroads. He crossed a green canal where the folk in the barges were stirring. A baby was wailing, and a mother was crossing a plank-bridge, tottering on rush sandals from the shore. The inns with their tables and benches seemed to be waiting for people. A man with a yoke balancing two baskets trotted beneath Nai, disappearing under his straw hat. And so Nai came to the Imperial Avenue, and the road that led to the ferry Northwards.

But as the poet came to the widespread crossroads, and the road that would take him towards the foreign realms, he saw some horses standing with men on them against the sun, and he saw pack-horses and servants and a chariot. And the two horsemen stared at him, as though waiting for him to come along, so that his mind fancied fearfully it boded ill for him. And he searched about to think of some reasons to explain his going in a lone cart with luggage on a summer morning.

And a deep voice cried out to him, 'Xie Nai, where go ye in the dawn? Why does the poet have his house on his back? You have come now to the crossroads. Which way is it that you will take? To the imperial palace of home or North towards the frontiers? You recognise my voice, I think? Your old tutor Kun? And this beside me is the mad monk Lun himself. We go towards the ferry to leave Jian kang for the North. To the kingdom of Chin we go and the ancient capital.'

Now when the dull Nai had heard these words, he could

not believe his ears, and he stared for a while at the two shapes high on horses against the sunbeams, and indeed he saw it was Kun and Lun as had been said. But then he said, 'This is a strange meeting, come so early in the day. And how should it be you two go on such a journey? For indeed I purpose to hie to the great Chang an. But surely it cannot be that Fate has meant us to journey together? What, my old tutor and monk, of cantankerous memory? Oh, are we to debate again, as we rattle along the road? Has heaven awarded us this bounty on our leavetaking?'

But Confucius did not reply to him, but jerked his horse to start, and led his own party from the crossroads, and so did they ride together, long shadows now to their left, and take the river-road by the wall and the gardens. And they came to the Yang zi, where the fishermen were launching their boats, poling themselves out to fade in the river-mist. And they joined the yawning porters, and the farm-wives at the quay, and the lugubrious man with the curtained booth of his puppet-show. And the crowds began to stir, as out of the sky it seemed the ferry-boat approached, sideways floating.

Now when the carts were loaded on the ferry, Nai stood about anxiously, gazing back to the town. And the bell was clanged then to signal it was time to go, and he was called by Confucius and Lao zi to embark. But then there was a bustle by the customs-house and innyard, and thronging servants came and guards on horseback. And a mandarin's carriage with flags and banners flying rattled now splendidly towards the ferry. And Nai went forward happily, and he waved his hand to Wei, who dismounted from his horse and took his hand. And together they talked on the quayside as the things were loaded, while Kun and Lun looked on impressed.

But when the ambassador's things were loaded, and the carriage in all its splendour, with curtains closed, deep-hung and mysterious, Wei took Nai towards it, and opening the curtains, showed him that Jen after all was travelling with him. And Nai exchanged greetings with her, as she sat

193

there timidly, and she kept a reserve in his presence. But when Wei was gone she said, 'Yes, I am coming too. For his sake, I am to brave these troubles. But once we are on the other side, in this carriage I will remain, enclosed and curtained for the whole journey. Be good enough to leave it so. If I step forth in the country, there is death. Do not, I pray you, seek me to leave the carriage.' And Nai nodded, gazing at her, the mysterious maiden. And then the ferry put off from the shore.

But as the ferry approached the further shore, the two disguised gods, Kun and Lun, stood leaning on the rail, watching the North come towards them. And Lao zi said, 'Well, the travellers are assembled. Ambassador Wei is a welcome escort. But now what's going to happen? Before us are the wild ways of China, and a long road we must crawl upon her bosom. But will we win this poet from his journey? Will we dissuade him from his faith? Will we turn back the march of China? Ha, old fellow, my learned friend, you've got a tough task ahead of you!' And the gods watched the approaching bank with sobriety.

Chapter Thirteen

Now the journey of the travellers commenced in brisk style, for upon the opposite shore were all hopeful. With cheerfulness they clattered down the wagons onto the banks, and with vigour got ready the grand procession. The proud Wei gave orders to his guards, his grooms, his servants with their carts and carriages, an impressive party. Nai hitched his humble cart to his horse, a solitary voyager, and poor, beside the rich ribbons of the ambassadorial carriage. And so did the travellers make off into the North, with Kun and Lun riding at the rear and watching everything.

At first the land they rattled through together was easy, flat and fertile. As the mists fled, the paddy-fields were revealed, green and chirruping with frogs. Beneath the flaglike palm trees the chariots trundled, and among the thickets of rustling bamboo. The parrakeets swooped over the farms with their soggy fields, embankments and wicker gateways. All China hummed. Ordered were the ways of men, and the female overcame the male with stillness.

But that night when they came to the market-town of Nanchao, it was difficult to find an inn to accommodate them, for there was a sale of horses that had brought farmers from all around, and the inn found room only for the ambassador's party. Kun and Lun were forced to sleep in a dilapidated annexe, and Nai had to make his home in the stables. And as he went to bed that night through the dewy garden, the cool evening air made him melancholy. For this was the very inn he had stayed at with Xiang, when they had stopped on the journey towards Shou chun.

But when he came to the stable, and sat among the hay,

he sighed and said, 'How different is this journey! When I was last here, I laughed before the wars, and Xiang, my sweet companion, was with me. Now I am alone again, too poor for the good rooms, and sickness crazes my wits and my body. O Xiang, Xiang, how bleak it is now that you are gone! How life is dull, unlighted, unfunny! Oh, will I live in happiness ever again? Each day the pain comes stronger and stronger. And yet I make my destined journey. The vision of you urged me on. We can but make our actions and have hope.' And Nai lay down sighing in the brittle straw, and sleep soon took him.

Then in the depths of sleep, Xiang came to him again, her image, hovering faintly in his slumbers, and she looked at him, white-faced, and called with a distant voice, 'Nai, Nai, can you still hear me? I am fading, alas, from you, my love. No longer can I live in your dreams. The inevitable distance of life prevents me. Yet herein let me warn you, Nai. Beware, beware of dragons! For there is a serpent still snuffles after. Beware, beware of his snaking pace, beware of his scaly eyes. Oh! Flee, my sweet, flee speedily beyond the Middle Kingdom! Have good courage therefore. Persist in your hope. For in Dun huang, beyond the border, is reunion. Farewell, my sweet, farewell.' In tears did the spirit cease, and it seemed a great stretch of waters came between them.

But the next day as they rattled along, the two old disguised gods decided to begin their assault on Nai, and so Confucius rode near and said, 'Well, we have lots of time to chat, as we roam through the centre of the Central Kingdom. You must tell me and my friend here, Nai, what takes you to Chang an. You did not mention this journey when last we were with you. Are you fleeing your disgrace at court, or perchance on a secret mission? I only ask because we have heard absurd rumours, for some of your servants said you had become a follower of the Buddha, and were thinking of beginning a Buddhist pilgrimage to India?'

And Nai looked at Kun, and nodded as he said this and said, 'I am India-bound indeed.' And the poor old scholar

196

nearly fell off his horse with the suddenness of this blunt reply.

But Lao zi was enraged and cried, 'Has disgrace turned your brain? You can't be serious about such mumbo jumbo! Has there ever been anything crazier than this faith of vegetable fools, whining and snivelling after extinction? Are you a man or what? A little trouble at court and you seek to run out of the country! Go into the hills by all means. Contemplate the Dao. But why hurry off to a land of brown barbarians?'

But Nai shrugged his shoulders and said, 'Well, say what you will. That is my destination.'

And Lao zi now looked with eyes popping out of his head, and even the horse stopped in astonishment beneath him.

The travellers wound their way forward, and the hills came now upon them, winding their paths through clustering woods and outcrops. The coloured carriage creaked on the tracks, climbing the green hillsides. The horsemen glided beneath the branching chestnuts. Wei came alongside now, and they talked for a while, the horse nodding its tassels by the cart. And the stream from the misty heights clattered among its boulders, and the stag looked up amazed at the procession.

The afternoon was waning, as they crested the top of the range, and the sun-gorged grass and flowers smelt ripe and lazy. Nai in his cart was lagging behind now, and some way up the slope were Kun and Lun whispering together. It was quiet in the woods, and at their back the evening mists were forming in the lowlands, as though to engulf those that rode in the rear in a great sea of oblivion.

When he came to the place where the road turned a corner, and the view behind would be shut from them, Nai stopped the cart a while, harkening to the others rattling into the distance away from him. He turned then and looked, to take a last glance at the country where he had been happy with Xiang. But the mists were engulfing it,

197

glittering river and orchard, seeping away the bases of the hills.

And then Nai noticed that the mists were sliding after him, snakelike, brimming in the valley. And they wound towards him like a silver serpent, congealing its body from vapours. The forest was all about him silent. In the dusky light, he thought he saw the head of the mists rear up at him. Most like a dragon it was. Nai turned round in fear, and whipped his horse briskly after the others.

But that night at a tree-ringed farm-house, that gave them rustic shelter, beneath the slopes of Tai Pie Shan, they sat in the yard, eating their meal, as the summer evening sunk about the acacias. And as they looked forth idly, gazing into the golden light, they saw, casting up the dust of the road, another traveller coming, swinging along jauntily, with a pole and sack dangling from it. And the traveller came towards them, and stared at them quizzically in the half-formed light. It was a youth with tawny hair, and a gap-toothed grimace, and a brown face, cheery and cheeky, and he stood with one hand on his hip, pointing a finger at them, and counting the figures of Nai, Wei, Kun, Lun.

And when he had assured himself, the youth came up and said, 'My masters, you seem a sober lot, sitting dribbling there over your dinner, though one or two of the party has a certain intelligence or shrewdness at least in his eyes. If it happens you are travelling West along this road in the general direction of Chang an, perhaps I may accompany you, for you could be what I have been seeking, in my long quest for a promised prize. For I was told by a wizard once I would discover a great treasure, if I could but follow four honest men all together.' And the youth stood grinning then, eyeing the great and senile, nonchalantly waiting for an answer.

But Confucius answered him, 'Rash speech loses friends, and undermines the confidence of your superiors. It should be obvious to you that we have with us a person of ambassadorial rank, and yet you brazenly approach us *en masse* as if we were schoolchildren. You seem to be a boy still. You should speak scrupulously to your elders, and not give way to urges while your pulse is still unsettled. I have my own servant, thank you, as has my religious friend. And a person like yourself would bring shame on the ambassador.' And Confucius turned away then, haughtily from the boy, and nodded at Wei in gracious formality.

Now the youth pulled a face at the scholar Kun's rebuke, but did not seem unsettled by it. Instead he turned to Nai and said, 'What about you, ginger-top? You look as though you haven't got any servants. Us non-black-haired people of Han should stick together, you know, and I reckon I could be useful to you. I can run errands, and forget why I've been sent, deliver courteous messages abruptly, burn dinners, and pack things creasingly. But at least I have a go! So I reckon I'm just the lad for you. You look a bit of a misery who could do with cheering up. What about it then? Don't listen to old po-face. My name's Tawny.' And the boy stared at Nai, who at last chuckled and nodded his head.

The next day when they set off, the rain came down, and the roads were full of puddles. The high ones threw about them their oiled capes, but Tawny and Nai like the servants got out straw coverings, and as they rattled along, both sitting in the cart, they looked like two travelling haystacks. The boy still kept cheerful. He gave Nai a big grin from his melon-split and gap-happy mouth. He was always doing something: making a flute out of a reed, weaving a hat to go over the horse's head, hanging upside down with a block of fat, trying to cure a squeak in the cart. To Nai he seemed to be crawling everywhere. It made him feel sad, yet somehow comforted. They came to the ford of the River Fei.

When the old ones were over, and the guards were struggling with the carriage, which had got stuck in a rut in midstream, Kun and Lun returned to Nai's side as before, and stood by him staring out over the rain-prickled waters. And Lao zi said, 'How the stream flows for ever! It washes

199

away the blood of the battle. Men's clashes are soon forgotten in the highest good of water, that gives life to the ten thousand things. Can you really desert the land of Dao, where wisdom has met its balance, and go into the rash, uncivilised lands of the foreign devils? I think you will not. The place for the poet is alone among the hermitage hills and torrents.'

And Nai looked at him, and nodded his head and said, 'Indeed such a life would be ideal. But how can I settle for rest in a land where there is no place for me? I have tried to fit in here, but no one can see the worth of the things which I have always been pursuing. Sooner or later I must physically take the road, which my mind has always been on in secret. What beauty indeed have the hills and lakes of the Middle Kingdom! But in quest of the sterner mountains I must go beyond.' And Lao zi looked at him, puzzled and stilled by his resolve.

Now when they settled that night at the wayside inn, the innkeeper was impressed by his official party. Busily he bustled to look after the mandarin Wei, and Nai found himself with his servant stuck in a barn once more. He made his bed among the sweet hay, then went to the hostelry and tried to get in to supper. But the crush was so great that the innkeeper rejected him, and asked him to come back when they were less busy. He returned to the barn, and lay forlornly without his food, grieving again at Xiang's disappearance. But then Tawny came in jauntily, carrying a tray, and on it were rice and beans steaming.

And Tawny said, 'Come on, my mâster. Don't sit there glum like a pudding. You'll never get anywhere along the road to Chang an, if you languish about like a limp piece of celery. Eat up this supper I've brought you. Put spirit into your heart. What is all this mooning about anyway? Did you leave a nice, fat wife behind in a featherbed in Jian kang, or are you fancying there's someone else in it already? If you're going to be my master, you've got to be tough and true. So eat your beans and spill them.' And Nai gave a chuckle at Tawny's prattle, and began to eat hungrily.

Then at last he said, 'Little urchin, you are young, and you have not yet a man's heart in your breast. Little can you know of the affairs of love. But I, alas, am something of an expert. Women are like stars for me: they draw up my soul, and from their bosoms I breathe the air of the cosmos. And Tawny, in Jian kang not these three months ago, I had such a love of the constellations. Alas, I had not looked for it, but she was everything to me: sister of my soul and twin of my body. And we were bound together not in the chains of marriage but on life's unofficial highroad. But then she was snatched from me. I lost her in the wars, my friend. We were caught in the midst of the fighting. A bout of concussion and lunacy intervened to be my saviour. But she, she – where is she? I think I will search for my love, my sweet Xiang, for ever, and my soul will never rest without her.' And Tawny listened to this with all his ears, and for a while he stopped eating.

But then he laughed and said, 'Oh, my moony master! You're too old to be lovesick! You ought to be married now, and settled down, not having teenage love-affairs! Yet tell me about this wonderwoman? How did you meet her? To what did she owe her celestial character? I ought to warn you, master, that from what I've observed of the world, paragons are just biding their time till they're married. But come on, fill me in a bit: how did you encounter her? What did she do, this sweet, fair, virtuous jewel?'

'Another time,' sighed Nai leaning back on the straw. 'You will have to wait till you are older.'

The next day was fine again. The carriages clattered on through countryside washed with summer rains. The woods were loud with monkeys, and the pheasants gave their calls, as the guardsmen with their bows and lances trotted to the fore. In mossy dells they passed the century-tempered trees, pines whose trunks were gnarled and knotted, and the ferns in the sun smelt warm and rank, as the chariot-wheels crushed them by the roadside. Nai rode beside Wei. They spoke together. But the curtains of the carriage stayed tightly shut. Tawny watched at the back of the cart. Even he was pensive, as the miles rattled on towards the hills.

When they stopped for a noontide meal, they perched on a cliff, which overlooked the strange, twisted mountains. Again the rain seemed to be approaching, for clouds were formed on the peaks, and lazily the grey vapours drifted across the slopes. The ambassador's coach was out of sight with all its guards and servants. Yet Kun and Lun ate their meal near the cart of Nai. Tawny was leaning against a pine tree trunk, picking at the bark, which came off in flakes.

'You know,' he said, 'master, the countryfolk believe that old pine trees turn into dragons. You see these bark-flakes? They are already turning into scales. I'd give it a century, then, watch out. The serpent will pounce upon you. It's very dragonish weather, you know. All these clouds! A thunderstorm is dragons fighting. And then after a thunderstorm by dragon-haunted pools you find the red-cloud herb, all mysterious. It's a wonderful magic plant, formed from dragon-fight tempests. But I'm not sure what you do with it.'

Nai looked at him and laughed. 'O Tawny,' he said, 'you're an idiot. I must admit I feel quite upstaged. You undoubtedly make me merry though. And a merry heart is healthy. I swear I feel ten times better for you and this journey. Yet do not joke about dragons, boy. Your master has a great madness, and one of the symptoms is seeing dragons. Look at those clouds now. Could you not imagine a silver dragon forming amongst them?'

Nai pointed to the clouds now, and Tawny looked out startled, and he shrieked because there he could see a dragon. The billowing grey was lined with silver, and snaking up from the vales, it seemed to twist and undulate towards them. Tawny leapt up from his seat, for even as they gazed, a head with cloud-horns reared up before them, and a sunlight shaft of eyes seemed to peer at them menacingly, examining them for food.

Tawny ran over to Kun and Lun. 'Masters,' he called, 'help us. Look, there is a dragon coming after us. Save us, masters, save us!' And he pointed to the valley, where Kun and Lun looked, and got up from where they were sitting.

Now the two old gentlemen went suspiciously to the edge, and they peered out where Tawny was pointing, and they saw indeed a grinning shape, lying along the peaks, winding its camel-face round towards them. Whereat their faces darkened, and Lao zi fetched his hand into his robe, and he pulled out a fan, and shook it, pretending to fan himself. And the cloud hovered a while, but then seemed to lose its shape. And Lao zi clapped his fan back into his tunic.

But Confucius laughed and said, 'What, boy, do you have wild dreams? These are only clouds you see before you. Comrade Nai, have you been telling this imp of yours fairy tales? Can you not leave off spinning these absurd narrations?'

But Nai looked and said, 'No, Kun. I have told no tales for weeks. When I speak now, it will be truth embodied. But surely I think you two old men have a way with clouds. The phantoms of imagination flee before you.'

'Ay, keep your feet on the road, my boy,' said Lao zi returning to his lunch. And there was a pop as he pulled the stopper from his wine-flask.

Yet when the rosy evening had come, and the woods of buzzing summer had staggered home with their branches filled with honey, the travellers having found no inn, raised their tents in a clearing of the woods, with a fine view over the songbird valley. Tawny, after supper, sat with his master beneath their cart, while the smoke of their fires went up into the leaves of a chestnut tree. All the camp were quiet in their various tent-doors, so that the moon came up and peered at them over the hill's shoulder.

And Tawny said, 'Well, master, here are four men, leading your expedition, and from what I have seen so far they seem to be honest. But yet I have found no treasure. I wonder what my wizard meant? What sort of treasure was he intending? Yet surely, I think, this is a strange group and strange things stir amongst you. For take Wei for a start, riding boldly on his horse: why does he keep his carriage so closed-up? Anyone can see and tell there was a woman in it. What is he trying to hide and from whom?'

And Nai only shook his head at this and sighed. Wherefore Tawny sat with his brow still thoughtful.

'And then,' he said, 'we have also the mystery of these two old sages who travel with you. The one mad. I like him: he's a man after my own heart. But the other so pompous and so laid down with morals, you would think he was Confucius himself. But what do they here with you? Always they are questioning you, trying to probe and test what you believe in. What's the great attraction? You're my master, I know, but they dog you like you were some famous person. What's behind this, master?'

But Nai again shrugged, and could give no answer.

Tawny frowned at him and said, 'And then the other scholar. The great conversationalist, Master Nai: if only he would stop talking! Chatter, chatter, giving opinions on everything all the time! Why, it's difficult to get a word in edgeways.' And at that did Tawny pick up a loaf and chew, and he said no more on these subjects.

But Kun and Lun, as night fell, went out into the woods, and when they were alone, they moved to the side of the wood's edge, and they looked out sternly to where the moon shone and lit the mists breeding from the night air, and together they raised their arms up, and Confucius called, 'Dragon, whatever may be your nature! Appear to us plainly now, for we know what you are, and surely we would hold talk with your mightiness.' And as the words went echoing over the empty vales, the silver dragon formed before them.

And Lao zi cried, 'It is he! Emperor, what do you here? How can you come sniffing like a dog at our heels? Do you think to seize Nai? Well, we will protect him. Do you think he'll find your daughter? There's a hope! What object is in you hounding us as we go upon this journey? Have we not enough to do to seek to sway the poet? If you snatch him to death, remember, that way you plunge China. Why do you not leave it to us, this mission?'

But the silver dragon answered them. 'Tell not your king his duties. I shall devour that Cowherd if I wish. But still I creep behind him, hoping to read his thoughts, seeking to see where he has hidden my daughter. For do not you believe but that he and the dragon are in league. The star-dragon has been corrupted by him. I shall seize this slippery poet soon out of sheer impatience. You two old men have not the power to stop me.' And the vapours poured below them now, boiling with silver fury, and snaked away under the sickly moon.

Now next day as the travellers roamed, they came to ominous forests that hung black and sooty-scented about them. No huts or villagers were here, and scarce grew their supplies, and hunger began to pinch them. When they came to mountain clearings, they would pause a while and pick what fruits and berries were shyly burgeoning, and grim were these regions, for though protected by Wei's guards, they could see bandits watching from their lairs. And Nai met a group of them, who threatened the rear-guard, and while Tawny cowered in the cart, the poet spoke to them reprovingly, like a dull schoolmaster, so that the bandits did not know what to say.

Through the dripping forests at last, when Nai and the sages were in front, they came upon the frontier of the empire. Past a ragged border-post, with a decayed customs-house lay the turbulent kingdom of the Chin. The fir trees clustered dark about. Gloomy clouds were above. Into the dim air tumbled the border guards, and drunk and belligerent they set on the few travellers, and menacingly went through their carts. Having searched without effect, they loomed and demanded bribes, forbidding entry and threatening imprisonment. The two old sages looked alarmed, and kept staring back along the road, waiting for Wei's arrival.

But Nai stood by the guards and said in a dull voice, 'It is wrong to demand bribes with threats. We are going to Chang an, and we could report there that the guards of this post are drunken and corrupt. You ought not to drink so much, nor threaten innocent travellers. You are abusing your positions.' But as Nai looked at them gravely, there came Wei's guards riding round the corner, and the drunken soldiers refrained from setting about him.

Now the hills grew steeper as they came into the heights of the Qinling range, and the going was ever more difficult. The mules and horses laboured to pull their burdens up the slopes, and their hoofs misplaced themselves on the pebbles. The travellers dismounted and heaving with their shoulders, shoved the carts on bodily. But it was hard work, and the deep forest all about seemed closed in and airless. Hot was it in the daytime, though the clouds hung close. Thunder sounded dryly in the distance.

'Master,' then said Tawny, as they rattled along again, sitting now in the car on the level, 'it seems you have a kind of death-wish, for ever you are opting to rebuke and provoke villains. What is it makes you take such chances?'

Nai shrugged and sighed. 'I don't know, Tawny, but something makes me do it. It is rather against my wishes, but the impulse drives me on. Still, we've so far been lucky.'

'So far, yes,' said Tawny. 'You're a strange man, master. Yet I fear danger is hanging over us.'

The hills and streams of China now drew the travellers on with ever increasing weariness and trouble. The carts fell into disrepair. The horses shed their shoes. The roads became impassable. The little procession of wheels and men would creep up the forgotten paths, and plunge down into the stream-fed valleys. In fords they would stride over, wading up to the waists, holding staffs against the current. By cliffs they would go creeping, perilously overhung by steepy crags and boulder-balanced chasms. But still they made their travel forward through the Qinling Shan and ever towards the crest which would bring them to Chang an.

But when they came to Neisang, a mountain town, with pagodas rising into the clouds, the mayor himself came out to greet them, and was overjoyed to welcome an ambassador. The streets filled with well-wishers. From the balconied houses the people came forth to view the Southerners, and the mayor himself offered the hospitality of his mansion to house the whole party.

In the festive halls of the town-hall that night, with its pillars twirlingly painted, among low tables crammed with steaming bowls and dishes, the travellers feasted thankfully. Even Jen came out now in the town to show her face, to the marvelling of the mountain-people. And Kun and Lun chatted, as Tawny darted about, waiting at table and spinning the bowls round on his finger, till Nai told him to settle down, and behave like a guest, and all the travellers together clattered their chopsticks.

But when the banquet was over, Tawny and Nai left, and seeking their room walked along the walls of the mansion, for the town-house was built on the side of a precipice, with the cliff in darkness falling away at their side. They walked along the slippy path with a melon-shaped lantern, and in the muggy silence smelt the jasmine, and thus did they dally at this break from their journey, as the moon struggled to come through the clouds.

And Tawny said, 'Well, master, this is better than toiling up hills, and soon we will be in the grand capital. We will be able to put our feet up for a while and have delicious rest. You look as though you need it. But master, are you really going to see this monk, Fa xian, and join his strange pilgrimage to India? Do you know how far India is? It's the other end of the world! Do you think you've got the strength to do it?' And Tawny shook his head, as they leaned together on a rail, surveying the moon-filled valley.

But Nai said, 'I hope so, Tawny. I am not as bad as I was. Your horrible company has somehow made me feel better. But even so, it is hard, I only hope I can keep going. For Fa xian's pilgrimage: yes, I must be on it. And strive I must at least to get as far as Dun huang. But oh, it is hard, striving, forging, grasping, toiling, faltering! It came upon me once before, this sickness of exhaustion, when I strove with things beyond my capacities. But now I hope better to know my strength, and the wisdom of India will help me.'

'Well master, let me ask you now,' said Tawny quietly. 'Let me come with you also to Dun huang. I would come there at least, for I would get you to your goal, and maybe also there I'd find my treasure.'

Nai smiled to hear him say this. Then he sighed and said, 'You are not alone asking that, Tawny. For Kun and Lun, the old men, today also told me they intended to go onward. It seems the whole crowd of us is venturing to the limits, assuming Fa xian himself can take us. Well, you are welcome, Tawny. You are dear to me. Though a boy, you and I are alike, I think.'

As they loaded the carts in the morning, Tawny dodged about, helping everybody with their own affairs. In the dawn light, the gloomy guards took forth their axe-spears, and Tawny was there, handing them their helmets. While the cockerels crowed, the old men, Kun and Lun, spent some time coughing, and Tawny was there, patting them on their backs. As the mayor's own servants brought from the kitchens provisions for the ambassador's travel, Tawny was there, helpfully sampling the pies and directing the best morsels to Nai's cart. But when he came to Wei escorting Jen to her carriage, Tawny went up to them and intervened.

'You're not putting her back in that laundry bag, are you?' he said, taking Wei by the arm. 'The poor girl's likely to stifle in this summer weather. It's cooler in the hills, but even so, we've all seen her now. She was out in the banquet with us. It's a crime to shut her up, and keep her wrapped up in curtains like a boiled pudding!'

But Wei looked at him sourly. 'You are an impudent youth,' he said, 'and know nothing whereof you are speaking. Have a care to your own affairs, and curb that audacious spirit, which seeks to fidget ever your superiors. Be gone, vile boy!' And Wei frowned at him, so that Tawny shrugged his shoulders and sauntered off. But then Wei turned to Jen and said, 'You see what they say? They think it is my fault I keep you hidden. Can you not risk appearing and being with us, while we journey in these hills? Will you always seek to hide yourself from us?'

But Jen sighed and answered, 'Do I need to remind you of the conditions under which, Wei, I came to live with you? Do you not remember in Jian kang, when you asked me in that inn-yard, I said that I would consent to live with you, if you did not ask me to travel, for it was in the country my nature came into the most danger. Well, you have brought me out of the town, and I have consented to it, but at least in my panoply I can rest hidden. It is hot and unsociable in that place. But, my sweet, a fox is safe there.' And Jen climbed up to the chariot then, and looking at Wei seriously, closed the curtains.

Now the company set off with promises from the mayor that they were not far now from Chang an. The pass was before them, cresting the Qinling Mountains, and then they would be descending towards the ancient capital. As the morning came on, clouds bred still in the mountains, stealing away the foundations of the summits, so that they trundled from Neisang to a mysterious country, where peaks on peaks rose like slumbering sea-beasts. And the clouds seemed to follow them, boiling at their heels, coming up from the valleys.

But as they went along, Lao zi said, 'Ah, see how Feng-yang towers on our right! And beyond those ridges there, Taibai Shan touches heaven, highest peak of the Qinling Mountains. There are four great mountains on which this square earth is set, with Kunlun in the West and Tai Shan in the East where the mighty mulberry tree sends forth the sun each day, and the Yellow Springs take the soul to the underworld. In the spirit of these mountains and streams the very Dao is hidden. Can you not feel the breath that hums through all the ten thousand creatures?' Lao zi sighed inspired, and the rest of the company respected the perception of his words.

209

They moved along the mountain-tracks. Perilous were the ways now, and the pebbles skidded off and into the valleys. The pack-horses laboured under their burdens. The carts went slithering with the mud-slides. The travellers threaded through the crags and beneath the over-hangs, by the copses of stunted spruce, whose twisted branches clutched at the muddy vapours, by the gorse bush and broom perfuming the air with its nutty fragrance. Meanwhile, in the distance the waterfalls plummeted, spuming the black descents and cliff-hangs, and always behind the travellers the clouds came on, scaling the passes after them.

But as they paused to drink, Confucius spied a memorial of stone, celebrating the rites of the Western Zhou, and he said, 'Why now, we near the capital, for see already here: the remains of the rule of the great ones that had their capital at Chang an. For first did the Zhou reign here, the wise kings that governed with virtue, routing the hard, wild soldiers of the impulsive Shang. And next did the Emperor Chin, whose name lives on in China, begin his An Fang palace here, wicked tyrant and burner of the books. And after him the Han came, fosterers of the grand empire, whose like in riches we have not yet seen again. Thus pass the dynasties. Yet Zhongguo endures all kings, all faiths, the Central Realm everlasting!' And Confucius shed tears at that, and the others were still, for this was truth that he had uttered.

But now, as they prepared to make on again, the travellers looked back a while, for weirdly the clouds behind had been assembling. And as they looked upon them now, the clouds seemed grouped together, in a boiling line that snaked its way through the twisting valleys, as a road climbing a mountain curls back on itself and back again, sliding with sideways gait ever upward. So did the clouds follow. And it seemed they were like a snake, and beneath them the jaws opened as if grinning at them.

Wherefore Tawny pointed and shrieked, 'See, the dragon again! Save us again, great masters, save us!' And he ran to Kun and Lun and hid among their robes, as the masters looked abashed at what he was pointing to. For now the dragon was there again, boiling from the clouds, his silver eyes dazzling with anger, the pearls upon his forehead gleaming, spit spewing from his lips, sun-patches of scales on his sides of cumulus.

But Lun stepped forward now. The monk threw up his arms, and searched again in his red and yellow robes. And he produced the weird fan and clapped it, brushing the serpent away. But the clouds merely boiled with fury further.

And Tawny called aloud now, and called on the others of the travellers, Wei and his carriage who were a little along the track. But Kun when he saw this, himself stepped forward to the edge, and he drew forth a rod and held up it against the dragon. And he called out, 'Have home, have home! Clouds must not seize here! All will be torn if you have forward.' But the clouds piled up higher. Black they were now and threatening. A huge dragon-head seemed like to fall on them.

But far off from the North there now came a noise of thunder, that boomed and fell rumbling around the mountains. The clouds that were before them now shocked and winced at the sound, and the snaky trails began to turn and slither. The thunder rang again louder, exploding like a bolt, flickering sparky lightning down upon the cliff-face. The mules and horses in the train whinnied and stamped with fear. All was blackness about the travellers. Now Wei came running. The guards appeared. All the travellers were there, grouped beneath the towering clouds of fury. And it seemed a sparkling dragon of fire came bounding from the peaks and prowled about the silver vapours.

With horror did the travellers watch as the silver dragon lashed his tail to see the other. He followed him, as the fiery serpent rolled along the crags, his silver head watching the snaking flight. For an uneasy calm, the storm was still, a hush having caught the twilit mountain. But then the fiery

211

serpent lunged and snatched at the grey vapours, tugging them away in his teeth.

Now did the silver dragon howl, and momentous thunder clanged about, flattening the travellers on the ground with fear. Now did the whole mountains bellow, reverberating the valleys with bombastic clangs and precipitous armies of air. The silver dragon towered up. The fiery dragon crouched. Once more the two sky-serpents surveyed each other. Then flickering lightning, the silver fell. The two snakes rolled on the hills. Bellowing they tumbled clawing among the valleys. The travellers crept up. Shielding their eyes, they looked down the way they had come. Roaring with the blast, the dragons fought up again, sending the humans running.

The fiery one was free again. Slithering over the peaks, he once more menaced the white-faced clouds. The silver serpent hissed with rage. Waterfalls spouted from his nostrils. Lashing rain and hail came flattening the hillside. He dodged about his head. The fiery serpent watched. Then lunging once more he sunk in his teeth. With hideous howls of agony, again he tore away vapours, and again he mouthed and mumbled the silver sky-serpent. The travellers winced. Whole crags came away. From the hilltops came bouncing boulders and landslides. The dragons a while drew apart seething and panting, then closed with clangs for the crisis.

Huge was now the rattling battle of the fighting dragons, as the fiery met in combat with the silver. Like cats that fight in alleys, like stallions tearing with their teeth, like eels that come wriggling onto the bank of the fishermen, the serpents of the sky fought biting, clawing, stabbing, tearing, from the black clouds casting down the pearls of ice-sweat. From boiling, murky towers in the heights of the sky, precipitous descents of lashing rain, from singeing streaks of clanging thunder, making the travellers cower, sheltering from the deluge beneath rocks and capes, the serpents churned and toiled and struggled contorting their clouds, agonisingly locked in contest, until the silver

212

vapours now spread thin about the hillsides, and the fierier clouds were pressing upon them.

Then did the flamy dragon with his sparks set about his foe. Up the crags he drove him, casting to the winds the mists. Now did he long pursue the silver down the reeling valleys, and disperse with mouthings the vapours over the fir forests. Chasing each little wisp of the fog, the fiery dragon now roamed again, writhing in the mountains and scattering the thunderstorm. And a sense of peace came then, a quiet to the rain-washed dales, as the last fog-banks slipped away over the cliffs. The sun came gleaming. In victory in the pass, the serpent rolled with rainbow scales. And the birds began singing again, as the way lay clear, and the road to Chang an shone in the light.

'Now have we seen a mighty storm!' then said Wei to the others. 'Surely it was as if the dragons themselves had combat. For never in the thunderstorm have I seen their presences more, nor sensed the mighty clashes that are in Nature. A wonderful immenseness it is, these shows of the elements' powers. How puny and pointless seem the ways of man beside them! Yet let us go on again. For the cities of men await, and the sun, see, gleams upon the path to Chang an!' And Wei gave the signal, and the others picked up their things, and Tawny looked up from his sheltering beneath Nai's arm. And fearful was the boy, staring with eyes huge and round. And Nai also had a ghastly gaze.

When the travellers marched again, awed and full of wonder, taking the downward path towards the capital, Chang an before them spread its square, gridded with avenues, filling the plain with its mighty highways. Its courtyards clustered the streets, its canals reflected the sun, its shimmering gardens bowered the shores of the West Lake. Pagodas and great fortresses reared up amidst its walls, drum-towers and great pavilions and palaces, and splendid were the towering gates to which the riders came, to pass through to the largest city upon the earth.

But when they came within the gates, ruin and decay did

213

they see, dilapidated shops and buildings fallen. The gate-
houses were open to the sky, the roads were full of pot-
holes, the walls themselves cracked and eaten inwardly.
And the fireweed grew in rosy clumps everywhere in the
streets, and fig trees sprouted from the battered walls. And
the shadows of the palaces that loomed across the squares,
with bronze and copper roofs and gilded tiles: why, now
they had great holes in them, viewed from the closer eye,
and creepers grew green upon the spires.

'O great and mighty capital,' then exclaimed Confucius
with fervour, 'O seat of the Emperors, well-named Everlasting Peace! O hugest court upon earth, wherein a thousand thousands had dwellings, O centre of riches and trade
by ocean or Silk Road! How about you in undying homage
do the tombs of the mighty Emperors cluster in these
wrinkled hills! The builder of the Great Wall, the jade
princess of Han, the eight-thousandfold earth-army of warriors: all these lie kowtowed before you, square symbol of
government. Yet ah, yet ah! How are ye fallen! Tibetan
hounds vaunt over ye! Usurpers neglect your courts. The
wallflower and the humble moss now cling to ye. Alas, alas,
Chang an the Grand! How sadly are ye passed away! How
soon the leaves blow through the sumptuous throne-
rooms!' And Confucius now led the pilgrim's sighs amidst
the city. But then the travellers went their separate ways.

Chapter Fourteen

Now in the city of Chang an, Fu jian sat once more on his throne, and his courtiers and generals sat about him. And Fu jian addressed them and said, 'Warriors and mandarins, we have heard the reports of the troops who regrouped after the battle. We have also had the painful duty of hearing of these regiments who gave way and fled before the Southerners, and how indeed they suffered! Far better is it to fight, than to show cowardice and invite carnage. Wherefore since we ourselves are returned, from escape and ruin saved, starving among our people and sharing their shame, it is now time to think again, and plan what designs we may, and to take steps and stern ones too, to keep order. Yet where is Wang Zhia, our esteemed Court Astrologer? Let him be sent for, while we continue with our deliberations.'

And thus did the monarch fall silent, while Mu jung Wei stood up, and grim-faced he addressed him. 'Great victorious monarch,' he said, 'we congratulate you on your return, and honour the bravery with which you survived the defeat at the Fei. The General Fu jung, who allowed the Southerners to cross the river, and negotiated with them to fight on our Northern side has been suitably punished for his absurd manoeuvres, without which the day would have been ours. And may I salute in this court my own cousin Mu jung Chui, who kept his army intact throughout the heat of the warfare? As you know, great monarch, the Mu jung clan has served you inestimably through this difficult period. I therefore ask your majesty's permission to be granted full command of the capital's defences.' And thus did the General Mu jung Wei stand firmly before the face of his master.

But Fu jian frowned at this and said, 'Mu jung Wei, I have no cause at all to doubt your loyalty. Your cousin indeed fared well, and his army still is under his command, but I have yet to hear from it new oaths of allegiance. There is also your other cousin, the General Mu jung Chung. Of his intent there is much suspicion, for he loiters near the gracious capital, among the tents of the Xien pi, and these are generally recognised as impulsive barbarians! How shall it be if Chung decides to attack our capital Chang an, and his own cousin is in charge of the defences? Better is it therefore the command rests still in my hands, though I am grateful to your loyal suggestions.' And the monarch ceased then, and stared from his throne Eastward out of his fretted window, where above the walls of the courtyard there could be seen the distant hills beyond the Wei River.

Yet among the hills of Qinling Shan, where the travellers had now passed, the clouds were now pulling themselves together, and the angry dragon who had been dispersed, assuming the shape of clouds, biting the crags and clawing the stunted trees, now dragged himself serpently beneath the heights of Feng yang, and painfully put together his vaporised parts. And he drew back his cloudy claws from the crevices of the hills, and he clawed back his scales scattered on the rocks, and he worked again together his cloudbanks of silver sides, so that once more he was a working dragon. And then did the silver dragon glower all around with fury, and sigh hissing steam from his foggy nostrils.

And the silver dragon said, 'Well, we have found the star-dragon at least. Wo Long Wang has not disappeared from the earth. And truly I see now that in the fogs of Zhongguo he has been hiding from heaven's messengers. No doubt he has been stirring things, during his Emperor's absence, embroiling the bowl, setting mischief running. But also he has been watching me. Else how could he have attacked? How could he have known the moment I planned

216

engulfing? Why, I had deluged those creeping pilgrims in the sluice of the crags, had he not appeared with sharp-stung thunders. Well, I must beware of him. Wo Long Wang is awake. The Jade-King must proceed by indirections.

'Why now then, to spite him I will stir things up in the dragon's way. Ay, in this city there is plenty I can rouse up. The pilgrims have gone into the capital, the two philosophers protecting Nai. But there are ways I can still assault him. Who knows not that the dragon's king, Fu jian, is uneasy on his throne? Who knows not that revolts are near the surface? And out to the East there lie the Xien pi, barbarians under rebellious guard. And also in the city itself there are bands of them. The Mu jung clan are strong. They slobber over the throne. They and the Xien pi might make some mischief. I will go to their camps and stir them, and then into the city, where secretly I'll work these Mu jungs to revolt.' And the silver dragon thus flowed away, while the evening came, and he joyed to set about such earthly plots.

But when the dawn had banished the shadows from the twelve-cart-wide avenues, and the Buddhist monks had gone with their clappers announcing another day of the Buddha, then Nai awoke in his sultry bed, where the sun tinged the dust pink in the sunbeams, and Tawny already was busily dressing himself. So Nai shouted to him to go and make them some tea, for now they were to arrange for the pilgrimage.

When they had dressed, they went downstairs from the room, and Kun and Lun were up already awaiting them, and since the old men refused to desert them, they all went in a bunch out into the city. And they came into the great avenue, about which the buildings rose up, with steep roofs, glittering with flaking gold, and they searched among the avenues for the temple of Hung fu, and when they found it they marvelled at its grandeur, for the mighty gate rose up with pagoda-towers and fluttering prayer-flags, and beyond the gate they could glimpse great courts and statues.

Now when they had come there, Nai spoke in the gateway to the monks and said, 'From Jian kang, the capital are we come, my servant and I, devout in the faith of the Buddha, at the behest of Guan yin, the goddess, to seek the monk Fa xian in this temple, and to join in his mighty pilgrimage. Tell us where he is that we may present our greetings, and seek his favour for the voyage.'

But the monk replied, 'Fa xian is not here today. Let your spirit be at peace. If you have alms for us, place them in these patras, and they will go to the proper places. But as for the pilgrimage, Fate alone can assist Fa xian in his transcendent mission. Calm yourself, sir. Examine your soul. Refuge is in the Buddha.' And the monks then shut the travellers out of the temple.

Now when afternoon had come, and the travellers sat in the inn, despondent at what they had been told, Confucius said, 'Well, this rebuff is a blessing, for you did not wish to journey to India truly. Your words to the monk were a kind of sham, my son, for you have no such strong faith in the Buddha, and improper would it be to go on such a journey for any other than devout motives. Back then to Jian kang. Rejoice to be saved much trouble. And let us all be at peace with our heritage.' But Nai sat thoughtful, plunged in doubts and complexities, wondering what should be his way forward.

Yet as they sat there gloomily, there came into them Wei, who wore as much a long face as his comrade. And when they had sat him down, and given him food and drink, sitting among the tables under the awning, Wei sighed and said, 'Well, my friends, I know not how you fared, but my day was most unsuccessful, for I found that the Court Astrologer was too busy to see me, and that the mandarins were far from impressed by their recent conquerors. I went to the Western palace, where the observatory lies, and the courtyard built strangely to study the

218

stars, and there I spent the day fruitless, chasing officials about, attempting to find someone to take me seriously.

'And when I came to one who would – it was a supervisor of the imperial music, who had negotiated with us over the canonical musicians – he told me that my quest was fruitless; the Great Tortoise could not be returned, for it had died over a year ago. I wish that I had known of this before I left Jian kang. I might have saved myself a whole leg of my journey. And there seems little point in my trying to see the Court Astrologer. I have now nothing to claim from him. Such, O my comrades, has been my dispiriting day. What a vanity is this official business!' And the others sighed and gazed at him, for his mood reflected theirs. There was no triumph in the ancient capital.

Yet the business of the silver dragon was proceeding more brightly, for he stirred up the Xien pi outside the city walls, and then going into the city went with the commander of the Xien pi guards in revolt to Mu jung Wei, minister to the monarch, and they found he had also had messages from his brother on the readiness of the Xien pi to revolt. Wherefore they sat together and worked on a plan, whereby the failing Fu jian might be toppled, and the conspirators sat in a room by the palace courtyard, where a few leaves began to blow from the trees.

But the very next morning Nai got ready with his friends and once more they went to the Hung fu Temple. And though Confucius and Lao zi tried to dissuade him, he approached the monks again that guarded the gateway. But again he was refused. Wherefore Tawny came up hobbling, and said his leg was broken by a mad Buddhist, and tottered into the temple, creating such diversions that Nai and his reluctant tutors could walk in unhindered. And they came again to the courtyards, and saw the great hall with the statue, and about the golden figure the rattling prayer-wheels turning.

Now it happened that Fa xian was in the courtyard at that moment, and moving to pay his devotions. But Nai went up to him and said, 'Sir, may I speak a little, for it seems to me

219

that you indeed may be Fa xian? Wherefore I would wish to tell you that from Jian kang have I come, inspired by Guan yin to join your pilgrimage. Nor am I empty handed, for many taels of silver I bring, the savings of my life back in the Eastern capital. Good sir, long was my journey to reach you here. Do not send me away from your mission.' And Nai finished his speech, and bowed his head before the monk, who stared back at him with thoughtful expression.

And Fa xian said, 'Your devotion is impressive. But Southern stranger, little can I help you, for the pilgrimage that was planned long before this has been continually delayed because of the wars. Yesterday I heard also on my visit to the palace that the guard who had been promised me now cannot be spared. And with these uncertain times, and the turbulence of the Xien pi, the Huns, and the other barbarians, it would be hard to travel. Moreover, the summer nears its end. The vast Pamirs are cold and high. India cannot be reached in winter.' And Fa xian smiled at the poet with a compassionate look, and leaving him went on to the temple.

When the afternoon had come, and the travellers sat in the inn again, Lao zi hammered his hand on the table and said, 'This table is solid. So is the state of China, never mind how many Buddhists and usurpers it has in it. A great country is like low land, and it conquers by lying still. Xie Nai, you must go home again. India is not for you, nor are the ways of Buddha. A wise man knows when to stop. So we can all go home.' And Lao zi attacked his wine-cup, and downed it in one gulp, and then clanged it on the table with a shout.

But as they sat silent, there came a noise from the street, and the carriage of Wei appeared to them, and wearily he dismounted, and then helped down Jen, who came forth boldly in the city. And when they had been greeted, and settled at the tables, Wei said, 'Well, once more I can't know what success you have had: from your faces I would say not much. But I have again accomplished nothing this day, though strange and deep things have I witnessed.

220

'For I went again to the monarch's palace to seek the Court Astrologer, Wang Zhia, since I was determined to fulfil the letter of my mission. And I found in the palace that day greater accommodation, so that I was led to the throne-room where he was present. But here I found, by chance, that I had come upon the monarch himself, for there sat Fu jian, the man we defeated. He was smaller than I thought. He clutched the arms of his throne. His eyes were fiery, but not much focused. A minister was with him. Mu jung Wei was his name, and was asking him this next day to his son's wedding. And Fu jian agreed, and then did the monarch turn to the Court Astrologer.

'"You have heard," said the monarch to him, "the honour in which I am held even by great families who have been opposed to me. For this Mu jung Wei, who has just left the presence, is head of that family who were my rivals. But you see he still cherishes me. He asks me in my imperial carriage to visit the private residence of a liegeman. A great one is compassionate. I shall attend his son's wedding, in spite of all the troubles of our harassed city. You understand then, Wang Zhia, your warnings are not always purposeful. With compassion much can be moved forward."

'But Wang Zhia looked at him, and he did not reply directly, but instead walked before the monarch, and then in a half-singing voice he recited to him a strange poem in a kind of peasant metre.

You'll not get much milk from stirring this whey.
It's not a good Wei you keep.
But down comes the rain on the way to the Wei,
And he'll not slaughter the sheep.

And Wang Zhia said no more, but left the throne-room, and a long silence behind him, for all were puzzling upon his words, and trying to see meaning in the prophecy. As I was for a while, but then I ignored this talk of rain and

221

riverside slaughter, and delicately slipped myself from the sovereign's presence, and hurried after the seer.

'And when I cornered him I said, "Wang Zhia, you have heard perhaps of my mission, for on business of the Jian kang court of Imperial Rites and Ceremonials, I have represented our plea for the return of the Grand Tortoise. Yet also I have heard the news: the tortoise is no more. My mission has proved foolish and a vanity. Yet duty urges me to fulfil the letter of my mission, which was to deal with you in this matter directly."

'And Wang Zhia looked at me, and again he did not speak, but sang in his weird peasant quatrains:

> Where goes the Wei who takes the wrong way?
> After a tortoise' ghost!
> Vain are all journeys in silk for him.
> The cotton offers most.

'And again the weird astrologer left abruptly, having spoken the strange words of a fortune. And all day I have pondered just what his verse might mean. Jen says she knows, but will not tell me.'

But Nai smiled and answered, 'I too see what it means, and Wei, I have always thought this of you. He means that you are bound not for the silks of imperial service, but for the cotton of a Buddhist. All other travel is vain for you, until you take that path, wearing the orange of renunciation. And indeed this suits your nature, better than this pursuit which has led you only as far as an empty tortoise-shell. But listen, my comrade, your next embassy in any case is along the Silk Road towards Liang province. Will you not come with me tomorrow, and visit the monk, Fa xian, and inform him you are bound with your guards on such a journey? For he has lost his escort. He is in need of such things as you and you alone can furnish him. Offer him your company. It is all he needs to prompt him. And let us all go West together.' And Nai looked at Wei eagerly. And

Wei nodded his head. But the two old men closed their eyes in horror.

Now when the third day had come of the travellers' stay in Chang an, the day dawned gloomy and overcast. The clouds hung thick and creased over the centre of the city, where the bell-tower rose with its huge copper bell and suspended striker. Across the hill-hung river the darkness was of pitch, and the cracks of lightning glimmered over the water. The old men rose wearily. This was no day to go forth, they said. But Nai was up and eager. He waited with Tawny as the rain began to fall, bringing a smell of damp earth to the dusty backstreets.

But when Wei's carriage arrived with its canopy streaked with rain, the downpour was splashing the puddles like needles. There were channels in the streets, with the silt of loess streaming in ochre. So heavy was the rain now, that Wei and all came into the inn, and they stood in the leaking verandah, and watched the deluge. There was a noise of trumpets sounding and music in the streets, which came and went as the wind blew them.

And Wei said, 'The wedding procession of the son of the minister has been caught in the tumult of the rain. The monarch has cancelled his outing. He is staying in the palace, and his guards mass in their ranks without being led forward. A strange day it is in the city. There is news from outside that the Xien pi are stirring in the Hua marshes. The scouts are alerted, and they man the lookout-towers. The walls are heavy with bristling archers. It would seem to be prudent to leave on our mission without much delay.' So Wei spoke, and the company heard his words with fear, the old men sighing in the rain.

When the downpour had slackened itself, the travellers braved the wet, and they made off again together towards the Hung fu Temple. And Kun and Lun still followed doggedly, yet with anxiety in their hearts, and they kept their eyes always on Nai as he splashed forward. But as they crossed the main avenue, they saw the guards were out, and riders hurrying off towards the palace, and a commotion came to their hearing of shouting regiments, as though of some mock battle. But once again at the monastery, all was holy, and the monks this time welcomed the official party.

For when they came to the Hung fu Temple, in the steam of the drying rain, they heard the clash of gongs and bells tolling. Entering the courtyard, they found the monks in rows, intoning psalms to the Buddha. With deep and growling voices the chant *Om mani padme Om* echoed among the red pillars, and the smoke of incense went up before the glowing gold of the great statue. Palms pressed together made their holy tents in the darkness of the sanctity. Some great spell was working, corkscrewing up into the heavens in supplication.

But Fa xian was passing on his way to attend the rites, and thus did the travellers come across him. And Nai put his hands together, imploring him to spare them some words, while the sight of the imperial envoy made him stop also. And Fa xian came towards them thus, and said, 'You have come again, Southerner, and this time do you bring with you an ambassador? You come at a good time. We are deep in our special rites to help prevent bloodshed in the city. Now perhaps the action of a foreign power would have a stabilising effect.'

But Wei answered him at once. 'I am indeed an envoy, sir, and to your Court Astrologer was my fruitless mission. But hearing of your predicament from my friend here, I have come to you with an opportune offer. My next business as ambassador is with the Province of Liang, whither I am bound with an armed escort. I hear that you have looked in vain for an escort of this sort for a journey along the same path to the Silk Road. I am come, Fa xian, to offer you my protection as far as Dun huang for your pilgrimage. I hope you will accept it, and my comrade here as a pilgrim. If you do, it would be well to leave immediately.' And Wei was silent, and all among his troop stared at the monk, some with hope and some with anxiety.

But Fa xian turned impassively towards the statue of the

Buddha, and for a while his eyes were closed in prayer. And then he answered, 'I will take up your offer, envoy. Blessings on you and your friend for suggesting it. Let us try to leave tomorrow. I would request that you meet us here, to depart at once after the dawn prayers. Perhaps you have not heard? There has been a revolt in the city. A plot has been discovered to assassinate the monarch. It seems that Mu jung Wei planned to kill his sovereign at a wedding today, but the rain prevented him going. Wherefore the throne is safe. Yet vengeance is planned for the conspirators, and this may well brew trouble. Have you heard the further news that the Xien pi advance towards the city? We must use haste to leave before the siege.' And the monk stared at the others, who reacted with amazement to this news, and the pallor of dread descended upon their faces.

Now when evening was approaching, all the travellers were at the inn, for Wei had moved his party here for safety. And when the afternoon was fading, there was nothing left to do, for the packing was finished, and the carriages stood ready to leave before first light. Wherefore the voyagers idled, sitting in the eating-place, staring with disquiet at the empty streets, and a hush seemed to hold the town of sultry menace, so that each noise was heard with dread and misgiving. The roofs were dry again. The streaks of the rain-channels lay in the roads still from the morning. But the distant noise of hammering, as stakes were sunk by the gateways, had the tone of a weary dream.

But Nai was glad in the city to see Jen taking the air, not skulking hidden as ever among the curtains. And as they sat in the inn idle, he went over to where she was, and sat down to talk with her. But she seemed nervous. She would not speak openly to him. So Nai asked her if she would care to walk. And Jen looked about to where Wei sat with the two old men, but he did not seem to be heeding her. So quietly she spoke to him of what she was doing, and then went out with Nai from the hostelry. But all the time Tawny watched, staring with anxious eyes, and when they had gone, sighed quiet and broody.

The streets were empty and all the town had a forlorn air, as they passed the boarded-up stalls and closed shops. Folk had flown for their homes. The avenues were ghostly, like dawn on a holiday. None but a few dogs loped about in them. Afar off on the walls, the guards were massing, and towers were being reinforced and gates. They strolled through the streets aimlessly, and after a while Nai sighed and looking at Jen he spoke.

'It has been strange travelling with you,' he said. 'And with you closeted away I have never really had a chance to speak to you. After what we discussed that day in Jian kang, there have been many things I felt I could say. I must thank you for your advice. I did what you told me, and though not from Guan yin, I had a certain guidance. Where it has led me, I am not sure. But I am going on the way I intended. Sometimes by indirections we are forced out of our road to discover we have taken a short cut.'

As they sauntered along the avenue, they saw down by the palace troops of soldiers forming outside in the square. They saw some horsemen ride swiftly towards the gates. Others were hauling great cauldrons across the road. Nai and Jen decided to turn back. There were noises coming now of the murmur of troops marching in distant avenues. As they moved back down the road, which was wide like a square in itself, enough for twelve carriages to drive alongside in it, they saw a strange figure standing far off in yellow robes, and the maiden gave a start of anxiety. She took Nai a different way, along streets parallel to the main avenue, and thus they walked more briskly back towards the inn.

Yet Nai was unsuspicious, and at length he said, 'It is a shame that Wei's mission here has been so pointless. To negotiate for a tortoise may seem ceremonial enough, but to come all that way for a dead tortoise! Perhaps in Dun huang, his embassy might meet with something more smacking of success, something which might lend him a little more kudos than he had attracted in this affair. Yet it is good to see him so proud now. He wears his robes well. I think he will have a distinguished career in office.'

But Jen was shaking her head. 'No,' she said. 'It is not so. He is perplexed and dissatisfied with his responsibilities. Have you forgot already the prophecy spoken to him, which you corroborated? He has been a scholar a long time now. He is happy with his books. These absurdities of office are disheartening for him. And the affair of the tortoise has more firmly rooted his dissatisfaction. As I told you once before, Wei is near to the point of renouncing the world, and if he does, my task will have been successful. You, Nai, are different. You relish things so much. You lust to possess and transmute everything. But Wei is a pure soul. He would be happiest leading the life of the Buddha.' And Jen was silent now, staring sadly at the road. Nai looked at her admiringly.

As they moved along a pleasant road, where there was a pagoda that had obviously suffered damage in an earthquake, they suddenly saw and heard along the avenue they had left a great troop of cavalry rushing and spurring. The horsemen were making no war-cries. Yet the jingle of harness and creak of leather and thud of hoofs came floating to them, suspended in the dying afternoon air. As Nai chanced to look behind him, he noticed the figure in yellow walking with a strange, winding gait.

'But you, Xie Nai,' said Jen at last, 'you seem to be on the path of the Buddha, and yet I hope you will excuse me if I say it does not seem likely. Your old tutors, Kun and Lun, are always criticising you over it, but they have sense with them. It does not seem a wise step for you to be taking. It is difficult to see if you are serious. You are going with Fa xian, and yet somehow you don't seem to be committed. What is your secret, Nai? Somehow I always feel with you, there is some explanation lurking behind it all.' She stared at Nai puzzled, but though he seemed willing to reply, he stopped, for something had caught his attention.

When Jen turned to see what it was, she uttered a cry of dismay, and stood for a while stuck on the spot. Nai was also puzzled, for before them on the road now was the man in yellow that he had seen behind him. Jen took Nai's sleeve and pulled it, indicating that they should go off down another street. The man stared at them weirdly, with snarling snake-lips, his hands folded in his imperial yellow sleeves. Jen pulled Nai's cloak again. But Nai shook her off. What was the point in running from this strange figure? He wondered if it was the monarch? There was something regal in his presence, standing alone, erect in a deserted street.

Jen tugged his sleeve desperately. 'Nai,' she whispered, 'flee this man! I implore you to flee him! Do not let him seize hold of you. Come quickly and firmly away. We must get back to the inn before this man can work his mischief. Oh why will you not come?' she cried tearfully. 'Trust me for this instant! Xie Nai, Xie Nai, come away, come away from him!' She spoke to him in weeping whispers. But Nai merely stared at her puzzled. And beside the man was coming towards them.

The man stopped and bowed to Nai. 'Xie Nai could it be?' he said.

Nai bowed his head assenting.

The man advanced a few steps. 'What luck to meet you in Chang an!' he continued. 'It has taken me a long time to track you down.'

Nai felt himself grow cold.

'You must be wondering who I am?' said the man. He paused for a moment peevishly, for Jen had suddenly left Nai's side and run away. But then he looked again at Nai. 'I'm an old acquaintance really.' He sighed and smiled. 'But it's now so long ago, I think you have forgotten.'

Nai stared at the man. He had a weird silvery face, and his hair was silver and misty. The yellow robes that he had on gave him the air of an emperor. There was a sudden noise of shouting and battle.

'Do not worry about these disturbances,' said the man. 'The bodyguard of Fu jian have just gone to massacre the Xien pi. It shouldn't take long. There are only a thousand

228

of them. Fine men too. I was with them just now, and shared some of the spirit of their revolt. But it seems the rain came from some clouds and frustrated their attempt on this Fu jian's reign. "The rain on the reign by the shores of the Wei –" Well, I'm not good at these rhymes like Wang Zhia. But at any rate they failed to obliterate this monarch, Yung ku, Wen yu, son of Fu xiun, this impostor who had on his back at birth red marks that spelt out a message: Xao fu chen yu tu will rule Xien yang! Well, I am sick of all of these impostors! And if you ask me this rain came down by the help of a traitorous cloud-dragon. And if I could find him – Have you ever seen a dragon by any chance – They are very powerful creatures!'

The man looked madly at Nai, as though lusting after something. Nai felt his hair stir in terror.

'I note that you are nodding,' said the man. 'A man of few words, I see. I suppose you save them up being a poet? What most people scatter freely, you want to make pay. What a very plebeian idea! And you haven't perfected it, have you? If you had, you wouldn't be running away from China. I hear you're going on a pilgrimage. Just exactly what are you after? Just exactly what are you searching? Come, you can be frank with me. I'm from your part of the world. Are you looking for someone you can plot with? Are you looking for someone to gang up with against the Emperor, the true Emperor, not this upstart? Where is this person you are looking for? Where are they?' The man looked madly at him. 'Have you ever been to somewhere where they don't write poetry, and no one tells any tales?'

But a voice called, 'Excuse me one moment.'

And the man turned about, and Nai also, to see Jen returning with Kun and Lun. The old men hurried up to Nai, wheezily panting, and once they were there they drew him back towards them. Meanwhile the snake-lipped man stared at them with pale eyes, and a hiss came forth from his teeth reptilianly.

And Confucius said, 'Excuse me, gentleman, but I saw you about to lay hands on our friend here, and I thought I ought to explain that it is best if he stays with us at the moment. He is a pilgrim friend of ours, and at this moment in the city it would not be advisable for him to accept any invitation, no matter from what quarter. We have to be off early tomorrow. We wish to escape with all speed. We must apologise if this does not suit your arrangements.' And Confucius stood against Nai now, tall and dignified. But the man stared back, twitching his robes, his eyes roaming menacingly.

'It seems, my friend,' he said, 'that you impute to me a haze of dubious motives. Just what do you think I intend to do with our friend here? I regard him with as precious esteem as you do. I have the feeling he is looking for someone, and I am just fascinated to see where this person is. I wish him all speed. I follow his movements with interest. I am wholly with him in his endeavours. But I must say, moreover, that I shall be disappointed if he hasn't found what he seeks before the border. I couldn't bear to think of him leaving the bounds of China without this happy discovery we all wait for. Indeed, if I chance to find him one day from Dun huang, and still the mission not accomplished, then that would be another case. I should think seriously then of grabbing his hair and tossing him into Hell.' The man stared at the two old men. 'And I have to say it,' he continued, 'I don't think you are strong enough to stop me.'

But Nai took courage now and he said, 'It seems to me you are menacing me with these suggestions. Yet you talk in riddles, and before I make my conclusions, perhaps you could speak more openly. Why do you talk of dragons? And what makes you think that I am seeking someone? I'd like to know more before I answer your insinuations.'

The man looked at him angrily. 'Do I have to speak plain?' he said. 'I think you know what I am referring to. I do indeed menace you. To speak in a figurative fashion, I'm threatening to have you carried off to Hell. Does that make it plain? You are all alone with me here. Nothing restricts my actions. Nobody would ever see what I do to

230

you. So to put it plain to you: yes, I am threatening you. Tell me what you know.'

'Then it is as I thought,' said Nai. 'Whatever you are, you are indulging in menacing behaviour. You are seeking to extort from me information under the threat of physical violence. This is not polite behaviour. I think you should consider whether a man wearing robes such as your own, should give himself to criminal acts in an ancient capital like this, where in days gone by lived the noblest of emperors.'

A strange hiss came from the man. He looked at Nai with eyes blazing. Restlessly his hands stirred and rippled. A weird flickering seemed to flow over him, making his robes wave, as though currents of life were stirring in them.

'Give me a straight answer!' he said. 'This person you are seeking: what do you know of her? Where is she hidden? You must know something. You have this last chance to tell me, or I swear the ground will open beneath your feet.'

'You are doing it again,' said Nai. 'Can you not see that this behaviour of yours is unacceptable? A man such as yourself should not stoop to menacing in a public street as if he were no more than a bandit.'

'Thus it is!' hissed the man, and he stretched out his hand to seize Nai by the shoulder.

But Lun now leapt forward at the man. 'You old windbag!' he shouted. 'Do you threaten to do that? Well, remember who you are, and remember who we are as well. And remember who he is, for what you do to our friend here, this is not a minor matter. You think you are invincible because you wear those yellow robes. You have the mind-poisoning of the Emperors. They all think they're invincible, but what is in our Annals but a succession of Emperors kicked in the dust? This will happen to you, my friend, wear the yellow how you will. And I might fetch you one myself!'

'You have neither the rank nor power,' then said the yellow man fiercely. 'I could overpower you both in this street.'

231

But a voice said, 'Good day to you all. This is a quiet town. I'm glad to meet some life at last.' And a stranger approached them. Also dressed in strange clothes: long flowing robes, embroidered all over with fiery dragons, he came to them with a serpent-face, with snarling snaky lips, and a golden and flamy glow to his hair. And when he came to the group of them, the man in yellow stepped back, and he stared at the newcomer aghast and amazed.

'I think I must be in Chang an,' continued the newcomer, 'but it is so much more quiet than I expected. It is almost as if someone were planning to stir up a rebellion in the town, and everyone had taken to their houses. But who could be doing that? Someone with a grudge no doubt. Someone who resents the recent wars. But I shouldn't think it'll do much good. What's the point in ditching Fu jian? No one can do much with the Northern kingdom now. I heard some rumours recently that both North and South were done, for they say an even greater force is descending. I don't know what this force can be – some elemental fury? – but it threatens to sweep away the whole of China.'

'You!' now exclaimed the man in yellow. 'You, here again for battle! You that I have searched the very globe for! What have you done with them? What have you done with the prize? What have you done with the thing, the object you snatched from me? You must forgive me, masters, if my speech is a little obscure and strange. You must forgive me if I talk not quite like a passing townsman. But I have known this man before, fought with him in sudden fight, searched for him, but he flees me. And well I met him last in another place: to the East, where he stole something from me! Where has he put it, eh? That's what I must know! Where has he put my prized possession?'

'Possession?' said the newcomer. 'I think there must be a mistake. I didn't take anything that actually belonged to you. You seem to speak as though the heavenly law were on your side. Surely, my friend, it is the other way round. I took away something which you were stealing from some-body else, something which naturally and legally belonged

232

elsewhere. I don't think you can upbraid me with any action of that sort. I wonder if these gentlemen will agree with me? I don't know if any of them know the case to which I am referring, but I imagine some of them will have a guess at it.'

'What brings you here?' then said the man in yellow. 'What makes you appear on this street? You know everything, and you have no mind to tell me, and yet you come here meeting with me, brazenly among these others, of all men in the world my enemy. What are you plotting now then? You know this poet here, don't you? I can't believe you are not plotting with him? For sure that's it. It's all a plot. You're hiding and he's seeking. Well, give him it fast before you get to Dun huang!'

The newcomer looked astonished. 'What wild accusations!' he exclaimed. 'I assure you I have spoken to no one here recently. And as for him: is he a poet? I really wouldn't know. If he's seeking something, good luck to him, that's his business. But I assure you what you suggest is totally unfounded. But now: it's late. Should we look for some tea somewhere?'

The man in yellow stared back. 'Let there be no third time,' he hissed. 'I shall not cease my vigilance.' And he turned and went away from them, and off down another street, where as they watched there came horsemen: the guards of the beleaguered monarch, pursuing the rebel Xien pi, and bloodthirstily cutting them down in the road.

PART FOUR

Dun huang

Chapter Fifteen

But in the Western heaven, meanwhile, beyond the Jade Gate, at the farthest reach of the Kun Lun Mountains, beyond Guan yin's West Paradise and the Pure Land, in the heaven of the great nine-tiered city, surrounded by gold walls, by the orchard of the peaches which renders the juice of immortality, now sat the King of Tai, presiding in another court, ready for Pan Dao Hui, the feast of peaches. And he sat upon a terrace watching the courts of heaven spread before him, ceremonial ways, ornamental moats and bridges, and he presided among the courtiers, the immortals of the various grades, wearing the seven categories of colours: scarlet, azure, black, mauve, and the fertile hues of grass, lush and burnt, and nature-colour.

But there marched into the heaven-court now the gods with their attendants, arriving for the great gathering of the peaches. And first there came Guan ti, the chief god of war, he who fought on earth in the Three Kingdoms. Frowning was his scarlet face, red as the jujube fruit, and yet measured and firm, with the strength of integrity. He strode in the court in mighty boots, with curled tops and curled arm-shields, and his green clothes flowed among his twisted armour, while on one side his equerry, and on another his son, marched briskly, and his horse nodding behind them.

Next came the god of wealth, Xai shen, with his attendants, that sweep the coins up from the floor by the money-tree. About him came his footmen with strings of cash, his butler with the inexhaustible chest of silver. They came bearing fruit-ingots of gold from the wealth-boughs, and nuggets of electrum from the trunk-furnace, and in the midst the god himself, with black cap and pouch in his hand, laughing beneath his wind-twisted moustachios. And still he rolled and fanned himself, while all about him shimmered, clinking, jingling and rattling the trophies of treasure.

Now when these gods had kowtowed to the King of Tai and taken their places on the platform, there came into the court next three gods together, that were the gods of happiness. For the Xings arrived, that were Zhou, Fu and Lu, inseparable mandarins marching together, and about them fluttered the symbols of their cause, as they progressed over the flagstones. For first came Lu, the god of salaries, in his scholar's cap, holding a scroll, and a deer capered behind him, which was the sound of his name, stepping dappled in the summer sunshine. Next came Fu, the god of cheer, that smiled with his round, sleek face, and since the sound of his name in his language was bat, the happiness bats winged and twittered pink above his head.

And last of the trio there waddled an old man, that was the god of longevity. A staff he walked with, bowing in his steps, holding a peach of immortality, and a crane flew over him, with red head bent back, elegantly sitting on the winds, for the god of longevity had power over men's lives, and could sometimes twist the figures of allotted years, as he had done with a young scholar, fated to die at nineteen, who giving him a jar of wine, had the numbers reversed, and lived till ninety-one, singing the praise of the star-deity. Thus waddled on Zhou xing, and the sun sparkled upon him, his huge, bald, domed head like an egg.

And when all these gods had kowtowed to the King of Tai, then rose the deity and bowed to them welcoming, and he said, 'Great gods of Zhongguo, you have come to this great festival, and I in my humble fashion welcome you, for few are the festivals of the peach-gathering, and rare and rich is the honour to taste that immortal fruit. Yet it is with trepidation that I bid you welcome, for this task was to have been that of the Jade Emperor, but as you know urgent personal business has contrived to keep him from us this day. Wherefore have the goodness to accept me as his

238

substitute. In his name be you welcome. Move into your mansions, and prepare for this first day's banquet. Tomorrow will others come, and we will greet them. Tonight let there be rejoicing.' And the King of Tai ceased, and all murmured assent, and the gods left the square for their rich pavilions.

But as they went a mandarin came, and approached the King of Tai and said, 'My lord, I come to you with troubled brow. For though the gods are gathered here to feast and make merry, yet ominous reports have come in from the frontiers. Great king, we have heard that strange things stir out in the wastes beyond, and that the tribes of the wall are restless and hungry. I have sent more scouts to observe and report. Meanwhile, we sit here idle, debating faith, while the kingdom crumbles. Should we not rather cancel the feast and cancel the great council, for Buddhism has no urgency against these matters?'

And the King of Tai said, 'Find out all you may, and come to me again. Indeed I have urges to the defence of the empire. But let us not alarm these deities, but rather be glad they are here, for what are all gathered may be more easily deployed. I have martial instincts, more so than the Jade-King. Should there be sudden attacks, away will these talkers go to man the borders. Yet keep all quiet now. In military matters, one mind planning secretly is best.' And the King of Tai winked at the mandarin, and together they went, and joined once more the massed gods climbing the stairs.

But the fiery dragon, Wo Long Wang, raged about the land of China and he said, 'Why now, the Emperor is a dragon! He walks in the common street! The Jade High King sniffs about the backstreets, accosts solitary travellers! Low is the high king. Yet I have dug my teeth in him. I have mouthed his silver clouds. And there in the streets I have outfaced his menace. A king has little strength out of office. But he said he would come again. He would not let Nai out of China, and the day before he reached Dun huang, he would take him. Well, I must watch and guard, and be cunning as I slide along across this little land of China.'

Now the dragon went floating from the East, and stirred by his scaly tail, the night came on behind him. It fell on the seas, where the fringe of the coasts dipped dust-bowl and jungle into the deep. It fell on Hua dong, on the lakes and streams, and on Mount Tai and Mount Huang of twisting shapes. And the dragon went over paddy-field, over buffalo-trodden bog, over the great gorge-channelled river, where merchant ships spread their battens and ride to sink into the colourless dusk.

And Wo Long Wang said, 'Well, I have stirred up his kingdom surely, and that will keep this silver rival troubled. For the civil war I spread about lingers still in the North, and the state of Liang receives the attacks of the braving Southern forces. Moreover, now the rabid pirates have I hurled at the shores, for the Zhe jiang raiders at the coast of the Yang zi, these have I roused under their manic leader Sun en. And here will all the Southern empire have ports and trade disrupted. Yet these are but petty things to what I have also done, for all the barbarians within the wall I have now given scope to bring chaos. No longer Fu xian is my champion. I have chosen the true barbarians.'

Now when the dragon had proceeded with the night upon his back across the weird grooved pillars of Yunnan, from the Central South up towards the dry lands, he flew to the roaming pastures and there did he see the roads that lead to and from Chang an. And gazing down he saw on the road that leads West from the capital, the travellers hasting with carts and carriages, with guards and monks, Buddhist prayer-wheels encoached, and Fa xian on his white horse riding in the fore. And Wei he saw there with his ambassador's chariot swaying still, its curtains for ever closed, and Nai and Tawny rattling on in their cart, sitting wearily bounced about by the road.

And the dragon said, 'Why there again, the poet and the pilgrims that fled from Chang an, the caravan that escaped, as the very gates closed before the siege came down upon them, hurrying away in the dawn, while the Xien pi made their bidding to have the town. These must I guard, for my rival dragon, he shall not have their eating. Blessings upon you, little cart, clattering on the track! I hunted you through the land, but when I found you, the hunter and hunted shifted their rôles. Hie ever to Dun huang, and the day before you get there, I will come back and guard.'

Now the dragon when he had passed the travellers moved on to the West, and came soon to the rocky pass of Gansu, and there did he behold the Great Wall that snakes along the hills, and divides the known world of Zhongguo from the grim regions. And the dragon went hungrily, and slithered over its stones, and he mounted and fell and twisted and roamed like the wall, and when he came to a point of vantage, he hung there with the dusk, and swayed his great head staringly this way and that, sniffing the air, for he was thoughtful, and a long while he sat on the fence pondering.

And when the dragon threw about his gaze to the vast wastes he said, 'What a world lies there beyond the wall, as great as any stretch that is within it! See how the Mongol regions lie stretching into limitless space! See how the Gobi lies half in the moon, gasping with eternal thirst! Look now at the pine-clung Altai, where the Huns have their central kingdom, the prairies of the wastes whose riches could feed a million million steeds! And see, even yet, in the sultry afternoon, midge-haunted, the steppes pour on to the West, rolling towards the Roman lands, strange people, strange faiths! Ah, surely vast and grand is the land beyond our marching wall. Such views I get, as I cruise by the moon.' And Wo Long Wang hung silent, cloudlike in the twilit air, and he pondered the question of going further.

With slowly shifting limbs then, as a cloud changes its shape, transforming its stretched vapours and piled-up billows, as if blown by the evening wind, fragrant from phoenix-rich China, in sleek jade skin gliding over the grasslands, Wo Long Wang moved Northward, drawn by long-puzzled reach, in the hovering hour of dusk, beyond the great Wall, and he flew about the Mongolian plains, where the Huns ranged in their hordes, and he coasted above the gold-rich Altainula, and he flew North over the prairies where the summer-dry grasses waved, floating above the fir forests. He reached even the tundra, blooming briefly with lichen, browsed by reindeer, hung with midges, and even into this cold he went to where the world holds its breath, for this Hellish vast of all places on earth is the coldest.

And he saw there in the evening light a vast ring of sky-touching mountains, a range of bare peaks, barring the path, a square of fortress summits. And he saw in the clouds that hung above the mountains a strange glow of fire from within, a reflection of burning that seemed to arise from the midst of the guarded cold. And the dragon stared amazed at this far-off strangeness, this burning imprisoned, this fire in the dark at the end of the world.

And the dragon said, 'What then? Whence is that strange light? Whither comes that burning in the permafrost? For of all eerie things I have seen in my sliding about earth, that flame on the edge of the land in the deeps of the cold . . . Well, I will go to it. I will see what I will see. I will go to the world's worst country. For Fate has perhaps led me here, the very waves of Fate, to seek and stir the very base of kingdoms. O wide and everlasting heavens, my old home, whose stars even now come peeking at me, wait but a little while now, but a little while. Your master comes soon, well fed, his tasks accomplished.' And Wo Long Wang slid on again over the tundra's cold, and into regions where man cannot follow.

Now when a new day had come to the world, rising from the mulberry tree of the East, staining the horizon with mulberry-juice and flinging bright gold at the zenith, then in the Western Heaven above the Kun Lun Mountains, the gods arose and washed and drew on their raiments, and they moved from their apartments among the nine tiers of the celestial city. From the bounds they walked then, where the aureate walls fall towards the Kingfisher's River, and they came to the great courtyards through the Meridian Gate of the mighty Western Palace, and here with the King of Tai they sat to watch the arrival of the newcomers.

First then stepped the moon-goddess, beautiful Cheng O, wife of I, the primal archer. To the moon she once flew, having eaten the pill of immortality, to live there on the dew and cinnamon trees, for she found the pill by the white light coming from its hiding-place among the high beams of her cottage, and eating it she left, her husband stretching out his arms to the vanishing phantom. To the yard thus came the beauteous one, clothed in white, with long pink sleeves and ribbons floating, and before her there hopped busily a white rabbit, with long legs like the hare of perversion.

Next into the parade-ground came Tou Mu, the Bushel Mother, that was the goddess of the North Star. Two dogs ran before her, a grey and a brown, snuffing about the joins in the flagstones. The goddess entered in a gay cart, richly painted, with high red wheels, and in the balustraded enclosure, on a lotus of shading pink, the goddess sat waving her eight arms. In one hand she held a flaming disc, in another a lotus, in a third a wand with red tassels, and so there progressed this colourful lady, smiling at the assembled dignitaries.

But when these goddesses had been received, there came a famous trio to the courtyard, for the gods of literature marched in next, revered by the land where the text is sacred. First came Wen chang, seated in his palanquin, dressed in the grey robes of a mandarin. A crook in his hand, a pile of books beside him marked this man of the incarnations. But holding his brush and ink-stick, trotting by his side came a weird demonic figure. Grey all over, with wrinkled skin exposed and muscles standing in gnarled bunches, Kuei xing hobbled grinning, a tiger skin round his loins, god of examinations.

Last in the trio, running with a scroll in his hand, there hurried up late Redrobe, for Redrobe is the man who scrapes in at the rear with last-minute passes. For in the

243

examinations, the student who has not worked, and who fears that his efforts will meet with defeat, he prays to Redrobe, and the old man, if he is pleased, nods his head and gets the papers accepted. So did the three gods process into the courtyard, and were received by the Jade Emperor.

But as the King of Tai Shan looked about now he said, 'Gods of the air, the peaks, the waters, welcome are you all, both those that arrived yesterday and those who have just entered our heaven. Our meeting is begun, this great peach-festival, and the days before us are given over to feasting, and then when we have dined and entertained ourselves with music, dancing, with interludes, the grand ceremony is to be acted, where, from the ancient peach-orchard, we immortals pluck the fruits of immortality.

'But gods, I must tell you now that you have been summoned here this season not alone for snatching fruit from branches, not alone for songs, music or sleeve-dancing, not alone for friendship and conversation. Indeed our meeting this month as the autumn comes on, and the White Tiger begins his prowling, is dedicated to hard things, serious matters, and your voices are to be heard in a council.

'My friends, this year dire peril has come to our land, and long-sewn things have flourished in evil. Wherefore we are to discuss a foreign invasion of our kingdom, an influx of faith not natural or national. The question of Buddhism, my lords, that philosophy and ritual path: this is to be debated amongst us. Do we consider it sound? Do we honour its beliefs? Do we wish its faith to take root in our country? Do we rather not consider its nature too strange, too alien, too eclipsing for our traditions: these things, great deities, are to be faced by us in the council. So think upon these things, great powers, discuss them amongst yourselves, and let us give them an ear in the midst of the rejoicing. Now has there been forgot some last, great deities? I think I see them coming. Wherefore let us welcome these, and then, let us in to the banquet-chamber.'

244

And the Jade Emperor ceased, for he saw coming into the courtyard, a final great parade of colourful figures.

For there floated into the courtyard then on a ship borne on clouds, shaped of the stumps of trees, knotty and gnarled, the Pa Xien, the Eight Immortals, who in such a craft made the great voyage to view the ocean's wonders. There was Han Chung li, and Chang guo Lao, and Lan Zai ho, the street-singer. There was Tie guai Li, and Han Xiang zhu, and the damsel Ho Xien gu. They sat in the ship, pot-bellied, fair-faced, wand-twirling, bristly bearded. And Zhao Guo chiu and Lu Tung pin sat also, mandarin-robed and coiffured and embroidered, in the peach-laden, fan-bearing, sword-holding, flute-hearing ship of magic. And the gods floated forward and were greeted with cheers by the assembled, and all then rose and followed the Tai Shan King towards the great feasting-places.

But as they went, the mandarin came again, and spoke to the King of Tai secretly and said, 'Great King, I have busied about the land, and drawn up all the reports about the barbarians. And true it is what we feared; the Huns are already marching, they descend from the North upon the Empire, and long it cannot be before the barbarians threaten our borders and begin again their devastating attacks. Yet also have I been to the guards and prepared them as you bade me, and they are gone out each man along the Great Wall, and the preparations they have begun to man the grand defences, and they but await your signal to arm the ramparts.'

And the King of Tai stared at the mandarin and said, 'You have done well. All this has been secretly accomplished. And truly now the deities of Zhongguo have all arrived at our heaven, and the great mass of the pantheon is already assembled. It is like an army coming softly, mobilising unawares, beginning even to form the battalions for a battle, and yet none of the generals yet has heard that war is in the air. Such things are good. This is the way to win wars! When the barbarians attack thus, we shall be ready. I have but to order the gods to battle. And along the Great Wall a bastion of divinity! Yet we must tread still secretly. Tell no one of these things. Meanwhile, all the deities are assembled. And yet we lack two gods; two old gods. Well, let them go their ways. Our plans and our force are enough to shield us.' And so the King went with the mandarin, and once more across the courts, they joined the other deities at the hall's entrance.

But while these gods entered the halls of the palace, there left the Western heaven a goddess swathed in cloaks, closely hooded, so that none there might know her. And she quitted the Kun Lun Shan, and flew out first over Turkestan's arid sand dunes. And she flew then towards the Gobi, known as Shamo, where Mongolian nomads stray and leave their skeletons, and the dry winds howl on it, for here rain never comes, and the sand eats continually with gritty teeth. And she came upon the turfy plains where the horses of the Huns go roaming, and the vast pastures washed by Irtish and Selenga.

And the cloaked goddess said, 'Why now, these regions seem calm enough. The sheep and the goats dot the untroubled prairie. The yurt-tents of the Huns hump their skin backs over the grass, and I see no blood-thirsty fiends issuing out of them. The Huns are indeed a vast race. Squat and vengeful are their natures. They of all our enemies could wound the deepest. Yet here is no commotion, nor Westward towards the Altai, nor further into the steppes and the grassy oceans.' And the white goddess made on again, gathering her robes about her, for now the autumn winds blew mean and sharply.

There the grass of the wastes became thicker. Blanched from the summer, it hummed below, mothed and daisied. There came a smell of warm earth, of seeds from feathered herbs, and the rivers reflected the clouds among the herbage. She came towards the Serenga River and the old biding-place of the King of the Huns, and now she saw the hordes massing and stirring. For there were tribes of the Xiung nu, with their comrades, the Xien pi, and the related nations of Rong and Di in Hunnic alliance, and the horse-men on their squat steppe ponies, swirled and thundered among stockades, and flocked in their regiments, eager for slaughter. And they were like ants there, that jingle and teem, glittering the face of the rocks and ant-hills, intent on milliard battle, their caustic ready in their tails, their beetle minds rejoicing in the thought of onslaught.

And the cloaked goddess sighed at this and said, 'Well, there is some threat. If I were a messenger, this would set me running. For how many are there of Huns on those plains? Enough to make many nations, enough to round the Great Wall, and sink their teeth in Zhongguo. Yet alas, have we had not enough of them? Did the Huns not just sack Chang an? Is it hardly a mortal's life since they toppled the Northern rulers? But these mean more mischief! Oh alas, Zhongguo, Zhongguo, how is your wealth prey to so many robbers! Yet what is it that stirs these barbarians? I see more shadows to the North. I see beyond the mountains' darkness and dire flickerings.' And the deity was silent again, and pulling her robes about her close, she sailed forth on her cloud to the wild regions.

So did the great white mother pass above the Lake of Baikal, hugest of fresh pools in the width of Asia, and she winged above its shiny depths, where the pine trees fall to its banks, and the silent forests cluster its sturgeon-haunted waters. Then did she wing above the ranges of Irkutsk, where the glossy martin and sable live among the fir trees, and as she floated Northwards in the bleak Siberian realms, the cold got greater, the lingering light lesser, and the sun was slung low in the frosty September sky, making the shadows of the prowling bears fall vastly. And beyond an icy river that flowed towards Arctic realms, she saw a great wall of square-ranged mountains.

And the goddess stared upon this realm and said, 'What is this at the end of the world? What mighty fortress of peaks is this before me? Now surely nor I, nor any of the gods of Zhongguo, have set our eyes before on such a forbidding place. What are those dark summits? See where

247

the forests cease about it: the boglike tundra spreads its midget life-forms, while brooding in the clouds lie these enclosing mountains. Who dares think what lies within them? And in this dusky light of the timid sun's low arc, do I not see there flashing and rustling and glowing? What are the fires hidden in the peaks at the end of the world? Dare I go discover?' And the goddess dallied a while, set on a streaky, sunlit cloud, and feared to descend into the abyss.

But as she stared at the mountains, she saw a terrible change, for there happened there what never happens fairly, for a mountain rose up itself, rearing behind the others, a crag, a peak, a summit arising from the earth, and it grew upon the horizon as volcanic fire trajected, glittering many lights, reflected in the cloudbanks. And there came a dragon's head now, horned and camel-like, cresting the hills, hung about with stars. And Wo Long Wang thus stared at the goddess, his snake-form glimmering along the horizon like the final sunset.

And the dragon said, 'Welcome, goddess, hidden in those cloaks. Well may you seek to hide your nature! For all the gods of Zhongguo are seeking your guilty head, and best is it you hide from their gathering, for now do all deities gather at the Mother of the West's, ready to eat her feast of peaches, but I brew a surprise for them to wreck their little sports, and blow away their kingdom.

'Well, do you like my new home? It is fiery and hot in this pit. Yet the air is cold. Verily a home from home here. For gloatingly I sit in the fires, like a desert dog in a puddle, and truly the people here like me. Of all the ways to Hell men find dotted about earth, this is the widest and greatest. Wherefore great knowledge is mine, and things I have discovered here, which shall shake not just China but the world. But what will you, Guan yin? Do you come seeking Xiang? I have not got her. She is hidden from us.'

And Guan yin said, 'No, great dragon, we do not seek her now, for the mighty Mother has spied where you have hidden her. Rather does she send me to seek what is

248

pressing now, for dire things are happening in these waste-lands. And what do *you* sitting here? For that also we would know. What is brewing among these wastes you have taken to? Have you not done enough? Is it not time to go back to the stars? Can you not leave the world to silence?'

But the dragon laughed and said, 'Dear goddess, you overestimate me. None of these things is in my control. Xiang is her own girl. She is a spirit not to be dominated. And she has gone where she wished to go. But as for these exploits: I do but sit here. I am but a witness of these stirrings, for here in this pit there is burning enough to set the world in ashes. I lit by chance on these mountains, and through them I discovered that there is power in the mass of matter far beyond dragons' power, even here in the bowels, in the hot Hell of the world. Wherefore is it strange that from this place there pour forth continually the barbar-ians? On China they rush, and from here onward, trans-figuring with terror the whole world.' And the dragon thus sunk down again, and the goddess watched him go, and when he had descended below the mountains, great fire and cloud came billowing, reaching up to the sky, and hung there like a tree in the heavens.

Chapter Sixteen

'You know,' said Tawny as they travelled, 'I think Wei'll become the Buddhist and you'll run off with Jen. It's much more fitting and suitable. Yes indeed! I can't see why you can't see it.' They were rattling on in the morning sun beside the loess terraces, which were shaped into strange rock-forms by the wind, Nai and Tawny, sitting in their cart, with Kun and Lun wearily journeying alongside. 'I mean, Wei is interested in Buddhism,' he went on. 'You don't seem to be at all. All you care about is pondering on these deep, mythic plots, and then every now and then bleating about Xiang. But Wei rides there thoughtfully, and talks with Fa xian, the great master. I wouldn't be surprised if he doesn't shave his head tomorrow. And everything that happens seems to strike him as the great vanity of the world.' Tawny fell silent for a while, and nodded his head sagely.

They were coming down from a detour now, which had taken them on the goat-tracks, and the mules were stepping gingerly until the plain road greeted them again. They found themselves in a valley now where the farmers had planted hemp-fields, and the harvest was on for the tall plants, the peasants scything the lush foliage, and off in bundles it went to be stripped and shredded and bludgeoned into the sacred paper. The sun was rising to its height of noon, yet dwindling in the arc of autumn.

'Well, it's nice to be on the level again,' said Tawny looking about, 'though I can't see the others. I suppose the ambassador has got a long way ahead. But these uneven hills! It's like trundling along on a cart made with square wheels. Poor Kun and Lun: they can't hear me now, but just look how miserable they are! They've done their best to stop this journey with something new every day. I don't know why they carry on with us. They're too old for this sort of bone-shaking. Yet they were talking with Wei a lot this morning, ever since that messenger came. Now that we know – what was it he said? – that the state of Liang is fallen to the South, they seem to think that Wei's mission is pointless, and that he might as well turn round and go back. And they've got a point, because if Liang is now the South's, how can you negotiate with your own forces? Poor old Wei's missions; they have a great way of turning out to be utterly futile! I suppose he takes it as a great confirming of Buddhism. I tell you: he'll become a monk.' And Tawny stared ahead now, trying to see along the road, where the rest of their party might have got to.

As they moved along the dusty tracks, trekking their way through the wrinkled face of old China, they came now where in little rows of huts the caterpillars munched on mulberry leaves. Tawny stared round interestedly as he saw the foreman cooking the little grubs in their cocoons, and others unwound the glossy threads and cared for the spun finery, which would go to the looms to be woven into pelts of deep-dyed lilac and rose. The mulberry trees shaded with their thick leaves the fruit that grew crimson in the branches, and all about the tree's floor, splodges of dye there were where the berries had been squashed in the dust.

'But how long is this journey of ours!' sighed Tawny after a while. 'We've been travelling for weeks now, ever since we scrambled, with them clapping the gates all round us, out of the besieged Chang an! But Dun huang seems no nearer. Is it just an allusion this journey? Are we really just staying in the same place? One by one it's wearying us. Kun and Lun are dropping. And you: look at you: you are a wreck and hobble about like a cripple. Kun and Lun have been saying: perhaps you'd better winter at Lintao. They make great ink-slabs there. That ought to please you. You can write a thousand epics while you're recovering.' And

251

Tawny sighed, and thwacked his stick down on the side of the cart. 'You don't have to answer,' he said to Nai sadly. 'I'm just amusing himself.'

After travelling a few more miles, they saw before them thankfully, the ambassador's party drawn up and taking a meal. They rattled towards them, and stumbling to the ground, fed their horses and joined the group to rest. The ambassador's carriage was pulled up, and the curtains were open, but no Jen was there inside. Instead on the ground and fully open to the air, she sat and feasted with the guards. Wei was a distance off. He and Fa xian, the monk, were talking seriously together. The old men and the younger sat wearily down, got out their food-baskets and brewed tea.

Tawny was at Nai's side still. 'It's nice to see Jen out,' he said. 'I never thought he'd allow her to do it. He's been keeping her cooped up for months as though she were some embarrassing freak. Now suddenly he releases her. You know, I think it's ever since he heard the news about the state of Liang having been conquered by our own forces. There's probably some deep, Buddhist significance behind it all. He has let go his desires. Are you feeling all right, master? You don't look it. You look like a sort of green jellyfish. Here, have some of this bread, and let me get the tea. You're enough to frighten a ghost.' Tawny moved away from Nai, and bustled about with the things, and soon he was guiding some tea into Nai's mouth.

But when Fa xian had finished with Wei and had gone aside to sit lotus-fashion beneath the trees, the two old men, Confucius and Lao zi, bustled over and sat alongside the ambassador. There was anxiety on their faces, for after long observing him, they had not liked what they were watching. So now they pinned him down, while the other pilgrims were dozing after their meal.

'Ambassador Wei,' Confucius said, 'we have travelled now since dawn, and still you have given us no indication of what is your answer to our request. You remember what happened? Yesterday at the ferry, we met a messenger hieing to Chang an. He brought them news that the state of Liang had fallen to our own forces of the Jin. Three commanderies have been taken, and now the province is no longer in enemy hands. This being so, your mission now is pointless. You have no one to deal with. We urged you to turn back therefore. You said you would think upon it. May we now know your answer?' And Confucius ceased and stared at him, as did Lao zi beside him, keen to know if their trials could be over.

But Wei said, 'My friends, scholar Kun, my dear friend, monk Lun, I have thought on your words and spent an anxious night wrestling with my conscience. It is true what you say. Now that Liang is ours, there is no need to try to negotiate agreements. The orders from the capital can be carried out. Ambassadors are not needed. I could well turn back. But what struck me last night again was: look at the people who depend on my company. The monk, Fa xian, for one. He would not have begun this journey, if I could not have assured him of my military escort. And then there is my friend Nai: he is anxious to get to Dun huang, may be he is even anxious to get to India. If I desert the party now, how would they fare forward? These war-torn days are the sport of brigands. As far as our party goes, it seems it is beholding to me to carry on with my journey.

'But my friends, there is another point. You recall how yesterday the news of the messenger struck me with dismay? My first mission in Chang an proved to be a delusion. It seems that now my second mission was also. These failures seemed to weigh upon me – poor Wei weighed down on his way! – and moved me to see my own life's utter futility. What have I been doing these many years, studying to succeed in the examinations, merely to take up tasks that are wholly pointless? I looked beyond myself to the monk, Fa xian, bound also upon a journey. How wise was his way compared with my own! How right was the path that leads to nirvana. I longed for the extinction which his faith alone could bring. Thus I decided I could not desert him.' And Wei finished his speech now, and turned his gaze to the monk, who under the great tree was meditating with serenity.

But Wei turned back and said, 'Yet my friends, one other thing I thought of in the night. You have noted that from this morning on, my concubine Jen is riding on horseback. This means her carriage has now nobody in it as it goes on its stately and comfortable way. You two are distinguished, and old men such as yourselves should not travel long in a rattling cart. Will you not therefore honour me by taking my carriage and henceforth journeying on cushions?' And Ambassador Wei smiled at the gods, who looked at each other a moment, but then nodded, eager for comfort.

Nai sighed and spoke at last, as he sat with his boy, leaning against the mossy tree trunk. And he said, 'Well Tawny, thanks to your tea, I am feeling a little better. Forgive me for being so glum, but my joints are all seized up, and rattling along, it seems as if always I shall vomit. A horrible sickness is in me ever, as though tottering a last mile, and all my strength I need merely to stay the travel. For indeed we have come far. How many days, how many weeks, since we were in Chang an, rushing from the capital, with the barbarians at our heels, and off along the Wei by the Nine Pinnacle Mountain! I had some strength then, but now so far, such high hills, such toil and such striving! Why, it beats me how you all can do it, and what a weak thing am I. And yet I have the greatest lust to go forward.

'Oh, Tawny, we have followed the Wei, and passed the Tien shui Commandery, and threaded the yellow-tinged trees of the Five General Mountain. And by Chen zhang to the hilly province of Chin we came, and took the detour through the deserted ranges. By dank mill-houses have we rattled, churning the white water, by log-cutters in the pine-stacked mountains. We have forded across the snow-fed streams, hugged the precipices, crested the gloomy-shouldered borders. Yet only now we approach Gansu, and the Yellow River. Only now we pass into the true wildness. How far, how far still seems Dun huang! How far

254

its hope of Xiang! Oh, Tawny, long is the way to our soul's sweetheart!'

And Tawny said, 'Ay, master, so you tell me every day, and telling me does not make the way shorter. You journey sick, and journey blindly, yearning ever in your soul. And yet how like the state of man is your journey!' And Tawny turned away, and did not show his face, but beat with his stick on the ground, raising the red dust.

Now when the pilgrims had eaten and drunk, Wei stood up and said, 'Comrades, it is time we were setting on again. For before us are the hills, and once those hills are crested great sights should greet us on the other side. For my friends, do you see it? Almost invisible from here there yet creeps a sandy line over those blue ranges yonder. That is the Great Wall, that ruined branch of which was set there by Qin Shi huangdi, the first Emperor. Wherefore good pilgrims, the end is in sight, for the pass of Gansu begins there, and tonight if we hurry, we may shelter in Lanzhou, and for the first time feast our eyes on the Yellow River.' And Wei then turned to get his horse, and the others sprang up from their rugs, and with high hearts they recommenced their journey.

But when Wei came to settle Jen that now braved the air, he smiled at her as he lifted her into the saddle, and with love and with pride did he hand her the reins to hold, tapping her gently on her trousered thigh. For Jen was in riding gear. Fair-faced she looked, among the furs and jerkins of a traveller. And Wei at last slipped her tiny feet into her shoes, for two red slippers she had tied by ribbons to the stirrups. And then he leapt himself in his saddle, and pulling in his reins, prepared to lead the pilgrims forward.

Meanwhile, as Nai went to get into his cart, his sickness came back with startling results. For as he went to climb up, he came over dizzy, and fell back, causing Tawny to shriek with alarm. The two old men, however, were approaching at that point, and Nai's fall made Lun throw his arms up in amazement. Confucius's hat was knocked off, so that confusion broke out, as they all tried to sort themselves back into good order. But as Nai climbed a second time up into the cart, the others heard him murmuring, 'O Xiang, Xiang, wait for me. I will get there I promise. Wait for me. Only wait for me!' And so he sat down on the bench and took up the reins. But the two old men were thoughtful, and a while they stood, wondering on what they had seen.

But then their new conveyance lit up their eyes, and they went towards the carriage. Eagerly did they gloat on its silken-covered seat, and the springs supporting the body. First with a glad cry, Lun leapt in, flung himself on the seat, and kicked up his feet to the canopy. Then Confucius, tall scholar, heaved himself aboard, and smiled to sink down into the cushions. But there came a twang, and the carriage lurched to one side, so that it scraped the axle. Cries of dismay went up, Tawny ran round in circles, and everyone stared baffled at the accident. But then Wei called for the servants to fix the cart, while he exhorted all else to carry on without them. The pilgrims thus moved on again, leaving Wei, Jen and the two old men, biding the repairs of the struggling guardsmen.

While they waited beneath the trees, Confucius spoke to Lao zi and said, 'Did you hear what Nai said, as he got into the cart? He was murmuring still about this Xiang, the bewitching sleeve-dancer, who lured him off to the country. It is absurd to think of her. She has long gone. She was stolen surely by the Northern forces. But it drives him in his illness. If we wish to get him to stop, we will probably have to face this compulsion. It is a pity Wei has decided to go on. We lost a chance there. But we must keep working on this poet's sickness. What do you think he suffers from? He is a strange type. His desires seem to wear out his body.'

But Lao zi said, 'Oh, I grow weary this task. I know not, old friend, if I can go much further. To travel in a carriage will at least ease the way. But why do we fool any longer with this poet? To Hell, alas, with the prophecy of the Duke of Zhou! To hell with the life-march of China! I want to go home. Let us leave this idiot to the dragon. We can't shield him for ever.' And Lao zi sighed and walked away.

But the carriage was fixed now. The old men climbed in gingerly. The carriage remained steady. Amazed with their new comfort, with blissful sighs the travellers then made on again.

The pilgrims were moving forward now through the morning plain, to where the crags of loess marked the hills' beginning. The day was cool and sunny. The clear air rang with the call of rooks, and the streams babbled through the yellow poplars. As they came to fresh country, they encountered a fresh sight: camel-trains loaded with cotton, the lumbering beasts lunging with their long necks swaying, and behind them the ochre woods on the slopes. Yet above on the wrinkled ridges with winding serpentine gait, the Great Wall of China had its trailing fragment. And Nai's heart leapt to see it clearly now, and his spirit went roaming with it.

Yet Wei and his party rode tardily out of sight from the others, and they trundled along beside a stream coldly clattering. There was sadness in the autumn, and the berries ripe on the haws, seemed poignant like a last feast before the winter. Wei was troubled. He noted now Jen's nervousness, but did not unduly think of it. But she smiled upon him, and the soft light lit her face, showing her to him as everlasting beauty. There was a sound of a horn calling. Jen gazed at the ground and sighed. A shiver of frosty wind made the trees hiss above her.

But Wei gave a laugh, and pointed with his whip, for there were huntsmen riding over the leafy hills. Through the crisp, sunny air came the melodious sound of hounds, belling to the echoing valleys. The horsemen looked gay, their legs clashed on their blue felt saddles, their reflex bows and quivers rattled behind them. The hounds had the scent. They were hurrying towards the pilgrims. Wei looked about to see their quarry. Out of the corner of his eye he saw Jen slip from her horse and a flash of russet flit away from him.

With skin prickling with horror he leapt from his horse, and ran to where the hounds were yelping. They were

257

worrying the fox, tugging it limb from limb, and fighting over the bloodstained fur. Wei jumped in among them, striking them with his boot. The brush he seized and wrested it from them. Over his head he held it, and as the hounds surrounded him howling, the huntsmen arrived and cheered him good humouredly. The hounds were whipped away now. Wei stood in the midst of the sacrifice, blood staining the ground and his hands and sleeves. The huntsmen spoke with Kun and Lun. Then they rode away again. Wei was left with a fox's tail.

Confucius came to Wei and said, 'My friend, we must hurry forward. The servants have left us, and the pilgrims are well ahead now. There is no time to delay. Bury what remains of the fox, and let us strive forward again on the road. None of us needs speak of this act. What is gone is gone. We may speak the truth of a fall from a horse and a grave. Ambassador, you have been touched by spirits. Yet here was no evil. Bury your love now, and come away.' And Confucius stood firm, staring at Wei with compassionate eyes, and the man dazedly did what he had been told.

Wherefore Wei took out his sword now which he carried in his saddle, and he dug up the dusty loess by the babbling stream, and where were red berries of the wayfaring tree, he made a grave for Jen's torn, foxy limbs. And he set her in the earth, and strewed the mound with autumn flowers and leaves. But when he returned, as the others watched, he saw Jen's horse standing forlornly, and her little red slippers dangled from the stirrups just as she had slipped out of them. So he took the slippers, and set them on her grave, and shed there his tears, alone. Then did he take up again the reins of his road, and stay on the way he had chosen.

The weary sun was sinking to their left, as the pilgrims came over the hills at last towards Lanzhou. The firs on the sandy track opened a way for them to see, and the great valley stretched out before them. Of resin smelt the warm air, and dusty pine needles, as they looked across to the peaks in the North beyond. But the others caught up with them there, and while Wei rode at a distance, Kun and Lun gave the pilgrims their grievous news. How bitter it was thus to hear of death at the very moment at which they stared upon the pass of Gansu! How bitter to taste of grief as the route was before them that led the ancient path towards the West. And beneath them with its silty flood, unseen by the pilgrims till now, the Yellow River flowed, the backbone of China.

But when they sat together at evening up in the gallery of the inn at Lanzhou, and the room on one side overlooked the central courtyard, but on the other, built out with timbers and eaves, gazed out over the Yellow River, they spoke of the sad events of the day, and sighed to think on them. For Nai was there, plunged in dismay, with Tawny at his side, and Kun and Lun sat over their steaming wine-cups, staring forth to sigh at the Huanghe. But Wei was not amidst them, for the Buddhist had taken him away, and they had gone to meditate together.

Wherefore Nai sighed again and said, 'That girl! She was so good! I cannot tell you her virtue! To be thrown from her horse like that and trampled under cruel hooves! To lie forlorn in a wayside grave! Could we not have brought her to Lanzhou! Should we not go and dig her up again? Would it not be best to find a better grave in this city? To leave her where she could gaze forth on this great seaward river, that sumptuously floods the plains of the ancient empire!' And Nai was silent again, and they all sat there thoughtful. 'Could we not?' he said suddenly reawakening them.

But Lao zi shouted, 'Leave her! She is beneath a red-berried tree. There is traveller's joy with feathery blooms just by her. Will you pitch her into a city, where men grasp and snap all day? Oh, she is alone with the great dream of Nature. She was a rare spirit, and has gone to virtuous rest. And she had little cause to show charity. But there! The Dao trembles among the thorns of the rose, and love is her fragrance.'

But Nai now burst out weeping and said, 'Oh Lun, why did you speak? Is not my love's name in our language

259

Fragrance? Does not Xiang bring me fragrance? And what if she is gone like Jen? When shall I ever see her again? When? When? To come all these miles like Wei here, and to have her snatched from him! How may I not know that my fate is not the same? To come all these miles in hope and to reach at last Dun huang – and where is she? To have been led by a phantom! Oh, cruel, cruel! How Fate bewitches us! How will come an end to my yearning?' And Nai put his head in his hands, and his whole body shook with sobs, so that the others stared amazed.

But then Confucius said, 'Well Nai, if this is truly the reason for your journey, I doubt not but that you are deluded. If you have come through half China in the expectation of a reunion with a girl you left in Shou chun, I can only marvel! You are bound to be dismayed! How can it be otherwise? What possessed you to think that Ling Xiang could be at such a distance? Indeed you should be weeping, for this is prize folly to ride so far and to drag so far your old masters after you!' And Confucius stared at him, while Nai stopped weeping, and he returned the stare with grim expression.

And Nai said, 'When I left my home, I left it alone, nor did I ask that anyone should accompany me. I neither strove to align myself with my comrade, ambassador Wei, nor seek your dogged fellowship for such a long travel. I made my own way forward, and on my own quest was I bound, and I had no duty to make justification to anyone. You chose to think that I had devoted myself to a new faith. I will not deny that I had leanings. But how could I have told you that I journey because of the promise in a dream? I cannot even be sure I dreamt it. And even if it all proves vain, still do I go forward. What is it to you if I lay unto my soul a little comfort?'

And Confucius stared back at him and said, 'Your words are just. You have not to answer for this journey. But I would that I could plumb that strange region of your soul where the spring of your actions is even beyond your own comprehending. My son, my son Nai, I have known you two years now. Some slight freak of foolery brought us first together. But ever as I know you, do you slip ever from my grasp, and from Lun's, until you drive us both to distraction! We are old men, my boy! You have led us a desperate dance. I wish you had the means to have mercy on us. But still we must follow. And do you come all this way for a dream, for the dreamed fancy that with Xiang you will have some reunion?' And Confucius stared at Nai, as did Lun with glaring intent, and Tawny also, leaning his elbows on the table.

And Nai said, 'No. I came in quest of the Great Tale. This has been my lifelong journey. My soul is linked with Xiang because she also is in pursuit of it, the Great Tale of all men, all gods. I would not have let myself pursue her, if I had not thought that she and I were destined for some such purpose. It was easier to abjure. But through hard hillsides and torrents Fate takes us all her way forward. You say that Xiang is gone. It pleases you to dismay me, so that I might return home again. But if I have to go without her, still I will go. The Great Tale waits for me. I suppose I seem mad. Well, I am a poet. But long ago this mission came to me, when there came a visit to the Southern capital by twelve strange foreigners.

'It was over ten years ago, and there arrived in the court of Jian kang, twelve musicians from India. My uncle being a courtier invited them to our house, and I hung about and talked to them. They had weird singsong accents, and their tones were confused, but I managed to find an understanding, and heard rich things among them: they spoke of their ancient poems, epics, they call them, of the Aryan. Huger than fifty books, it seems, they have in their lands Great Tales that sum up all India's heritage. Grand are the narratives, of gods and heroes, battle, and exile, and hard journeys. When the musicians had gone, I spent long thinking on these things, convinced that in the days of the Shang we had such. I caught then the fire to revive these ancient forms, and to find and sing the Great Tale.'

The night came down outside. The chill of the autumn

seized them, the sunset fading on the Yellow river. As Nai ceased his tale, Tawny reached in a bag he carried, and brought forth a shining cup. He placed it on the table, and Nai with growing amazement looked on the golden cup he had seen in Shou chun, the cup that Xiang had showed him, at whose vision the heavens opened, gods came, dragons thundered.

And Tawny said to him, 'Ay, I thought you would recognise it. It does indeed come from Xiang. You need not fear that she is dead. She lives, that is for sure, and was taken Westward. The forces that seized her on that eve of the Battle of the Fei took her off to the mountain regions. There was it I talked with them, and took from them this cup, slipping out on the road like a beggar. Have faith then, master. Whether in Dun huang or not, you will meet Xiang on your journey.'

Chapter Seventeen

In speckled robes, in brocaded silks, in black hats with tassels, in tiaras with dangling pearls, with attendants with fans and guards with maces, with animals symbolic and bats and bluebirds buzzing, with a clattering and a chattering, and a drumming and a trumpeting, the deities now congregated in the great council-chamber, and rustling like the wind in the poplars at last got themselves seated.

The King of Tai himself swept in, stern and proudly swaggering, and made his way with a canopy over him, musicians blowing at his sides, great capering grooms who rushed upon the other gods and roughly pushed them aside, and liveried others who debated with others liveried as to which gods had precedence: all these made their way into the thronging halls, beneath the great red and green rafters, and sat at last in quarrelsome peace, frowning at each other.

The council-chamber was huge and steamy. Clouds of incense billowed about. Red-faced lesser deities by the tripods were choking. The mass of heads went in rank and rank to the sides, and a thousand hats were turning this way and that eagerly, and gossiping fairies leapt up and down from their seats, craning their necks to see if their friends or enemies sat close, and important officials suddenly remembered important things and swept regally and seriously down aisles, to mutter with concerned frowns and conspicuous business to other officials as concerned and equally busy. But the King of Tai now banged his gavel, and thousands upon thousands cried hush! And there was even more din in the hall.

But when a silence had come truly, the King of Tai spoke

and said, 'Great gods of Zhongguo, now is come the time for our council, and we are to hear your voices concerning the issue of which I spoke to you before. The debate is to be of Buddhism. Do we desire it in our country? Do we oppose or welcome this faith from India, which has no roots or origins in our soil? Let us hear your views on this. Wen chang speak first, for all princes should listen to the voice of literature.'

The King was silent as Wen chang, in his robes as a mandarin, rose and addressed the assembly. Wen chang said, 'We are to debate if Buddhism stays. No one can deny that Buddhism is here. From our conquests of Turkestan, and our victorious campaigns against the Huns, we established contact with the West which brought it to us. It is, however, a foreign belief. It derives from the Hindu tradition. There is no basis for it in the Middle Kingdom. And worst of all it is for us merely a faith of air, for there are no sacred texts for us to ponder. How can there be, therefore, support given to a teaching which has not the means for it to be taught? I am in favour of Buddhism being outlawed. It is not what we hold holy.' And Wen chang was silent, but next arose Kong Mu, the ugly god of chemistry.

And Kong Mu said, 'I agree with Wen chang. What purpose will it serve, allowing in this religion? It says all life is suffering, therefore avoid it! This is merely life-denying. How may knowledge be promoted, things be discovered, the progress towards perfecting the pill of immortality be fostered, if we are to harbour these defeatists in our realm, continually sapping the energy of the people?' And when Kong Mu had said this, the other gods agreed with him, including the kitchen god who murmured, 'Ay, banish these monks, for they are always at the kitchen door, begging for food just as you are cooking.'

But Pan ku, the creator god, stood up now, that was a dwarfish, rough-looking fellow, and he had young horns sprouting from his brow, and he carried in his hand a hammer and chisel. And nothing much the god wore but leaves and a bearskin cape, and thus did he speak to the company, 'Gods, you are not generous. What is all this mealy-mouthing? Is this the way to build a great kingdom? I acted not thus, when I hewed out the sky and earth, and laid down the great water-courses of China! If this faith appeals to the people, why then, let them have it! A little of what you fancy does you good. And so I counsel to let Buddhism have its day, and allow that pretty goddess to go her ways.' And Pan ku sat down again, nodding his head, and there were some murmurs for him.

But now spoke up the hearth-god, Zao Wang, and said, 'Ay, let them all come and be welcome. Is it truly our way to ban anyone from our hearth? Do we usually refuse hospitality? No, it is in our traditions to allow everything to come, for we know China is big and can eat anything. So it has been in the past, so it will be again. This Buddhism will give us much refreshment. Old maids they are who fear it will eclipse their power. Good men assimilate and prosper. I agree with Pan ku: the goddess should be made welcome. Why was she not asked to this festival?'

But at this there leaped up the Chamberlain who said, 'It is erroneous to suppose that such a personage was uninvited. The court invitations were issued to Guan yin just as they had been to all other divinities. You may recall that at the beginning of the year, the honourable Buddhist goddess was given a state reception of several days' length. The deity of compassion is absent today not through any calculation or incompetence of our office, but because she is not anywhere. She was not in her heaven when we sent for her. She was not to be found in any of the heavens. We have summoned her continually to appear and answer our charges at the council. But it merely seems the Buddhist has run away.' And the Chamberlain sat down again, nodding at the company, while the King of Tai gave him a glance of approval.

But there arose now the goddess Tou Mu, the Bushel Mother, who held up three of her eight arms for silence. And the goddess said, 'I am happy to put here the views of female deity, because we seem to be discussing principally

265

a female. And I would maintain, great gods, that this is a serious consideration, and that all here who are Daoists should automatically agree with me, for surely we have only to look around to see that China is weighed down with men, and it needs a balance of femininity in its pantheon. Wherefore I say: let us admit Buddhism, since it restores the harmony to the land. But also I'll say this: it will come in anyway. For we gods have no power to banish it. The gods but live on men, and since the mortals have espoused it, it is here to stay.' And the goddess sat down then, happy in her comments, though there was much murmuring and bustling at what she said.

Zhou xing arose next, with his great domed egghead, the long-speaking god of longevity. And there were some who saw him and groaned inwardly and yawned, for of old they knew this god's stretch of oratory. And Zhou xing said, 'Great gods of Zhongguo, I am reminded in rising here this day of an occasion now some two or three thousand years ago, or no, perhaps I exaggerate, for in the march of time, one's mind tends to wander happily hither and thither, but at any rate I distinctly remember such arguments as we are having here exercised the gods at the time of the great sages. For of Confucius and Lao zi we had arguments of their merit, and whether such mortals should be allowed into the natural pantheon. And I remember then the choice that faced us, for then we had to choose either to go forward or to go back, and what we had concluded in that debate, I am not entirely sure, for as the Bushel Mother says, it all happened none the less.

'But my lords, there is a further point, which your divinities should consider, and one which makes our debate here even more urgent. I refer to the distant past, and to something which many here are not old enough even to remember. The Duke of Zhou's prophecy! It has been spoken of much of late. And with good reason has it been spoken of. For the Duke of Zhou said shortly after his translation to the heavens, and in my own hearing was it spoken, that the path the Cowherd treads will be the path

266

of China. That is to say now: a Buddhist pilgrimage! When we consider then what attitude to take to this extra deity amongst us, and to the other deities and saints which are attendant on her coming, indeed to Buddha himself, who let us not forget, lived very close to this Western heaven in these very mountains, when we consider these things, we are deciding not just for now, but for the very future of the Middle Kingdom. Do we want it to take up Buddhism? Do we want it to worship Guan yin? But more important than that: do we wish it to march Westward? For this is what this journey means which the Cowherd is taking: the inevitable Westward march of China!' And the querulous old Zhou xing thus finished his speech, and tremblingly the great domed head was lowered.

Now after he had spoken, there leaped a number of gods to their feet all at once, and one by one the King of Tai called on them. For one of the Eight Immortals said, 'I would just like to make one point. The Cowherd in human form has not utterly committed himself. We know that he goes on a pilgrimage, but he has not become a Buddhist. It is not even certain that he really believes in it.' And another of the Eight Immortals said, 'In any case he goes to gather Buddhist texts, so it will not be true to accuse Buddhism of being textless.' And another one said, 'It is good to go on journeys. Did not we eight achieve great fame from our enterprise?' And a fourth said, 'Westward great things are to be discovered. It is time we looked beyond our frontiers.' And there came a great murmuring after these remarks, until the King banged his mace down and silenced them.

'I think,' he said, 'we have heard enough. Zhou xing put the case most reasonably. Considering each point that the ancient deity made, how can there be any decision but the inevitable? I propose, my fellow deities, to issue orders forthwith banning Buddhism from all corners of the mighty Middle Kingdom.' And a great resounding of talk and clamour greeted this sudden announcement, as the gods in their rows of seats burbled to each other.

But just as they were talking, and the noise of them rumbled on, like the boom of bees that live in the chrysanthemums of autumn, hurrying before winter to pack up their stores with sweetness, and prime the hive with pollen against the frosts, there came a sudden silence, for at the far end of the hall between the great banners of red written with mottoes, there entered a slight figure, flowing in robes of lilac silk, with delicate step, white-faced, and humble. Thus did the congress of gods view the maiden of mercy approach, and Guan yin herself stole up to the throne of the Jade Emperor.

And Guan yin said, 'My lord, great Tung yueh ta ti, highest king of mounts, King of Tai Shan, forgive my late arrival at this imperial assembly, and overlook I pray any neglect of duty, for I was away from my heaven in another place, and did not get your summons until this minute. So I have hastened to put myself before you, for I hear many voices have charged me of many crimes. I am a lone woman. Against so many learned ones I could not hope to sway by rhetoric. I merely come therefore to say I mean no harm, to admit my sins in stealing the lovers, but to say before you all I am as innocent as any here of this further act of stealing the Weaver-Girl, nor do I know where she might be, only that she is safe, and will when the time comes be brought forward.' And the goddess was silent then, standing before the throne, with a thousand deities staring at her.

Then there rushed in a messenger, who kowtowed before the King and said, 'One Thousand Years, urgent news I have for you. The Xien pi have revolted and seized Chang an, and Fu jian is driven out of the city.'

Another guard rushed in, who kowtowed alongside the other, and he cried, 'Below the footstool, may I address you? There comes urgent news, great monarch, from North of the wall, for in Manchuria are the barbarians seething.'

And thirdly there hared in another post, who flung himself before the throne, and he cried, 'Tai King, the Huns,

268

the Huns are marching!' And all in the court heard these things and were chilled by such messages, and at last there came in a mandarin in a strange livery.

And the mandarin said, 'Ay, sir, these reports are all true, and more also, for all the steppes are teeming, as the Huns and their confederates ride to make the great attack and to throw more might than has ever been used against China. Wherefore, sir, I am sent to you by the goddess, the Queen Mother of the West, by Xi Wang Mu, in whose palace are you conferring, and she bids me say to you: the dragon has done all this, the dragon sent down after the Emperor's daughter. Wherefore she advises the gods to band together while they may, for only the gods together can face this menace.' And the mandarin was silent.

And the gods were silent too, as silent as a still night when it is snowing. But the King of Tai said, 'Why then, my fellows we must fight. Send forth the orders for all gods to be in arms. We shall go down to the Great Wall, and man the fortresses. We shall place ourselves all about Zhong-guo's borders. We shall defend the mighty kingdom against all attacks, and by our powers deflect the Huns onto others. I am glad, sirs, that this news has come while I hold the throne. We shall be equal to this moment.' And the King paced out then, galvanising the gods, and with a great murmur they in fervour followed.

Now when the evening had come down, and the gods in the heavens of the peach-orchards had bustled and rushed to the orders of the Tai King, then from the gardens of Xi Wang Mu, while the night descended, there floated forth a goddess above the fruit-tree walls. And Guan yin went in fairy gait away from the peaks of Kun Lun Shan, and through the still air she glided to the North and came towards the great pass of Gansu. And herein did she find the slithering sands of the duned Gu dong, and so did she descend and hug the dust-hills.

And when she had floated for many a mile, she saw at last far off, by the cliffs of Dun huang the smoke of the camp-fires of travellers, and she came to the place where the horses and camels were tethered, and the rickety carts and carriages were surrounding the little fire, which glimmered in a ghostly landscape. And Guan yi sunk down then, and hovered a while, surveying the pilgrim's station, peering to see in the twilight the ones she was seeking.

For she saw among the travellers Fa xian, the Buddhist father, sitting cross-legged and meditating in the desert. And she saw now beside him the ambassador Wei in his official's robes, gazing with devoted eyes at the placidity of the master. And she looked about the rest of the pilgrims, but could see no Tawny or Nai, for their cart stood there, but they were neither in nor about it. But at last she saw two weary old men on the edge, staring forlornly across the dusky dunes, and with a smile she coasted towards them, and glided onto the dust, and without stirring it landed with ivory feet.

And the goddess whispered to them softly, 'Hail, O venerable pair. I bring you greetings from one you used to think your enemy. For not since the night in winter at the Emperor's banquet have we three been together, and I hope by my deeds I have earned a better opinion of you than I had then. But I come now with messages, urgent pleas. From the Queen Mother I descend to you. From Xi Wang Mu, and the King of Tai, from all the gods united, I am come to summon you for this night towards an urgent action. Will you come with me, gods again, resuming your divine powers, and will you for this night defend your country?'

Now when the goddess had spoken, the old pair looked at her amazed, and their eyes for some time were unused to the light of divinity. Wherefore they stared astonished at the goddess, dragged from their human forms, and painful at first it was to adjust to the celestial. But then they looked about at the camp of mortals, and the pilgrims with whom they had shared their long journey, and their eyes returned once more to the goddess, dubious at what she had said. But at last Confucius coughed and addressed her.

'Great Buddhist goddess,' he said perplexed, 'you must

excuse our delay. But it is indeed poignant to see you before us again, with whom we sparred at the outset of this adventure. Are we to think all is forgiven? Do you hobnob with all the gods? Do they send you, and the Queen Mother herself on their biddings? What changes have been happening in heaven while we have been away? And what then is this danger you seek our help upon? For surely, goddess, you come to us now at the very end of our journey, and but one day more sees us in Dun huang, our destination.'

And the goddess replied, 'Ay, that we know, great adviser to the ancient kings. Nor do we seek to deflect you from your journey's purpose. You plan to reach Dun huang tomorrow, and that tomorrow you will do, but for tonight, your divine help is needed. Great things have occurred, terrible actions, movements that threaten the world. All power of heaven is needed to deflect them. Therefore am I come to you, to bid you both away, and to come and join the rest of the gods of your country, for now indeed this night the deities of Zhongguo are all amassed in the defence of the empire.'

But Lao zi looked at her and said, 'This is not a plot to beguile us? You are not in league again with the Jade Emperor? For you know he has followed us, dogging our steps, seeking to snatch Nai away, and we two deities alone have been his protection. You seek to waylay us, to lure us from the path, to leave Nai naked to the mist-snake, and so you come to us with these colourful tales, while the last night before the border is upon us.'

But the goddess of compassion sighed at this and said, 'Well, if you would, this you may believe and hold to. But surely as I look about here, I cannot see Nai guarded, nor is he about for you to have a care for. But you must realise, my lord, we Buddhists have our great edicts, and one of them is never to lie. If you can believe a god would err against the faith he embodies, then stick to your sands, and leave your country to be ravaged. But this night I tell you the gods have flown, and they stand along the Great Wall, and their influence goes out to protect Zhongguo from the barbarians.' And the goddess was silent again, staring at the old men, and the smoke of the fires smelt ashy in that wilderness.

Wherefore Confucius said, 'We will go with you along. I trust your faith, and there have been developments. For these great stirrings of the steppes: there have been rumours here, and here even in Gansu is the greatest danger. Perhaps if we would protect our charge, this is the greatest way, for what now if the Huns should descend upon us? Chang an has fallen once to their blows not many years hence, and another strike would be annihilation. We will come with you, O Buddhist goddess. But the gods are now your friends? And Xi Wang Mu: she is your own director?'

Guan yin smiled back. 'She sent me to seek you. She was foremost in this plan. And she also gave me a message to deliver. For the Queen Mother Goddess wishes me to tell you that she cast the *I Ching* this night, and the judgement she deems fitting thus to tell you. For the goddess threw her yarrow-sticks, and she cast the hexagram Chen! and the *Book of Changes* gave this judgement upon it. "Shock brings success. Shock terrifies for a hundred miles. Shock comes: oh, oh! Laughter follows: ha, ha! But he does not let fall the ritual cup." This was the writing on the coming time. The Arousing. Thus she bade me tell you.'

And Lao zi leapt up then. '"Shock comes: oh, oh!"' he cried. '"Laughter follows; ha, ha!"' The Dao thus speaks to us! Oh, wonderful judgement! How it pleases my soul! In this case, goddess, we will come with you. Whatever shocks will come to us, we will follow the Dao, for the shock pushes us into the Dao herself. And the barbarians will be deflected, and those we cannot deflect: these will be taken up into the Dao. Well, goddess, you are a woman, and women and the Dao have an affinity. And so let us all go hand in hand on the path of Destiny together.'

And they all took hands then, and floating forth, the three gods cruising towards the moon.

But Nai and Tawny far from the camp sat quiet on a cliff

above the pilgrims, and together they stared out as the dusk grew deeper across the sea of dunes. The smoke of the fires lay idly in the valley, but they were above the evening mists, and afar off beyond the sands, they could see the cliff-face, and the ranges that held the monastery of Dun huang. In the hesitant moon the crag-face glimmered, and the caves carved therein showed huge and dark, and the curled roofs of the monastery and a pinnacle beyond the cliff stood silent. Meanwhile the paths of the stars now unravelled high above their heads.

And Nai said, 'Well, Tawny, journey's end. Dun huang is within our grasp. Our long, long pilgrimage through the heart of China has here its frontier with infinity. Through Zhongguo we cannot seek further, and what we have sought, if not in Dun huang, will not be for us. I fear to know. I fear to enter those walls, and see if what I seek is ever to be with me. But you, my boy, what are your hopes and fears of this final voyage? You have travelled a long way with four good men, but have you any treasure?'

And Tawny sighed and said, 'Well, master, that I'll also see tomorrow. And if I find none, then one of you four is not honest! But truly, master, I also have fears, for I fear you might not meet Xiang. And I fear also a change if you should meet her. For a long way I have gone with you now, and served you faithfully, and got used to your mad ways, and what will become of me, when you are reunited?'

But Nai said, 'Why Tawny, you may serve us both. I hope you will not go back or leave me because of her. You have been a good lad to me, cheerful and willing, and have kept my heart light along the way. A perfect companion, with wise head for a boy, and a subtlety well beyond your years. But you will not be excluded by Xiang. She will love you as much as I do. She will love you, little freak. Yet surely before you meet her, you must do something to clean yourself up. Why so grubby, boy? If I had my strength, I'd clean you all over with sand. And this gap-tooth of yours, it's not a gap, is it? Just that the two teeth there are black. You need a thorough scrubbing. Your teeth as well. Tomorrow may be. Oh, tomorrow! Are we there at last, Tawny? I dare not think of it. Take my mind off it. I dare not know if she is there.'

But Tawny stared at Nai for a while and said, 'We are up on a cliff. The mists rise. No one in the valley can hear us. You have come a long way, master, somewhat in pursuit of Xiang, and full enough have your thoughts and talk been of her. Yet never have you truly told me what sort of girl she is, or how you met her, and how took to her. And surely I need to hear this, before our journey's end. Tell me the tale of your meeting. For this is a good time, while the night descends, and we sit on the edge of China.' And Tawny ceased here, and looked on his master soberly, and all the landscape was filled with silence.

Nai sighed then, 'It was a year ago in Jian kang, as I sat quiet in my chamber writing, a Buddhist nun came to me with a strange request that called me forth on a great adventure. She said that in her nunnery there lodged a certain lady passing now her first youthful days, intelligent and sensitive, very gifted, who needed to finish her education. She had heard that I worked as a tutor, and took pupils in the Five Classics, and that I had in life no demanding position. Would I be prepared to teach the lady? It was an unusual request, but she hinted that I did not have too much to lose. I smiled at the implication that a nobody fears no ruin, but hesitated before accepting. The fears of scandal did not cow me, but the thought of a blue-stocking for a pupil, a sober, old, probably bearded lady: this was what caused my delay. Yet I agreed to it, and the nun went on her way.

'I was writing at this time, Tawny, a version of an old myth: the tale of the Cowherd and the Weaver-Girl. I was versifying a section in a new metre I was trying out, where the Cowherd goes walking by the Silver River. On the walk he takes that day, over on the further bank, he suddenly sees a maiden picking flowers. He straightway falls in love with her. Her face dives into his heart. It is the face of the Weaver-Girl. When I had finished this passage, to clear my head of the whirling words, I went for a walk in the city. In an idle reverie I strolled along the green canals, and vacantly stared across the water. Then I saw a woman there, dressed in lovely silks, beautiful, bewitching, waving at me.

'It is difficult to catch, Tawny, the stabbing shaft of pain that went straight to my heart from that girl's face. Her beauty bounded at me, with dazzling life and energy, breathtaking to have her smiling at me. She stood there in her scarlet silks, her eyes blazing so brightly, and called to me, calling out my name. She explained that her name was Xiang, and that she had been told of me, and that she was my pupil for the Five Classics! I tamely mumbled something back, and was preparing to say more, when she walked away, and with a busy wave was gone. And so I stood there transfixed, reeling from the meeting, and took some time to draw my breath. But then the fit passed. Strange to say, I even then forswore her. I somehow knew that my days for such pursuits were past.

'Now you may think it odd, Tawny, that I would make such a vow, or at least you would if you had known me from my younger days. For I have always taken sickness from the eyes of girls, and many times have been reduced to slaves to them. There is a fiery weakness in the bottom of my heart that flames easily and inspires me vaunting, and many times with such a flame I have pounced upon maidens, only to retire at length a mass of wounds. This woman was too undreamed fair to think even of love. And I was old and wise enough now to shun it. It was not till long afterwards I was stricken by the thought that I had seen this girl just as I was writing of the Weaver-Girl.

'When she came to me at first, I was very impressed academically with her powers as a student. Her mind was super-subtle, and her powers of condensation and analysis formidable. I taught her dutifully, and since she was an unusual case, gave her some extra attention. But thankfully I found that, whether due to my vow or not, I was not in the slightest measure in love. Rather I felt sorry for her. Here

275

was she in Jian kang, an exile from her home city, with no friends of her own to talk to, a beautiful girl set so strangely on a life that was full of unnecessary austerity. It seemed rather as we parted from our various meetings that she was sad to part from me. Out of a strange compassion then, I began to talk with her. We went to a little tea-shop on the corner.

'And truly I found it comforting, that for all her beauty, I was no way in love with her. I treated her with an easy detachment. I even asked her out for an evening, so that she could meet some of my friends. I even confirmed to one of them, as we sat gossiping at a playhouse, that he was free to make a bid, if he wished. I went home thinking gloatingly how finally I had made it: the charms of beauty and life had no power on me. I had crossed the sea of passion, and after so many storms, was safe on the other side.

'The next day she came to me to read me her work as usual. It was an essay on the humorous *Zhuang zu*. And she referred with subtle distinctions to the famous passage where the philosopher dreams he is a butterfly, but then wakes to wonder if perhaps he is the dream, and the butterfly is his reality. As she read the essay to me, softly in that reverent voice, carefully differentiating the nuances, her voice flowed in my very soul, awoke something within me, and when she finished, I was in love.'

Nai broke off his tender tale in reverence a while, and sighing gazed forth again over the moonlit landscape. But then he noticed Tawny beside him bowing his head down, and strangely shaking. He squinnied in the dim light, and then saw to his surprise that Tawny was in fits of laughter.

'Oh, my dear master,' exclaimed Tawny, hugging himself with glee, 'has anyone in the world had a funnier master? You fell in love not with her beauty, but with her mind! Oh, classic clinch! Oh, master how I love you! But go on now with your tale. I won't laugh again. I love to hear your warbling story.' And Tawny gazed up at him, trying to

276

keep a straight face, and his eyes were radiant in the moonlight.

Nai went on. 'Well, Tawny, you may laugh, but once you have fallen in love, you put yourself down for a course of suffering and you expose your tenderest soul. The first lash that came to me happened soon after this, when Xiang abruptly cut one of my classes. A tutor does not happily bear the absence of a pupil, having a useless hour with an empty chair, and the note she sent me, unsuitable for pupils or for lovers, said, "I'm throwing it in. Too busy preparing the dance to cope with philosophy." And so was I put down before I had hardly begun.

'It went on like this. Another time, touching this wicked lapse, she asked me if I was angry about it. When I said a little, she replied she was more angry at me for setting her such difficult subjects. I winced at this unreasonableness. Just like women, you see, Tawny, and here I was putting myself into her power. And she was sharp, you know. The very flames came out of her eyes. I was not dealing with a cabbage.

'Yet there were compensations. This dance she mentioned, it turned out that my grand uncle found out about her, and banking on what he had heard of her reputation from Hangchao, he engaged her for an evening's sleeve-dancing. She prepared for it studiously. She had various maids helping her, and other dancers. She directed the whole entertainment. And when it came, I was fascinated by her skills. And from her reactions too there came some benefits.

'For after the dance had taken place in the Chief Minister's palace, among the willow trees and green-painted pillars, and Xiang had danced all alone to the castanets, and twelve-stringed lyres, in peacock robes – how languidly her swooning movements ghosted over the floor, how did her sleeves fall like cataracts into chasms! – yet when the music pounded, how like eagles did she dive, and flash with feet pattering in passion! – at the banquet afterwards, I was standing by Xiang, as the Chief Minister himself drank to

277

her, and "Hold me!" she whispered leaning against me with a swooning look, and how it seemed home to embrace her!'

Nai ceased a while, for strangely among the hills as the stars came forth, there was a rumbling sound of thunder. He and Tawny exchanged a glance, then looked out over the wastes, but nowhere could they see any sign of thunder-clouds. The mists lay below them, thicker now, and Tawny stared at them wide-eyed. A moment he turned, and seemed about to speak. But then he settled down again, and Nai went on with his tale, and frowning spoke on in the gathering darkness.

'I was not to know it then, Tawny, but there were trou-bles in Xiang, and a dangerous place was it to venture into love with her. So far I had winced at her tongue when I was supposed to be her teacher, how much further I could cringe, if I submitted myself her suitor? Yet I told her that I loved her one day, all unwittingly, and put my head on the slab beneath her, after she spoke to me long, quizzing me in the tea-house, as to why I was unmarried and unattached. We went out in the rain together, and under my sheltering cape I told her what I could not say by the listening fire-side, and then Tawny, I saw her alter, and a dread harsh-ness came in her, and we bargained as over some bitter matter.

'And so did the story follow, for what I would find loving, she, Tawny, would fiercely come to strike against. Take when she gave a tea-party, after the dancing was over, and my uncle came and Kun and Lun to the Xie apartments, and in the drunken caperings, though I tried to woo Xiang away, we all went out to a country inn in my carriage. There by romantic ruins we walked, looking up at the stars, while Kun lectured, and Lun sang out his insults, and I kissed Xiang first beneath the Silver River and by the weirs and falls of the Yang zi's tributary. What I thought was the sweetest moment, she bathed in fire, and roundly she condemned me later for my trespass. So was it, Tawny.

278

Fire was in the rose, and for all this fragrance I suffered penance.

'And I suffered indeed, for from the first, the blaze of love was in me, greater than in my life I had ever known it. Each day my body brimmed up itself with delicious fever and trembling excitement. Each hour my heart beat continually loud and fast. In the mornings I woke up to it, wracked in bliss. At the nights I sank down to its embrace. And my body lost its vigour: my arms became thinner, my appetite fled, I grew light and scrawny with the passion. It was indeed a tumultuous time for the little world of my soul, and yet hardly had I alone embraced her.

'Yet that time came. For Fate had set aside a time, and all seemed fitting for an encounter, for we were in the very month in which I was born, and on the very nativity day I was bidden to a party. There was a group of poets to which I satirically belonged, called the Begonia Club, though I was a rebel to their preciosity, and they were holding one of their meetings on my November birthday, out in the country in an enchanted old house. I asked Xiang to this party. She did all she could to refuse. But being my birthday, she at last accepted.'

Nai paused, for as he spoke thus, there came a trembling in the ground, and at first they looked round to see who had approached. But there was nothing. They sat on the cliff, with nothing about but stones. The rock shook again, and it seemed an earthquake made it tremble. But the hills were all silent, and no more sounds came, and the pair of them gazed about puzzled, while the slithering mists lay below, and the dunes were enwrapped in the coils, all ghostly under the light of the moon.

And Nai sighed and said, 'Well, Tawny, we must rest, and try to sleep before tomorrow. The mists come thick about, ominous for us, and time is we went down into the valley. My story must have ending, and end I will with my birthday, and the party which we attended at last together, with Xiang being nice to me, and tender for the first time, and magic in the palace of November. For what a fragrant night it was: bonfires on cold hills, secrecy in forgotten chambers!

'Yet what a fury Xiang was in at the beginning of the evening! She gave a display of incandescent anger. And what was its great origin? The sedan-chairs in the city! You could never get one when you wanted them! She greeted me with this when we met. But I was teaching all that day. Eight hours I had, and Xiang being my last pupil, on my wretched birthday, and she all in a rage. I thought to myself: here's fine party manners! And as she fumed against my city, in my mind I counselled: Nai, you are not taking her anywhere. And yet she won me round at last, promised to behave. In fact gave me sweet tokens for my name-day. So I silently revised my plan of ditching the scold, and off we flew in a rattling carriage.

'How soft were the woods of November with their ghostly twigs lying in hills misty under the moon! How sweet was the house, with lofty roofs curling under the stars, and melon-shaped lanterns lighting the fairy terraces! How warm were the chambers: they smelt of wine, mulled with cinnamon, and log-fires of sweet cedarwood crackling in ashes. The music and the poets' laughter boomed about the verandahs. Inside: rich silks, green-painted eyebrows, and welcome.

'At a break in the rites, I stole a chance to show Xiang over the house, to idle among fur-coats and mirrors and halls. We tiptoed upstairs to the canopied bedrooms, and peered in screen-rich studies, where lutes were lit by moon-beams on dusty sills. We found a chamber that smelt all apples, with trays of them mellowing, we rested in rooms with featherbeds soft and silent. We kissed amid the frosty house, in horizontal conversation, while outside in the forest the foxes called. But now I must break off my tale, for I see to my dismay, we have been joined by an old acquaintance.' And Nai stopped speaking here, and they both turned to gaze into the valley.

And there they saw with horror, sliding among the mists, the fog-scales of the momentous serpent. The slithering form again of the vapour-snake they saw there, enwrapping each hillock and cliff in menace. With the silver sides of billowing fogs he circled about the dunes, and roamed from the blurred sand-horizon towards them. And the head of the serpent arose once more, congealing from the vapours, and once more the dragon that had dogged them before Chang an gazed on them. And it loomed right up to them, huge and threatening, breathing into their faces and grinned at them with its mist-dripping jaws.

And the dragon thus spoke to them. 'So I have you all alone, I have you safely perched on the cliff before me. Dun huang dies in the moonlight, beyond your last grasp, and the mighty sniffer-dragon is upon you. Ah, a long way have I trekked you from Jian kang, slithered after among the forests and the mountains, confronted you in the public street. But here I have no rival. I look all about: there is no other dragon in the landscape. You have no biting protector, no one to give me wounds, no one to dare to tear me with his teeth, but sit all alone, in a bare country, bereft in sight of your goal.

'Nor do not look down the hill, or seek to call those below. Fret no more to cry out for your tutors. Those that have protected you over the long miles, those that have opposed me in the woods: they are gone from you for ever! Ay, you missed their leavetaking. Suddenly in a hurry the old men departed. While you strolled upwards, thinking on a wild spot to avoid my hounding, Kun and Lun received a sudden summons. Their peers await them. Their strength is called for. Their interests are under attack, and they have flittered away to other wars. Goodbye to your defenders then. Teachers now have you none. Just you are to feed the dragon's spite.

'But do not grieve yourself too much, poet. You would not have found Xiang. For she was not awaiting you as you supposed. For I have gone snuffling endlessly about that wretched Dun huang. I have scoured those monks, and there is no woman there. She has not been abiding you as your dreams foretold. She has deserted you like the others.

281

Fruitless then in any case would have been your journey, and the world must do without the Great Tale.'

'Dragon,' then said Nai bitterly, 'you are a miscreant wretch, and you do dishonour to your breed, for serpents such as yourself should be above these petty modes, nor skulking sniff about ever at the heels of humans. Do not you have great storms to attend? Is not the earth to be pregnated? Are there not growing things and floods to break forth? But you like some ignoble dog come cringeing at our behinds. Well, have done then. Do your worst! Leave this toying. What is this weakness gloatingly prodding those who are in your power? Oh, abject grovelling pastime of office! Be done with your spite. And be ashamed. And scoff you not at the Great Tale. It will eat you, fins and talons!'

Now the thunder again came, as Nai said these words, as the silver dragon stared at him with malice. The creased horizon flickered with alien lightning, and the very night grew black with a breed of sandstorm. Then did the pattering pebbles fall speckled all over the paths, and vultures were blown about, lit by light-shafts. The mountain gave a shuddering lurch, the earthquake coming as before, and the vengeful dragon stared perturbed.

Then did the pair on the cliff feel the ground they stood upon draw back. The whole spine tottered from the dragon. The mortals could only stare, and hold amazed to the bulging rocks, as the cliff-face inched away, as if walking. In seismic shudders it crunched apace, convulsing and jerking from within, as though in fear of the serpent before them. But then with cataclysmic trembling it humped forward into the mists, and the silver dragon began to gaze with fear.

With alarm and amazement then the mortals sat on the hill, as it chased after the mist-serpent. The cliff-face leapt forward, and the mists drew away, and the crag cantered horselike on the sands. The backing fogs hovered up to the sky. But the humping hill lunged forward: it bumped, trundled, speeded, jumped and at ease sat on the air with

282

triumph, thwacking the winds, spewing the sands about, yet cruising air-borne after the slithering mists. And the crag put forth horns, and they saw it was a dragon, and the humans were seated together upon its neck.

Now the dragon Wo Long Wang that bore the pair of mortals up into the night sky first pursued through cliff and mountain. Eastward he chased the fleeing snake. Above Nan Shan he flew, where the Great Wall runs to Taiping Bao. Next hurried he down to Wuwei, where the pilgrims made their path, and across the great loop of the Yellow River. Next then again to Lanzhou, gateway of Zhongguo, and over the moonlit land the two serpents raced. The other ran along the wall, capering with busy legs, through Jingbian, Laoying, Ying xian and Xi xian, and at last to Nanjing, the Mongol town destined for capital power, fled where the wall goes down to the East Ocean.

To escape the huge pursuer now the lesser dragon changed its path, and sped North into the bleak Manchurian wastes, and here he circled round where on Mongolian plains, the mortals saw Huns ranging in their hordes. The restless barbarians poured towards them, as the dragon-head forged its way, the teeming ponies and slaughterous warriors unending. And then they saw the Gobi and the tundra, bitter and drear, and beyond these sights the vast wall of square mountains. And it seemed that the fires that burned from thence but poured the hordes on the plain, but hurled the forces of malice towards civilisation. And the dragon swept before it, and still pursued, doubled back towards the South, and riding with the Huns now made haste to China.

Now the frontiers of Zhongguo flinched at this assault from the boiling pit of earth, and over the mountains the wall could be seen again trembling. And the silver mist-dragon swooped towards it, flattening himself in the moon-lit clouds, seeking its home limits again with panic. But when the mortals came towards it, all along the wall, they saw glowing, coloured and pure in the night-time, the gods of China, the hearth- and wealth-gods, the armoured gods of war, the helmeted door-gods in chainmail guarding the kingdom: these hovered in fragrant forms with their arms raised, their benedictions protecting the Central Realm. And the barbarians there thundering were turned away, deflected towards the West, whither the sky-snake shimmering once more glided.

At the limit of the wall, where by Gansu the roaming stones reach their rest, two great gods stood, barring the gateway into China. In royal robes they hovered together, ancient men of tradition, in garbs of scholar and monk, the mighty sages. As the dragon flew above them, Nai looked down, reverencing the forms, and stared into the faces of Confucius and Lao zi. But such a shock he got from them that he nearly fell off the snake, for Kun and Lun they were, his tutors, unmistakable! And Nai looked marvelling lost in puzzlement at this amazing vision, till the dragon now swept to take his breath away, for soaring perpendicular, nosing the stars, the dragons took their chase, and the mortals held tight, zooming into the sky.

Now did the surging dragons ride glittering to the stars, through the clouds of the strato-cumulus and cirro-stratus. Now did they forge amazingly up through the stratosphere, and into the circles where fall and sizzle the meteors. Yet even higher they made their chase through the curtained Northern Lights, up through the ion- and the ex-ospheres, and then into the night sky, where sang the planets and galaxies, so that festal lights were tinkling all about them. And they came to a star-land, where a silver river ran by a little hut, and the sky-cattle roamed through star-trees unattended.

But here as in the speckled meadows they sped in desperation, there came a lilac star glowing in the distance to which they flew, and nearing it, they saw the rose and sapphire light increasing, so that a figure hung there, softly glowing mauve in the vasts of space. Flowing robes she wore, that ruffled in the space-winds, a coral comb in her jet hair, tender glowed her ivory face with compassionate smile. And Guan yin was before them, holding a peach blushing in her fingers, and the silver dragon was slowed and stopped by this sight.

And Guan yin said, 'Ay, Emperor, you do well to cease, for here I bear your reckoning: the peach of immortality plucked this day from the celestial peach-orchard. You cease your flight here, for in such fruit the gods have their continuance, and without this refreshment even their long lives sink low. And I have brought it here to uphold you by command of the great Queen Mother. Ay, your imperial matriarch, Xi Wang Mu, bids you cease here. Wherefore if you would have your life, she bids you leave this form, resume again the form which is yours surely. And at once she demands that you hurry down from the stars, and seek her in her palace in Kun Lun Shan.' And the goddess smiling looked at him, so that the silver dragon hung brooding. But then was he overtaken by wild rage.

For he writhed back on his own spine, uprearing a flushing crest. He scrabbled at the stars, his jaws cracking wide. Then coiling monstrously convoluted, knotting about himself, he reduced his misty circles to tight bunches. Then did his scales fall. The glittering silver cascaded into the night. And the lump himself began sinking from the planets. To an emperor he changed, taking on again the imperial yellow silk, dropping from the night sky, burning like a meteor. And now on breeding cloud he slowed, and stood again like a god, and drifted down to the twilight of the mountains. And the mortals and deities saw the cloud-borne Jade-King thus return to the snowy heavens of Kun Lun Shan.

But now beneath the mortals, the dragon-head jutted up, and shaking them in their seats, clapped up and down with loud laughter, and the booming voice of Wo Long Wang cried, 'Ay, emperor, run to your mother! This is a fit end to the chase of the Imperial Jade King. Let it be a lesson to you: do not seek to play the dragon. And note now how as an emperor your strength is lessened. For you have seen without you, king, how the hordes are stirred to the West, and without you how the gods have manned the

285

defences. Wherefore be you humble. And thanks, O goddess. A woman's touch like yours has long been needed.'

And the goddess replied, 'Thanks, Wo Long Wang. Hail, to you sky-gliders all, O haunters of the rare stratospherical regions. I think there are some of us here who have met before, by a lake of Shou chun, smoking with ruin. But Wo Long Wang, I bring you greetings, greetings from Xi Wang Mu, who has watched you making grace stealthily. Wherefore she salutes you, and bids you peace now, for now you can return to the stars, and fulfilled has been the destiny of your coming. Yet this she requests, and I also, dragon: these mortals you bear on your back: you have guarded them well, and protected them from the Jade-King. One task remains then, one last toil. As you return them to earth, take them so that they may see the vastness. Let them see the great earth turning. Let them watch the continents. Let them have high view of all the way Westward. And to speed them further, let your dragon-breath breathe on them with inspiration, and give them vision of the grand abodes of the gods. All peace upon you, therefore, O faithful, sleepy dragon. Blessings for when you come again to the stars.' And the goddess smiling ceased there, and carrying the immortal peach, sunk after the Emperor from the night sky.

But the dragon himself was sinking now down towards the world, and the swirling clouds of the blue globe came towards them, and China they saw bulged and immense, spreading its vast square, and the pass to the West, and the Kun Lun Mountains below them. And afar to the South they saw from this height the sky-scraping Himalayas, and beyond them the hills and smoky jungles of India. And they stared with wonder at the world of men so unified to behold, and they looked further West to see the unknown countries.

Thus did they see glittering, rich and rare, beyond the quick Arabian sands, and the highlands of the purple courts of Persia, the huge and wealthy spaces of a great turquoise sea, ringed with ports and speckled with foam-frothed islands. To the South of it lay a mighty continent, ochre with baking desert, and a leafy river snaking of length unparalleled, and North were the islands, and other lands, a host of varied shapes, dense-wooded, and peaked in the midst with snowy ranges. And beyond the sea, and its perfumed shores, cut through a narrow strait, there lay on the curve of the earth a vast, grey ocean.

And the dragon said, 'Behold the world! Pilgrims, see the riches. Such are the mighty sights the goddess bade me give you. And there you see the empires of the Indians, the Persians, and the Romans, and the war-plains of the Teutons. And there are hasting the steppe-barbarians lusting for blood, for you must know the Huns are ever thundering. But sit now, for here will I puff from my breath the smoke to give you vision, a power to see deep into the spirit of these things. For here you see empires, but soon you'll see heavens upon this globe: the lands of men with the pantheons that inspire them. For with these fumes you'll see each continent serving the gods they create, swaying below the cities and mountains celestial. And mark them well, for on these empires thunder the hurrying Huns, and soon this splendour you see will all be stricken.'

And Wo Long Wang now breathed from his nostrils a fume of perfumed smoke, and it billowed up with glinting opal and diamonds. Wherefore the two travellers breathed it in, as they sat fast on the scales, and Tawny behind clung to the waist of the poet. And when they had smoked it, their minds grew sharp, and richer the stars became, and gleaming bright the dappled earth lay below them. And they looked again at the marbled lands, the continents and subcontinents, and there grew things like flowers within the substance.

For where were the mountains and airy clouds, now could they see further, and the heavens of the gods came forth in the sunlight. And Meru they saw, the mount of gold, with its terraces and peacocks, a fairy city high above the Himalayas. And Westward beyond the lofty Pamirs, gardened paradises they saw, and Persian fields of

Zoroastrian cosmic battlers. And cloudy Olympus gazed at waves, shuttered with blue pillars, neglected high and threatened by a tempest, while the towers of jewelled Zion lay angelic above Jerusalem, on sandy crags spread out by the turquoise sea. All these they saw, amazed at the sights, drinking each honeyed cup, and it seemed indeed the world had become heavened.

But Wo Long Wang said, 'Yet these sights, sparkling their little gems, have but a frail hold on the peace you see in them. For I may tell you there is hasting upon them barbarians of destruction, and in the bowels of Hell the blasts of doom are stored. Wherefore look closer, for you will see there the foes of civilisation, and the lovers of fire, who would bring the world to ashes. Nor are those heavens at peace with themselves or with each other, for truly the gods love strife and altercation. See a last sight then, and then to sleep. To your cliff I will you restore. And these visions will seem but a dream when you have passed from them. Yet remember them, poet, for herein lies much to feed the soul, and the deeds to come well enough will make your Great Tale.'

And the dragon thus hung a while, as they looked once more in yearning on the heavens, and yet saw the plains blackening with the Huns. And the serpent coasted, while they stretched their eyes, and saw the barbarians thronging about the empires of India, Persia and Rome. And they saw also the Teutons marching, streaming in vast fields, and Northwards over a cold land of sea-gnawn fiords, they saw the walls of Asgard rearing up, brazen in the clouds, and a rainbow bridge arching towards the grassy earth. Beyond the continents lastly they glimpsed over the vast, grey sea, a giant serpent looking down in thunder. But then did their troubling visions fade, cut by night and cloud, and a forgetfulness of dreaming stole upon them. And the serpent set them down again in the sands of Gu dong, and they descended the hill in the mists together.

But when the Jade Emperor, now himself again, flew down to the heavens of Kun Lun Shan, he tumbled to his

288

mother's palace, among the rich peach-orchards, and went through marbled halls in yellow robe. And he came through the jars and statues, and libraries and lanterns, and went to the living-quarters of Xi Wang Mu. And thus was he ushered to the silent room in the depths of night-time, and he knelt and kowtowed before the yellow screen. And there was a long silence then, except for the clepsydra, the water-clock, which plopped away the seconds.

Then a voice from behind the screen said, 'Well, you have come at last. You have finally ceased from your process of self-degradation. And my son has seen fit to resume his shape as an emperor again, and slide no more about the world like a great worm. Do I detect a change of heart in these more noble measures, or is it but a slavish and servile obedience? At any rate, I hope that you have now quelled this degrading passion you have harboured too long for your own daughter! You have seen that you can never have her. You cannot suspend nature. And so you return to your throne.

'Yet you have observed that your absence has not been an entire disaster? Indeed, it has been most fortunate that you vacated your place. The King of Tai is a martial spirit, with a fervour that comes from strength, no whit the sort of energy that streams from weakness. And he indeed has proved a warrior equal to this present menace, and has roused the gods to unite against their foe. Thus do they defend now the ancient borders, and man the length of the Great Wall. And the Hunnic marauders are shuffled over to the West. The Empire of China has taken strength as it often does, and your own weakness has in this instance been most helpful.

'Yet hark you, Jade-King, the times are coming, when our own strength will not be enough, for what can we do when the whole world is threatened? We can defend Zhongguo, but as we have seen, even the Central Kingdom has limits, and the weakness of others in the world far beyond our concerns, may pull us all to destruction. Dire times are coming. The world's empires are threatened in

289

themselves, and there lies in their gods the unwisdom that brings chaos. We must wait and watch. But it is perhaps well that these new faiths draw us West, for there seems to lie the Fate to destroy or redeem us.' And the goddess fell silent then, as the night's clock dripped on, and the Jade-King knelt before her shamefaced.

But the Emperor of Jade spoke then and said, 'Great Queen and Mother, some words you have spoken were indeed just upon me. You are right that I demeaned myself. Never again will I shake off this imperial shape, nor bring my dignity to slither in the dust. And you must know that even I could not discover my daughter, even I searching the empire could not find her. Wherefore I have fancy now that Fate wishes me to treasure her dream, for truly when I found her first, she turned against me. She spoke indeed bitter words. The Weaver-Girl has changed. Her long haunt with the Cowherd has corrupted her. And so I renounce her. Yet tell me, Mother, for you seem to know so much: where is it Xiang is truly hiding?'

And the voice from the yellow screen sighed and said, 'As to that, my son, men are always fools and dreamers.'

Chapter Eighteen

Now when the grey-eyed dawn had broken in the East and coldly lit the sands of Gu dong, the pilgrims stirred about the embers of their dying fires, and packed their waggons for the last day's journey. And Wei was up bright and eager, directing his embassy servants, and Fa xian briskly also roused his monks. But Kun and Lun came buggy-eyed from their toilsome night, and yawned to be back in the sands and men again. And poet Nai stirred with dread, and fearfully stowed his things, while Tawny walked about sighing and silent.

Now when the caravan made forth, they travelled the shifting road, and difficult was the going among the drifting dunes. Yet by the noon they had made good way, and in the autumnal sun, they saw well now the cliff-face and caves of Dun huang. Beyond the poplars that by a stream fluttered their yellow leaves, the great rocks loomed up from the smooth sand-hills, and mighty Buddhas were carved in the cliffs, hollowed in canopied caverns, and painted were the arhats that flew around them.

When they came to the crest of the hill, and approached the monastery itself, then did dread seize the breasts of many, for the monastery bells boomed keenly, filling the air with woe, and the travellers wondered what this doom might bode. But then servants came, bearing the news that the Grand Abbot had died, and that the monks were lamenting this day his funeral. Wherefore Fa xian was stricken aghast, and Wei and the monks with him, and gloomily did they march the last of the road.

But now the gateway was before them. The cliff-hewn walls reared up, and the terraces with their rafters ranked to the skies. And great prayer-flags fluttered, red and white, tied to lines and steeples, and down from spires glared the painted eyes of Buddhas. Weird was the Buddhist hall, throbbing with iron, filled with the cries of weeping monks, and ominous came the entrance to the citadel. But the pilgrims passed through the gate, and entered the spiritual world. And the Dean and his staff came hurrying to greet them.

But when Nai came within the walls, he shuddered and said, 'Tawny, my heart is vexed near to dying. For I look about this thronging place, filled with a thousand monks, and I think: how, how can Xiang be waiting? A voice surely stirred me in my dreams, saying she was not here, and now I am here, the hope itself seems foolish. What can I do? I have come so far! I am on the edge of our world. To what grim strangeness have my dreams led me?'

And Tawny said, 'To Dun huang, master! Just look at all these orange-clad eggheads! I can see what you mean. How can it happen? They dart about like rows of ducks, fattening on a farm, and unless Xiang is bald, she is not among them. Where would she be, do you think? Did she give you a message? Did she in these dreams tell you what room she was renting? And Kun and Lun: look how they stare amazed at so many Buddhists! To have you here must confirm all their nightmares. But you better get searching. I'll stay with the others, but keep my eyes peeled. Meanwhile, O master, good luck. Tell me when you find her.' And Tawny went off with the others then, as they were led by the Dean, and escorted to the guests' apartments.

When Nai went roaming, he scoured each way the faces of the monks, seeking to see if Xiang were disguised among them. He looked about the courtyard and up the alleys, and peered at the windows of the buildings, searching each face to see signs of his beloved. No sign did he see. The monks were hurrying to the great temple of the Buddha, whence rang the funeral chants for the Abbot. And Nai could find no joy in them, and leaving the square he turned aside, and went to the remoter parts of the monastery.

Through narrow roads and passages he then threaded his way, emerging into yards where all was silence. The prayer-wheels turned at little shrines, and flags fluttered aimless from walls, but nothing did he see of Xiang or anyone. He searched the porches. He peered into dark cells, where sutras lay open. He looked and mounted winding stairs that led to the sky. But nothing did he find there of any feminine thing, and it chilled him to feel here was a world without women.

Coming to the caves then, Nai studied the forms of the holy holes. Some were still carving, with half-formed stone arhats. Some were half-painted, and the rows of spirits suddenly faded into colourless drawings. The brooding Buddhas gazed at him. They only had one message: fruit-less is human activity. The source of all suffering is desire. The tubas boomed firmly from the temple. Nai returned despondent, and in the square he found Wei coming towards him.

And Wei said, 'Nai, you must come to the temple. Wait with the others in the portico. We are to witness the funeral rites of the Abbot. This hour are the monks electing another to succeed his Holiness, and we are privileged to be here at such a moment. Where have you been roaming? Join Tawny there. And do not let him misbehave. At last we have achieved the holy ground of the Buddha!' And Wei went off then, into a building, clearly at one with the monks, and Nai was left with a lonely feeling.

But he went to a servant then, whom he saw sweeping a verandah, and Nai thought a while and said, 'My friend, it seems you look after these buildings which are the guests' apartments? I want to ask a question of you. Can you tell if these last few months, there has been a woman staying in any of these chambers? I am looking for a beautiful woman, with a smooth, radiant face, and clear, almond-shaped eyes?'

But the servant stared at him and said, 'You want a woman? You won't find one here! Go back to the border-town where the camel-trains stay. You will find them in the

293

caravanserai. But here: no women! Here they are all monks and holy.' And the man went back to his sweeping, while Nai sighed and thanked him, and went away again from the central square.

But still he did not go to the portico, but instead he saw a monk, meditating, bald-headed under a tree, and he went to the monk and stood for some time in his light. But the monk did not turn to notice him. But Poet Nai at last said, 'Excuse me, holy sir, I do not want to interrupt you, but truly I am feeling desperate. I have come here searching for a friend. I have come all the way from Jian kang. Could you not describe to me what visitors you have had from the East, say in the last three months or so?'

The monk opened his eyes, and calmly smiled at the poet, and said, 'Have you not yet done with these concerns? To seek for satisfaction in the fabric of this world is doomed to failure. To act from worldly motives is to bring sorrow after, as a cart follows the hoof of an ox. There have been no Eastern visitors to Dun huang these months, in spite of the sudden change in the government of the province. You must look elsewhere. Here our only visitors are mind-training and wise morals.' And the monk closed his eyes again, while Nai in dismay walked back through the leaf-blown courtyard.

So he came to the portico, and Tawny was there waiting for him, staring into his face to see what he had discovered. But Nai could not speak of it, but went into the portico, and found the others sitting there. Yet still he could not settle, and staring behind at the temples, he went to a monk that stood by the door, and spoke to him. And Nai said, 'Holy sir, I am in great need. I desire more than anything to pray to Guan yin. Could you tell me where the temple is of the goddess of mercy? My soul is in need of comfort from this great Buddhist goddess.'

But the monk laughed at him when he said this, and replied at once. 'If you want these peasant idols, friend, you must go elsewhere. Here we are all monks devoted to the great fourfold path. There is no room in our minds for

294

any goddesses. You will find the worshippers of Guan yin among the humble people and farmers. Here we plumb the depths of the soul and intellect.' And the monk turned back to look at where the ceremony took place, and the pilgrims were then bidden into the temple.

Into the rank-reeking hall then went Nai and the others, to the darkness where the light hung curling with plumes of incense. The air was loud with the swaying mantras of the monks, as they sat in their rows with their sutras open. Breaking the swell of deep-throated prayers, the clash of cymbals came, the howling of trumpets and long-held booming of mountain tubas, so that the very walls themselves seemed to shake under the onslaught, as the frescoed thousands of Buddha-souls swayed in their painted colours.

Nai stared at the statue of the central place, which smiled down on these rituals and psalms. The statue of Siddhartha Gautama, become the enlightened one, shimmered with light from the door on its gold-leaf surface. Its sad, compassionate smile floated above the monks, and gleaming on its forehead shone gold wisdom, beneath which the sweaty bald heads in a sea of orange robes bobbed up and down with mesmeric prayers. The Abbot's corpse lay covered. Its head was towards the door. It bided the illusory burning.

Nai wearily stared about, and once more he studied the monks, once more he peered at their faces for traces of Xiang. Tawny sat beside him staring, following his eyes, earnestly helping his master in his search. The ranks and ranks of monks flowed by. Nai felt himself grow giddy. The rumbling chants went on monotonously. Face after face flickered past like the hordes of a dream, riding in waves endlessly fervid forward. Nai felt himself faint, and then he knew no more of prayers, monks, world, tubas, mantras, statues, heads, anything.

And yet in his swoon, he still saw faces riding in ranks ever forward, the faces of the Huns, with their skin hats and twisted bows. They surged ever forward, hungrily pouring.

There was no end to their driving. They ate the very world with their lust.

But when morning came to the cliffs of Dun huang, the tawny-haired Xie Nai awoke and shivered with the cold. And seeing his breath steaming, he gasped and tried to reach the coverlet, but his hands were stiff, and there came a remembrance to his soul, and he fell back on the pillow as black despair seized his heart in triumph.

Yet hearing him stir so, his servant-boy, Tawny, came up, and he brought near a charcoal brazier, that smoked a little from its chain. And he set it close, and stared into his master's pale face. Then rising from this task, he fetched the fragrant tea, which he boiled on a fire out on the verandah, and he brought it to him, and pulling up Nai's head, made him drink.

And Tawny said, 'Come master, you must not mope so. Be of good cheer, and have courage! For though you found not Ling Xiang awaiting as you hoped, yet still there is this mission you told us of the Great Tale. Get better quickly, master, for if you dally here, you will most probably be forgotten, for I have heard Fa xian and his pilgrims intend not to winter here, but to press on with their journey. And surely they will leave you, my master, if you are sick. Wherefore get ready soon, and let us go on again!'

But Nai replied, 'Will you make me giddy? Have we not had enough of this travel? For months and months we have rattled on until my bones and joints will clatter for ever! No further can I go, Tawny. Go on without me, if you must. But here where the vision told me, here will I winter. But where am I, Tawny? What is this room? What happened? I have had a night of visions.'

'Well master, you do embarrass me,' said Tawny, giving him the tea, 'for you have so little sense of decorum. But I suppose I had better tell you how we arrived in this hut, so that you learn to restrain yourself in future. There were we in the hall, harkening the bellowing monks, rolling our eyes up in holy frenzy, and you started your impressions of dying fish, gasping and glowing green over everyone, and the next thing I know you have stretched yourself out on the floor, all in the middle of a pile of monks. Well, we took you away from there, and I propped you up against some bags, and I did my best to keep you quiet.

'Well, while you were out cold, looking as if you were drunk, and raving in a sort of delirium about hordes of hurrying faces, it seems that all the important monks had had a big meeting, and big things were decided. You happened to be lying quite near their council-chamber, and what with this, and the burial service in the temple, it was quite a commanding spot. Anyway, the big monks made their decision, and what do you know? They chose another Abbot. And not an ordinary Abbot either. In fact I'm sorry I got here so late. Otherwise I reckon they'd have picked me. Because this Abbot is just a lad, smooth-faced, quite feminine-looking. Why a lot of grown-up monks picked him I dread to think!

'Anyway, there you were in a faint, raving about hurrying faces, just as the monks come out from their council. The Abbot himself with his high squeaky voice looks down on you thunderstruck. "What's he?" he says, pointing with his finger like a baby. I stare at him coolly. "This," I reply, "is the supine form of China's greatest poet. So great is his genius that none of the literati at the moment are anywhere near recognising it. He has fainted at the sight of so many monks. And I have brought him out of the temple." "Carry him away!" says the Abbot. "Look after him. Lay him in the pinnacle pavilion." That's my story, master, and the pinnacle pavilion is where you are, and where you've been all afternoon, evening, night and this morning.'

'And is a whole day passed,' said Nai, 'since I fainted away?'

'Ay,' said Tawny, 'and you've been in a very boring sort of delirium. I'm fed up with hearing about these little yellow faces whom you seem to see pouring all over China!'

Nai stared at him white-faced. 'Yes!' he said. 'Yes! I saw

297

them. Millions of barbarians and warriors! They are coming. They are coming.' And Nai struggled out of bed, and reeling sickly went over towards the rope-latched door.

The day was dark with cloud over the barren ranges, and the wastes of dune and desert were empty. The monastery rose on its slope, presiding over the caves, its pagoda hovering ghostly before the grey sky. There seemed the smell of snow in the air. The whole landscape was quiet, as though all but the two of them had departed. A lost goat went running down the ribs of the slope and out bleating and calling towards the dried-up river. A melancholy outpost at the onset of a hard world. Nai sighed. They were beyond the wealth of China. He turned and went back to his bed. He sat against the wall. He wept with misery.

'Come, lie down again,' said Tawny going over to him. 'Are you warm enough, master? Would you like to hold me for warmth like you did on the road? You said it made you feel easy.'

Nai shook his head. He lay down and sobbed into his pillow.

'Oh, master,' said Tawny, 'don't give way to your grief. There may be some catch, some trick you have not thought of. Perhaps Xiang is here, and somehow you just can't see her.'

'Tawny!' said Nai. 'Will you torment me? To have come all that way, sticking to such a silly hope! So far, so far, and yet futility!'

'Ay,' said Tawny nodding. 'You are a bit of a fool. But men can never see what's under their noses.'

Nai groaned and was quiet. But he saw then at the door two figures softly enter into the pavilion. And they wore Buddhist robes, and he recognised when they turned to him Fa xian, the leader of his pilgrimage. But the other Buddhist was strange, for he wore the robes of an Abbot, and yet had a young and girlish face, so that Nai became confused by the sight of this holy boy, who it seemed could be either a man or a woman. But then the figures came forward, and sat near his bed, and studied him with kindly interest.

The Abbot spoke, 'Xie Nai of Jian kang, I welcome you back to consciousness. I am the Abbot of Dun huang, yesterday elected, to serve in this venerable post. There have only been two Abbots of this holy place, since Luo Zun had here his vision. Both were old men. But I – it has been decided – I am the reincarnation of the visionary. The first thing I saw after my election was, sir, you in a swoon. I considered it our duty to care for you, setting you here in the pinnacle pavilion. Your servant I see also is physically grimy. I shall bring cleansing implements. You are here, sire, on a cliff, a bluff of its own summiting, just beyond the ancient frontier of Zhongguo. You have therefore left China, and are in a suspended state, between two worlds, prey to many visions. But here is Fa xian to speak with you, that came with you along the road. He has come to say his goodbyes.' The Abbot ceased, his high womanish voice warbled quietly to an end, and Nai looked at Fa xian with worried eyes, wondering what he had to tell him.

'Indeed,' said Fa xian, 'I have come to bid farewell, for we members of the pilgrimage have come to a decision. Since in truth we have arrived in Dun huang sooner than we intended, due to the fast pace of the latter parts of our journey, before the winter closes round us, we feel we could reach further to Lo Lan, Turfan, or even Kashgar, before the snow enwrap us in its stillness, and makes impassable the menacing ranges. We are pressing on therefore. You, Nai, have reached your goal. Your thoughts, I think, never stretched much beyond here. You are also too ill to travel. Now I will send another to bid adieu. After that we will no longer trouble you.' And Fa xian nodded to Nai, and quietly left the room. Nai felt overwhelmed with loneliness.

But the Abbot remained a while and said, 'Indeed it is well that they go, for theirs is an important mission for Zhongguo. If they should return with the Buddhist scriptures, then our faith may take root in this land. Without such texts, it would command little respect. Yet dangers attend our outpost here at the very gate of China, for there

299

have been rumours of stirrings in the wastes of the barbarians. Should there be a sudden attack, the pilgrims would be caught in it. It is well if they get as far as they can to the West. And you, sir, I think have had intimations of some such hordes descending upon us? I read in your mind the flashes of that future.' And the Abbot stared calmly, while Nai looked back startled to find his visions read by this holy stranger.

Then there came a tap on the door, and Tawny darting over, let Wei into the room from the grey air. And Wei came in shamefacedly, wearing robes of the Buddhist orange, and he knelt by Nai's bed in quiet humility. And Wei said, 'Old friend, I come with fateful news, for now is Wei to leave you. For the third time he comes to you, in third transformation, restored to the way you knew him. Dear Nai, we have shared many things together, from the rare delights of the old capital, when I was your junior, your poor cousin you treated to the tea-houses, to this long journey, when in my train you went, a nobody in the progress of a mandarin. But now my third state berefts me of all power, and I bide even the shaving of my hair. Wherefore, my friend, I come to you to bid a long farewell, and to fare forth wholly on the way of the Buddha.

'It seems, Nai, you shared with Jen the reasons she kept from me, and you were privy to her unrecognised guidance. To you, I think, did she confide her appraisal of my faith. To you, I think, she made plain the steps of my progress. You could see what I could not: the trappings of a mandarin satisfied me less in having than in dreaming. From poverty to wealth, the sense of futility never left me, and was underlined by the fatuities of our travel.

'When Jen saw me released from any further worldly ambition, she knew I was on the way towards the Buddha. When she thought of my journeying amidst the Buddhist pilgrims, she knew I was in the safest company. At this point I heard that the State of Liang was ours, and I was pointlessly going as an ambassador to our own people, and Kun and Lun came to me, and pointing out these facts, urged me to turn homeward. I spent the night upon it.

300

What home was I to choose? By morning I had chosen the true one. Jen knew then she could leave me, for her work was done, and she emerged from her protecting carriage. Oh, Nai, how am I blessed to have found such sacred love. Surely her soul was that of a bodhisattva!' And Wei took his friend's hand, and held it then in tears, as Nai gazed back at him sadly.

And Nai said, 'You found that soul who brought you to yourself. How can there be further blessing? In the merry streets of Jian kang, you made encounter with her who brought you to the desert home. Well, yours is the fortune! Once it was I that was fortune's brocaded wonder! Fare forward then, thrice-realised Wei. I shall weep to see your departure. I shall weep good tears to see you voyaging towards India. Yet all is fair, my friend. The balance of Fate is just. And look: I have left Tawny.' And Nai, as he said this, held out his arm to the boy, and Tawny came and sat with him.

But now there came a servant who tapped at the door, and the three by the bed turned to gaze at this. But the Abbot who was sitting cross-legged in the corner said, 'Ah, this is the monk with the lotion. I must trouble you, sir, to surrender your servant, while I attempt to make him more worthy. Rarely have I laid eyes on such a grubby boy! And perhaps also your visitor should leave you. I think that you should sleep again, for sleep in a holy place brings both vision and blessing.' And the Abbot seized Tawny by his ear as though a dog, and dragged him out onto the verandah.

Yet just as the Abbot got outside, there came two other figures, and they and the Abbot exchanged friendly greetings, for it was Kun and Lun who bowed and smiled at the frowning monk, who still held Tawny by his ear, unnoticing. Wei looked at Nai with sudden sadness, seeing that he must go, and for a while the two friends regarded each other, Wei in his robes of orange and russet, Nai in his old jacket, the red satin embroidered with blue roses. Their faces were rough with travel now, no smooth shaves or oily

301

perfumes, and for the quiet moment they looked at each other, Wei's long thoughtful visage, that contrasted with Nai's round, widespread face, with lively eyes and nose hooked like a parrot. But now the old men entered the room, and Wei got up to go, and went without turning beyond to the grey mountains. And the Abbot was there now, sponging lotion from a tipped-up bottle, and scrubbing it over Tawny's face.

'We are come to bid you farewell, my friend,' then said Kun smiling. 'You could not know, but we have been called forth on urgent business. The tasks which we have neglected long are in dire need of our powers, and our duty is to go to the beyond. We have been with you stoutly, my son. Diligent as ministers, we have sought to sway you from your foolhardiness. Well, we have failed. Yet content ourselves we can that if we have failed, so also have the thousand Buddhists!

'My son, you are a remarkable fool, and the great faiths of our land have not been able to dent your triumphant folly. In spite of the best powers of sages, you remain serene, ever steadfast in your brilliant ignorance. Wherefore we leave you. Yet remember, Nai, all this is but a show, all this and you and we have a deeper reality. In the very cup of grossest matter the drink of the gods is held, and the body in beauty holds in her breast all heaven. Wherefore remember, keep fast the cup, even when thunder comes. On fortune and misfortune a gentleman looks alike. These truths you'll find in the *Analects*, a copy of which I leave you here, and so farewell, my son. Fare well in the West.'

'Ha! Indeed!' Lun said suddenly. ' "Laughter comes: ha, ha!" But you, my son, remember the way. And though great sights may come to you: respect your end, which is to say: remember your fundament! For whatever the wild dreams may say, there are still two ends to a man, and neither of them particularly savoury. But now, go on your way again. You have led us a long dance. You have driven two old men mad with frustration. But it is good for sages thus to toil now and then in the world. Respect your end:

302

remember your fundament! So imp, farewell. Keep ever upon the way. And have a care of Tawny.' And Lun smiled at Nai then, as Tawny came into the room, his head in a towel with which he scrubbed himself, and the two tutors went to the door, and turned to bid farewell, as the clouded mountains lay in dusk behind them.

But when they turned to look on Nai, a fog seem to breed at their feet, and billows of clouds bred about the floor. Then did the monk and scholar seem to hover above the ground, and float up into the air framed by the doorway. With kindly smiles and waves of their hands, the tall and the squat then bowed their heads in their red and azure robes, and borne on clouds they floated away, like the blessed gods, and left the dusty patch of earth behind. And Nai sat gazing, lost in wonder, while Tawny on the bed, still scrubbed his face with his head in the towel.

But when he had finished he said, 'Oh, master, such a lotion the Abbot had! Why, he's half flayed the skin off my face with his lousy liquid! I'll keep it hid yet, for truly, master, I would not you saw it so. I think the poor visage needs to recover in quiet. But the Abbot tells me you'll like what you see, for he says you'll find me fair, and what you see will cheer you after your disappointments. For not every man, master, that treads the earth can achieve his dream, and some of us must be content with reality. I must give my face some minutes to cool. But while we sit here idle, perhaps, master, I could tell you a story?

'For up on a cliff last night you told me of your wooing of Xiang, your heroic wooing of this impossible beauty! And so stunned was I by the heroic forbearance you showed in so many cases against the wild moods and unreasonableness of this monster, your saintly fortitude in the face of such impossible provocation, that I thought I'd continue the tale in your praise a little, for you may remember, as you were narrating me this inspiring epic, we were suddenly interrupted by an earthquake. You broke off at the point when you and Xiang went to a house in the woods. But perhaps you should have gone on to another place: a

303

circle of stones? You may stare at me, master. Indeed, for a boy, I have unusual insight. Yet hear me on and you may marvel even more at my intelligence, and maybe even marvel at your own.

'For on a later occasion, you and Xiang took another journey, rattling onward as ever in your carriage. Midwinter had come, and midwinter's night settled on the countryside, when you went on a journey you had planned together. On the solstice of December, you drove through the hills to visit the Ba zhen tu: the Eight Formations, a Giant's Dance of stones. And there to the ancient circle of monoliths you came through the frosty woods, tethering your horses, and walking across the fields.

'Xiang was afraid to come there by night, as if the gods were looking, for the place was sacred to the ancient earth-spirits. You bounded on happily, bouncy as ever, knowing nothing of her dread. You both stood together, the looming colossi circling. You gazed up to the circling planets overhead. And the Silver River flowed above, like a frost of stars. How deep and quiet was the whole universe!

'It was there, as night faded, as you stood by the stones, you put to her your strange proposal. You asked her to come with you, to fly with you on a journey, to hie to the West, to seek a Great Tale! And the round year was turning, the heavens moved, and the stars themselves forced us – I mean you and her – to the sacred place.

'Ay, master, hear now the final moments of my tale, and see if this does not stir you to some realisation. See, if with these words, the truth does not dawn, which has dogged you on the road, holding your hand so close, and yet unnoticed! For as dawn was approaching, and the night grew colder, as it does near its end, the dome overhead glowed grey and sharpened the stones. Wherefore you both stood in the hallowed spot, and gazed through the mighty columns, to where a glory trembled on the distant hills. And when the sun rose, it came as a crescent first over the crest, and grew to a disc soon of burning gold, and climbing a channel exactly held between the monoliths, it surged up on its journey to the West! Such is my story. I had it of one that seemed to know Xiang well. But few of us know what we really are.'

'Indeed, indeed,' said Nai then sighing. 'Alas, for the foolishness of men! Alas for those who cannot see what is beside them! They search the world, yearning for the touch of the very one who helps them in the travel forward! They sit in Dun huang, on a magic pinnacle, while under a towel hides the blessed and unexpected revelation. A common comedy, I think, in other veiled forms. But here is one of the great clowns of the cosmos! What may be said of him? And what may be said of her? What tale could ever tell of her blessedness?'

And a soft voice said, 'Well, sweet, no doubt you'll pen one soon. Yet there is a Great Tale that calls us forward. And what, you stayed me patiently amidst my strivings, and I with patience your long journey. But in the Eight Formations you pledged us on a path that henceforth we must tread stoutly. So let us fare forward then, for the road is long, and at least we have each other. Yet love, the autumn has gone today. The frosts they are come. And the earnest pilgrims have delayed their pilgrimage. In tranquillity a little while we travellers can rest that take the great quest together.'

It was colder in the dusk as they spoke, and before them on the bed, the frozen light lit the chamber strangely. All things had come to stillness in it: the statuette and the incense-sticks, and the book and the leafy twig left by the masters. Across a little chest there lay some embroidery of scarlet, with silk threads tangling their fiery colours. And suddenly beyond the crimson satin in the gloom of the doorway, Nai saw that it was snowing. Hiding the rocks and monastery, steeped in the green twilight, the flakes were teeming down like flowers from heaven.

But now he drew the veil away from the hidden face, and there he saw at last at the end of China, in the light of the lamp his love, and at this the travellers kissed, and they were still together, Xiang and Nai.

interzone

SCIENCE FICTION AND FANTASY